TO CAPTURE A REBEL'S HEART

Heart's Rebellion
Book 1

Madelyn Grey

ARE YOU SIGNED UP FOR DRAGONBLADE'S BLOG?

You'll get the latest news and information on exclusive giveaways, exclusive excerpts, coming releases, sales, free books, cover reveals and more.

Check out our complete list of authors, too!

No spam, no junk. That's a promise!

Sign Up Here

www.dragonbladepublishing.com

Dearest Reader;

Thank you for your support of a small press. At Dragonblade Publishing, we strive to bring you the highest quality Historical Romance from some of the best authors in the business. Without your support, there is no 'us', so we sincerely hope you adore these stories and find some new favorite authors along the way.

Happy Reading!

CEO, Dragonblade Publishing

Foreword

Ever since I was a young girl, I've held a fascination for the American Revolution. It's the ultimate underdog story, and, in essence, America's very first civil war. Despite my interest, nothing ever truly ensnared me until February 2020, when I saw a spy exhibit at Mount Vernon. I was fascinated by the methods of espionage (especially the video featuring Lydia Darragh, a pacifist-turned-patriot spy, sewing intelligence into a button).

Later that same year, I learned about the Culper Spy Ring, and how they operated so efficiently that to this day, we still don't know all of the members. Although I didn't reference any of these historical figures, I'd like to think that Robert Townsend, in particular, will forgive me for lifting the majority of his intelligence and giving it to my characters. In addition to the "stolen" intelligence, I also took creative liberties here and there for the sake of the story, i.e. inventing a made-up estuary (I didn't want my characters traveling through the Devil's Belt and risking imprisonment), and putting a sleet storm in the middle of December (I wanted a romantic, rainy romp, so sue me—but also, please don't!). In short, all historical inaccuracies were made for the sake of moving the plot forward. A cardinal sin, I know!

In the back, you'll find *a glossary featuring the historical words in this novel*, most of which were referenced from Francis Grose's *Dictionary of the Vulgar Tongue*. I truly hope you enjoy this passion project of mine—and if you do, will you please be so kind as to leave a review on Goodreads, Amazon, Bookbub, or any book platform of your choice? Reviews are the life blood for authors, and help us reach more readers!

To my parents, who never stopped believing (and are allowed to read everything but chapters 9, 13, 24, and 26, which they must skim in order to keep looking me in the eye).

PROLOGUE

ORDER OF EXECUTION
Take heed.
BE IT KNOWN that
DANIEL ELIJAH HOSKIN,
having been found GUILTY of Treason against the Crown,
shall hereby be EXECUTED,
and hanged by the neck until DEAD.
May God have Mercy on his Soul!
GOD SAVE THE KING.

February 1779

THE FIRST TIME Benjamin Hoskin saw a dead body, he was only nine years old. Devastated by the sight of his mother's sunken cheekbones and wide, gaping eyes—that wasn't her! That was *not* her!—he'd turned mute for three whole months until his older brother, Daniel, successfully guided him back into speaking as before.

Fourteen years later, Benjamin found himself speechless again at the sight of Daniel's cold, lifeless body hanging from a gibbet. He'd always warned his brother there was a price for freedom; he just never imagined it would be Daniel, his shining beacon of hope—*Daniel*, the man he endlessly looked up to, being reduced to nothing more than a cautionary tale to those who enacted treason.

The redcoats swarmed their hometown of Freyview, Long Island, two years prior. Even with the threat of death closing in, Daniel proudly upheld his patriotism, whether it be through pamphlet readings and discussions, hosting secret meetings after their father's church services, or rebellion to one of the highest degrees: smuggling. Over the past several months, Daniel and his best friend, Amos McQuinn, had taken to traveling up and down the colony of New York, stealing from bloodybacks, and anonymously giving to their own.

Why had he let this go on, Benjamin wondered? *Why* had he turned a blind eye and allowed his brother to throw away his life?

With a weary grunt, Amos McQuinn plopped down in front of him, nudging Benjamin's foot with his boot. "How's your arm there, lad?"

Benjamin pulled back his leg. "Never better," he muttered, wincing as he assessed the stinging, angry red welt beneath the torn fabric on his upper arm. "You have any whiskey?"

Amos laughed, though the sound was strangled. "Whaddaya think there, Moony-boy? Me without whiskey's like bein' a milkless cow." Retrieving a flask from the inside of his coat pocket, he handed it over while the other men in their hideout shuffled about, each tending to their wounds and recuperating.

Expression devoid of light, Benjamin uncapped the flask and took a long, hard swallow, then dribbled the booze over his graze mark. "You said Dan's other friends would show up today…that there would be enough of us to fight."

"Aye, well…" Amos shrugged, lifting a carrot from his satchel. "Not everyone wants to risk their life—their *families'* lives—for a friend." He bit into the vegetable. "I'm real sorry there, lad. Y'know Dan was like a brother to me."

Benjamin froze, his limbs trembling as Amos took another bite. Though innocent, the stark, crisp pop was akin to being at the gallows, to hearing Daniel's neck snap while he and the other men arrived too late to save him. Even while riding in like a bunch of masked bandits on horseback, it hadn't been enough.

"You all right then?" he pressed.

Benjamin drew a breath, the churning in his gut growing worse. "I'm fine."

"Oi, c'mon now," Amos coaxed. "Y'don't hafta lie…"

"I'm not lying," Benjamin countered. But he was. He *was* lying, if only to suppress the catastrophe deep within his very bones. The thought of being separated by six feet of dirt left Benjamin with a sour coil of bile in his throat. Daniel was dead— *dead!*—and when Benjamin realized he would never lay eyes upon his brother's friendly, impish face, nor tease him about his infatuations that changed with the moon phases, nor eagerly tear into his witty, clever letters, nor even embrace him again, he felt completely hollowed out…*empty.* So empty, in fact, that it took him a moment to realize he was having trouble breathing.

With a quivering hand, Benjamin smoothed his palm over his chest and drew in several slow, unsteady breaths. "He's gone," he whispered, trying to come to grips with this truth. "Dan, he…he's *gone.*"

Amos winced. "Aw, c'mon there, Moony…"

"Don't call me that!" Benjamin snarled. "Only Dan has that right!"

Amos sighed, then rose from his perch to come sit alongside him. At thirty-four, the cabinetmaker was eleven years Benjamin's senior, but looked far older due to working outdoors and his queued, silver-streaked black hair. The exaggerated crow's feet around his eyes always crinkled like starbursts whenever he smiled, yet that comforting sight was presently nowhere to be found. "Y'wanna talk about it?" he coaxed.

Benjamin laughed, but there was no mirth in his tone. "What's there to talk about?" he bitterly asked. "Dan chose his hill to die upon, and now I get to *bury* him on that hill." A spark of resentment burned within Benjamin's breast, and his limbs shook while he set aside the flask. "He should've kept his big mouth shut. He should've—"

"What?" Amos fired back. "Ignored his beliefs? Been lowly an' subservient to the Crown? We can't all be neutral in this war like you, y'know."

Benjamin scoffed. "At least that way he'd still be alive. He would still be here with…!"

Me.

Swallowing the word, hot tears filled his vision, and angrily, he swiped his forearm across his eyes. "He was being selfish."

"That ain't true," Amos replied, his voice uncharacteristically soft. "Dan was a lot o' things, but he sure wasn't selfish. Y'know that, lad."

He did know. Once the King's Men came after Freyview's sole church—the one ministered by their father, Josiah—and stripped it of pews for kindling and British fortifications, it had been the ultimate nail in the proverbial coffin. It drove Daniel right into the enemy's snare, because above all, his brother was helpless but to lend his aid. He'd always done the right thing.

"So, what now?" Benjamin miserably asked. "Father may agree to help us hide, if asked, but unless he moves away from Freyview, he could also become a target."

"I sent Timmons to fetch 'im 'til things're safe," Amos promised. "Danny may be gone, but his fight's far from over."

Benjamin squinted. "How do you mean? What good can he do for your cause now that he's dead?"

"Funny you should ask that," a deep voice spoke from behind.

Jerking in surprise, Benjamin looked over his shoulder at a broad-chested, imposing man with dark hair and sharp, cunning brown eyes—a major general in the Continental Army, and the very reason they were able to assemble that morning—yet he was presently wearing plainclothes rather than his uniform. He was another one of Daniel's patriot friends.

"We haven't been properly introduced," the man said. "My name is Major General Edwin Bishop."

Benjamin turned around more fully, appraising the other man with caution. "Benjamin Hoskin," he replied. "Dan spoke of you often."

"If he confided in you, I trust he also spoke of plans for our future," Edwin continued. "Those plans are precisely why I was in town and able to arrange this attack. In addition to reconnaissance work, I've been recruiting help along the side. Daniel was preparing to go undercover for me to infiltrate an influential, successful Tory family."

"Aye, in Upper Manhattan," Amos affirmed. "Jedediah Boyd aids that pifflin' lout, Mayor Mathews, an' other barmy, good-for-nothin' lobcocks like Major General Tryon, so we were hopin' if Dan ingratiated himself, the family might get cocky an' start flappin' their lips."

Benjamin blinked at them in shock, overwhelmed by this sudden influx of information. "But that's impossible," he snapped. "Dan, he…h-he only spoke of smuggling exploits…" Unbidden, a spark of nettled fury burned within his breast. "Are you saying he was to be a spy? A spineless, lowly blackguard who does everything in secret rather than out in the open like a man?" Livid, he scoffed and shook his head. "A pox on you both. He would *never* do something so cowardly."

Edwin's expression remained blank, though there was a slight twitch in his cheek. "I know spying is frowned upon, and considered gutless by many; but Hoskin, if intelligence helps us win this war and end all the bloodshed, would you truly be so bothered?"

Benjamin swallowed, his throat painfully raw. "No," he rasped. "No, I suppose not."

"I understand your reservations," Edwin continued. "I, myself, would've never dreamt of turning toward such underhanded channels, but the British enacted these tactics first. It would be asinine of us not to reciprocate."

"Aye, well it don't much matter now, does it?" Amos grumbled. "The plan's all gone to shite. Dan'll have died for nothin'."

"Not if *he*—" Edwin pointed toward Benjamin. "—goes in his place."

Amos rocketed up from the floor. "Are y'dicked in the knob, man? D'ya want poor Reverend Hoskin losin' both his sons? Find someone else!"

"I don't recall asking you," Edwin replied. "No one else here is eloquent enough to blend in with the target, and Hoskin is clearly a smart boy…a bookkeeper who attended college, if I'm not mistaken? So surely, he can answer for himself."

Amos turned his head and spat. "You really wanna fight me, uh? Don't be fooled by me size. I could tear ya limb from bloody limb!"

"All right, that's enough!" Benjamin growled. Shakily, he rose from his perch off the floor, the blue of his eyes burning like the center of a candle flame. "The major general is right; I can speak for myself. And Amos, if you feel responsible for my life, I hereby absolve you of any such charge. I am *nobody's* burden."

"But Moony—!"

He speared Amos with a sharp glare, his upper lip curling while looking between both men. "Who else knows of this plan?"

"Just the men in this room, and Major Oliver Yates. Whenever I'm indisposed, he's the one you'll send word to," Edwin explained. "Everyone here was supposed to take part in aiding Daniel, whether serving as his courier, or acting as part of the intelligence gathering itself." He shrugged. "Alas, half our team died during this failed rescue, but the smaller numbers work in our favor."

Benjamin's mouth twisted. "I'm so happy to hear you think of your own men as expendable, sir."

"That is *not* what I meant, and you know it. Every man in this room knew precisely what they signed up for when they joined this fight, and sacrifices can and do need to be made. Your brother understood that better than anyone. And you…" Edwin huffed, looking him over in distaste. "*You* are clearly here for selfish reasons: to help your brother rather than our cause. So why not continue that selfishness by going ahead with Daniel's plan? By honoring his final intentions?"

Amos spat again. "Don't listen to 'im, Ben. You ain't a bad man for choosin' family. If mine were still alive, I'd be fightin' for 'em too."

"No, uh…he's right," Benjamin replied, his hands curling into fists. "I owe it to Dan to at least consider the possibility…" *If I'd only supported him from the start, perhaps he would still be here.* Drawing a sharp breath through his nose, he looked back at Edwin. "If I agree to help—and I *will* need time to think this over—what would I have to do?"

Edwin's mouth tipped into a grin, a hint of yellowed teeth peeking between his lips. "How good are you at improvisation?"

CHAPTER ONE
Mistaken Identity

May 1779

I N NEW YORK City, Clara Boyd and her family lived in Upper Manhattan on a grand, secluded estate with livestock and lush, expansive fields. Despite many homes being used for billeting soldiers, her father's constant donations and close ties with British officers, and Mayor David Mathews, himself, spared them of this inconvenience.

Alas, their life was far from perfect.

Ever since Clara was quite young, her parents held her out at arm's length, only truly doting upon her elder sibling, Charlotte, and paying minimal attention to the youngest, Catherine. Their mother, in particular, ran Clara through with insults, each snagging against her heart like brambles—*undignified; brazen; trollop*—and with the continuous verbal assault, scar tissue was quick to form in a protective shield. Nothing could harm her; nothing could sway her, and sometimes, the only way to feel beyond that scab was to misbehave and get cut all over again. It felt *good* to be different; it was comforting being seen by her parents, if only for those brief moments of disobedience.

"Kitty?" Smoothing her hands along her skirts, Clara left the upstairs study in search of Catherine. It was early afternoon, and despite the quibble she'd endured with her mother that morning, she was in a rather pleasant mood. "Kitty, darling, where are you?"

"Down here!" a soft voice called.

Descending the staircase, Clara found Catherine sitting upon a bench in the grand estate's foyer.

A smile blossomed upon her features, warm and genuine. Her beloved sisters always eased her heart.

"There you are!" Clara chirped. "I was beginning to think you were hiding from me," she said in a singsong voice. "Not entirely *wise,* seeing how I know all your secrets."

As she stepped closer, she appraised her sister's downturned face and froze, her smile wiping clean. "What is it?" she demanded. Sinking onto the bench alongside Catherine, she touched the girl's arm and pleaded, "Tell me what's wrong."

Helpless but to obey, Catherine fell into a story of young love and heartbreak. At only seven and ten, she was prone to maudlin romanticism.

By the end of her tale, Clara was positively incensed. She wouldn't stand for this. Harm upon her own heart, she could handle, but her sister? Absolutely not.

"What a cad," she spat, her red curls bouncing. "Right after you throw yourself at his feet, he decides to sow his oats in *that* cow's pasture? It's unbelievable!"

Catherine blushed, anxiously wringing her hands. "I did *not* throw myself at him. That would be unsightly. Besides, Mr. Havenshire is a gentleman. I'd prefer not to speak ill of him just because I misinterpreted his affections."

Clara scoffed, all too ready to leap to her sister's defense. "Pray, allow me to speak ill of him then, because I certainly have no qualms dragging him through the mud! I'm surprised he hasn't bored his new mistress to death with his wealthy knowledge of arithmetic."

Catherine soured, insulted on his behalf. "I like to learn."

Clara huffed. "That may be so," she agreed, "but he didn't allow you to learn the one thing you were *truly* interested in, if you get my meaning."

As she'd hoped for, Catherine gasped, pink outrage flecking

her cheeks. At least in this way, her sister's focus was no longer on that good-for-nothing suitor.

"Good gracious, Clara!" Catherine exclaimed. "Do you ever tire of your perversions?"

"Of course not!" the redhead exclaimed, happy to play along. "The day I tire of men and their attributes is the day I no longer have a pulse."

Lifting a paper fan from her lap, Catherine began to cool herself, her cheeks growing progressively hotter. "Have you learned nothing from your shame?" she snapped. "It's bad enough that your scandal delayed proposals to our Lottie, but now you wish to delay mine, as well?"

"Oh, fie!" Clara waved a hand. "So long as Father keeps lining pockets, no one will give a single whit about my dalliances."

"That is *not* true," Catherine hissed. "Do you wish to see me an old maid? No man will desire the sister of a morally loose woman!"

Clara snorted, the corner of her mouth lifting in wry amusement. "I'm afraid you have much to learn about men, dear sister." Gently, she fixed an errant lock from Catherine's honey-blonde updo. "If you are so concerned about courting, I've just the idea! Why don't you send a letter to Mr. Hepplewhite instead?"

Catherine paled, anxiously shifting on the foyer bench. "I really don't think that wise…"

"Whyever not?" Clara volleyed. "You need a worthy suitor, correct? The man is smitten, and he's not nearly so boring. Well…I suppose *all* men are rather dull, when you get down to it, but he at least has excellent hands."

Catherine's brow creased, confusion flashing across her wide gray eyes. "What on earth do his *hands* have to do with anything?"

"Why, everything, of course! If a man has nice hands—agile fingers, in particular—he should be an excellent lover, indeed," Clara replied, winking.

"Good Lord… Clara, I have told you time and time again:

Please do not speak of such filth!"

She sneered, unimpressed. "How is it *filth?* Procreation is wholly natural! If it were not, why would we ever wish to lie with men in the first place? Why would the very Bible tell us to 'be fruitful and multiply' if we were not, in fact, intended to give in to such urges?"

Catherine cringed, fanning herself harder. "But what about Charlotte? She has found a man of fine breeding to court, and seems quite content, judging by her letters. She's mentioned nothing to me about *hands.*"

"Ah, yes…the ever-elusive 'Mr. Philip Ashby,'" Clara agreed, rolling her eyes. "Were she to actually return from Philadelphia and show us his face, I might be more inclined to believe in his existence."

"But Aunt Martha's written about the match," Catherine reminded her. "Why would you doubt his existence when she's always been forthright about gossip?"

Clara flicked a hand. "Fiddle-faddle! 'Match made in heaven' or no, it's complete fudge that Father hasn't even met Mr. Ashby *or* his family. Granted, it's only been a few weeks of Ashby and Lottie's acquaintance, but she has flooded us with letters. Her intentions are quite clear."

"Yes, but you know how things are," Catherine said. "The war has everyone so terribly nervous. Is it any wonder Lottie wishes to move things along? Father would only need to see the Ashby monetary figures to agree!"

Clara shrugged, unconvinced. "Of course, but does money outweigh character? In Father's eyes, the answer will always be yes, but our Lottie is a sensible sort."

Catherine nodded. "Indeed, she is. Charlotte has excellent judgment," she affirmed, only to wince at her mistake.

Clara pursed her mouth, her green eyes flashing. "Oh, yes. How could I forget? Perfect little Lottie would absolutely *never* let any man enter her carvel's ring before marriage."

Scandalized, Catherine swatted her arm. "Do not speak like

that!" she warned, blushing fiercely. "I cannot believe you even know such words!"

"Why? *I* have a carvel's ring, and so do you."

"Stop it, *stop* it!"

Knock. Knock. Knock.

Jolting to attention, both women looked toward the door in surprise.

"Is Father expecting someone?" Clara asked. When Catherine shrugged, the redhead glanced at the far end of the foyer and nodded to the lanky, thin footman dressed in blue-and-gold liveries and a powdered wig—William, his name was—and he nodded back before opening the door.

Eager, both Boyd daughters tried to see around William's shoulders, but couldn't quite get a good view. They could hear a pleasant, masculine voice requesting Jedediah's presence, and Catherine gasped in delight.

"Oh, it must be Mr. Ashby!" she crowed. "See? I knew Charlotte wasn't lying!"

"Mr. Ashby?" Clara echoed, her interest piqued. "How ever did you come to that conclusion? Is any old fool Mr. Ashby now?"

"I heard him say he traveled from Philadelphia!" Catherine said, annoyed. "Though I'm loath to break my vow, Lottie told me that sometime next week, she is returning with Aunt Martha and Mr. Ashby. It's to be a surprise!" Furrowing her brow, she added, "Though from the look of things, he's arrived early...and without our dear family."

"Yes, well perhaps they sent Mr. Ashby first to earn Father's approval," Clara said, ignoring the sting over being excluded. As the black sheep of the family, she was rather accustomed to it. Allowing the new snub to roll off her shoulders, she rose and folded her hands over her floral stomacher, adapting an air of superiority as she called, "Show him in, William."

The servant hesitated, muttered a soft, "Yes, Miss Clara," and then stepped aside to admit their new guest.

All at once, Clara's eyes lit up, and her rosy lips twitched into a sly, lopsided smile. If she didn't love her sister, she supposed she might actually be a bit jealous. This Philip Ashby was not only young, but very handsome. His eyes were a warm, enchanting cornflower blue, his features both sharp and soft, and his dark-blond hair was braided in a queue at the nape of his neck. The gray riding coat he wore, though perhaps a bit drab, further brought out the forget-me-not quality of his shrewd gaze, and Clara simpered, stepping forward with an extended hand.

"A pleasure, Mr. Ashby," she purred.

The man's eyes widened and his face grew ashen, and for a long moment, he appeared genuinely confused. "I-I am—"

"Mr. Philip Ashby," Clara said again, nodding. "Why yes, I know. Despite her best efforts, Charlotte's failed to keep you hidden from us. We know all about your not-so-secret intentions to marry."

If it were possible, the man paled further. "I…am he, yes," he allowed, taking her hand. "I'm so pleased to finally make your acquaintance, Miss…Clara, was it?"

"Ah! A man who is not only handsome, but capable of listening? Why, I'm smitten already!" Clara teased. Nodding to him, she withdrew and gestured to her left. "This is my sister, Catherine. Mother's presently napping, but I can wake her, should you desire it? Father is in court, so I imagine he'll be detained for quite some time."

The man quickly shook his head. "No. No, no, that won't be necessary."

"Splendid! If that's all there is to it, William will take your bags and show you to your room," Clara said, folding her hands. "Although you have arrived a sennight early, I am certain our parents will be thrilled to house you. The supper gong goes off at six, so do make sure you aren't late. Father detests unpunctuality."

Mr. Ashby bowed, and Clara and Catherine both curtsied.

While William led the newcomer toward the guest bedroom, Clara leaned over to her sister and whispered, "He has the backside of a Greek god."

"Clara Boyd!" Catherine hissed, mortified. "Have you no shame?"

"Why no, none that I'm aware of," she said, beaming. "Shall we read for a bit? I've grown rather bored." Linking her arm through her sister's, Clara grinned and spirited Catherine off to the downstairs library. Things were suddenly far more interesting in New York City.

BENJAMIN WAS IN a state of absolute panic. Pacing in his assigned guest bedroom, he pressed a fist over his mouth and exhaled through his nose, his head ducking as he moved from one side of the floor to the other.

This wasn't happening. This was *not* happening. After all the research he'd done on the Boyds—the father, the mother, the three girls—how in God's name had it escaped him that Charlotte was courting some mysterious suitor? And why had he leapt at the opportunity to pose as her soon-to-be betrothed?

Well done, jingle brains, he furiously thought.

As promising as the lie seemed at first, Benjamin was quick to realize he was a complete dunderhead for changing his story. Initially, he'd written Jedediah as a "Mr. White from Philadelphia," offering his services as a bookkeeper. The man had accepted, given his present lack of supporting staff, and invited Benjamin to come to his estate for a proper interview. From there, Benjamin planned to ingratiate himself with the family and befriend them. Now, however, he'd fallen prey to the allure of instant access, and thus, completely condemned himself to the gallows. Not only did he know absolutely nothing about this Philip Ashby, but he also didn't have a wardrobe beyond what was in his travel bag. The meddlesome daughters had ruined everything!

"Blood and thunder," Benjamin groused.

Just as he was concocting a new plan, a knock came at the door, and Clara Boyd poked her head into the room.

"Pardon me, Mr. Ashby," she chirped, "but have you gotten yourself settled?"

Stunned, Benjamin gaped at her in shock. Checking on the welfare of a guest, let alone one of the male persuasion, was most certainly *not* something a female member of the elite would do. It was inappropriate—scandalous—and a faint flush overtook Benjamin up to the tips of his ears.

"Miss Boyd," he greeted. "Though I appreciate the concern, this is hardly proper."

To his surprise, Clara snorted. It was a coarse, unladylike sound, and she shrugged, stepping farther into the room.

"I wished to lend my assistance," she said. "I noticed you don't have any accompaniment—not entirely wise, if you want my opinion."

"I don't," Benjamin snapped, only to immediately regret his tone.

Clara, however, seemed charmed by his brusqueness. "Well! At long last, a man who isn't trying so desperately to pucker-up at my backside." She folded her hands. "I imagine in your haste to acquaint yourself with your lady-love's family, you must have forgotten everything: your servants, your carriage, your..." she trailed off, appraising him uncomfortably close, "...*fiancée*. Where is our darling Charlotte?"

"Philadelphia. With your aunt, Martha," Benjamin said, praying for this to still be true.

Clara arched a brow. "You decided to come to town separately?"

"Yes. I wanted to do the honorable thing and ask for your sister's hand, face-to-face, man-to-man with your father." Palms sweating, Benjamin composed himself with a taut smile. "I adore Charlotte, Miss Boyd. I intend to do right by her."

"And so you shall," Clara said, sounding bored. "Father worships the very ground Lottie walks on, so you are assuredly in good company, sir." Again, she appraised him. "Part of this mystery still remains unsolved; whyever did you travel without accompaniment?"

"I was nervous," Benjamin fumbled, lifting his shoulders. "I do my best thinking by myself, so…I informed the hired help I wished to be alone. I decided to travel via horseback."

"And your horse is…?"

"In the stockade with your farmhands. To be frank, I am lucky to still have her." Feigning humility, Benjamin ducked his head and lied, "At the end of my trip, I was robbed by highwaymen. Despite my best efforts to present myself as a commoner, they took nearly everything I own: my money, the majority of my luggage, my very dignity, and yet I managed to pull ahead and escape."

Finally, Clara's unruffled demeanor developed a slight chink. "Highwaymen? Oh, good gracious! You are fortunate your entry passport was not stolen!" Concerned, she inspected him with a different sort of invasiveness. "Are you hurt? Should we send for the constable?"

"No, no, I trust they're long gone," Benjamin dismissed. "With my lack of coin, I was forced to ride the rest of the way without stopping."

Clara fluttered a hand to her throat. "Lord above, why didn't you seek help? You're completely mad!"

I truly am, he bitterly thought. "I trust this was all you needed, Miss Boyd?"

Pursing her mouth, she stepped back and nodded. "I will have William lend you whatever you need. Name it, and it shall be done. You and Father aren't so different in height, so I trust I can find you some extra raiment."

Benjamin frowned. "Will your father not notice?"

"Notice what, a few missing garments? Goodness, no!" Clara said, waving a hand. "He never wears the same outfit more than twice, if he can help it."

With a swell of relief in his chest, Benjamin bowed his head. "Then I would be much obliged, thank you."

She hummed. "Remember, Mr. Ashby, the supper gong is struck at six." Slowly, Clara's good humor returned, and she smirked. "Might I make one small suggestion?"

A stab of unease filled Benjamin's chest, but he nodded.

"Whenever you do speak with Father, please try and appear as if you don't have a giant stick lodged up your bottom. It's rather unseemly." Breaking into a sly grin, she winked and offered a curtsy. "That is all, Mr. Ashby. I look forward to seeing you at suppertime. Lottie's been rather secretive, so I simply cannot wait to learn more about you!"

When Clara ducked from the room, smug and with her head held high, Benjamin exhaled and sank onto his canopied bed with a heavy bounce.

CHAPTER TWO

The Boyd Family

As PROMISED, THE mealtime gong struck at six, and Benjamin mentally floundered while heading downstairs to join the family. His new backstory was simple enough. He was aware the Boyds had friends in the maritime business, and thus, decided on the Ashbys being a shipbuilding family. Despite the proud demeanor he'd adopted for this role, he felt an uncomfortable, nettled heat burning beneath his collar while William showed him into the sitting room.

Both Clara and Catherine curtsied upon his arrival, and were bedecked in ostentatious ruffles and skirts. Benjamin knew absolutely nothing about fashion, so all he could discern was the former was dressed in a flashy green gown that brought out the stunning jade fire in her eyes, and the latter was wearing an equally flashy gown of pale yellow.

Jedediah Boyd—who hadn't even spared him a friendly glance—was tall, thin, and sour-faced, with a powdered bag-wig and sharp, beady little eyes beneath a pair of spectacles. He snorted through his bulbous nose, retrieving his pocket watch to check the time. This, unfortunately, seemed to aggravate him all the more. "No good upstarts!" he exclaimed, startling all present company. "The nerve of some people!"

"Is something wrong, Father?" Clara asked, arching a brow.

"Never you mind," he snapped. "Just know that in this world, you are never to trust the word of a commoner. They make plans and immediately break them."

Awkwardly, Benjamin offered a thin smile as his condolence. He had a feeling "Mr. White" was the cause of Boyd's turmoil. If this was, indeed, the case, his persona wouldn't be welcome back any time soon.

Grumbling to himself, Jedediah led the group into the dining area, then hotly claimed his seat at the head of the table. The foot of the table—where his wife was to go, Benjamin presumed—was empty, and Deborah Boyd was nowhere to be found.

After servants pulled out the remaining chairs, Clara seated herself next, and once Catherine was settled across the table, Benjamin hesitated before moving to sit alongside the haughty redhead. Catherine hadn't spoken a word to him, and thus far, Jedediah was a no-starter, so Clara's foul openness seemed his safest bet.

"You look like a fish out of water," Clara teased him, unfolding her napkin after Jedediah led the custom.

Gaping at her, and probably resembling the fish of which she spoke, Benjamin tied his own napkin around his neck. "I feel a little ill," he said, which wasn't far from the truth. He did feel hopelessly sick, what with everyone's eyes darting between him and Jedediah. Was he supposed to do something? Was everyone waiting on him?

Mercifully, Jedediah spoke and recaptured everyone's attention. "You must accept my apology, Mr. Ashby," he said. "I wasn't aware you'd be coming to town, so I have not yet prepared a proper welcoming party. I can arrange something for next week, if you can afford it into your schedule."

Benjamin forced a smile and nodded. "But of course, Mr. Boyd; this is beyond sufficient. Thank you, sir."

Jedediah seemed mollified, and tilted his head in acknowledgment. "Alas, we normally would've had other guests, but again: I did not know of your pending arrival."

And thank God for that, Benjamin thought. He wasn't sure he could withstand an audience beyond the three—five, if he counted William and the other servant—gathered in his presence.

"Perhaps I can invite some gentlemen over for a drink tomorrow evening," Jedediah decided. "That, at the very least, can get you acquainted with the very best in town."

Despite Benjamin's inner panic, he perked up. A night with the wealthiest, most influential men in New York could prove promising. "Yes," he agreed, trying not to sound too eager, "yes, that would be wonderful. Thank you, sir."

While his mind raced with the possibilities, four servants of European descent entered the room and served vegetables and soup from tureens. Benjamin thanked each in turn, which earned him a sharp, disapproving glare from Jedediah. The paling servants appeared startled by his politeness, and they ducked their heads, doling out everyone's portions while sweating faintly beneath their powdered wigs.

Clara chose to lead by Benjamin's example, and turned to the servant at her right. "Thank you, Harrelson," she said, beaming in a bright, beatific way. "It smells heavenly."

"Clara!" Jedediah snapped.

Mulish, her green eyes cut toward him and she pursed her mouth. "Yes, Father?"

"There are certain *hierarchies* that must be kept, and you are currently in violation. Ladies do not speak to the hired help." Jedediah waved a hand. "Not beyond one's requests, of course."

"Oh, dear." Feigning ignorance, Clara pressed a hand to her cheek and gave an overdramatic gasp. "Why, I suppose I am in violation! Silly me, thinking that a distinguished gentleman such as Mr. Ashby must surely know hierarchies, and therefore the proper way to address them. After all, I am only a foolish, bottle-headed chit. How could I possibly hope to know the ways of the world?"

"Clara, don't," Catherine hissed from across the table, shaking her head.

Discomfited, the servants all exchanged glances, and it was

William who stepped forward with a tray of pre-carved mutton. He set it down before Jedediah, then backed away upon seeing the older man's contemptuous look.

Jedediah lifted the knife and fork for serving, and irritably set a piece of meat onto his own plate.

Benjamin's mouth was suddenly much, *much* too dry. Clearing his throat, he deflected, "And what of your wife, sir? Is she unwell? Charlotte speaks of Mrs. Boyd quite often and fondly, so I'd been hoping to make her acquaintance."

The furrow between Jedediah's brows softened, however slight. "She's presently resting," he muttered. "Dear Deborah is a lady of society, so she tends to fall into exhaustion quite often."

Clara snorted. "That's Father's romantic way of saying Mother is in her flowers. She always works herself into a state, so I trust she won't be coming down until tomorrow morning."

Jedediah tossed his fork in disgust. "For God's sake, Clara, how many times must I tell you? When your mother is—"

"What?" Clara refuted, equally annoyed. "A woman's monthly blood is hardly a scandal, Father, so I wish you wouldn't treat it as such! Why, if anything, it's wholly natural and as God intended!"

Benjamin's mouth dropped. Never in his life had he ever heard such open, bold-faced talk, aside from men jeering about lying with women during their cycle. Slowly, a flush from secondhand embarrassment stained his cheeks, and when he caught Catherine's gaze from across the table, she shared in his blush and looked away.

By this point, Jedediah was positively seething. The vein at his left temple pulsed along with his indignation, and muttering about wayward girls, he turned to Benjamin and apologized, "You must forgive her, Mr. Ashby. My daughter suffers from bouts of unruliness; all curable, from what I'm told, but the war hasn't allowed us much luxury for tending to her problem."

"My *problem* is this is the only way I gain any acknowledgment," Clara snapped. "How else am I to earn your oh-so-fleeting attention, Father?"

Jedediah ignored her, encouraging William to pass around the mutton. While the young man served the meat, other servants placed dishes of shellfish, corn, beans, and fruit onto the table.

Benjamin's stomach rumbled, yet he felt disgust over the superfluous spread. While the Continental Army, not to mention the very residents of New York, had meager meals, these blustering peacocks ate, and they ate well. How did they manage it? Did Mayor Mathews guarantee their full bellies?

Realizing he needed to blend in, Benjamin swallowed his pride and indicated to the servants for more food; at his request, each helping spooned onto his plate was as scant as possible. Every morsel sent a pinprick of guilt into his heart.

While Catherine engaged Jedediah in conversation, Benjamin took one bite before abandoning the meal in favor of his wine.

"You have the appetite of a bird," Clara observed, smiling at him. "Surely, you cannot be courting my sister. She is a regular knight of the trenches."

Benjamin set down his glass and chuckled, though the sound came out strained. "You're too hard on your sister," he said. "There is nothing wrong with a healthy appetite."

"Especially in the future, when she's carrying your spawn," she agreed. Humming in thought, Clara added, "Lottie has it in her head that that's all she's good for. And in a way, I suppose that *is* a woman's place. But I'd rather dive head-first into the sea. I couldn't imagine anything more dreadful."

Benjamin looked over at her, aghast. "Child-rearing? Dreadful?"

"You're right," Clara said, pursing her mouth. "It's hardly dreadful. Terrifying, perhaps, is a much better word."

Glancing toward Jedediah to ensure he and Catherine were still chatting, Benjamin looked back at the redhead and frowned. "But you would have a nursemaid," he reminded her. "You're afforded a luxury most women are not."

"And *you* are afforded a luxury my *sister* is not," Clara hissed, the fire in her voice astonishing him. "While you'll inevitably rake in the spoils from Lottie's womb, *she* will have to worry about whether or not it'll be her last year on earth." Furiously, she stabbed her fork into her piece of mutton, her knuckles turning bone white. "There is a reason we womenfolk turn our wedding gowns into burial shrouds, you realize."

Paling, Benjamin appraised her in stunned silence. This woman was confounding. Who on earth had raised her? Surely not the proud, taciturn man at the head of the table...

Clearing his throat, Benjamin shifted in his seat. "Forgive me," he said, careful to keep his voice low, "for I meant no offense. I'll admit I've never thought—"

"No," she agreed, "I suppose you never would think of such sentiment, and that's precisely the problem." Expression softening, she heaved a sigh. "I beg your forgiveness as well, Mr. Ashby. You're actually...tolerable, truth be told, and as far as suitors go, you are not the worst to cross our path."

Benjamin ignored the not-quite-apology, and instead, succumbed and lifted the mutton off his Wedgwood china. After weeks—nay, months—of not having eaten properly, it was difficult to resist ripping into the meat like a glutton.

Discreetly, Clara moved her hand over his thigh to stop him, commanding his attention. Benjamin nearly choked at the brazen gesture. To his surprise, the look on her face was that of amusement and not seduction, nor ill intent.

"You're not using your knife and fork," she whispered, the words delivered from the side of her mouth.

A jolt of panic blitzed through Benjamin, and he stiffened, swallowing his mouthful with difficulty. "I...I-I do not much care for frivolities," he whispered back, "so I'm inclined to only use silverware whenever necessary."

"And why should you do otherwise?" she agreed, smiling more freely. "Why, with being a man of such vast import, I imagine you hardly have time for silliness such as cutlery."

Benjamin couldn't tell if she was agreeing or making fun of him. Nevertheless, he grudgingly set the mutton onto his plate, then lifted his fork and made a show of stabbing it into the meat. If only he could stab it into his ear canal…

The first course came and went, and after the servants changed the dinner cloth—such a ridiculous practice!—a second course arrived and was set before them. Fruit tarts, jellies, and creams were tantalizingly on display, and Clara gleefully requested a peach tart before it was set upon her plate.

Jedediah no longer seemed quite so taciturn, and, just like before, was ready to engage the entire group in conversation. "I pray this war will be over any day now," he said. "As a man of Philadelphia, Mr. Ashby, how does it feel being surrounded by so many traitors to the Crown? Those ungrateful rebels should show gratitude for being granted the protection of His Majesty's Finest."

Clara groaned. "Oh, Father, must we always circle back to politics? It gets so tiresome!"

"No, no, I don't mind," Benjamin interjected, relieved that the subject had been broached naturally. "In fact, as well as getting to know your lovely family, I had every intention of seeing how I could aid you in the loyalist cause."

"Oh?" Jedediah eyed him over his spectacles. "In what regard?"

"Any regard you see fit, sir. I am but a lowly, humble man at your service—at the king's service." Smiling, Benjamin bowed his head and moved a hand over his heart, as if pledging his very allegiance. He heard Clara snort, but didn't spare her his attention.

Taking a sip of madeira, Jedediah hummed to himself, then set his crystal glass off to the side. "You'll have to forgive me, Mr. Ashby, because I must confess I was only lured in by Lottie's promise of your family's wealth. Your business is in what, again…?"

"Shipbuilding."

"Ah. Well, that could be quite beneficial to the cause," he allowed, his eyes gleaming. "In light of Billy Tryon's good fortune last year—becoming major general of all the British forces on Long Island!—I imagine he'd make great use of your ships."

"I'd be honored, sir," Benjamin agreed. "I could also smuggle items for the mayor, whether it be here or abroad—the soldiers, as well. So long as you act as our liaison, I imagine New York will be none the wiser."

Jedediah lifted his glass again. "Hear, hear!"

Clara huffed. "Now far be it for me to douse this oh-so-happy occasion with misgivings, Mr. Ashby, but I thought your family business was a different sort? Specifically, textiles?" Smugly, she added, "Charlotte's always going on and on about how your father is such a superb businessman. Many a Philadelphian tongue is wagging about his draper shop, and how he's dressing the wealthiest elite in Pennsylvania."

A heavy silence befell the table, but ever quick to action, Benjamin grinned and leaned back in his seat. "Alas, it seems you've caught me red-handed, Miss Boyd!" he exclaimed. "My father *is* a mercer—I've admired and studied underneath him my entire life—which is why I was inspired to embark upon my very own business. After all, what sort of man would I be if I relied upon my father's wealth? If I, heaven forbid, failed to uphold his values of hard work, commerce, and success?" Benjamin waved a hand. "I recently employed a crew of shipbuilders, and started offering my services to loyalist groups. I'd be remiss if I didn't offer the very same to your family, would I not? You are, after all, the ones my darling Lottie loves most."

Jedediah pursed his mouth, considering this. "A cloth merchant? Well now, that's very interesting, indeed…do you think that in addition to ships, you could get me a new suit tailored, Mr. Ashby?"

Benjamin nodded, tasting bile from his near slip-up. "It would be my highest honor, sir."

Clara looked at her sister and sighed. "All this talk of business has me rather vexed, and desirous of some much-needed stimulation." Expectantly, she turned to face Benjamin again. "Would you care to accompany me for an afternoon walk tomorrow, Philip?"

For the second time, Jedediah threw down his fork. "For heaven's sake, Clara, can you at least behave as if you and Mr. Ashby are not familiar?"

"But we are!" she cried, her chin stiff with annoyance. "He is the man Lottie loves, so that makes him family!"

"I don't mean to be an imposition," Benjamin quickly spoke. "I'll gladly welcome myself as a familiar to this family, Mr. Boyd, but if it insults your sensibilities, I will just as gladly denounce it."

Jedediah huffed, mopping at his glistening brow with a handkerchief. "Spoken like a true gentleman," he muttered. "I thank you for your patience with my daughter, Mr. Ashby—nay, Philip. Seeing how you're the man who caught our Charlotte's eye, I am glad to extend the offer of deeper acquaintance."

A seed of relief bloomed within Benjamin's breast, and as the servants came out and changed the tablecloth for the third time, he finally felt in control of the situation.

As was customary, the menfolk stayed in the dining area for more drink and conversation, and the women retired to the sitting room. Despite Clara's vulgarities, Benjamin was sorry to see her go; she'd provided a much-needed buffer between her father and himself, and anxious, he swirled his port while Jedediah moved on to his third glass of sherry.

"It's no wonder you've swayed me into this," he muttered, motioning at William to pour him another drink. "I'm no fool, you realize. I know every great family in the area—some parts of

Philadelphia, too—and with what I've learned tonight, I am of the mind that you are from good, sensible stock; the very best, in fact! I'd be a complete loggerhead to dismiss this while taking Lottie's future into account."

Benjamin swallowed. "Thank you, sir… But as a true Philadelphian gentleman, I've come all this way to request Charlotte's hand, and on *your* terms, not mine."

"Hmph." Swallowing his sherry in three gulps, Jedediah gave a pleased hum, then made another impatient gesture to his servant. While William refilled his glass, the lawyer rolled his eyes in thought. "The match is sudden, though not ill-advised. I can scarcely say no to little Lottie. I trust you feel much the same. So all in all, I'm compelled to acquiesce to this union. And why not? A fine, shipbuilding empire coupled with my renown as an attorney will get us far in this world, my boy."

"Oh…yes. Of course you're right, Mr. Boyd," Benjamin stammered.

"Please! Call me Jed." Gesturing to William, he indicated that he refill Benjamin's glass. "Drink up, my boy! This calls for a celebration!"

To your death or mine? he bitterly wondered.

BENJAMIN COULDN'T SLEEP. Ever since he was a child, it had always been difficult for him to glean rest in new places; perhaps it was some type of primordial survival tactic. If he lay awake, he wasn't in danger of attack. And there in the Boyd manor he was completely surrounded by an unknowing enemy. The thought left a sour taste in his mouth.

Earlier that afternoon, Benjamin recalled seeing a library on the first floor. He would read a bit to settle his troubled mind, he decided. So after lighting a candle, he quietly made his way downstairs. To his alarm, he discovered the library was already occupied.

Sitting on a plush, high-backed chair by the fire, Clara Boyd was curled up with a book and bedecked in a dressing gown, her feet perched on the cushion's edge, and putting her legs in a most unladylike position. Benjamin flushed and quickly moved to retreat, but she'd already spotted him.

"Have you come to escape your thoughts?" she asked, a wry smile on her lips. "I couldn't sleep either, if it's any consolation. I've been too fraught with grief over my behavior."

Benjamin mirrored her smile. "You regret your behavior?"

"Ah. Fair enough. I don't," she agreed, simpering. "Not truly, anyway—not where Father's concerned. That old goat deserves every bit of my vitriol." Brow creasing in annoyance, she set aside her book.

Benjamin read the cover and arched a brow. "*The Taming of the Shrew?* How relevant."

"You are not clever, you realize." A more genuine smile filled Clara's face, belying her irritation. "I've been told I am a lot to handle on a first meeting, so I suppose I should apologize. I doubt woman's blood is one of your favorite subjects." When Benjamin's face burned a brilliant scarlet, she laughed, her eyes sparkling while she drew her covered legs in toward her chest. "Why are you being so modest? Have you never read a book on the human body?"

Benjamin hesitated, wondering if he should be truthful, before he decided to lie and shook his head.

"Ah, it's just as well," she said. "Charlotte's as pure as they come, so you needn't worry about venereal disease, or any of the other topics in those books."

Benjamin gaped at her, completely stunned. Clara was so crassly forward, and yet she was also soft and refined. How had she managed it? If Jedediah's earlier claim was anything to go by, the war had brought any plans of remediation to a halt. Perhaps

Clara's misbehavior stemmed more from recent events, as opposed to a gradual build-up since birth.

"How did it go?" she asked, dragging his thoughts to a close. "That is, how did everything go with Father? You were talking for quite a while."

Hesitant, Benjamin set his candle onto a small table, then moved over and had a seat in the chair directly across from her. "Rather well, I'd say. He approved the marriage."

"Oh! 'Rather well,' indeed!" Clara crowed. "Welcome to the family, Philip—or should I say, the death of your dignity?" She grinned and hugged her knees. "As an honorary member for the past twenty years, I can assure you that sanity is only a state of mind. Unfortunately, *insanity* is the only state you'll find here with us Boyds."

Benjamin reclined in his seat, mirroring her tranquil posture. There was something wholly disarming about her—*freeing*—and he found himself envying how easily Clara flitted from one subject to the next. Nothing bothered her. After growing up as a reverend's son, he craved that lack of guilt. Her father clearly was ashamed of her, but she didn't care, and *that* was what he coveted.

"Do you love my sister?"

The question slapped Benjamin to attention, and a sharp stab of panic took root in his stomach. "Of course I do…yes. Undeniably."

"It's all right if you don't," Clara softly said. "Many don't marry for love…they do it for family, or duty, or a little of both. I suppose I just want to know why this engagement came on so suddenly, and under the utmost secrecy. Despite my teasing remarks, I really do love my sister. I'd do anything for her…Catherine, too."

Thinking of his own siblings—his estranged sister, Ruth, in London, and Daniel, cold and dead in the ground—Benjamin offered a knowing nod. "Family is important," he agreed. "In the end, they're all you have…all you can count on."

"Then you understand," she affirmed, nodding. "Despite my parents being dreadful people, they've sired true gems—except for me, the diamond in the rough." Sighing, Clara rose and grabbed her book, curling it across her breast. "I should retire. Will you still be accompanying me tomorrow, Philip?"

Rising from his seat, Benjamin bowed and nodded. "It would be my highest honor."

Grinning, Clara teased him, "You really *must* love Lottie, seeing how you're so eager to earn my good graces." Slapping the book of Shakespeare against his chest, she quoted, "'By this reckoning, he is more a shrew than she.'"

Bewildered, Benjamin moved to reply, but she'd already turned and left him with the tome in hand.

CHAPTER THREE

Tensions Rise

18 March, 1779

My Dear and Treasured Son,

It aggrieves me to learn of your intentions through a courier. Did you fear I'd say no? Did you think I'd forbid you from answering the call of your heart? I am proud *of what you've decided to undertake. Although you once resolved to remain impartial in this war, you've sacrificed your comfort and safety for the love of family. You enlisted as a soldier, first and foremost, and have God's Light to guide you through the rest. Your brother would be so very proud. Surely, you must know this.*

In terms of lodging, the redcoats occupying Freyview have at last relocated, so I've finally felt safe enough to return. I shall never again abandon my flock. Running away is for cowards and thieves, and I am neither. And what's more, I intend to live by your brother's example—by your example. After the previous war, I vowed to never again raise a musket toward my fellow man, but in this conflict, I can at the very least support those who are in need. Washington petitioned residents of New Jersey, Pennsylvania, Maryland, and Virginia to provide cattle for the army, so I intend to arrange for one of our bulls to be donated. It's good and right to give unto others.

One day soon, I hope to embrace you, to look into your eyes and witness firsthand the brave, brilliant man you've become. I implore you to not write me under any circumstance. Any ties to our family could compromise your alias. Although it pains me, I'll be content to wait for your safe return. Until then, remember your teachings, and above all, the unfailing love I shall have for you always.

Please burn this upon receiving.

Your Most Humble and Affectionate Father,
Josiah

Trembling, Benjamin smoothed his hand across the dog-eared letter, his heart shattering and reassembling with each bolstering word. Although delivered to him two months prior, he often took it out and reread the lines for encouragement, reminding himself that his father did, indeed, love him, and didn't harbor any ill will toward his failure to mitigate Daniel's passions.

When Benjamin lived in a boarding house in Huntington, New York, he'd only heard from Daniel and Amos every one to three months. Despite not being foolish enough to state their intentions outright, Benjamin read into their plans with little to no effort. Unfortunately, it seemed someone else had as well, and entrapped Daniel upon one of his returns to Freyview.

Exhaling, Benjamin pressed the letter over his heart. He could do this. He *had* to; if not for his brother and father's sake, then for all the *other* Daniels and Josiahs whose fates lay in the balance.

With his resolve bolstered, Benjamin said a quick prayer, then set the letter across the flames on his hearth. "I'll see you soon, Father," he whispered.

Knock. Knock. Knock.

Startled, Benjamin turned toward the drumming at his chamber door. Why was he being disturbed?

Nearly toppling, he clumsily rose and strode across the room, sparing the hearth one last glance. "Yes?" he called.

"Good morning, sir," came the muffled response. "It's William with your clothes."

Instantly sobered, Benjamin opened the door and blinked at the freckled younger man, relieved to see a travel trunk in his arms. The poor servant, however, appeared a bit unsteady beneath the chest's weight.

"This is from Miss Clara," he explained through gritted teeth. "She said her father wouldn't mind."

"Yes, that's what she told me, as well," Benjamin replied, retreating to allow him entry. "Thank you for this."

While William awkwardly crossed the threshold, Benjamin showed the servant where he could set the trunk. Though once it became evident the man wasn't leaving, he frowned in curiosity. "Was there something else you needed?"

Equally bemused, William asked, "Don't you need help getting dressed, sir?"

Oh, sweet merciful Lord…

With a grimace, Benjamin reminded himself that in order to keep up appearances, he had to play along, so with a tight smile and nod, he watched William open the trunk and set all the necessary raiment onto his bed.

The room grew painfully quiet. Judging by the night's prior commentary, the hired help truly didn't speak unless spoken to. So Benjamin cleared his throat and asked, "If it isn't too much trouble, do you think you could show me around?"

William straightened. "*Around,* sir? You mean the grounds?"

"Oh, no, I can manage that on my own; I meant the house," Benjamin explained. "I was hoping to explore. But if you think it unwise…"

"No, sir, I think that would be fine," William assured him. "First, I must seek approval from Mr. Boyd. After that, I'll be sure to come fetch you." Stepping forward, he took Benjamin's nightshirt and tugged it over his head.

All at once, Benjamin winced, stricken by the morning chill washing over his naked skin. With the clothing discarded, he flushed with humility while William fetched the ruffled shirt from his bed. Avoiding the servant's eyes, Benjamin poked his head through the offered linen shirt, and slipped his arms through the sleeves, relieved once the long garment covered any indecency. After swiping a pair of stockings, he sat upon the bed and tended to them himself, not wanting more assistance than was necessary.

"Accessories, sir?" Holding a wooden box, William indicated the cuff links inside, and Benjamin pointed to a simple gold set, unsure of what was the most tasteful.

"How long have you worked here, William?" he asked, extending his arm.

Applying the left cufflink, the servant moved on to the right. "When I was very young, my mother and I searched for employment. I had all my teeth, and a sound enough head for learning, so Mr. Boyd took me on. He has his manservants tutored."

"Does he?" Benjamin asked, trying to mask his shock.

Fetching a pair of breeches off the bed, William nodded. "Yes, sir. He's one of the richest, most powerful men in New York. He wants his hired help to reflect himself."

Accepting the breeches, Benjamin rose and stepped into each leg, then fastened his fall front while William knelt to secure the shiny, ornate buttons along the knee bands. "Do you like it here?"

William stood and helped Benjamin into a tan, silk brocade waistcoat before fetching a cravat. "I have the Lord, sir, so therefore, I very much enjoy my life."

It was a well-practiced and diplomatic answer; Benjamin could respect this, but found it far too convenient. Allowing William to wrap the silk fabric around his throat, he held still while the servant tied and knotted his cravat. "Since you can't be spared until later, would you mind telling me about the rooms here?"

William shrugged, fluffing out the tails of Benjamin's cravat. "Although hardly standard, it's what you'd expect, sir: bedrooms abound, a foyer, the sitting room, a drawing room, Mr. Boyd's office, the dining room, a libr—"

"An office?" Benjamin cut in, his interest piqued. That was surely where Jedediah was originally scheduled to meet him. "Does Mr. Boyd take clients there?"

"Sometimes," William allowed, "but usually the special ones. He does most of his dealings in town at his place of business."

When William rummaged in the trunk for a pair of shoes, Benjamin tried not to smile. If Jedediah headed into town often, that meant he had ample time to explore the man's home office, because surely, more private intelligence would be found there?

Mood considerably lifted, Benjamin started fastening his waistcoat buttons, then extended his left foot when William returned. The servant slipped the shoe into place, the black leather a little snug around his toes. A thick brass buckle shone brightly in the morning light.

While William tended to the second shoe, the servant apologized, "Begging your pardon, sir, but Miss Clara didn't lend you a wig. She said it'd be a shame to cover your nice head of hair."

Benjamin nearly snorted. He *never* wore a wig, and was grateful this Tory doll didn't expect him to play dress-up. "It's no matter," he assured the younger man. "You've both done more than enough. Thank you for your help."

"If you insist, sir." Satisfied with the job he'd done, William rose and helped his superior into the ornate, blue, wool frock coat from the bed. "Breakfast will be in about fifteen minutes, so I can escort you to the library before the gong is struck, if you'd like?"

Already, Benjamin could feel his stomach curdling. A meal, though a great pleasure for his tongue, also meant the *displeasure* of yet another encounter with the Boyds…

AFTER CLARA'S HANDMAIDEN helped her get dressed in a blue damask silk robe a l'anglaise, complete with a floral-patterned underskirt and white muslin fichu, Clara came downstairs in search of her sister. She found Catherine in the drawing room, expertly tinkling the keys of their well-polished harpsichord. But rather than sit and listen, as was her usual custom, Clara stormed over and stilled her sister's hands.

The blonde jerked away from the intrusion, her brow pinched and expression sour. "What on earth has gotten into you?" Catherine demanded. "I was finishing my—"

"We need to talk," Clara interrupted. Her eyes were sharp like unweathered sea glass. "It's about that man...Mr. Philip Ashby."

Bemused, Catherine shook her head. "Why are you saying his name like that?"

Checking around to make certain they were alone, Clara had a seat alongside her and took Catherine's hands. "I believe that man is a liar," she said. When the girl moved to speak, Clara shook her head, cutting her off. "Don't talk over me," she warned. "Though acceptably polite, and quite handsome, Mr. Ashby is woefully out of his depth. When I spoke with him yesterday afternoon, he told me he didn't have many clothes, nor any servants, nor a carriage at his disposal."

Catherine shrugged, unimpressed. "Surely, he had a reason for that."

"Indeed, he did! Complete hogwash, too," Clara said, annoyed. "Philip claimed he was robbed by highwaymen, and that they stole most of his belongings."

"But what if it's true?"

"And what if it's not?" Clara countered. "Could you live with yourself, were we to welcome some stranger into this family?"

"W-well—"

"He's like an awkward fawn," she continued. "Any time we speak, he gets all shy and tongue-tied. That is not the man Charlotte described in her letters."

Catherine bit her lip, perplexed. "You are right about that," she allowed. "Lottie said her Philip is blond, tall, and has a commanding way about him. There's hardly anything commanding about this Mr. Ashby..."

"Nor is he witty and dry," Clara agreed. "I understand that we all have different personalities with certain people—little masks, if you will—but I cannot imagine this Philip being anything but reticent in the company of others. Why, he is far too quick to take orders. Father may appreciate it, but Charlotte would not. She's always been a fan of the brash and domineering sorts." Clara shrugged. "Not to mention, this whole shipbuilding nonsense. Why would Lottie have never breathed a word of it?"

With a hand lifting to her throat, Catherine whimpered. "Oh, goodness, I wish you wouldn't spin such stories... You've always been the imaginative one in this family, and this is by far your worst tale yet!"

"I pray you're right about that," Clara said. "But truly, can I be blamed for having concern for my family? For our dear sister?"

"But what do you intend to do?" Catherine pressed. "Even if he is an imposter, you can't just accuse him without proof!"

"Leave it to me," Clara said. "Last night, I first became suspicious of him during supper, so my invitation to walk was but a ruse. I intend to get to know him, to earn his trust, and perhaps he will put our minds at ease."

"I don't like this," Catherine said, wringing her hands. "What if he figures out that we know?"

"We don't know anything," Clara reminded her. "Despite my suspicions, I don't actually believe him a nefarious sort. When I spoke to Philip last night, he was far more interested in my reading material than the family itself."

Catherine's brow furrowed. "Reading material? When on earth did you speak to him about books?"

"After bed last night," Clara said, dismissive. "Don't look at me like that! I don't need a chaperone to read." Rolling her eyes, she continued, "Neither of us could sleep, so he joined me in the library. It was a rather uneventful affair, truth be told, and I gave him some half-hearted apology for how I'd treated him."

Catherine snorted. "If he actually knew you, he'd recognize that all your apologies are faulty."

"Slander! I actually am a little sorry..." Shrugging, Clara offered a sheepish smile. "Even if he *is* putting on an act, he's by far the most interesting distraction we've had in months. Father's law friends are all so boring, and the British soldiers aren't much better. Their vanity is a huge nuisance."

Catherine's mouth grew pinched. "You are working on my nerves, and I do not appreciate it. Firstly, you imply that Philip Ashby is not Philip Ashby, and now you are speaking as if he is at the very height of your social calendar!"

"I am not!" Clara exclaimed, defensive. "I'm merely saying he is not a huge nuisance...which, coincidentally, is what I named that one soldier's pego."

"Clara Boyd!"

Giggling, the redhead hid her grin behind a hand, her eyes flashing with mischief. "What?" she asked, grinning more broadly. "Am I not to have a bit of fun? I already said I don't believe him a danger!"

Sighing, Catherine irritably turned and closed her music book, all desire to play having fled with her sister's perversions. "I suppose we should head in for breakfast. What are we to do once we encounter Mr. Ashby?"

"Nothing," Clara said as if it were obvious. "He is our guest, so we are to act naturally. If he thinks something is amiss, he'll become all taciturn...or rather, more so than he is already."

Twisting her hands, Catherine rose from the bench. "Tell me honestly. Do you believe him a man of ill repute?"

Following after, Clara stood and took the girl's shoulders, her eyes shining with fondness before she kissed her brow. "Of course not," she soothed. "It's as you said; I have an overactive imagination. I just wish to exercise caution, is all."

Catherine's brow creased. "Should we tell Father? Or Mother?"

"No." Shaking her head, Clara brushed back a lock of her sister's hair. "There is no need to worry them. I should've spared you the same courtesy, but I want you on guard, should he try and deceive you."

"He won't," Catherine promised. "I intend to keep to myself."

"Good. That's a marvelous idea," Clara agreed. "You leave all the talking to me." She took her sister's hands. "Now come! We have ourselves a breakfast to host."

WHEN BENJAMIN TOOK his place at the dining room table, he was somehow more agitated by the Boyds' customs than the night prior. The rules of dining etiquette, though simple enough, rankled him since they were clearly done more for show than necessity.

After thanking William for helping him get seated, Benjamin grudgingly watched the servant place small portions of food onto his plate. Even breakfast was superfluous: eggs, bread, fruit, nuts, and various jellies were laid out before them, and guilt lanced through his heart when he once more thought of his fellow soldiers.

While Clara prattled on about some party, and Catherine spared him several cautious, furtive glances, Benjamin sighed and picked at his eggs—and yes, this time with an *actual* fork.

"Where are your parents?" he asked them.

Clara pursed her mouth, not appreciating the interruption. "Father rarely breakfasts with us," she said, feigning nonchalance. "He prefers to eat early, and then rushes off to meet with his clients. And Mother..." She sighed, checking the hands on their tall case clock. "If I'm not mistaken, she should be barreling in here any moment. She'll probably be a bit lushey, but that's nothing unusual."

"Clara!" Catherine hissed, appalled.

Clara shrugged. "*What?* He is to be family. He might as well know what he's getting himself into." Turning to Benjamin, she flashed an impish smile. "How did you sleep, Philip?"

"Terribly, truth be told…though I appreciate you lending me that book." Benjamin speared a bit of egg onto his fork, then shoveled it into his mouth. He didn't bloody well care about trivialities, and now that he knew Jedediah was no longer in the house, he pondered his best course of action. It'd be foolish to search Boyd's home office without familiarizing himself with the layout, so a potential visit into town seemed wisest. Or rather, he wished to meet Boyd's clientele, should they also be linked to the Tory cause.

Suddenly, a shrill, unpleasant groan rose above the clink of silverware, piercing through Benjamin's thoughts and making him cringe. In the entryway, a comely blonde woman stood holding her head between her hands, her brow furrowed and her pretty mouth pursing as she groaned yet again.

Lushey, indeed, he thought.

Despite her cry for attention, it was already evident by her well-coiffed updo and gold-threaded green muslin that she was fully prepared for receiving guests.

"What's all the racket?" Deborah Boyd moaned, still rubbing her temples. "I can scarcely hear myself think!"

"Neither can we," Clara muttered. Falsely perking up, she added, "It's so good of you to come down, Mother. You've missed the event of the season. Charlotte's fiancé has come calling!"

Squinting at the trio, Deborah looked between each face with difficulty before she exhaled, dropping her hands at her sides. "I did hear of your arrival, Mr. Ashby," she said. "Do forgive my absence! I've been plagued by a dreadful, *dreadful* ailment, and didn't feel well enough to come downstairs and make introductions."

Rising from his seat, Benjamin offered a courteous bow. "I wouldn't dream of making you come down for me," he assured her. "Your presence now more than makes up for your absence."

"Oh…" Deborah tittered, a pretty pink blossoming across her

cheeks. Clara made a gagging face, but the woman ignored her daughter and strode across the room, her grin genuine as she took Benjamin's hand. "A pleasure, Mr. Ashby. Once you wed Charlotte, I trust our home will be filled with handsome, strapping young boys such as yourself."

Clara snorted. "Why? Do you intend to form a harem?"

Curling her upper lip, Deborah shot her daughter a warning glare. "I meant grandchildren, you vile doxy!"

Catherine paled at their mother's chastisement, and Clara laid a hand on her sister's wrist, sensing her distress.

Deborah looked back at Benjamin. "I must say, I hadn't realized our Lottie's beau was so handsome," she purred. "In her letters, she didn't go into much detail. It must have been to keep you all to herself!"

Benjamin forced a weak laugh. "Yes, undoubtedly."

"Your humbleness is something to strive for, Mr. Ashby," Clara muttered, rolling her eyes. "You are a true beacon of modesty!"

"Ignore her," Deborah snapped. "Clara is a lonely, wretched girl who only wishes to douse the happiness of others."

"Yes. I daresay I am all of those things, what with having withstood living here my entire life," Clara growled.

Benjamin looked between both women, genuinely shocked by the vitriol and lack of respect. He knew Deborah was owed deference from her daughter, and yet he felt a sharp, inexplicable pang of pity for Clara, perhaps because he, himself, knew what it was like to strive for perfection in the eyes of a parent. Benjamin loved his father, but with that admiration came the compulsion to never disappoint him.

Deborah, clearly a fan of theatrics, feigned a swoon and pressed a hand to her forehead. "I need to sit down," she whimpered. "All this senseless chatter has aggravated my condition."

"Allow me," Benjamin offered, quick to pull out a chair. As he seated her, he caught Clara's gaze, and she responded with an eyeroll. "Er...are you feeling any better, Mrs. Boyd?" he asked. "Should I fetch your lady's maid?"

"No, no," she said, waving off the idea. "I'm much better now that you're here. A big, strong man is precisely what this household needs!"

Clara shook her head, furiously cutting up her eggs. But rather than eat them, she just as furiously shoved aside her plate. "You are free to fawn over, ingratiate, and even flirt with Lottie's intended, yet *I* am the doxy?" Livid, she glowered at the older woman. "Father may not be home as often as it pleases you, Mother, but at least have the decency to keep your desires secret!"

Deborah drew up from her seat, clearly forgetting her feigned ailment. "Why, you miserable doggess! I should have you thrown into the street!"

"Please do!" Clara seethed. "At least then I'll become the harlot you've always claimed!"

Catherine burst into tears, and despite the look of regret in Clara's eyes, the redhead steeled her shoulders and stalked from the room.

Awkwardly, Benjamin lingered near Deborah, unsure of his place now that the natural order had been disturbed.

"Well!" the matriarch exclaimed. "Let us conclude all this nonsense, shall we? Catherine, stop crying. Such weakness is unsightly. And Mr. Ashby..." She turned to Benjamin with a bright, wolfish smile. "Might you tell me about your business?"

Benjamin flinched at her close proximity, but nodded. "Of course," he agreed.

"Splendid! Let us reclaim our seats."

As he followed her example, his eyes strayed toward the dining room entrance, half hoping to see Clara in the doorway.

THE MORNING CAME and went, and without any true progress. Although Clara bribed William to listen in on Philip's conversation with her mother and sister, she was disappointed to find it lacking. The man didn't say anything worthy of note. According to William, Deborah had commandeered the conversation to be entirely about herself, so it left very little chance for Philip to catch himself in a lie—not that the servant knew of her suspicions, of course. Whenever making her request, Clara claimed she was trying to determine if Philip was "the perfect gentleman" for Charlotte. Thus far, she still had no earthly idea if this was even the case.

Frustrated, Clara paid William, and he alerted her that Philip was presently in the library.

After asking the young man to join them as a chaperone, she went downstairs in search of her target.

Philip sat reading unawares. He flipped through her copy of *The Taming of the Shrew,* his eyes scanning the text while he jiggled his foot.

"Good afternoon, Philip!" Clara exclaimed.

Philip jerked, not having expected her greeting. "Uh…good afternoon, Miss Boyd," he said, clear caution darkening his eyes. When she stalked toward him, he pointedly returned to reading her book.

"Ah-ah-ah!" Just as pointedly, she yanked the novel from his hand and tossed it aside. When he scowled, she placed her hands on her hips. "You promised to accompany me for a stroll, remember? Or are you one of those 'yes men' who only says what we Boyds wish to hear?"

"If I choose to lie, I do so for a just reason," Philip coolly said.

"Oh?" Eyes alight, Clara teased, "Then you don't find kissing my father's bottom to be a just cause? Good for you, Philip!"

Annoyed, Philip tried to reclaim the book, but she pushed it farther out of reach.

"Why are you being so stubborn?" she pressed. "Father isn't here, and neither is your darling Charlotte, so I can't imagine you actually wishing to dwell within this stuffy old house."

Take the bait, she inwardly pleaded. Men were all the same, so surely, he would cave…

To her delight, a grudging look flashed over Philip's eyes, and he ultimately acquiesced.

"Where are we going then?" he wearily asked.

"Just along the grounds," she assured him, triumphant. "And you look quite dashing in Father's clothes, if you don't mind my saying so. I daresay he won't even realize they're gone."

Philip scrunched his brow. "You didn't tell him?"

"Heavens, no! Father isn't the acquiescent type." With a wink, she gestured for him to follow, so he rose and accompanied her to the foyer, where William was waiting for them. "How do you find the garments?"

Philip winced. "A bit tight, actually."

"Perfect!" Amusement flashed across Clara's eyes, and she appraised him over her shoulder. "Just remember, Philip: *I am the one helping you out of the goodness of my heart, so you'd better be nice to me.*"

As she peered up at him with her bright, coquettish smile, Clara allowed him to ponder the hidden meaning behind her words.

THE BOYD ESTATE was boundless. A long, uneven dirt path extended from the manor toward their gardens, and several proud, sturdy ginkgo trees dotted the landscape. Cattle grazed in the fields, and storehouses were tucked along the forest edge with a smattering of daffodils, crocuses, and flowering dogwoods, while directly behind the manor, the Harlem River flowed placidly like a silver skein.

This was surely how it felt when one entered Heaven, Benjamin thought. It was a true, untouchable paradise, giving off the impression that the world was still beautiful—that it wasn't on fire and trapped within a cruel, winnerless civil war. And while Benjamin talked to Clara, his passions fueled by the desire for change kept him vociferous and excitable.

A deep sigh drew him to attention.

"Good gracious, Mr. Ashby, I hope you are quite finished!" Clara complained. "Must you keep asking about Father? I grow so bored of it all!"

She hid her face from the sun beneath a parasol, her hand pressing into the crook of his elbow while William followed at a respectable distance.

Benjamin snorted, a bit thrown. "I'm to be part of your family," he reminded her. "Wouldn't it be beneficial if we discussed these matters now rather than later?"

Eyeing him skeptically, Clara adjusted her straw chip hat and huffed. "But wouldn't you rather talk about me, sir? I am perfectly interesting—marvelously interesting, in fact—yet you're barely paying me any attention at all."

Benjamin sneered. "Forgive me, but it would seem that my interests deviate vastly from yours."

"Well! There is no need for that tone," Clara snapped. "At least I am not a clodpate."

"You believe me a clodpate?" Despite his prior agitation, Benjamin's lips curved into a smile. "If I'm so dull and stupid, let it be known that you're rather eager to be in my company."

Clara's mouth pursed, her eyes flashing. "I'm a woman of society in need of a respectable male acquaintance; as fate would have it, *you* happen to be the only eligible man available." She shook her head. "I hope Mother's fawning inclinations haven't muddled you. I do not share in her sentiments."

"Then I have been blessed," Benjamin muttered. Her fingers dug into his arm, but he didn't acknowledge the gesture. "Do you think I could stop by your father's town office sometime? I'd enjoy seeing him at work."

"Ugh, more talk of Father?" Rolling her eyes, Clara groused, "And to think, womenfolk claim men only reason with their hornpipe, when in actuality, they're far more obsessed with business and economics. Such a bore! Truth be told, I would much rather you speak to me about your hornpipe." She spared him a sly smile, which Benjamin vigorously ignored. "Why so interested? Are you intending to study law?"

"I admire your father a great deal," Benjamin supplied. "As a future in-law, I intend to contribute to the Boyd success story, whether it be through shipbuilding, or following his example. And in order to do that, I need a decent knowledge of the goings-on of his office."

Clara elevated her shoulders. "Oh, very well…it certainly won't be an enjoyable walk now, but I cannot argue with your reasoning."

"Oh, no?" In spite of himself, Benjamin smiled.

Clara turned up her nose. "How old are you, Mr. Ashby? For being such a young man, you are quite confident in your arrogance. Is there a reason you believe yourself so charming?"

Sighing through his nose, Benjamin rolled his eyes skyward. "I'm three and twenty, Miss Boyd, so I don't presume to know anything. I only hope that in time, I can acquire as much worldly wisdom as your father."

Clara's expression grew feline. "Well, that's rather interesting, isn't it? In Lottie's letters, she said you were seven and twenty."

Oh, blood and thunder.

"I lied to her," Benjamin quickly said. "As unscrupulous as it was, I wanted to impress your sister, so I embellished my life's story. If Lottie believed me older, and therefore more sophisticated, I thought she would desire me in the way I desire her."

Clara huffed, though her stance softened. "She does love older men," she agreed, twirling her parasol. "Still, you needn't lie. Mother's nearing the end of her prime, and even she was willing to throw her legs over her head."

Benjamin choked, unable to return her gaze.

"What?" Clara jeered, playfully poking his ribs. "Am I not speaking like a lady? I'd argue that you haven't been much of a gentleman, what with all your lies. I don't much care for deception."

"How do you mean?"

She harrumphed, twirling her parasol more vigorously. "Since you're reading *The Taming of the Shrew,* allow me to enlighten you with a likeness you might understand: you remind me of Sly donning the garments of a lord."

Benjamin's heart stuttered in his chest, yet he managed a hearty chuckle. "Although it pains me, I must admit, I don't follow your logic," he treaded carefully. "Unlike Sly, I am not at the center of anyone's cruel prank... Or at least, I hope." He glanced her way. "However, much like many of the characters in that production, I do wish to change my socially defined role—though in my instance, I yearn to play a part in ending this war."

"By what means? A disguise?" Clara challenged, causing his pulse to drum erratically. "Quite a few of those characters masqueraded as other men. Is that what you intend to do? Become someone else, just as Tranio dressed up as Lucentio?"

Benjamin forced a laugh. "If I can aid in the king's cause by becoming someone else, then yes, absolutely. When I told your father I would do anything to help, I meant it."

Clara pursed her mouth. "And how far are you willing to go, exactly?"

"As far as it takes." Looking down at her, he vowed, "I would do anything for our king—even degrade myself to the highest degree."

Clara hummed under her breath, sparing him a disbelieving

glance.

Desperate to deflect, Benjamin reminded her, "Wasn't it you who said I lack modesty? Perhaps I should demean myself for the king, if only to lower my sense of self." Glancing at their chaperone, he looked forward again before asking, "Speaking of our king and his devotees, do you know who your father's invited tonight? I've heard quite a bit about Mayor Mathews, so as you can imagine, I'd very much like to make his acquaintance."

Clara pouted. "Why? The man is an eel. His own supporters find his character questionable."

Trying not to sound too eager, Benjamin prodded, "And your father doesn't?"

She shrugged. "Father is an eel, too," she replied. "To what regard, I do not know, but they're old school chums. That merits a sort of loyalty, I suppose…they studied law together, and thus, help one another break said law." She eyed him shrewdly. "I imagine these secrets will all be passed on to you, seeing how you're about to become part of this family."

"Oh, I don't know," Benjamin replied, feigning dismay. "Your father's rather taciturn. I doubt I'll be privy to the family secrets any time soon."

Clara shrugged again, brushing back a wayward lock of hair that spilled free from her updo. "Perhaps you're right," she agreed. "The truth is, Father only confides in Mother and Lottie, so I have to get my news from hearsay, and what little fragments he mutters at the dinner table. I have no idea who he's inviting."

"But surely you've met his friends before?"

Peering at Benjamin beneath her parasol, Clara flashed him a look of bored exasperation. "I've tolerated this long enough, Philip," she admonished. "You may be our guest, but it just so happens that I have some questions for you now. For starters: How did you meet Lottie? I never quite got the full story. You don't exude 'fine dining and parties,' so I can't imagine how your paths might have crossed."

Benjamin tensed his hands, not having expected the deflection. Clara was far, far too good at questioning his motives. "You give me too little credit," he said, waving a hand. "We met at a party hosted by a mutual friend. While Charlotte inquired about my business, I happened to fall in love."

Clara snorted. "You fell in love because she asked about ship-building? Men truly are all the same, aren't they?" He ignored her, so she continued, "And who was this mutual friend?"

Oh, rot it all…

Straightening, Benjamin shrugged as though it were of no consequence. "You wouldn't know him."

"Wouldn't I? She is my sister, Philip. I make a point to know everyone she meets." Canting her head, Clara appraised him with clear interest. "Unless there is a reason you don't wish for me to know?"

"Of course not, I…I beg your forgiveness." Fumbling through the Philadelphian names in his mental stock, Benjamin plucked one free and said, "It was Augustus Winthrop. He's rather partial to matchmaking, so I failed to realize it was a set-up until…w-well…I was already smitten, naturally." To his surprise, Clara appeared startled. "Was that not what you were expecting?"

"No," she admitted, frowning. "I daresay it wasn't."

Benjamin found it a strange response, but wasn't complaining. At least her suspicions, whatever they might have been, seemed diverted. Readjusting his tricorn, he continued his furtive appraisal while they walked at a more leisurely pace.

"Why do you suppose Mr. Winthrop was so eager for your match?" Clara asked. "He's always been rather smitten with Lottie. I imagine if he weren't so terribly old, not to mention, if he were far wealthier, he would've already married into the family."

Benjamin shrugged, hoping his eyes didn't reflect the brief stab of panic between his ribs. "Change of heart, perhaps?" he asked. "Maybe Winthrop is a romantic. If he can't have her, then he wants to make sure she's well taken care of."

"Oh, hogwash," Clara replied. "Male vanity wouldn't allow

such a thing."

"You don't think so?"

"I know so. Masculine pride is the very reason we are ensnared by this horrid war to begin with."

"Among other reasons," Benjamin countered. "We entered this fight for economic motives. Many businesses, loyalist ones, are suffering from the lack of trade with our king."

Clara snorted. "I hope you're not trying to explain what I already know, sir. I may only be expected to hold court, but I am well aware that everyone's suffering."

Not everyone, Benjamin thought, looking her over in disdain. "Forgive me, Miss Boyd," he said. "I didn't mean to suggest you were uneducated."

"Perhaps not in the way you are educated," Clara agreed, appraising him with a sly smile. "Since you're a Philadelphian gentleman, I presume you attended the College of Philadelphia?"

"Yale, actually," Benjamin replied. "My father and its president were childhood friends, so the choice was inevitable."

"You're an Eli?" Clara asked, a playful grin lighting up her face. "Oh, yes, of course; I see it now. One of my old beaux went to Yale. You educated sorts are in constant need of someone to keep your vanities in check."

Benjamin snorted. "And as a woman who holds an endless supply of said vanities, I trust you are the primary expert?"

She simpered. "You are sharp, I'll give you that. Any man who can eviscerate me within a moment's notice has my respect. However, no, I don't find myself presumptuous enough to teach you a lesson. That is Lottie's job. And what a trying job it must surely be!"

Before Benjamin could reply, the sound of horse hooves thudded hollowly against the earth, and both looked up as a British officer rode toward them upon a sleek, beautiful black horse. The man had a cocked hat, dark hair, and an aquiline nose, and was bedecked in a full regimental coat with white facings and gleaming, polished buttons bearing the number 17 on each surface.

The sight made Benjamin's mouth go dry. In his mind, all he could picture were the soldiers lined up at Daniel's execution, each of them dotting the terrain like freshly spilt blood. Major General Bishop gave a whistle like a bird, and then Benjamin and the other patriots descended upon the scene, mindful of the screaming civilians as they attempted to reach Daniel in time.

"Major Markham!" Clara greeted, startling Benjamin out of his trance. "What a pleasant surprise!"

The man clicked his tongue, then rode to a stop alongside them, gently crooning to his mare while she nickered in displeasure. As he pulled firmly on her reins, the harsh tug reminded Benjamin of a tightening noose.

Beaming, Clara gestured to her right. "Have you met Mr. Philip Ashby yet, Major? He is Charlotte's betrothed."

The officer's eyes lit up, then he looked to Benjamin. "At long last. The man of the hour!" he exclaimed, extending a gloved hand. "A pleasure, sir! I am Major Adam Markham, officer of His Majesty's 17th Regiment of Foot. Though I suppose we'll be getting to know one another rather well, seeing how Jed's invited me to your party tonight."

Clara perked up, watching the two shake hands. "Ooh, will any other officers be in attendance?"

"But of course, Miss Boyd."

Quickly, Benjamin retracted his hand. "It's so good to make your acquaintance, sir," he said. "Anyone serving the king is surely serving the Lord, as well."

"Hear, hear!" Adam agreed, drawing back with a grin. "Are you able to watch the cockfight this afternoon? It was arranged last minute, but the boys and I wished to give Jed a surprise in light of your good news. Word travels fast in these parts, you know. My highest congratulations!"

Not wishing to be thwarted from his original plans, Benjamin laughed and waved a hand, feigning embarrassment. "Oh, no, no, as thoughtful as that all is, I'm afraid I grow faint at the sight of blood, any blood, which is precisely why I won't enlist."

"Truly?" Adam asked, amused disbelief brightening his face. "Alas, that's what we get for orchestrating a surprise. You must beg my forgiveness."

"A surprise you were all too happy to divulge, I see," Clara teased.

He winked. "Secrets are no fun if they cannot be shared!" Stroking his mare's neck, Adam added, "I suppose I'll continue on to the house. Jed isn't due back for another couple hours, but I figured I'd start assessing the hay and livestock set aside for the King's Men. Perhaps I might even help myself to that apple pie your cook is so exemplary at, Miss Boyd?" He tipped his hat with a jaunty grin. "It was a pleasure making your acquaintance, Mr. Ashby."

"The pleasure was all mine, Major," Benjamin replied.

As Adam rode off, Clara nudged him and jeered, "It would seem he thinks you're a fribble. Well done, Philip."

Benjamin said nothing. It was only when the major became a small, barely visible red dot that he was fully able to breathe again.

CHAPTER FOUR

The Gathering

LATER THAT AFTERNOON, Clara was brimming with nervous energy. Due to her ability to wield her charms against men, she considered herself an excellent judge of their character, but this? It was unlike anything she'd ever experienced. Despite Philip's satisfactory answers for each of her questions, there was still a nagging, sour sensation in her gut that could not be shaken…

And yet, it would have to be. For Catherine's sake. Even if she didn't completely believe him, she needed to ensure her sister did. Philip wasn't a danger, of that much she was certain, so it would be unkind to keep Catherine fretting and embroidering so madly that she pricked each finger.

"Kitty?" Entering the sitting room, Clara noted Catherine still stitching, and strode over to her with a sigh. "Where is Mother?" she asked.

"In the garden with her lady's maid," Catherine replied. Setting aside her work, she rose and moved to her sister, anxiously wringing her hands. "What of Mr. Ashby? You took a stroll with him, did you not?"

"Shh!" Clara hissed, agitation sparking across her eyes. "You must learn to keep your voice down! Only the two of us know about this suspicion. Understood?"

"But—"

"Yes," she cut in, taking Catherine by the shoulders, "yes, I did speak with him earlier, and I learned quite a bit."

"Oh?" Expression apprehensive, the girl chewed her lip. "What happened?"

"Nothing of immediate import," Clara assured her, "though I did make it plain I suspect him."

Catherine gasped. "Oh, Clara… You didn't!"

"Take care, would you?" Lowering her hands, she continued, "My accusations were veiled at best, because I wished to see his reaction. And, though I am loath to admit as such, he remained unruffled, and dodged each one of my parries…and all with valid answers."

Catherine softened with relief. "I say that's wonderful news!" she declared. "Perhaps Lottie failed to properly describe Mr. Ashby, after all. Of the three of us, she *is* the weakest at observation."

Clara snorted. "That's because she needs spectacles, darling."

"You know what I meant," Catherine snapped. "This isn't funny, Clara, and least especially since you were the one to act as if this is some great concern!"

"Yes, but it's better to be safe than sorry, wouldn't you agree?" Feigning joviality, she draped an arm around her sister's shoulders. "With Mr. Ashby no longer an immediate concern, why don't we discuss our gowns for the party this evening?"

Catherine blinked, incredulous. "You are trying to distract me," she accused.

"No, I am trying to ensure that you're an absolute vision, as usual," Clara deflected.

Unconvinced, the blonde shook her head. "Very well, but…Father won't wish for us to be there," she said. "You know it's true."

"Yes, but suppose they call upon us to entertain? What then?" Clara challenged.

Catherine huffed. "You cannot play the harpsichord—not well, at least—and I cannot sing. Is it any wonder Father prefers to keep us hidden away?"

"Ah, yes," Clara dryly agreed. "We merely serve as two pretty dolls. Better to look at, but never to touch. Well…" She smirked, lifting her shoulders. "Better not to touch you, anyway."

"Clara, please."

"What? Can I help that men enjoy their playthings? If you're not careful, you will end up tattered and broken." A bitterness curled the corner of her mouth, but quickly evaporated. "Come along then. I'll fetch the servants so we can get started with our preparations."

Catherine moved to protest, but ultimately succumbed, and as Clara escorted her sister into the hallway, her mind danced with the possibilities of what the night could bring.

LATER THAT DAY, William gave his promised tour. The house was precisely what one would expect for a Georgian style manor: elegant parquet flooring; grand, sweeping rooms; well-crafted paneled walls; expensive heirlooms that Benjamin feared even breathing around; and opulence—so, so much, that left him oddly numb and unimpressed. After all, what was wealth when the very world was falling apart? Who was this benefitting, beyond a pitiful echo to yesteryears' past when halls were filled with song and dance, while now, only the most well-to-do could hold such affairs?

When William motioned him onward, Benjamin sighed and followed after.

He'd been forbidden to see the daughters' rooms (something about impropriety), so the last place on the list was Mr. Boyd's office. William was reluctant to enter this room unprompted, given Jedediah's strictness about who was allowed to do so, but after a bit of coaxing, he ultimately gave in and led the other man inside.

"You mustn't touch anything," William warned. "If you do, it'll be my head." With a wince, he amended, "Begging your pardon, sir."

Benjamin smiled. If nothing else, at least the servant was becoming more forthright. "Worry not, William," he replied. "You wouldn't be of much use to me without a head."

"Very funny, sir."

Appraising the great room, Benjamin admired the office with a calculating eye. The tall walls were a simple gray-green, with two large windows that let in a massive amount of natural light, and at the center of the room was an ornate, mahogany bureau plat desk. Benjamin's pulse quickened. Surely, something of use lay within those drawers? The only problem was getting it alone…

All at once, he feigned a swoon and stumbled in place, panting and tugging at the fabric of his cravat.

"Sir?" William asked, alarm flashing across his eyes. "Sir, are you all right?"

Gasping in response, Benjamin continued unfastening his cravat while pretending to greedily gulp in mouthfuls of air.

"I'll fetch some brandy," William quickly assured him. As he rushed over and grabbed the decanter off a sideboard table, Benjamin shook his head.

"No," he croaked out, "water…I-I need…water."

Practically dancing amidst his panic, the servant set the decanter onto its serving tray with a jarring *clang,* then held up his hands. "I'll be right back," he promised. "I'll fetch the water. Just please, sir, do not move!"

Poor William took off in a rush, nearly tripping over the rug on his way out, and once he was safely out of sight, Benjamin straightened and raced over to the desk with jittery limbs. Tugging on the middle drawer, he cursed once he realized it was locked. *Of bloody course it was.* Heaven forbid he deal with an actual idiot loyalist.

Exhaling through his nose, Benjamin mentally filed that away for later. He'd either have to find a key or break into the drawer by force. Instead, he moved over to the left drawer. Inside, he found a small leatherbound book. Glancing toward the entryway, he noted the empty corridor and was quick to snatch the ledger, his hands shaking while he lifted the cover. Inside, he found a list of names—all prominent Tories—and by every individual, Boyd listed a sum of money he'd paid, and what each man donated to the king's cause.

This is good, Benjamin thought giddily. If he only offered Bishop a few new loyalists, this could still lead to many opportunities.

From down the hall, the sound of slapping shoes echoed throughout the corridor, and in a panic, Benjamin hastily shoved the ledger inside the drawer, slammed it shut, and rushed back toward the middle of the room. He doubled over and started faking a wheezing fit, and that was when William made his flustered entrance. Flanking his sides were two other servants.

"Don't just stand there!" the boy snarled. "Help Mr. Ashby sit down!"

Allowing himself to be led to a scarlet wingback chair, Benjamin collapsed, and perhaps a bit too dramatically, onto the furniture while the men fussed over him. Accepting a glass of water, he dipped his fingers into the liquid and flicked it across his face, breathing heavily while swallowing low in his throat.

"Do you have a condition, Mr. Ashby?" William asked, anxious. "Is this to happen often?"

Trying not to reflect his amusement, Benjamin shook his head, slowly calming his breath. "No, no," he assured the younger man. "I think...I-I am nervous about tonight. I wish to impress Mr. Boyd's friends."

Slowly, William's face grew awash with relief. "Oh, is that all?" he asked. "I trust you'll do quite well, sir."

While one of the servants dabbed his face with a cloth, Benjamin mirrored his smile. Perhaps he would do "quite well," indeed.

DESPITE THE LAST-MINUTE preparations, there was no shortage of wine, spirits, nor desserts to be had that evening, and at least a dozen men milled around the drawing room laughing and making merry. Benjamin stood at Jedediah's side while the attorney bragged on his behalf, boisterously declaring the merge of their two families.

"Lucky you," Major Markham whispered into his ear. "The Boyd girls are all quite stunning."

"In more ways than one," Benjamin muttered.

By this point, he'd been introduced to each guest—various businessmen and preening peacocks, naturally—but most of them were sticking to their own favored social circles, rather than speaking to him beyond perfunctory politeness. Benjamin had always been quiet and bookish, so he was finding it difficult making conversation with these out of touch, conceited high-flyers. At least when a book's message agitated him, he could close it.

In his immediate vicinity was Jedediah, pompous and nettled as always; Major Adam Markham; Simon Falstaff, a middle-aged banker; Michael Collins, an agricultural merchant; and Ensign Eleazar Thomas, an ignorant boob.

"No, no, you are not listening!" the latter exclaimed. "If we ply these rebel cowards with a bunch of harlots, we won't have to outsmart them in battle!"

"Do tell," Adam said, hiding a smile behind his wine glass.

Not catching the man's scorn—or perhaps choosing not to acknowledge it—Eleazar continued, "It's a God-given fact that men are more submissive once they've had a good ol' grind, so if we buy them each a wench, they'll lose their drive to fight!"

The men erupted into laughter.

"El, that has got to be the stupidest thing I've ever heard," Simon remarked, "and the runner-up is your stance on the French. You're a prime example of why men in your position have to purchase army commissions to get ahead."

Eleazar huffed. "I just don't think we should be so dismissive of the Frenchies, that's all!" he exclaimed. His face grew nearly as red as his military coat.

Benjamin arched a brow. "Wait a moment…Ensign Thomas is the only one here leery of the rebel alliance with the French?"

"At this point, it's old news!" Jedediah exclaimed, puffing out his chest. "The French are no match for His Majesty's Finest, Philip."

Benjamin frowned. "But sir, they've sent arms and ammunition to aid in the fight, and that's not including their own soldiers, naval personnel, and warships!"

"What of it? Even if the French have a sizeable addition, they're fighting alongside rebels. That sort of alliance won't last against the royal army!"

"Hear, hear!" the group exclaimed.

Laughing, Eleazar chimed in, "I've got their 'sizable addition' right here!" and lewdly grabbed himself.

"Good Lord, El," Michael admonished, his upper lip curling. "Major Markham, can't you control your ensign?"

Desperate to rein back the conversation, Benjamin pressed, "But sirs, what about the newfound flow of supplies and coin? Surely, that will bolster the rebels and keep them fighting?"

Adam looked his way with a wink. "Don't you worry, Ashby! We'll find a way to stamp out their passions. Michael, here, has quite the plan."

"Oh?" Benjamin looked his way with intrigue. "What are you thinking, Mr. Collins?"

"Ah!" Jedediah crowed, waving his glass of port. "You two

could be of use to one another, Philip. You claimed you wanted to help with the loyalist cause, and that you've been helping *many* loyalists, in fact; so by God, this is assuredly the way!"

Michael brushed a thumb over his lower lip, assessing Benjamin with his dark, cunning eyes. "I have my own men," he allowed, "but a shipbuilding merchant could potentially get us ahead of schedule, if you have spare ships at the ready?"

"I am at your service," Benjamin affirmed. "Name it, Mr. Collins, and it will be done."

Crooking his finger, Michael indicated that he follow. "Take a turn with me, Mr. Ashby. I'd rather keep the specifics between the two of us, if you wouldn't mind. I'm sure you understand."

"Oh, absolutely," Benjamin agreed, tamping down his sudden burst of excitement. Could it truly be this easy?

Moving into step alongside the tall, scarecrow-like man, he kept his eye on the crowd while they strolled the perimeter. "How can I help, sir?" he asked. "I take it your endeavor requires nautical travel?"

"Preferably," Michael agreed. Lowering his voice, he added, "Throughout this bloody war, the rebels have been at a constant disadvantage with supplies. The French may be aiding them now, but they'd be absolute fools to deny further assistance after everything they've endured."

Benjamin nodded, his brow creasing in thought. "You wish to give them supplies, sir?"

"Tampered supplies," Michael corrected. "My business deals with farming, so I'm able to give them grain and flour—through hired men with patriot aliases, of course—but it's not of an ingestible sort." With a crooked sneer, he smugly confided, "I've already had tiny bits of glass put into each bag. These supplies could feed an entire army encampment. Just think of it, Ashby! We could end this war through their very food!"

The breath stripped from Benjamin's lungs, and he blinked, nearly stumbling when Michael looked his way. Forcing a grin, Benjamin feigned glee and exclaimed, "That is remarkable, sir! An ingenious plan, if you don't mind my saying so."

"I don't mind at all," Michael replied, chuckling, "because I wholeheartedly agree. And although I have men willing to bring these supplies to the rebels via cart, doing so by ship and then by cart might be safer."

"Most assuredly," Benjamin agreed, his mouth dry. "How would you like to arrange this?"

"Pray, why not make things easier for you?" Michael suggested. "I have a man in Philadelphia. If you give me your address, I can have him stop by for further instruction."

Benjamin shook his head. "No. My men prefer to be underground about dealings of this nature, and they never take 'donations' in the same place," he replied. "I'll get you the address once I've written home to verify. This is a bit last minute, so they may require some coin for their troubles."

"Fine," Michael agreed. "Have them name their price, and it will be done."

"Fifteen pounds should suffice," Benjamin said. "If you'd like, you can pay me tonight, and I will forward the coin along with my correspondence."

Michael nodded, appearing a bit put out, but no less invigorated. "Fine, fine," he allowed, "that will be suitable. How soon should you receive word?"

"Probably no later than a week or two," Benjamin replied, "so long as I reach out tomorrow morning. I'm sure I can find someone to ride out to Philadelphia posthaste."

"See that it's done," Michael agreed. "I'll give you the money before departing this evening. To do so now would be unseemly."

Nearly breaking into a wide, ebullient grin, Benjamin congratulated himself on a job well done. Not only did he have valuable intelligence to share, but he'd also gleaned some coin he could pass along to Bishop. Any amount of money, no matter how small (or in this case, large), could aid in employing additional blackguards.

His excitement, unfortunately, proved to be short-lived. A mere moment later, Deborah and her two daughters entered the room, preening beneath the attention bestowed upon them.

Oh, sweet merciful Lord…

"You're one lucky man, Ashby," Michael told him. "Each of Jed's daughters is a true sight to behold."

"A man could grow blind from taking in so much beauty," Benjamin agreed. *If their grating conversation did not lead to deafness first.* Falsely brightening, he added, "I can scarcely wait 'til I'm reunited with my Charlotte."

"Mm, I can imagine," Michael agreed. "And for your sake, I hope she has every bit the exceptional tongue as Miss Clara."

Benjamin blinked, scandalized. "I-I beg your pardon?"

"Alas, I haven't partaken myself, but one does hear rumors…" Clapping a hand onto the other man's shoulder, Michael concluded, "Now then! I must be off to greet our lovely hostess. Remember, Ashby. Fetch me the address, and I'll send along the supplies."

Benjamin nodded, dumbfounded, before finding himself alone by the refreshments table. Alas, this was the perfect opportunity for a premeditated ambush…

"Good evening, Philip."

Benjamin jerked in surprise, then turned and beheld Clara in all her coquettish, simpering glory. Her curls were piled into a high roll with ornamental jewels and feathers, and around her neck dripped a glittering spread of diamonds. Adorning her frame was a pale-blue gown with a low, lacy neckline—one so low that his eyes guiltily snapped back to her face. "Miss Boyd," he greeted. "Where is your chaperone?"

She snorted. "Mother's my chaperone, and with Father also near, I hardly consider this discussion a means for concern. Unless you plan on being untoward?"

Benjamin huffed, thoroughly mortified. "I…o-of course not. No."

When he flushed a faint pink, Clara grinned and mockingly

batted her lashes. "Are you not going to tell me how lovely I am?" she teased. "You certainly look handsome this evening." Waving a fan lazily beneath her chin, she pressed, "And how are you faring? I wasn't expecting to find you all alone."

"Why are you here?" Benjamin asked, choosing to ignore her questions. "To my understanding, this was supposed to be a gentlemen's party."

Clara snorted, her eyes sparkling with mischief. "Well, how unfortunate," she purred, "for I see no gentlemen here...present company excluded, of course."

"Of course," Benjamin agreed, resisting an eyeroll.

"Naturally, Mother's on the hunt for potential suitors," Clara explained, pointing her fan in Deborah's direction. "Unlike Charlotte, I'm afraid the matter of marrying up isn't quite so important in my case. She just wishes to see me wed and carted off to the highest bidder."

Benjamin hummed. "Surely, it's not all that bad? From what I can tell, you have quite a few men chomping at the bit."

Clara groaned. "I wish you wouldn't use a horse analogy toward potential suitors...though to your credit, you're not entirely wrong. Most of these men are a bit on the farm-animal side in terms of attractiveness."

Benjamin grinned. "How fortunate, then, that you have so much farmland to spare."

She gasped, swatting him with her fan. "You are cruel, Mr. Ashby!"

"I'm not cruel, I am honest—something you don't seem ready to accept."

The redhead appraised him sagely. "In regards to honesty as a whole, or yourself? Because you're right; I have encountered my fair share of men, and most of them say whatever I wish to hear, and almost always with an ulterior motive. I suppose I'm trying to figure out yours."

"My goal is to marry your sister," Benjamin replied. "Need I more than that?"

"Spoken like a true gentleman. With your silver tongue, I'll assuredly need to stay on guard." Eyes alight, Clara resumed waving her fan beneath her chin, only to falter once her gaze settled upon something across the room. "Who on earth is that?" she asked.

Intrigued by her disgust, Benjamin turned and beheld a surly, thick-browed man with dark, uncombed hair and filthy-looking raiment. "That's Kit Donnelly," he explained to her. "According to Major Markham, he's a commoner who hosted today's cockfight. When they discussed payment, this was what they settled upon."

Clara made a face. "What, to attend this party? These are my people, and even I wouldn't wish this upon anyone. Surely this blaggard isn't enjoying himself?"

"Clearly not," Benjamin agreed, bemused. The man's eyes were sharp and wolfish, and trained upon him with such fire that an immediate shudder lanced up his spine.

Clara hummed. "In any case, he certainly doesn't seem fond of you, Philip. Do you think he's taken offense to you skipping the fight? It was hosted in your honor."

"I…surely do not know," Benjamin replied, more perplexed than ever.

"Perhaps you should tip him, just to be safe," Clara decided. "You never know with the riffraff of this colony." A look of mischief overcame her face and she tapped his arm. "Let's not speak of such things any longer. How are your pipes?"

Benjamin blinked. "I beg your pardon?"

"Your singing voice," she clarified. "At these parties, it is customary to sing and make merry, so you might as well be the one to lead us. Maybe then your admirer will be far more amenable."

Benjamin sneered at her. "If your aim is to embarrass me in front of your father's friends, I am afraid you'll be sorely disappointed."

Clara raised her chin. "How so? Are you an accomplished

tenor?"

"Not in the least," he replied. "I have a dreadful singing voice—much like two feral cats wrestling in an alley, if I am being honest—but my song choice of 'Burrowing Yankees' will surely soothe any auditory assault."

Clara gleefully tucked her hand into the crook of his arm. "Well!" she exclaimed. "If that isn't a sign to head over to the harpsichord, then I surely don't know what is. Catherine can accompany you, and I'll use my singing voice as a buffer."

Benjamin huffed. "Yes, I daresay your voice could drown out anything," he agreed, smiling once she knuckled his ribs.

Despite her clear annoyance, the redhead leaned into his side and led him across the room, yet as they walked arm in arm, Benjamin swore he could feel Donnelly's dark, unwavering gaze searing through the back of his head, sharp and all-knowing in its intensity.

CHAPTER FIVE

Curiosity Killed the Blackguard

W HEN BENJAMIN AWOKE before dawn the next morning, he got dressed, wove his hair into a fresh queue, and then went down to fetch his horse. Since he hadn't stayed at the White Fox Inn, as originally planned, he needed to get word to his primary contact as soon as possible.

Just as Benjamin approached the stables, he heard the swift rush of feet, then two strong hands seized his coat and wrenched him into the large structure. He cried out before slamming against the interior wall. A few horses nickered at the disturbance.

"Have ya lost your feckin' mind?!" Amos snarled.

Overwhelmed by the ambush, Benjamin barely processed his friend's words before taking note of the clean, freshly pressed military coat of bright red. "Have *you*?" he countered, indicating the British uniform. "The 17th Regiment of Foot isn't so far away!"

"Aye, which is precisely why I 'borrowed' this 'ere get-up to help me pass through. In other words, I did this lil' thing called plannin' ahead—somethin' *you* could learn from, I see."

Irritated, Benjamin tried to pry himself loose, but to no avail. "An opportunity arose."

"Ah, an opportunity, was it? How good o' ya to share it with the rest of us!" Amos growled. "Our couriers haven't been able to find hide nor hair of ya in Lower Manhattan, so I had to do some diggin'. An' when I learned Charlotte Boyd's fiancé had come callin' from Philadelphia…well, I hoped an' prayed y'hadn't done somethin' stupid!"

Benjamin winced, still attempting to loosen Amos's grip. "I thought you were scoping Hempstead…"

"I was, y'bloody prat, but I had to come check on your addle-pated arse! Jesus!"

Despite the peril of their situation, Benjamin grinned. "Who's Jaysus?"

"Oi! Don'tcha start with me, y'snivelin' shite! If you weren't Danny's lil' brother, I'd lump ya right on the jobbernole!" Amos thumped his shoulder. "When I said to blend in, I didn't mean get a whole new cover!"

"It wasn't intentional!" Benjamin hissed. "Somehow, for some nonsensical reason, the Boyds believe me to be the eldest's fiancé. They didn't let me properly introduce myself!"

Amos gave a scornful hoot. "No offense there, lad, butcha ain't exactly 'man o' the town' material. How'dja pull that one off, uh?"

"It's…still a matter to be seen," Benjamin said. "They say Charlotte will return within a sennight, so I don't have much time to acquire information. You're going to need a new agent after I leave, but not around the Boyds. They'll be high on the alert once the truth comes out."

Amos released him with a huff. "Christ Almighty. Ain't all that Yale-learnin' supposed to help y'solve problems and not add to 'em?"

"Yes, well hopefully this will make up for it." Reaching inside his coat pocket, Benjamin withdrew a thimble and placed it into the other man's palm. "In there, I've folded a small sliver of parchment. It says: 'Tampered supplies. Don't accept.' I need you to get that to Bishop as soon as you're able."

Amos's brow furrowed. "Can y'gimme more than that? What's the story behind it, uh?"

"A Tory named Michael Collins has enough tampered grain

and flour to feed an army—specifically, a Continental encampment," Benjamin explained, careful to keep his voice low. "Inside each bag are bits of broken glass. From here on out, we shouldn't accept supplies from anyone but trusted sources." He paused. "In the meantime, with the shipbuilding merchant alias I've crafted, I convinced Collins to get that grain and flour to my men in Philadelphia. Can you send some of your privateering friends there for a drop-off? The ones onboard the *Joanna?*"

With a hearty laugh, Amos clapped Benjamin's face between his chafed hands and gleefully shook the man's head back and forth. "Moony, y'big, beautiful bastard! Perhaps there's a Yale brain in there, after all!" Giddy, he pressed, "So where do they gotta go?"

"Inside the thimble, there's another piece of paper with the address," Benjamin replied, "and, I swindled these high-flyers out of fifteen pounds." He withdrew a purse and tossed it into Amos's hands. "Get that to Bishop, as well. I figured with the extra funds, he could employ some new eyes and ears."

Amos whooped, practically dancing amidst his glee. "Moony, I could kiss you…"

"Please don't."

Guffawing, he crowed, "C'mere, y'long shanks goosecap!" Drawing Benjamin into his arms, the cabinetmaker squeezed him tightly and gave the space between his shoulders a warm, friendly wallop. "Y'did good, lad, y'did good! Have y'reached out to your primary contact?"

Benjamin shook his head, encouraging Amos to withdraw. "I haven't gotten to see Mr. Stewart yet, no. I was actually about to head out to his tavern and tell him I'm in the area."

"Go this evening," Amos advised. "Stewart's pickin' up a shipment, to me knowledge, so he ain't there yet. Besides, men're more distracted and well in their cups by nightfall, so it'll be safer." He lifted the thimble, then stuck it into his pocket. "In the meantime, I'll get this 'ere to one of our couriers. That way, I can stick close by, jus' in case y'need me."

Benjamin frowned. "But what about Hempstead?"

"Don't you worry 'bout that," Amos replied. "I'm not the only one there with a friendly leanin'. An' I know Dan'd never forgive me, were I to jus' leave his poor, hulver-headed lil' brother here all by his lonesome. I can spare a week."

Benjamin rolled his eyes, not wanting to admit he was comforted by having him around. "Right. In the meantime, I'm hoping I can get into Boyd's desk again. In an unlocked drawer, I found a ledger filled with names—all Tories, and all accompanied by expenditures. When the timing's right, I'd like to actually acquire those names." He straightened his coat. "The locked drawer might lead to something far more important, but I'll need to wait until closer to the end of the week, just in case my break-in is obvious."

"Use a bodice pin, if you can find one," Amos suggested. "O' course, that'd mean actually gettin' near a lass, so y'might be outta luck there."

"Arsehole," Benjamin dismissed, though he was smiling. "The middle daughter's a bit amenable to me…perhaps I can—"

"Oh-hoooo, no," Amos cut in, waggling a finger. "I don't think divin' into a bushel bubby's mutton is the best idea. Not when anyone in that house would delight in seein' y'hang for treason."

"Keep your voice down!" Benjamin hissed. Cheeks aflame, he amended, "Besides, I didn't mean I'd seduce her, I just…I-I thought I would try and befriend her. And along the way, perhaps I can find her collection of pins."

Amos's face twisted in consideration. "Y'know, that ain't too shabby. Give 'er a go. Or rather, give *it* a go. I really don't think it wise to get all bread an' butter fashion with one o' your targets."

"It'd be messy," Benjamin agreed, still pink cheeked. "My thoughts are only on the cause."

Despite Amos's leer, he seemed pleased. "I'll hafta change a few things, like gettin' our couriers over this-a-way for drop-offs. They'll either come by the front door, or leave notes in your horse's saddlebag."

Benjamin nodded. "Fine," he replied, "good. But how will I know the couriers from a regular visitor?"

With a grin, Amos nudged him. "Well, first, they'll request'cha by name—Ashby, o' course—and at some point, they'll say 'the rhododendrons are bloomin' nicely.'"

Benjamin snorted. "I'm shocked you can even say that word."

"Oi! Me ma loved 'er flowers, an' I made a point to mind me ma!" Amos drew back with a huff. "Well…" Chuckling, he held out his hand. "Here's to outsmartin' all these grout-headed gnatsnappers, eh? Godspeed, Moony."

Benjamin sensed the underlying sentiment and smiled, offering the older man a warm handshake. "May God's love favor us both."

CLARA HAD ALWAYS been an early riser. Perhaps she enjoyed being awake when nobody else was. The liminal space between sleep and the day's tasks kept her hidden away from chastisements, social responsibility, and each of her mother's harsh, bitter criticisms.

Her handmaiden, Angélique, also rose early to tend to her needs. Although they rarely spoke, Clara took comfort being around someone who didn't expect her to be prim and perfect. Four years her senior, Angélique had been her personal servant ever since she was eight. Despite the tensions between Great Britain and France, the towheaded Frenchwoman never once spoke of war, and Clara was relieved Jedediah hadn't grown paranoid and terminated her employment.

"Is this all right, mademoiselle?"

Barely processing her own reflection, the redhead forced a

smile and nodded, lifting a hand to touch the side of her simple updo. "Yes, this should be suitable. Thank you." Smoothing her palms over her embroidered bodice, she observed the lilac robe à l'anglaise with a cream, patterned underskirt, and hummed before asking, "Might you fetch my sister from her chambers? I asked her lady's maid to prepare her early, because I very much wish to speak with her."

"Of course, mademoiselle."

In five minutes' time, Angélique returned with a bleary-eyed, grumpy-faced Catherine in tow. It was clear that unlike her sister, the blonde very much did *not* enjoy being an early riser.

"Your sister, mademoiselle," the servant said with a curtsy.

"Thank you, Angélique. That will be all." Once the young woman curtsied again and made her leave, Clara eagerly stepped forward. "What did you think of the party last night, darling?"

Catherine shrugged, irritably grinding the sleep from her eyes. "This is why you demanded I rise so early? Clara, really…"

"Answer the question," the redhead pleaded. "I'd much prefer to discuss this alone and without prying ears, lest Mother become all besotted."

Flushing from secondhand embarrassment, Catherine warily asked, "Besotted? Surely, you are not speaking of Mr. Ashby…"

"Well, of course I am," Clara said. "He was an immediate favorite with his rendition of 'Burrowing Yankees' last night—a true inspiration!"

"Oh, I don't know," Catherine said, uneasy. "I'm still unsure what to think of him, truth be told, but he was quite impressive last night. Yet why should that matter? Mother was trying to set up something between you and Baron Wainwright, so I would much rather discuss that."

Clara gagged. "The hog merchant? Please! He's one of the few men who actually looks like his trade."

"Oh, don't be mean, Clara!"

"How is it mean? I know what I want in life, and what I want is *not* Baron Wainwright."

Catherine hummed. "Alas, that'll hardly matter to Mother and Father…they want you married off before—"

"Before I what? Bring more shame to this family?" Nettled, Clara straightened her neckline and released a breath. "I embarrass them just by existing, so I hardly have to worry about meeting with their approval. I will never have it."

Catherine winced, smoothing a hand down her sister's arm. "But surely, a sound marriage is a good start? What's so terrible about Baron Wainwright?"

"You mean aside from his appearance, profession, and utter lack of charm?" Clara asked, rolling her eyes. "They could at least saddle me with someone under forty."

"He's rich and would offer you stability," Catherine reminded her. "What more does a girl need?"

"What more, indeed?" Clara softly asked. Stiffening her chin, she admonished, "Enough of all this chatter. I summoned you to talk about Philip, not some fubsy hog baron." She flashed a hopeful smile. "Have your fears been assuaged?"

Catherine shrugged. "I must confess, I no longer feel uncomfortable in his presence."

"Nor do I," the redhead agreed, pleased. "I wasn't so sure about his Augustus Winthrop claim, but if he had any designs on our fortune, would he not have absconded with something by now? He only seems interested in our library and Father's business. The number of questions he asks is exhausting."

Catherine beamed. "Oh, well how wonderful of him to show such an interest! I imagine Father will wish him to take over someday."

"Undoubtedly," Clara agreed. "If Philip is to shoulder both the law firm *and* his shipbuilding business, I imagine Lottie will barely see him." Slowly, her lips lifted into a smirk. "How lucky for her!"

Catherine swatted her arm. "Oh, must you always jest like that? Surely, marriage isn't so ghastly!"

"Not ghastly, no," Clara agreed. "I rather enjoy having a man around. They're far better equipped for tending to certain needs than I am, though I'm not sure I would enjoy being tied to the same man for all eternity."

Catherine raised a brow. "Did you not feel such love for Mr. Shaw?"

Clara stiffened, her heart lodging in her throat, and her breath spasming in her lungs. "You know the rules, Kitty. We are never to discuss Mr. Shaw."

"But—"

"For once in your wretched, miserable life, do as you're told without asking a million bloody questions!" Chin wobbling, Clara pressed a hand to her chest and closed her eyes, startled by her outburst. "Oh… Oh, forgive me," she choked. "Oh, darling, I did not mean that…" Guilt-stricken, she cupped her sister's face and kissed her brow. "I didn't mean it," she said again. "I'd very much prefer not to speak of my past—not when Timothy is no longer capable of being my future."

"I understand," Catherine whispered, her bottom lip quivering. "Forgive me, Sister."

"Always, darling." Lifting her topmost petticoat, Clara dabbed the girl's face and encouraged, "Now dry those tears. I want you to head downstairs for breakfast, and wait for me there."

"But where will you be in the meantime?" Catherine asked.

"The library." Brightening, Clara explained, "I intend to give a book to Mr. Ashby as an apology."

"Oh? Do you have one in mind?"

Expression shifting into a more sly, impish demeanor, she allowed, "Why, yes. I daresay I do."

ALTHOUGH CLARA WAS coming to Philip with a peace offering, her motive wasn't quite so pure. She rather enjoyed making people squirm—it lent her a form of control she otherwise lacked. This was why, Clara supposed, she'd selected a book that would not only be an educational source, but perhaps rekindle that darling blush she'd seen in Philip once or twice. For being such a worldly man, he seemed quite easily scandalized.

"Mr. Ashby?" Lifting a hand, Clara rapped on his door. "Are you decent? I wish to speak with you, if I may."

There came a long pause, then the tread of footsteps. The door swung open, and Clara's smirk vanished once she took in the sight of Philip patting his face with a small, cotton cloth. Mid-morning sunlight streamed through the curtained windows, lambent and dreamlike, and backlit Philip like some sort of medieval painting. He had a demeanor that didn't quite match: a noble posture, a perceptive and all-encompassing gaze, and a softness that was perhaps intended to guard his heart. There was a sharpness to him, too—not just with his intellect, but his very soul, cutting Clara each time she gazed into his shrewd eyes of warm blue. They reminded her of the flowers she used to pick from the gardens when she was small—when her mother had a scrap of affection to spare, and the world still seemed so beautiful and full of promise.

Ridiculous, she thought. There was no beauty, nor hope, and certainly no true promise to be found within a man.

Souring at the thought, Clara opened her mouth to explain herself, only to take note of the soapy dollop on Philip's face. "Oh, um…" She tapped her cheek. "You missed a spot."

"Oh…" Philip wiped his cheek, then gestured with impatience. "What can I do for you, Miss Boyd?"

Ignoring the sharp edge to his tone, a hint of eagerness overcame Clara again, and she grinned before extending the book in her hands. "For you," she explained. "After our rocky start, I wished to apologize by offering something of assistance."

Bemused, Philip flashed her a distrustful glance, then took the tome before flipping through the illustrated pages. *"The Expert Midwife?"* he read aloud, more baffled than ever.

"By Jacob Rueff," Clara affirmed. "It has diagrams of women that showcase very specific organs. I thought this might help with your embarrassment over the female body."

Abruptly, Philip snapped the book shut. "I am not embarrassed."

"Oh, no?" Slowly, a wry smile filled Clara's face. "As I recall, you turned a very specific shade of red during our discussion in the library." When his cheeks grew aflame, she grinned and exclaimed, "Why, yes! Precisely the one!" Giggling, she continued, "You know, in certain circles, these diagrams are considered erotic, so I hope that regardless of your stance, you'll at least take some form of enjoyment from them."

Philip swallowed, his throat bobbing sharply. "Was this all you needed?"

"I've many needs in life, but yes…this was all I needed from you," Clara teased. "I hope you like it."

"I… Thank you for thinking of me," Philip stammered, clearly disingenuous.

Her bottom lip caught between her teeth and she grinned. Unable to resist teasing him—he was so delightfully easy to torment!—she said, "I'm rather partial to the illustrations on page 21. Perhaps you'll agree, should you find yourself curious what a uterus looks like."

Philip blanched. "Uter…uh…?"

"Uterus," Clara repeated, amused. "Surely, you've heard of them? I'd like to think you're not *that* naïve."

"Y-yes, but—"

"It's rather funny, isn't it? How the word *us* is in uterus? As if the man has any part in it other than sticking his pillock up a woman's—"

"Miss Boyd, please." Philip's face was so red that it nearly matched the color of his fine, ornamented frock coat. Taking her by the shoulder, he steered her toward the stairs. "I have a busy day ahead of me, and very much wish to retire."

Clara scoffed. "Isn't retiring the opposite of a busy day? You haven't yet had breakfast!"

Philip exhaled, ready to lose his temper. "I wish to be alone," he clarified, "but we can speak at suppertime, if it pleases you."

"Oh, but of course! I imagine reading that in mixed company would be rather unsuitable," Clara agreed, waving a hand. "I simply cannot wait for you to tell me all about what you've learned!"

Philip halted with her at the head of the stairs, astounded. "You think I intend to discuss this over supper?"

She shrugged. "Why not? Men have free rein over the dinner table, so they get to dictate whatever is discussed. And as much as Father may dislike it, the female body is far more interesting than politics." Her eyes gleamed. "Wouldn't you agree, Mr. Ashby?"

Philip drew a breath. "As I've said, I have a busy day ahead of me. Take care, Miss Boyd. And the next time you wish to speak, please bring a chaperone."

He briskly turned on his heel, and as Clara watched him practically flee toward his bedroom, she lifted a hand to her mouth and hid a smile behind her fingers.

BENJAMIN AVOIDED CLARA the rest of the day. He took all meals in his bedroom, feigning illness, and spent his time planning, reviewing, and rehearsing the exchange that would take place later that evening.

By nightfall, he sneaked through his bedroom window undisturbed, dropped to the ground below, and absconded with his horse before riding her spiritedly off to Lower Manhattan.

It was this urgency that brought him to the Grey Whale

Tavern. The moment Benjamin entered the building, warmth from the hearth and tightly packed room buffeted his face, making him shiver as he removed his tricorn and stepped farther into the establishment. Candles flickered in wall sconces and across the lit hearth's mantelpiece, barely serving as sufficient light; so much so that he had to squint to readjust. For this particular outing, he'd opted for his own clothes—commoner's clothes—so he felt comfortable blending in with the other patrons.

"I'll be right with you, love!" the barmaid called over to him.

Benjamin offered a smile and remained near the entryway. While he loitered, he spotted a man matching George Stewart's description in the far corner of the room. He was sixty-something with thin white hair on top of his shiny, balding scalp. As Benjamin stared, he and the older man shared a glance before the former looked away. Despite George not knowing his face, it was wise to avoid coming on too strongly.

The barmaid approached, so Benjamin fell into the ruse and ordered himself an ale. Seating himself in the front left corner of the room, he discreetly appraised the clientele while he waited for his drink. As was the usual case for Lower Manhattan evenings, there were several men present: five redcoats cursing loudly while partaking in whist, two gentlemen playing nine-pins, at least ten seamen well in their cups, and quite a few loners who hadn't arrived with any friends at all—Lady Liquor was all the friend they required. Thankfully, he didn't see anyone he recognized from Jedediah's party.

"Here you are," the barmaid purred, winking while she set the ale in front of him. "Anything else?" She placed her hands onto her ample hips, intentionally pushing up her breasts.

Distracted, Benjamin offered a weak smile and shook his head. "No, thank you...but thank you."

Disappointed, the woman shrugged her shoulders, muttered a terse, "Suit yourself," and sauntered off to check on the rowdy card players.

By now, Benjamin determined everyone was wholly absorbed with their own business, so he grabbed his stein and moved over to George. Despite being the tavern's owner, the old man often lounged about with the locals. Fortunately for Benjamin, George was sitting off to the side by himself, writing out his inventory.

"Good evening, Mr. Stewart," Benjamin greeted. George grunted in response, far too engrossed in his task, so the former took it as an unspoken invitation to sit. Sinking into the chair across from the tavern owner, Benjamin lowered his voice and said, "If Providence is kind, the winds will be easy for sailing tomorrow morning."

George froze. It was the secret message they'd all agreed upon, and with the pass code given, he licked his dry lips and responded, "Yessir, I have a shipment that needs taken care of myself."

With the second part of the secret message given, Benjamin relaxed and raised his stein. "To unmolested shipments."

George barely lifted his own stein before knocking it back, his throat working as he quickly swallowed the ale. He seemed nervous… Was this his first time dealing with actual intelligence?

Leaning on his elbows, Benjamin said, "I'm from out of town and have a letter for my lady-love. Will you see that it gets to the post rider?"

"Certainly…for a fee." George held out his weathered hand, and Benjamin placed a couple shillings into his palm. Despite the transaction not being necessary, both were determined to play out their ruse as realistically as possible. "All right," George said. "And the letter, sir?"

Reaching into his coat pocket, Benjamin withdrew the intel he'd acquired—a coded letter restating what he'd given Amos, as well as a few Tory names he could recall from Jedediah's ledger—before passing it across the table.

George gave it a quick once-over, swallowed, and stuffed the correspondence into his own pocket. "I'll see that it gets to your lady-love come morning's light," he promised. "You enjoy that drink, sir."

Benjamin smiled, relieved, before returning to his former seat, stein in hand. He intended to finish his drink to keep up appearances.

BY THE TIME Benjamin left the tavern, it was well into the late hours of the evening, just shy of the ten o' clock curfew. He felt a little overheated from being within the tight confines of the tavern, not to mention the extra drink he'd ordered, so he decided to take a walk and clear his head before returning to the Boyd estate.

With his tricorn pulled low, and his hands stuffed into his coat pockets, he trudged along the neighboring wharf, intent on remaining inconspicuous despite there being few people in the streets—no one beyond lowlifes and poor, desperate women looking to sell their wares. Despite the pang of pity he felt on their behalf, he didn't dignify them while he passed.

Edging closer to the dock's edge, if only to avoid the various people sparsely lining the cobblestone street, he started walking faster. That was when a figure descended upon him from behind.

"Mister, can you spare a light?"

Benjamin halted, not expecting to be grabbed. He looked at the hand on his arm, then up at a face eerily obscured by shadows. The moon was low in the sky, and there were a few lanterns in the street, yet he was only afforded the slight shine of teeth through the dark...like a wolf.

Uneasy, Benjamin shook himself free. "Apologies, sir, but I have no tinder box to lend."

He actually did have a tinder box—most resourceful men

carried one—yet something about this stranger unnerved him. He moved to step around the man, then gave a jolt once the shadowed figure swung an arm around his neck and squeezed.

Gasping sharply, Benjamin tried to drop to his knees and knock himself loose, but was punished by the entrapment of a tighter hold. The two men grappled, scuffling dangerously close to the edge of the docks.

"I have no money," Benjamin wheezed. Dark laughter followed, and the stranger's stale, pungent breath burned his nostrils. While the man giggled, Benjamin slammed his fist back and nailed his assailant in the gut. His attacker released him with a startled "oof!" and Benjamin spun around, fumbling through his pocket for a knife.

Unfortunately, the stranger was much faster. Wielding his own weapon of choice, the man grabbed Benjamin by the shoulder and yanked him forward, his breath hot and rancid as he hissed, "*Veni, vidi, vici.*"

Benjamin's eyes widened, and then an explosion of pain seared above his left hip. A sharp cry caught in his throat, and as the assailant yanked the small knife free of his wound, Benjamin's knees buckled, and he dizzily toppled from the wharf.

CHAPTER SIX

On Guard

WHEN BENJAMIN WAS seven years old, he nearly drowned. Stubborn and determined at that young age, he'd ignored Daniel's pleas to come ashore. In spite of the waves growing rough and sweeping his little body farther out to sea, he'd been too proud to cry out for help. And once he weakened and panicked, powerless to fight against the crashing current, he'd been unable to tamp down that pride and scream.

Daniel came in after him regardless, four years older and a much better swimmer. That marked only the beginning of his rescues. Between boyhood and adulthood, Daniel fended off imaginary creatures under the bed, town bullies, and absolutely anything that served as a potential danger to his little brother. And then once the time came to save Daniel in return, Benjamin found himself incapable—he did nothing.

He failed him. He had failed.

In the end, he'd been reduced to little more than a frightened, drowning child all over again, unable to do anything but watch his brother be destroyed by a dark, seething fate far too vast for his biggest hero to vanquish. There was no longer anyone there to lend a helping hand, no one left to pull his head above water...

With a wheezing breath, Benjamin emerged from the ocean's deadly embrace and greedily sucked in gasps of air, faint and disoriented as the stars blurred dizzyingly above him in smears of soft, lambent light. Treading the waves despite the pain searing through his midriff, he blinked the water from his eyes and scanned the docks. His assailant was gone…

Trembling, Benjamin swam up to the wooden structure and grabbed the edge. If that man did intentionally target him, he needed to return to the Boyd estate, and fast.

Miraculously, his horse was still tethered to the post where he'd left her, so with a pained little groan, he hefted himself out of the water and staggered toward his mount.

WHEN THE FRONT door opened, Clara didn't bother to investigate. She kept reading in the sitting room, absently worrying her thumb over her lips until a sharp, distinctive thud drew her attention.

Alarmed, she raised her head just as Philip staggered into a small table, soaking wet and barely able to hold himself upright.

"Oh…Mr. Ashby!" she exclaimed. Tossing aside the book, she gathered up her skirts and rushed toward him, her hands extending as he slumped to his knees. She caught his coat and drew down at his side. "What's happened?" she demanded. "How on *earth* did you get so wet?"

Gritting his teeth, Philip swore and lifted his hand.

Clara peered at the crimson stain and gasped. "You've been injured!"

"You truly are a woman of intelligence," he muttered.

Frustrated, Clara nearly struck him. "Why are you making sport of this situation?" she demanded. "You are bleeding all over Father's parquet floor! Not to mention, the torrents of water!" When Philip spared her a withering glare, she chewed her lip and amended, "You're right, that was unkind…" Touching his back, she pressed, "Can you stand?"

"I think so…" Wincing, Philip tried to rise again, but this time, Clara moved underneath his arm, bearing his weight while the two slowly drew to their full heights. "Miss Boyd," he implored, "I need you to stitch my wound."

"Me?" Wall-eyed, she scoffed while her face grew bone white. "I barely excel at my own needlepoint!"

"Please," Philip begged. "I would rather not wait for a surgeon…"

"Whyever not?" Frustrated, Clara spat, "No respectable man has a slapdash, ill-advised surgery, and of that I can assure you!"

"Yes, well last time I checked, *I* was the one stabbed here," Philip hissed, "so please leave it at that and help me!"

Clara flinched, nettled by his tone, but nevertheless heeded his command, and started guiding him toward the staircase. "We'll go to your room," she decided. "To stay here would risk making a mess—one that I would rather not explain."

Philip grunted. "Ah. And heaven forbid I ruin your father's precious floors, correct?" he muttered, stumbling alongside her.

She spared him a sidelong glance. "Alas, I am beginning to see why you were assaulted." Rolling her eyes, Clara gently squeezed his flank and coaxed, "Come along then…move your feet, one after the other. That's it."

Philip leaned into her side, his steps wobbly as they attempted to move faster.

"You are stepping on my foot," Clara groused.

Despite his tremendous discomfort, Philip laughed. "I have been stabbed, yet your foot is what's in jeopardy here?"

She huffed and helped him onto the first stair. "If you keep poking fun at my sensibilities, you'll soon find a lump on your head, as well." Looping her arm more securely around Philip's waist, Clara grew disgusted once she realized the bodice of her pink, floral-patterned zone front gown was streaked in scarlet and seawater. So much for not making a mess… Once it was safe to do so, she would find a place to hide her short gown.

Gripping the bloody spot above his hip bone, Philip instructed, "I am going to need a needle, thread, bandages, some honey, if you have it, and a bottle of whiskey."

Clara hummed, attempting levity as she teased, "Well, you certainly know how to show a girl a rousing good time. That sounds like the start of a good hazing."

Philip smiled—grimaced?—as they stopped at the head of the staircase. Exhaling through his nose, he implored, "The supplies. Please fetch them."

Clara was torn on what to do—stay by this clotpole's side and ensure he made it to his room, or leave said clotpole and head outside to the kitchen—before she frowned and ultimately slipped free of his hold. "Very well," she agreed. "Go to your room. I'll come by once I've gathered what you require."

She started back downstairs, only to turn and fearfully glance up at him. "Please don't die," she entreated, her voice uncharacteristically soft.

Before Philip could respond, she turned and rushed down the remainder of the staircase.

BY THE TIME Clara returned with the necessary materials, Philip was shirtless and seated upon his bed, pale and sweaty, and pressing on his clotting wound. Golden candlelight flickered across his features in a shadowy dance, making him look sallow and gaunt as her eyes drifted toward his breeches. It appeared he'd changed into a dry pair, thank the Lord. Ruining the silk sheets with his soaked, bloodied clothing would be difficult to explain.

"I collected whatever I could find from the kitchen," she told him. "Our cooks and farmhands get injured from time to time, so we keep a medical chest out there." Determined, she cut across the room and set everything onto his nightstand. "I see your breeches are already unfastened. Lower your fall front, if you please."

When she glanced over her shoulder, she frowned at the clear horror in his eyes. "Oh, come now," she admonished. "It's nothing I haven't seen before!"

Flustered, Philip was quick to shake his head. "I'm sorry, but I've changed my mind… Now that I've gathered my bearings, I feel it would be far more appropriate, were I to do this myself."

Clara turned with her hands on her hips. "All right, let's make this plain and simple, shall we? Either you open up your breeches, and I potentially see your pego and help you, or I let you remain modest and you die from a putrid wound." She gestured with impatience. "Hurry up and decide. I may not wish to do this, but I also don't want you dying in my home."

Disquieted, Philip shifted and swallowed, his throat bobbing reflexively. With a few strands of wet, matted hair obscuring his vision, he avoided her eyes and nodded in acquiescence, his body tensing once she took a needle and thread, then lowered to her knees.

While he held onto his fall front in a tight, unrelenting grip, Clara laughed thinly. "You know, whenever I'm usually between a man's legs, there is a far more pleasurable outcome."

Philip blanched at her quip, but was too weakened to blush or laugh.

Holding up a hand, she amended, "I know, I know. You think I'm a trollop. Just let me ramble, won't you? I'm bloody nervous!"

Slowly, Philip's grimace softened into that of disbelief. "I don't think you're a trollop," he said.

Ignoring his eyes on her, an unexpected warmth flowed through Clara's limbs and pooled into her stomach. "Yes, well I'm afraid you're the only one," she mumbled. Properly threading the needle, she exhaled, then gestured to his bloodstained hand. "Let go of your fall front," she commanded. "I can't stitch you up if your breeches are in the way."

Philip swallowed. "B-but—"

"Oh, for goodness' sake, you noddy! Let go."

Hesitant, his eyes darted in between her face and the floor with an acute, boyish panic she would've found endearing, had she not been asked to stitch up an actual man's flesh. At long last, Philip lowered the material from his stomach, opening his breeches and baring his wound. Despite the bloodied midriff on display, he kept his indecency covered.

"Keep your hands where they are," Clara instructed. "Don't let your breeches move while I'm working."

"See?" Philip quipped, swallowing past the dryness in his throat. "You're already sounding like a nurse."

Clara snorted. Admittedly, his attempts at levity were comforting. Glancing at him, she breathed in, breathed out, then earnestly entreated, "Try not to scream. I don't know what in God's name I'm doing, and I'd much prefer that you not startle me while I'm wielding a sharp implement."

Philip scoffed. "Believe me, I feel much the same way."

They shared a look of amusement, though both were tinged with apprehension as Clara took a cloth, dabbed it with alcohol, and then wiped away at the small, bloody laceration for a better view. Philip swore and gnashed his teeth.

Dear God. If he was behaving this way now, how would he react once she'd started stitching?

Trying not to focus on this, Clara exhaled before pinching the wound shut with her fingers. "Please don't move," she entreated him. "This is going to hurt."

"Yes, I figured as much," Philip gritted.

Chewing her lip, Clara attempted to stop the shaking in her hands—Lord above, why wouldn't they stop?—before she gave up and swiped the bottle of liquor, pressing it to her lips and guzzling a generous swallow. She coughed at the burning sensation, startled, before drawing a hand over her mouth. When she looked at Philip, a spike of annoyance blazed through her at the amused disbelief in his eyes.

"What?" she spat. "Am I not allowed a bit of liquid courage?"

"I didn't say a word," Philip promised. "If anything, I'm pretending my nurse isn't getting all muddled."

Drawing a breath, Clara shook out her hands, rolled her neck, and muttered a terse, "I am not muddled," before sharply sticking the needle through Philip's skin.

"Ouch! Zounds!" Stricken—at least a bit of color had returned to his complexion—Philip scowled and clenched his jaw. Tensing his hands around the fall flap, he drew in several sharp, shallow breaths through his nose, then growled low in his throat once she weaved the needle through his skin. In and out she worked, surprisingly resolute despite her aversion.

"You know," she said, deciding to provide a distraction, "for such a pig-headed sort, you're actually a decent patient. I thought you said you grow faint at the sight of blood?"

Philip snorted, though it came out as more of a groan. "I didn't wish to spend time with your father's friends, so I lied. Was that such a crime?"

Clara shook her head, then challenged, "Well no, not literally, but perhaps if you'd been kinder, you wouldn't be sporting a knife wound."

"Where is your family?" Philip asked, ignoring her barb.

"Everyone's asleep. And so long as you quit with your jawing, they should remain that way."

He sucked in a slow breath, perspiring faintly. "Far be it for me to disagree, but I seem to only hear your voice carrying above the quiet."

Clara hummed. "Indeed? Well, I could just forego your stitches and embroider *irreverent hob* across your stomach instead."

Philip cracked a smile at that, though it appeared as more of a grimace.

The shaking in her hands finally subsided, and Clara ignored how blood—*his* blood—oozed between the stitches like tear-drops. She laced his wound and pushed out a slow breath. "There, now," she soothed, "I'm almost done."

She forced the needle through a particularly stubborn section, and Philip swore anew, agonized and pounding his fist against his thigh.

"Sorry," Clara whispered, wincing. While he swiped the bottle and took a long, hard pull of whiskey, she worked up the courage to ask, "How did it happen?"

Philip coughed, clearing his throat. Lowering the bottle, he feigned ignorance and asked, "How did *what* happen?"

"Your *wound,* of course!"

They locked eyes, he alarmed and she exasperated, before Philip finally replied, "I was attacked at the Grey Whale Tavern."

Clara's mouth dropped. "The tavern? What on earth were you doing in town when you weren't feeling well?"

"Seeking to get stabbed," he snidely said, only to amend, "I wanted a bloody drink, of course! I thought it might soothe my nerves."

"All right, all right! There is no need for such nastiness. Fie, I would've thrown you into the ocean, too! Presuming that is what happened, of course." Scowling at him, she knotted her stitch-work and leaned back with a sigh. "It's going to leave a terrible scar, I think." Clara traced the line without touching it. "Men are lucky, though… Scars are a rite of passage, mapping out their masculinity. But for women? They're a blemish."

Dispirited, Clara rose from off the floor. Once she was standing, she tottered before toppling forward, not having anticipated how drained and weak-kneed this ordeal had made her.

Ever quick to action, Philip reached out and thwarted her fall. His hands slid to her waist and held fast, keeping her upright as she dizzily caught his shoulders.

"My apologies," Clara whispered. His bare skin was clammy beneath her palms, and as their eyes met, she swore she felt him tremble.

Philip promptly released her, behaving as if her very touch had burned him. Swallowing, he shifted on the bed and nodded toward the floor. "I believe I can take it from here, Miss Boyd. Thank you."

Bemused, she stepped back and smoothed a hand over her gown, flustered as she caught sight of herself in the mirror over his shoulder. Her eyes were wide and wild, and there were bloodied handprints on her bodice. She looked wretched, *claimed*, and briefly, she wondered if this was how her family viewed her—how the *world* viewed her: uncomely, unkempt, *unclean*.

Overcome, Clara tore away and moved to the nightstand. "Don't be ridiculous," she grumbled. "You don't want to tear those stitches, do you?"

Frowning, she lifted some strips of cloth and the jar of honey and moved to sit alongside Philip. Despite her thigh pressing into his, she felt nothing but determination as she uncorked the jar, then dipped her fingers into the sticky substance before smearing it over his injury. She'd once read that this practice was an ancient remedy, but she had never actually partaken herself.

After finishing, she set to work on wrapping the thin, frayed strips of cloth around Philip's lower torso. With the wound covered, she tucked in the tail end and smoothed her fingers over the cloth, the furrow between her brows softening as she looked to Philip with a nod. "That should do it," she said.

"I appreciate this…truly." Philip returned her gaze this time, though a painful shyness kept his eyes darting between her face and the floor.

Instigated by his response, Clara rose and turned her back on him. While she hid the whiskey and honey inside a trunk at the foot of his bed, she warned, "I'd advise that you be more careful, Philip. Between this misadventure and that highwayman from earlier, if you keep at it, there won't be any places left for your assailants to stick a knife."

In spite of himself, Philip's mouth quirked into a wry grin. "I'll keep that in mind, Miss Boyd. Thank you."

"Clara," she corrected. Catching his gaze, she shrugged and amended, "We are familiars, and I am quite literally witnessing you in an improper state of dress. I think we can lose the formality."

"Yes, I…all right," Philip agreed. Embarrassed, he moved to grab his soaked shirt. "I apologize if I've ruined your father's floor. Perhaps I can—"

"No," Clara assured him, "don't be absurd. It's not like you could've anticipated a knife to the gut, though I am curious what prompted the attack."

"Well, you know me…" Philip offered a feeble smile. "I'm sure you could think of a few reasons."

With a delighted laugh, Clara grinned and folded her hands. "Indeed, I could! Just be grateful I've never chosen to act on them myself."

A moment of soft, surprisingly comfortable silence passed between them, and she dipped into a curtsy. "Good night, Philip. If you need anything…" She hesitated, then blurted, "You may come to my room—it's the last one at the end of the hall. You, yourself said I've proven to be a decent nurse, so I'd like to think I could assist."

Holding his ruined shirt against his chest, Philip nodded in disbelief.

Smug, Clara teased him, "Perhaps I am not so silly and spoiled, after all?"

"I-I never said…" Catching himself, Philip's face melded into a sheepish smile and he chuckled. "Perhaps not," he allowed. "Good night, Clara. I hope you sleep well."

Despite it being a dismissal, the redhead beamed and felt a deeply sunny, befuddling feeling bloom within her breast. "You, as well," she replied. "Please be alive for breakfast tomorrow."

He gave an amused bow of the head, and then she turned and grabbed a quilt before rushing into the hallway. Unfortunately, now that she didn't wish to tattle on Philip for his misadventure, she had a floor to try and clean—more like blot with this poor, unfortunate coverlet—before anyone awoke and became wise to his accident.

BENJAMIN BARELY SLEPT that night. In between the aching throb of his wound and befuddling thoughts of Clara, he was also plagued with nightmares of his assailant. That stranger was the reason he hadn't sought professional medical help, fearing that somehow word of his survival might get back to him. Who was that man? And, more importantly, was his cover officially blown?

Despite the dread of a dawn reprisal, none ever came. Benjamin awoke the next morning, still leery and unsettled, and William came in to help him dress.

Since Benjamin had changed into a fresh shirt before bed, he quickly denied the offer, and instead encouraged William to aid in the other garments. He was terrified of his bandages being spotted. In truth, it was a great mercy that he was able to move without any signs of discomfort.

Once Benjamin was fully dressed, he followed William downstairs into the dining room and was surprised to find Jedediah at the head of the table. Thus far, he hadn't made many appearances for mealtime, so it was just Benjamin's luck that the patriarch decided to be there when he was feeling out of sorts. Fortunately, Mr. Boyd seemed far too distracted to bear him much mind.

The servant presently bent at Jedediah's ear withdrew and bowed his head, doleful as Jedediah spluttered and flapped his mouth. "Are you certain?" When the servant nodded, the attorney huffed. "Can you believe this?" he snarled. "According to Harrelson here, someone murdered George Stewart last night!"

The women all gasped, and when Clara glanced at Benjamin, he barely had time to reassemble his face and hide his shock.

"What a pity," Deborah said, drawing a hand to her chest. "He was from such a lovely loyalist family, too…it must have been rebel scum who did this."

Benjamin tightened his fists, then clumsily sat across from Clara. His wound throbbed from the graceless motion, and he exhaled, trying to minimize the pain on his face. "It's a true tragedy," he agreed. "I hope the man who did this suffers."

"Hear, hear!" Jedediah exclaimed. "The sooner those rebels are off the streets, the better. I'll have to speak with Mr. Collins about making his provisions plan more widespread."

Benjamin swallowed, but said nothing. He glanced toward Clara, who was eyeing him strangely. Did she suspect? Did she think *he* killed George Stewart?

Paling at the thought, he offered a feeble smile and nod, to which she frowned and returned to her eggs.

Oh, blood and thunder. Whatever her thoughts on the matter, she certainly didn't seem amenable to conversation…

"How did it happen?" Benjamin asked. Securing his napkin, he looked to Jedediah with what he hoped to be concerned expectance. "The man…Mr. Stewart, was it? How was he killed?"

Jedediah's mouth twisted, and he shook his head, getting worked up anew. "The poor soul was stabbed," he said. "The tavern must have been empty, because I cannot imagine anyone letting such a beloved man get attacked!"

"With all due respect, Father, I believe Mr. Stewart was only beloved by lusheys," Clara said. Her gaze pointedly cut toward Deborah. "As tragic as this is, it was probably some drunken dispute. Truth be told, I am amazed he wasn't killed sooner."

Catherine whispered a prayer under her breath, pale and trembling. "Please do not speak as such," she begged. "Even if Mr. Stewart was a drunk, he deserves our respect."

"Precisely!" Jedediah agreed. "I'll have to send his family my regards."

Clara snorted, her face an open mask of disdain. "If Mr. Stewart wasn't such a staunch loyalist, you wouldn't give one whit about his life," she snapped. "Far be it for me to support rebel trash when they are such reprehensible, violent beasts, but I do not believe in remaining silent when utter tripe is tossed my way." Jedediah moved to speak, yet she continued on, "You've categorized this town into 'traitors' and 'loyalists,' but I can promise you, Father: There are plenty of scoundrels in the latter class. A man's politics do not mean he has good moral standing."

Jedediah's face grew red. "Ridiculous!" he spat.

"I agree," Clara replied, "it is ridiculous. Why, this entire war is ridiculous, and I hate hearing about our neighbors, our former friends being divided over something so repulsive! We were so close with the Claytons, and now we never speak—and for what? Because they wish to be free of—"

"Enough!" Jedediah thundered, smashing his fist against the table. Catherine and Deborah both jerked, but Clara remained impassive amidst his rage.

Benjamin looked between both parties, equally fascinated and horrified. He wouldn't call Clara a sympathetic Tory by any means, but he also hadn't expected her to understand the damage the war had caused. Neighbors, friends, and family alike were torn apart at the seams, and sometimes underneath the very same roof. This abode was clearly a prime example.

Despite his own personal misgivings, Benjamin knew he needed to show his appreciation for the Tory cause. "Your father's right, Miss Boyd," he spoke up. "Although there's never an accurate gauge for honesty, it'll always be wisest to side with the loyalists. At least in this way, we can guarantee your safety."

Jedediah was still red faced, but softened at Benjamin's interjection. "An astute observation," he allowed, stabbing his fork into his eggs. "You'd do well to take his advice, Clara. No rebel would spare you—why, they would leap at the very opportunity to ravish and plunder, should you cross their path."

Clara paled, but her chin remained pointed and tense. "The male sex need not be rebels to accost me," she said. "I assure you, Father: That uncouth Ensign Thomas was *more* than willing during your party, and he's as loyal to the Crown as you and I."

Jedediah's eyes alit with anger, but it was clear by the hard set of his jaw he knew she was right.

"I've written a letter," Benjamin cut in, hoping to defuse the situation. "Once it reaches Philadelphia, my employees will be transporting Mr. Collins's tampered goods. In addition, they'll be sending a couple ships to use as you see fit. I apologize for lacking the foresight to do this prior."

As Benjamin hoped, Jedediah's contempt turned into something blissful and eager.

"Truly?" he crowed. "Why, that's marvelous news, indeed! I wasn't certain you'd uphold that vow, if I am being honest, but I'm thrilled you Ashbys are every bit as loyal as you claim."

Clara looked over at Benjamin, her eyes narrowing quizzically. "Come to think of it, why didn't you arrive on one of your ships?" she asked. "That way, you could've spared yourself the horrors of highwaymen."

Waving a hand, Benjamin deflected, "Father taught me that modesty is the key to business, and I didn't wish to embarrass you, nor your family with my riches. It'd be rather ill-mannered, especially since Charlotte is the only treasure I require."

Clara laughed, the sound musical despite her scorn. "Lord above, Philip, you truly are a hob! A treasure? *Please!*"

"I think it's lovely," Deborah crooned, her face melting into the flirtatious, dream-like simper she'd developed for Benjamin. "Why, I didn't realize that in addition to being a well-read, successful business owner, you were also a poet."

This time, Clara could scarcely contain herself. She howled with laughter, holding herself around the middle as tears filled her eyes. Discreetly, Catherine took away her sister's cider, believing the alcohol was the cause of her mirth.

"Oh, the whole world's gone mad!" Clara exclaimed. "Isn't it just…just marvelous how we're all players in this stage production of sheer twaddle?"

"Clara, that's enough," Deborah admonished. "If you're

unable to comport yourself, you may be excused."

Clara giggled, wiping her eyes with a finger. "Gladly," she agreed. Rising from the table, she spared Benjamin a disbelieving look before bursting into renewed laughter, rolling her eyes as she turned and left the dining room.

DESPITE CLARA'S MIRTH at breakfast, when Benjamin found her in the sitting room later that morning, she was nowhere near as pleasant to be around. In fact, once he offered a tentative smile, she snorted and deliberately returned to reading.

"Begging your pardon, Miss Boyd," he greeted. "Do you mind if I sit?"

Clara didn't look up from her book. "Do *not* presume to speak to me without a chaperone," she warned.

Benjamin breathed a disbelieving huff. Although he certainly agreed it *was* in poor taste, she'd never concerned herself with such airs in the past, and least especially last night in his room. This was how he knew she was truly cross with him.

"Forgive me, but I only wanted you to know I've read a bit of *The Expert Midwife*," he announced, hoping to win her good graces. "You see, you were right. I *am* rather puritanical when it comes to the human body, and that text did me a world of good."

This time, Clara sighed, rolling her eyes as she flipped to another page.

"Er…I thank you," he continued, sitting alongside her. "If it weren't for your insight, I daresay—"

"You were at the tavern," she accused, her tone crisp. "Did you witness Mr. Stewart's murder?"

Benjamin swallowed his feeble attempts at conversation, overcome by a lurching wave of panic. "I-I didn't, no," he allowed. "He must have been attacked after I was…or maybe before. I cannot be certain."

"And are you certain *you* didn't attack him?" Clara asked, lifting her gaze to nail him in place. "Because it seems rather convenient that you, yourself were injured, and yet managed to get away with your life."

And there it was. Although he hadn't been certain of her convictions before, her stance on his guilt was plain as she glared at him, her gaze sharp and cutting akin to a scythe. Every bit as viperous as she was soft and refined, this woman would surely be his undoing…

But not today.

Bolstered by this newfound resolve, Benjamin feigned contrition and shook his head. "I was attacked by a stranger," he asserted. "I'd been drinking, and he took me completely unawares. To be frank, I barely escaped with my life." Against his better judgment, Benjamin reached down and gently pressed her hand. "Clara, I hope you know I would never lie to you. As the sister of my dearest and most beloved Charlotte, my greatest wish is that we can become friends…that we can be family. You and your father, in particular, have shown me nothing but kindness during my stay here, and I wish to offer nothing but kindness in return. Please…" He squeezed her hand. "Please believe me. I am forever your humble servant."

Clara hesitated, a clear war raging on behind her wide, distrusting eyes. Finally, her stiff posture softened, and she extricated her hand before returning it to her lap. "Forgive me, Philip," she murmured. "Although I may not actively show it, I, too, wish for us to become friends… I imagine it must be Lottie's greatest wish." Wincing, she continued, "However, surely you can understand my reservations? There have been so many peculiarities as of late, and I cannot wrap my head around them. With the very world in a state of unrest, I am finding it difficult to trust anyone. And your attack…it's so strange to me. As much as we joked about it last night, there really is no good reason for someone to accost you."

"I agree," Benjamin replied. "The world's a lonesome, terrifying place right now, but that doesn't mean we have to completely shut down our hearts." Rolling his lips inward, he explained, "The ruffian wanted my money. Once he realized I only had a few shillings to spare, he stabbed me and shoved me off the wharf. Fortunately, he didn't stay to see if he'd finished the job. I imagine a similar fate befell Mr. Stewart."

"Oh, Philip…" A swell of emotion formed in Clara's throat, and she drew a hand to her breast. "I am so sorry. I feel dreadful for assuming the worst, especially since you've been…y-you…" Lips opening and closing, she amended, "You are a member of this family now, and as such, I never should've doubted your intentions. I'm glad you're all right."

Relief washed over Benjamin. So much so that he ribbed, "Truly? Would you have lost your favorite person to mock, had I died?"

Clara appeared startled by his response, but laughed. "You know, I think I much preferred you before the unveiling of your true personality." To Benjamin's surprise, she lifted a hand and touched his cheek, her thumb worrying over the spot he'd cut while shaving. "Please try and be more careful. As pleased as I am with my stitchwork, I don't wish to become your full-time nurse."

Benjamin gaped at her in stunned silence, instantly transporting back to when she'd toppled into his arms. Despite his ability to think, maneuver, and outwit in moments of dire circumstance, he'd been rendered helpless by the unexpected contact. It hadn't been romantic—no, no, she'd merely fallen—but for Benjamin, she was the first woman to witness him in a state of undress…the first woman to touch him beyond a dutiful press of the hand. He'd naturally experienced the glowing, fluttery rapture of attraction growing up, but after going off to school, he'd been far too shy to mingle with women. The fairer sex was always Daniel's forte, not his own. And Clara…

He swallowed. Despite her flirtations, Benjamin needed to stop thinking of her as his first anything. It was dangerous, unfathomable territory. But her hand—God, her *hand* was still on his face, and he *had* told Amos he'd glean a bodice pin, and since flattery *was* always a wise course of action…

Here goes nothing.

Taking Clara's wrist, Benjamin drew her hand from his cheek and kissed her palm. Despite his nerves, it was a perfunctory, easy gesture, and he ignored the slight flip in his stomach when they locked eyes. "I never thanked you properly," he murmured. "Despite the pain from your stitchwork, I only needed the whiskey once."

Clara flinched, clearly not having expected such bold-faced affection, if it could be considered as such. Slowly, an uncharacteristic pink flooded her cheeks and she scoffed. "I recall needing the whiskey far more," she muttered.

"What are you reading?"

Confused by the change in subject, Clara promptly withdrew her hand. "I'm reading *The Odyssey*," she said. "You interrupted the tale last night—rather rudely, might I add—so naturally, I was in no mood to read afterwards."

"I apologize," Benjamin said. "From the sound of things, I am ruining quite a bit."

"Yes," Clara agreed, sparing him a meaningful glance, "you most certainly are." Exhaling, she asked, "And how is your wound? You seem to be getting about well enough."

"Thanks to you," Benjamin replied, nodding. "In fact, I feel better than before I was stabbed."

"Oh, don't be ridiculous!" She laughed, lifting a hand to hide her smile. "Are you implying medicine is my calling?"

"You have a bit of a poor bedside manner," Benjamin observed, "but I've certainly had worse…even if that 'worse' was a literal dog."

Clara suppressed another laugh, both delighted and perplexed. "Now *that* sounds like a story worth hearing."

"Perhaps someday," he agreed. "Unfortunately, I'm far better at overseeing ship production than telling stories." Rising from the settee, he announced, "I must be off. I promised your father I'd visit a client with him later today, so I'd like to prepare myself."

"Poor you," Clara teased, smiling. "I wouldn't wish that upon anyone." Lowering her eyes, she added, "I would like to apologize for my behavior, Philip. I was unnerved, scared for my family, and it was wrong of me to blame you when you, yourself were injured."

Benjamin hesitated at her clear remorse, his gaze softening. "You weren't wrong to blame me," he said. "We have only just met, so your hesitance was merited. Truth be told, I'm impressed by your initiative. You have far more intelligence than you're given credit."

"Indeed?" Clara wrinkled her nose at him, amused. "You must really want something, given the needless flattery…"

Benjamin's smile turned melancholy. "No," he assured her, "it was just an observation." *God must never grant me what I want.* "Good day to you, Clara."

He bowed, then left before she could further ensnare him with her befuddling thrall.

WITH HIS UPCOMING meeting scheduled for later that afternoon, Benjamin decided to reinvestigate Jedediah's office. Deborah and her daughters were presently in the sitting room—one of the servant girls was singing for their entertainment—so he had a bit of time to spare. Although he still didn't have a pin for unlocking, he *did* have a small leatherbound journal to take notes.

Limbs jittery and heart pounding, Benjamin slipped undetected into the large office.

Making certain the coast was clear, Benjamin found the room empty and quickly opened the left-hand desk drawer. The ledger sat there undisturbed. With a relieved exhale, he retrieved the book and placed it upon the desk, then quickly set to work on transcribing the names into his journal.

Copying the shorthand notes left in the margins by each name, Benjamin was so immersed that he didn't realize someone was coming until it was too late. He heard the footsteps first, the heavy, unhurried tread of the elite, and in a panic, he shoved the ledger into its proper place, clumsily closed the drawer, and stumbled forward as Jedediah Boyd entered the room.

"What is the meaning of this?" the attorney thundered.

"Sir!" Benjamin greeted. "You're home early…"

"And a good thing, too!" Jedediah cried. "What in God's name are you doing in my office?"

"Uh…" Floundering, Benjamin pointed at the nearest window and staggered toward it, holding up his journal and pencil while he explained, "This room has the most natural light, not to mention, one of the greatest views available, so I came here to draw."

"To *draw?*" Jedediah echoed, incredulous. "Whatever for?"

"Charlotte, of course," Benjamin replied. "She's always been fond of my drawings, so as a token of my love, I wished to sketch for her."

Jedediah's face softened, though his eyes remained hard as flint. "Hmph," he grumbled. "I never begrudge my darling girl anything her heart desires, but I wish you would've asked me first, Philip."

"Yes, sir, of course. You're absolutely right. I apologize for taking such uncouth liberties."

"Goodness, there is no need to grovel," the older man said, "though I appreciate your sincerity." Perking up, he added, "May I see it?"

Benjamin's heart stammered. "You mean the drawing, sir?"

Jedediah nodded. "Why yes, of course. I am partial to those ginkgo trees out front, so I'd love to see them interpreted through an artist's eye."

He approached, but Benjamin was quick to tuck the journal underneath his coat and retreat, his finger wagging in admonishment. "Now, now, sir, it's to be a surprise! And as much as I wholeheartedly respect and value your opinion, it's my strictest wish that Charlotte's eyes be the very first to behold this piece."

Jedediah's lips pursed, but he gave a grudging nod. "Oh, very well. I suppose I can wait a few days more. Speaking of keeping people waiting..." He gestured toward the bookshelf. "Would you mind fetching that tome by the bust of our king? It's for you."

"This one, sir?" Benjamin asked, plucking the book free from its shelf. The words *Commentaries on the Laws of England* were printed along the spine.

Jedediah hummed in acknowledgment. "I came home to fetch it for our pending appointment—or rather, for a point of reference—but you might as well get a head start and skim over it during our carriage ride."

"I'm not sure I've heard of this," Benjamin admitted, flipping through the pages with vague intrigue.

"It explains common law in layman's terms," Jedediah replied. "I assure you, Philip, many a jolter-head has learned from this book, so if you're serious about your intentions—if you *do* wish to study law—I hereby welcome you into the fray."

Benjamin looked at him with a smile, his pulse slowly starting to calm. "It would be my highest honor, sir."

"Please! What did I tell you earlier? Call me Jed," the attorney admonished. Stepping forward, he clapped a hand onto the younger man's shoulder. "Come along, then. You have much to learn today."

I can only hope, Benjamin thought. He could feel the heaviness of the journal in his pocket, practically burning him with the fate he'd narrowly escaped.

CHAPTER SEVEN

Common Law

DESPITE THE CARRIAGE ride not being particularly rough, Benjamin's wound grew aggravated from the constant rocking. By the time they parked by a brick building with a well-kept, embellished wooden sign reading *J. Boyd, Esq.* in fine cursive, Benjamin was already in a foul temper. His upper lip curled at the sight. Even Boyd's bloody *sign* was ostentatious.

Taking the lead, Jedediah stepped from the carriage and inhaled the sultry spring air. "Ah, take that all in!" he exclaimed. "That, my boy, is the smell of success!"

More like the smell of hot air coming from your arse, Benjamin thought. Plastering on a good-humored smile, he eased himself from the carriage, mindful of his wound, before coming to a stop at the other man's side. "What are we doing first, sir?" he asked.

"Patience, Philip! Today's guest is someone you've already met."

"Oh?"

Considerably chipper, or at least, chipper for a man of Jedediah's usual temperament, the attorney led Benjamin into the building, then through a foyer for hats and coats before heading into his main office. "Ensign?" he called, opening the double doors. "I apologize for our tardiness…"

When Benjamin entered and beheld the back of a proud, swarthy redcoat, a seed of unease took root in his chest and he froze, watching in bemusement as the ignorant boob from the party, Eleazor Thomas, rose from his chair.

"Ah, Mr. Ashby!" the ensign exclaimed, grinning broadly. "To what do I owe the pleasure?"

"Today, he'll begin learning the ways of law," Jedediah said. "And if he impresses me enough, I'll personally see to it that he gets the proper schooling to become my right-hand man."

"Well, that's certainly exciting news! I know *I* already feel much better about America's future." With a throaty chuckle, Eleazor stepped forward and clapped Benjamin on the shoulder. "Are you abreast of Jed's latest endeavor?"

When Benjamin spared Jedediah a questioning look, the attorney said, "He is not, but it's never too late to start." He nodded toward his desk. "Ensign, in there, you will find the affidavits to deliver." To Benjamin, he explained, "David, or Mayor Mathews, to you, despite being able to draw up affidavits himself, has enlisted my help in taking off some of the heat. At present, he's under suspicion of visiting prisons and writing affidavits that deny prisoner abuse and neglect. Naturally, I don't mind putting my name out there. Because truly, is it so unlawful when these rebels have repeatedly broken our king's laws? If they wish to behave like animals, then they will be treated accordingly!"

Scandalized, a sharp twinge of anger swelled between Benjamin's ribs, his eyes blinking in shock. No words escaped him. If they had, he surely would have given himself away.

Eleazor nudged him. "As luck would have it, we've already had several British officers swear the American prisoners are well-fed and comfortable, and *I'm* about to be one of them." He flashed a smarmy grin. "I'm here to give my account."

Benjamin felt sick. How could God allow this? Men like Boyd and Eleazor were free to abuse innocent civilians, yet heroes like Daniel swung from the gibbet? While it was true that some patriots *were* violent toward their neighbors, he knew that surely, not everyone they were punishing deserved their sentence.

Daniel certainly hadn't.

While Benjamin fumed silently, Jedediah fetched his decanter of sherry and poured them each a glass. "Pray, don't just stand there, Philip!" he crowed. "Come drink with us. David is going to get what he's owed!"

As are you, Benjamin furiously thought. Forcing a grin, he stepped forward and accepted the drink. "To Mayor Mathews's good fortune!" he exclaimed, raising his glass.

The other men followed suit, then drank with gusto.

Lowering his glass with a long, drawn-out sigh, Eleazor grinned and tapped his stomach. "A good year, Jed! A good year, indeed!" Chuckling, he added, "While I'm here, might I trouble you about the produce pick-up?"

Jedediah set down his glass with a harrumph. "I thought I told Major Markham that Mr. Collins was tending to your produce needs. Is it not enough that I've supplied you with livestock, hay, and every other bloody requirement you see fit?"

Eleazor grew aghast. "But sir…it's for the Cr—"

"Our king would never be so careless with provisions, and of that I can assure you," Jedediah snarled. Sighing, he amended, "Forgive me, Ensign. You know I'd do absolutely anything for the Crown, but you are all bleeding me dry. Save some for my family, won't you?"

"Of course, Jed." Eleazor pursed his lips. "Sooo, Mr. Collins will be the one providing our produce?"

"Yes. If you send your men sometime within the next couple days, he'll have everything prepared."

Benjamin listened silently to this exchange. While the two men worked out the details, he worked out his own. If he couldn't save the prisoners from their fate, he would certainly ensure Eleazor's regiment went hungry.

CLARA WAS ANNOYED. Not only because of her perplexing encounter with Philip Ashby—why *was* that clotpole so charming?—but because for the past two hours, she'd overseen the proper care and maintenance of the household.

With Deborah hungover and unwilling to come downstairs, the title of "lady of the house" ultimately fell upon Clara's shoulders. When Charlotte was home, as the eldest, the job had gone to her. Deborah's drunken stupors were tragically commonplace; with Charlotte visiting Philadelphia, the servants had all turned to Clara for guidance.

After assigning the kitchen staff what she prayed to be suitable menus, she moved on to distributing the mending, laundry, farm and gardenwork, and general upkeep. This only further proved to her she wasn't suitable housewife material. Gossip, gowns, and hosting events were all delightful, but the actual upkeep of a manor was hardly entertaining enough to suit her tastes.

"Mademoiselle?"

The redhead sighed, her shoulders sagging as Angélique approached. Hiding in the library hadn't worked, after all… "Yes, what is it now?"

Wincing at her tone, the handmaiden said, "William's asking if you require the silver to be polished? It hasn't been done since the party, so—"

"Yes, yes, polish whatever fork, candlestick, and insufferable *knob* you all see fit," Clara groused. Catching the Frenchwoman's hurt, she quickly amended, "Forgive me, Angélique. I didn't mean to be cross with you. You all are doing an exceptional job, I just—" The door opened, then admitted none other than Philip Ashby. "—have a lot on my mind," she concluded. *He* being at the top of that execrable list.

Ever mercurial, Clara's agitation melted away, and her eyes glittered as she teased her guest, "You know, we really need to stop running into each other like this."

Philip snorted. "What, you mean in your own home? The mind wonders..." Looking between both women, he apologized, "Forgive me, I didn't mean to intrude. I only came to find a book."

Clara's expression grew smug. "Was Rueff's text not enough to satisfy your curiosities? Or did he perhaps inflame them?"

Philip flushed a faint pink, and Angélique was quick to intervene.

"Mademoiselle," she warned, clearly embarrassed.

"Oh, fie! It's all in good fun," Clara complained. "And with you overseeing our chat, I hardly think I'm speaking out of turn."

"But when you speak, who *does* get a turn?" Philip volleyed. Despite the clear barb, there was a certain warmth to his eyes that proved he wasn't sincere.

Opening her mouth, Clara was cut off by a brisk knock at the front door. She huffed, straightening her stance. "Angélique, please see who that is."

The Frenchwoman bristled. "With all due respect, mademoiselle, I cannot leave you two alone."

"Oh, I'll get it," Philip offered. "Really, I don't mind. I—"

"Don't be ridiculous," Clara admonished. "You are a guest, not a servant." Annoyed, she assured Angélique, "I will accompany you. Heaven forbid I am left alone with a man for ten whole seconds. Why, that's scarcely enough time for a woman to draw up her skirts!"

Pleased when both Philip and Angélique became sufficiently scandalized, she followed the latter out into the hallway, and remained by the staircase while her handmaiden approached the door.

After it was opened, Clara arched a brow once a petite, dark-skinned girl was revealed on the other side, her eyes guarded and a basket of freshly-cut flowers in hand.

"Yes?" Angélique asked, sounding skeptical.

The girl dipped into a curtsy. "Hullo, Miss," she greeted. "I'se here for Mr. Philip Ashby. Said he wanted to buy a flower."

Angélique hummed. "And who is the flower for?"

"I surely don't know, Miss. I don't make a habit of askin' strangers 'bout their business."

Humming anew, Angélique turned and called, "Monsieur Ashby?"

Philip was already in the hallway, seeing how he must have overheard the conversation. "I'm here," he assured them. His tone sounded a bit rattled. Perhaps he was still on edge from his attack?

Curious, Clara watched him approach with a brisk stride to his step.

Philip thanked Angélique before dismissing her, then lowered his voice so he couldn't be overheard. He and the young girl conversed, both of their tones equally hushed, and Philip passed the girl something, some coin, Clara presumed, before he received three stems of peonies in return.

Philip thanked the girl and shut the door, turning toward Clara with a sheepish smile. "Flower girl," he explained.

"Yes, so I saw," Clara wryly said. With an impish twinkle to her eyes, she asked, "Are those for me?"

"You, Catherine, and your mother, actually," Philip affirmed. "I saw the girl in town yesterday—er, before my incident—and I asked her to stop by today."

With a glimmer of intrigue, Clara asked, "And which one's mine?"

He chuckled. "Straight to the point, aren't you?"

"Always." With a sly smile, Clara stepped forward as he indicated the red peony.

"This one," Philip explained. "My mother was quite fond of flowers, and I know she only gave them to those she wholly respected…to those she admired for their strength and love." His expression turned shy. "I am aware we've only been acquainted a short while, but you're assuredly the strongest woman I've ever met."

Clara blinked at that, startled. "Me?" A scornful laugh bubbled in her throat. "How ever did you come to *that* conclusion?"

Bashfully, he shrugged. "You *did* stitch up my wound. If that isn't strength, I surely don't know what is."

Chewing her lip, Clara accepted the three stems and twirled them between her fingers, a skeptical pleasure brightening her face as she stooped to inhale the sweet scent. Humming under her breath, she straightened and smiled. "This is quite sufficient, as far as bribery goes. Thank you, Philip."

He laughed, though there was a hint of his earlier disquiet bleeding into his features. "I assure you, Miss Boyd, if I wished to bribe you, there would also be groveling."

Her expression turned feline. "Indeed? Then perhaps you should get on your knees."

A clearing throat interrupted their conversation—and a good thing too, seeing how dear Philip was ready to burst from embarrassment—and sighing, Clara turned toward Angélique behind them. "Yes, what is it?"

Despite her clipped tone, Angélique remained unruffled. "The cook would like your opinion on the sauces for Monsieur Ashby's upcoming banquet. Would you please accompany me, mademoiselle?"

Clara pursed her mouth. Looking at the peonies, her handmaiden, and then back to Philip, she apologized, "Forgive me, but it seems you will have to dirty your knees another time. You may return to your book search."

Philip spluttered, mortified, but she was already following Angélique with a pleased little smile on her lips.

DESPITE BENJAMIN'S VARYING successes that morning, he spent the rest of the day on guard, leery of everyone who crossed his path. That man, that stranger who'd accosted him was still out there. Even though it was doubtful he knew Benjamin was living with the Boyds, the overhanging quiet didn't sit well with him.

And then there was the girl from earlier, Ada, who was the youngest courier Bishop recruited. For today's particular exchange, he'd written a coded note about Stewart's death and requested a meeting with Amos, then tacked on an entreaty that the produce from Mr. Collins's farm be burned. He could only hope Ada passed that along in time…

Exhaling, Benjamin slipped into his bed and lay down, naked and uncomfortable. It was funny, he thought. Ever since the beginning of the war, he'd remained adamantly neutral about his political leanings, yet the moment Daniel was arrested for his beliefs and strung up without a trial, Benjamin could no longer remain upon the fence. He'd toppled headlong onto the patriot side, crashing painfully into his newfound allegiance. And by God, it *was* painful; not only because of his irrevocable loss, but because the more he infiltrated this Tory family, the more he realized the other side wasn't just filled with monsters. *Clara* wasn't a monster. She was intriguingly human, willful and alive, and whether or not he accepted it, he did admire her. He even liked her. Maybe it was because he was forever indebted to her aid, he couldn't be certain, but the lines between truth and pretend were officially starting to blur.

Dragging a hand over his face, Benjamin exhaled and attempted to settle into his bedding.

It was destined to be a long night.

CLARA, TOO, WAS ill at ease that evening. She paced around in her bedchamber, clasping her hands over her mouth as though in prayer.

What was *wrong* with her? Why had she become consumed by thoughts of that silly, insufferable clotpole her sister had chosen to marry? Although she'd started off tormenting and teasing Philip to prove he was truly loyal and devoted to Charlotte, and that he wasn't just in this for the money, she was quickly finding herself quite fond of him. And *that,* it seemed, was becoming a problem…

Oh, tar and sugar.

A sharp, painful slice of guilt twisted through her heart, and Clara exhaled, spinning about and facing her reflection. It wasn't as though she loved or desired Philip. She wouldn't be averse to physical entanglements, of course, but she actually found herself interested in what he had to say. Clara *liked* listening to his fumbling, awkward attempts at conversation, and, more befuddling still, she liked *him.* Ever since he'd given her that stupid flower, she'd found herself wholly endeared to Philip and his fawn-like eyes, bashful smiles, and bookish intelligence in ways she'd never thought possible.

Was this what it was like to enjoy a man's companionship, and without the sole desire for intimacy? Was this what it was like to respect someone's opinions other than her own? To yearn for their approval?

Groaning, Clara pushed back a loosened lock from her long, braided hair and once more glanced at her reflection. She appeared lost, tragic, and despite the leap of shame in her chest, she decided she needed to check on Philip. He hadn't changed his bandages all day, to her knowledge, so she'd go by his room and see if he needed any help.

Attempting to calm her nerves, Clara slipped into her dressing gown, then prepared a punched tin lantern to take with her into the hallway.

CHAPTER EIGHT
Muddied Intentions

A KNOCK CUT across the room and Benjamin jolted awake, panicked while glancing around in confusion. "Wh-who's there?" he croaked.

There came a pause, then he heard a soft, "It's Clara, Philip. Might I come in?"

Clara?

Squinting through the dying firelight, he sniffed and blinked the sleep from his eyes, suddenly remembering a very important fact: He was completely naked. If she came in, there would be far worse to deal with than her exasperating quips.

"Go away!" he hissed. "It's too late for a visit."

Silence followed, then the door clicked open. A faint spill of candlelight bloomed within the doorway, and Clara poked her head around the corner. "What was that?"

Benjamin lurched onto his elbows, shocked and spluttering. "I...I-I told you to leave," he snapped, scandalized. "Miss Boyd, this is—"

"Clara," she corrected.

Primary thought derailed, he flushed and curled underneath his blankets. "Whatever address you prefer, this isn't appropriate. Were your father to hear..."

"He won't," she assured him, her voice hushed as she shut the door. "My parents sleep like the dead, and they hardly concern themselves with the goings-on of my life."

Her tone was a little saddened, a rare moment of vulnerability on her part, and Benjamin hesitated, moved by her briefly exposed soul. Was she not nearly as indifferent as he'd always believed?

Swallowing, he amended, "Be that as it may, I am engaged to your sister. You shouldn't be here."

A look of guilt flashed across Clara's eyes, and gripping the small tray between her hands, she softly agreed, "I know this, yes... And I apologize greatly for my offense. But I cannot sleep, and you are still awake, so I thought...w-well, perhaps you needed your bandages changed?"

Benjamin balked. He wasn't quite sure how to safely explain that he was indecent underneath his quilt, and most especially when her eyes were so soft and pleading, and she was...*God*, she was coming right toward him.

He held up a hand, hoping to ward her off, but Clara ignored the feeble rebuff and set her tray onto his nightstand.

"Have you had any discomfort?" she asked.

With a barb of sarcasm, Benjamin asked, "What, you mean from being stabbed? Yes, I'd say a fair amount."

She speared him with a withering look, then picked up several linen strips and nodded to him with purpose. "Show me your wound."

"What?"

Exasperated, Clara commanded, "Show me your wound, Philip. I need to see if it's putrid. If it is, I am afraid I must call for a surgeon."

Hesitant, Benjamin slowly rolled into a sitting position, careful to keep his quilt up to his chin.

Clara noticed and laughed. "Why are you being so modest? I've already seen you without a shirt—congratulations, by the way—so what could you possibly have to be so shy about?"

He scowled at her, then lowered the quilt to just beneath his wound. As long as she didn't pull away the bedding, he knew he'd be safe.

Clara sat on the mattress and reached for his bandages. "I know all men are babies, but you are being quite difficult," she complained. Despite her sharp tone, she was very careful with him as she unrolled his wrappings. Benjamin flinched once or twice, but otherwise remained silent as the cloth fell away from his skin.

After the final strip was removed, Clara observed her stitch-work within the candlelight and frowned. "It...doesn't *appear* infected," she said. "There is a little bit of pink, but from what I've gathered, that is relatively normal for the first day or so. Has it been hot to the touch?"

Benjamin shook his head, regarding her in amazement. "I thought you claimed very little knowledge of medical science."

"Nothing professional," Clara murmured. "I read whatever I can...and perhaps too much." Rolling her eyes, she applied a fresh coat of honey to his injury. "Or at least, I read 'too much' according to my family. You're the first to seem impressed by my initiative. Don't you believe a woman's place is to keep quiet and produce children?"

Benjamin winced, shaking his head. "No, of course not...education is important. Whenever I speak to the fairer sex, I prefer stimulation."

She smirked. "You mean, stimulation from more than just your gingambobs?"

"Yes." He offered a soft smile. "Much more."

"That makes two of us," Clara agreed. Regarding him with a sly smile, she coiled the fresh bandages around his lower torso. "You know, this is the first time you haven't blushed during our chats. I suppose you've grown accustomed to my ways."

"Whether I wish it or not," Benjamin agreed, chuckling. She tied a knot on his bandages, and he laid a hand over her wrist, gently squeezing. "You don't have to keep helping me, you know. I was wrong to involve you."

Pulling herself free of his grasp, Clara lifted her shoulders, feigning indifference. "Yes, but I *am* involved, so that's a moot point, don't you think?" Amused, her lips quirked and her eyes glittered. "I rather like it. It's exciting being involved in something of which my parents would disapprove."

"With all due respect, isn't that everything you do?"

"There's no need for such impudence!" Laughing, the sound was light and warm as she fixed him with another grin. It was dazzling within the candlelight, and Benjamin shrank back, overwhelmed by the sudden urge to touch her, to capture that radiant flame.

Sighing, she tapped his knee. "I suppose I should retire. Are you in need of anything else?"

Benjamin quickly shook his head, far too afraid to speak, lest he voice his befuddling thoughts aloud.

"Very well." Glancing at the discarded bandages, she decided, "I'll take these with me...unless you'd prefer to keep them as a token of remembrance?" Despite the sneer in her tone, her eyes were warm as she gathered the strips and placed them onto her tray. Though once she spotted a few dark, haphazard drips of blood on his quilt, she offered, "Let me take your bedding, as well. I don't want anyone questioning how you've soiled my great-grandmother's hard work." She tapped his knee again. "I'll be out of your way momentarily."

"No!" Benjamin rushed up to stop her. "Please..." Cheeks burning, his mouth opened and closed soundlessly, unsure of how to explain his indecency. And although he expected scorn or laughter toward his over-the-top display, Clara surprised him once her gaze softened and she brushed the hair from his eyes.

"Oh, Philip," she murmured. "I didn't realize you were lonely, too."

Lonely? Clearly, she had misinterpreted his desperation. Although his initial response was to say that no, of course he wasn't, the moment her fingertips traced the strong curve of his jaw, his chin, and then over the soft, parted slope of his mouth, something deep inside of him fractured from the realization that yes, he *was* lonely—devastatingly so. He couldn't remember the last time he'd been spared a kind, gentle touch.

Help me, he thought. *Need me*, touch *me*.

Benjamin caught her wrist and Clara gasped. A tightness formed inside his chest. *Don't turn me away, don't, don't, don't.* And then his hand slid over top of hers, halting the path of her fingers. They remained pressed over his lips, firm and gentle as they locked eyes.

"Philip..." All at once, shame bled across Clara's face, and with a shuddery breath, she rolled off the bed in a rush, jerking once Benjamin's hand came around her elbow.

"Wait," he pleaded. When she looked back at him, her eyes were wild and verdant, much like a burning forest of evergreen.

"I must go," she told him, yet her tone shook and lacked conviction. "Good night, Philip."

Benjamin gaped at her, stunned. "Clara, if I have offended you—"

"You were wrong," she cut in, her body trembling. "I really *am* a trollop." A soft sob caught in her throat, and she tore from his grasp before rushing out into the hallway.

FOR THE FIRST time in ages, sleep did not come kindly. As a woman who was accustomed to the safety, comfort, and inevitable security that wealth tended to bring, Clara didn't often find herself weighed down with the troubles of most colonials. In fact, she usually slept much like a babe, dreamless and content. But on this particular night, with the memory of Philip's hand on her arm, and him beholding her with his deep, penetrating blue eyes akin to a midnight bonfire, she was spiraled into such a state that she could scarcely rest. At around three a.m., the first moment she blinked, she slipped away, and then it was suddenly morning.

Groggy and restless, Clara rose with her handmaiden's knock, and from there, allowed herself to be primped, preened, and dressed for the day. For once, Angélique was chatty and spoke of the town gossip, all of which involved Charlotte's upcoming nuptials. While Angélique inserted each hairpin into her curly locks, Clara hardly heard a word. She didn't wish to. Not when she found herself increasingly ensnared by a man *she should not want*.

"Won't that be wonderful, mademoiselle?" Angélique gleefully asked. "I've always loved babies. Perhaps with your sister's marriage, we shall soon have a lively home!"

With her heart dropping akin to a tree being felled, Clara's chin ducked and she swallowed back a low, shuddery breath. "I would rather focus on the present, if you wouldn't mind."

"Oh, but—"

"This is suitable, thank you." Shying away from Angélique's outstretched hands, Clara didn't dare assess her reflection as she stalked for the door.

WITH MORNING'S LIGHT upon him, Benjamin could no longer ignore what had happened. It was easy to hide his feelings in the dark—in the darkness Clara doused him with once she'd fled his room—but there, in the open corridors of the Boyd manor, was a certain emptiness that reflected the decaying chambers in his heart. He hadn't realized until last night how badly he yearned for love, normalcy, and as he entered the library for a respite, he felt an instant spike of heat at the sight of Clara sitting there, quietly reading a novel.

"Good morning," he greeted. "Where is everyone?"

"Father's at work, Catherine has a case of the vapors, and Mother is drunk," Clara snapped, promptly turning another page. "Why are *you* here?"

"I..." Incredulous, Benjamin cleared his throat and tried again, "I'm living here until Charlotte's return, in case you've forgotten."

"Ah, yes. Your 'treasure' whom you spoke of so fondly yesterday." Clara's gaze was sharp and accusatory, and her eyes grew wet before she quickly looked back down at her book. "I hope she knows what kind of man you are."

Benjamin flinched. "Clara..." Sinking onto the settee alongside her, he attempted to lay his hand over hers, but she abruptly shook herself free.

"I have nothing to say to you."

His chest grew tight. "Even if that were true, you *know* this was never my intention."

"Then what *was?*"

"Well..." Swallowing, he tried again. "It must have been the delirium. Surely, my blood loss and exhaustion affected my behavior."

Clara scoffed, abruptly snapping her book shut. "You don't actually expect me to believe that, do you?"

"I love your sister," Benjamin said with more conviction, "and I'd never do anything to betray her trust."

"Neither would I," Clara crisply agreed. "Good day to you, Philip." And with that, she gathered up her skirts and stormed from the room.

WHEN BENJAMIN STEPPED out for a much-needed breath of fresh

air, he aimlessly walked the grounds, reeling from his conversation with Clara. She was rightfully angry with him. What a *fool* he'd been! And yet, hadn't a small flame of yearning danced within her eyes? Wasn't he right to believe she might hold a scrap of affection for him?

While mulling this over, Benjamin heard the sound of briskly moving boots, and then two hands grabbed him and shoved. His back collided with one of the many ginkgo trees dotting the path.

"*Oof!*" His head knocked against the trunk, harshly, but not enough to wound, and once Amos came into view, it was clear he was wearing the same British uniform from earlier.

Infuriated, Benjamin ripped the other man's grip from his coat. "Will you quit ambushing me like this?" he growled. "It's not safe for you here!"

"Aye," Amos agreed, his eyes sharp, "though from the sound o' things, it ain't too safe for *you* neither."

Benjamin froze, his features sobering. "What do you know?"

"George Stewart," Amos replied as if it were obvious. "I gotcher message. Any idea who snuffed 'im?"

"No...I was hoping you might've heard."

The cabinetmaker snorted. "A bloody lot o' good it's done us keepin' you here. We need'ja at camp more than ever—where actual *progress* is bein' made."

"I *have* been making progress," Benjamin hissed. "Or have you already forgotten about Mr. Collins's tampered goods?"

Amos's jaw clenched. "Y'know I haven't."

"*Do* I? Because you're acting as if I'm not risking *everything* for this cause!" Lowering his voice, Benjamin pressed, "Has there been word from Philadelphia?"

"Aye. The drop-off's been made, so they dumped the tampered goods into the sea. So far, everyone's none the wiser."

Benjamin nodded in relief. "And my note...what are your plans for Mr. Collins's farm?"

"I'm headin' there at nightfall," Amos said. "You good here?"

All at once, Clara's bright, bewitching eyes came to mind, and cheeks warming, Benjamin nodded. "Yes…o-of course."

Amos mirrored his nod. "Good. I'll be done after midnight."

The cabinetmaker turned to leave, but recalling a very important detail, Benjamin grabbed his elbow and tugged. "Wait a moment," he pleaded. "I tried sending intelligence through Mr. Stewart, but he was killed in action…and now, I'm afraid whoever attacked him has my letter."

Amos's eyes went wide. "Zounds… Didja code it?"

Benjamin offered a jerky nod. "Yes, of course. I used our cipher key."

The cabinetmaker exhaled, holding his hands as though in prayer. "All right, good. Thank the ol' Man Upstairs! And'ja didn't go signin' your true name or nothin'?"

Benjamin scoffed. "I may be unlucky, but I'm not *stupid*," he grumbled. "I think we're all right, but I wanted you aware…all I included in the note were Tory names, as well as a rehash of what I'd already told you in the barn." Wincing, his shoulders drooped. "Unfortunately, there *is* one thing more. In regards to Stewart's murder, I feel confident he was killed by the same man who attacked me."

"Attacked you?" Amos balked, looking him up and down. "Whoa-ho now, when did *this* happen, uh? For the love o'…! Moony, why the hell didn'tcha say so?"

"Because I don't know who the man was!" Benjamin exclaimed. "I didn't recognize him, but he seemed intent on harm. His parting words were *'veni, vidi, vici'*—'I came, I saw, I conquered.'"

"Shite…"

"Exactly." Smoothing a hand over his mouth, Benjamin grimaced. "I thought for sure I would've been outed, but I haven't seen hide nor hair of my assailant since that night." Catching Amos's fiery look, he interjected, "I know I should've sent word, and I know I shouldn't have waited to tell you, but I needed to make sure that if I were apprehended, the trail wouldn't lead back to anyone else."

Cursing under his breath, Amos decided, "I hafta stay here."

"What?"

"I'll pose as your cousin from England," he continued, growing all the more determined. "Tell the Boyds how *important* I am to the king's cause, or whatever twaddle those high-flyers yap about, an' ask 'em to billet me 'til we can figure everything out."

Benjamin scoffed, tossing up his hands. "This is ludicrous, Amos. You can't just—"

"What's 'ludicrous' is leavin' this up to chance," he growled. "You're compromised, Ben. Lemme help."

He exhaled. "Be that as it may—"

"What?" Amos cut in. "Don'tcha think I can do anything?"

"Well, you're not exactly subtle."

He snorted. "In all our years o' friendship, I'd like to think y'could gimme more credit than that." Pointing toward the Boyd residence, he commanded, "Introduce me."

"Amos…"

"Introduce me, or I'll make the bloody introductions me'self!"

Benjamin steeled his shoulders, then nodded in assent. Whether he liked it or not, the Ashby family tree was about to get a little larger…

CHAPTER NINE

Lessons

SUPPER THAT EVENING led to a myriad of surprises. Not only was Amos welcomed by the Boyds, but Clara seemed wholly warm and jovial—even toward *himself*. Benjamin could scarcely keep up with her hot-and-cold mood swings: how she simultaneously held him out at arm's length and drew him close in the same breath.

To Amos's credit, he was able to adopt the posh, dutiful mien of a British soldier in far more ways than Benjamin expected. While he regaled the family with stories of war and valor, Benjamin forced himself to eat. Each bite went down like bits of cork, dry and tasteless despite the fact he was starving. He was far too nervous. Amos, or "Reginald Ashby," as they decided upon, was doing a marvelous job thus far, but the cabinetmaker had a flair for the dramatic.

As if proving Benjamin correct, Amos hoisted his leg onto the table, causing the women to cry out while Jedediah cleared his throat, torn on whether to adhere to decorum or honor a war hero. "And *this* is where I got grazed by a bayonet last fall," Amos said, unfastening the knee band on his right leg.

While he pulled down his stocking and showed Catherine a wide, grinning scar, Benjamin hid a smile. He knew the mark well. About three summers ago, Amos drunkenly climbed a fence during a prank gone wrong and caught his leg on the wood before falling over the side. The result had been a nasty cut, a cut currently presented as a bayonet wound to the wide-eyed, pale-faced Boyds. Fortunately, Jedediah himself was not a veteran, so no one could dispute Amos's various scars and injuries, one of which was the left index finger he'd lost while using a handsaw.

"Lord above," Catherine whispered, cooling herself with a paper fan. "Oh, Private Ashby…did you—?"

"Reggie," Amos corrected, causing her to flush.

"Ah…" Not wanting to list him as a familiar, and thus break the natural order, Catherine flushed more deeply and lowered her eyes. "You are so brave and noble, sir. I shudder to think what you must've gone through, and all for the glory of the Crown."

"Think nothin' of it," Amos said, winking. "I did it for our generous king, and would do so again in a heartbeat."

Benjamin yearned to scoff, yet froze once Clara openly showed her scorn at Catherine's side.

"With all due respect, Private Ashby, you strike me as more of a thrill seeker than a true man of the Crown. Why, your eyes positively glimmer every time you speak of battle," she said, smiling as she swirled her wine. "Soldiers are a fascinating sort. They either fall apart and grow taciturn, or they do as you have: open up and come alive at the talk of blood, sickness, and pain."

Amos snorted, though it was clear she'd thrown him. "D'ya think so little o' me, Miss? And here I was, already mighty fond o' you."

"Of course not," Clara said, "though I am curious about the family resemblance." She looked between Benjamin and Amos. "Philip is reticent, and fair-colored, and…well…tall. You are none of those things."

"I slouch," Amos grumbled.

"Relations aren't always identical," Deborah said, looking to her sullen husband for help. "Honestly, Clara, why must you always be so difficult? He may not resemble Philip, but how can one ever recreate such a handsome, masterful—?"

"*Mother.*"

"We're distant cousins," Amos fibbed, playfully socking Benjamin on the arm.

"Very distant," Benjamin agreed, sparing his friend a wry glance. "Truth be told, I've never been blessed enough to visit Reggie in London. Once the war is through, I'm hoping to rectify that."

"Oh, we'd be delighted to show you around London, Philip," Deborah crowed. "Jedediah has an uncle over there. Isn't that right, darling?"

Jedediah harrumphed, though it came across as an affirmative.

"Yes, I trust Lottie wishes to move there," Clara agreed. "She speaks of European society in nearly all her letters."

Amos finally lowered his leg. "And you don't, Miss Boyd? 'Cause I'd be happy to squire you 'round London…for a price."

She appraised him skeptically. "And what price would that be, sir?"

"A dance, o' course! Though you'll be gettin' the better deal here. I both excite and delight."

Clara scoffed, though she was smiling. "Someone needs to teach you how to flirt, Private. Alas, I am beginning to see the family resemblance: You both are woeful when it comes to female seduction."

Benjamin flushed all the way up to the tips of his ears, but Amos laughed and struck his arm again.

"Aye, Moony's not the best when it comes to womenfolk."

"Moony?" Looking between them, Clara said, "Now *that* sounds like an origin story I simply must hear."

Benjamin groaned, sparing Amos a wary look. "Please," he begged. "Is it not punishment enough that I had to live it?"

"Aye, jus' think o' everyone in town who had to live it, too, and with their own two eyes!" Gleeful, Amos leaned forward and explained, "I thankfully wasn't in town at the time, but legend has it that during a Bible play—Moses partin' the Red Sea an' all that—Moony-boy parted his *own* sea by runnin' buck-arse naked through the crowd. His poor mother was chasin' after 'im, tryin' a' spare the locals of his lily-white arse." After a dramatic pause, he concluded, "Moony was twenty years old."

"I was *not,* you arsehole! I was six!"

Catherine squeaked in horror, but Clara howled with delight.

Catching himself, Benjamin flushed and apologized, "Forgive me, I did not mean to shout profanity at your table. I only wish to appear my very best around this family, so…I overreacted."

Jedediah glowered in reply, shoveling a piece of chicken into his mouth, but Deborah and Clara tittered while Catherine reeled from the scandal.

Cleaning up with a finger bowl, Clara grinned and declared, "Be that as it may, you've both just shown a shocking amount of liberty. And as soon-to-be members of this family, I'd like to think you could offer something far better in terms of gentility." Pleased with herself, Clara glanced toward Amos and asked, "Perhaps you can prove yourselves this coming weekend? A family friend is hosting a soiree, and I'm certain they would be delighted to entertain a private of His Majesty's Army."

"Ah…er…"

"Some officers will be present," she assured him. "Do you know Major Adam Markham, by chance?"

"Reggie was just transferred," Benjamin interjected. "I'm afraid he doesn't know anyone yet, hence his request to billet."

"And we are happy to house him," Deborah promised. "It's an honor to have such fine, handsome men in our home…regardless of their colorful pasts."

Jedediah guzzled the remainder of his wine, then impatiently gestured for one of the servants to refill his glass. "So long as those promised ships come along, I'm willing to house whomever you wish, Philip," he muttered. "When are they arriving?"

"Oh…" Benjamin hesitated. "The end of the week, I'd say. Depending upon the weather conditions, of course."

"Yes, naturally." Jedediah's eyes cut toward Amos. "And what is it you do back in London, Mr. Ashby?"

"Smithing," Amos said with a grin. "I make the finest silver candlesticks y'ever did see."

"Does that include jewelry?" Catherine asked, intrigued. "I love brooches, in particular."

He winked and nodded. "Aye, o' course! Just ask me, an' I'll fashion one up upon me return."

"I stand corrected," Clara said, drawing a hand over her chest in a mock swoon. "It seems Philip is the only woeful flirt in this equation, because Private Ashby is speaking Kitty's love language."

Catherine flushed, but didn't deny it.

Benjamin caught Amos's smirk and rolled his eyes, though he was chuckling. "I'm afraid I am far better equipped for shipbuilding production than flirtations, Miss Boyd."

"Ships are similar to womenfolk," Amos assured him. "Both rock an' shudder whenever ya set into port, if y'get my meanin'."

Jedediah choked into his wine, but Clara threw her head back in a vibrant laugh, her cheeks growing pink as she hid her smile behind a fair hand. To Benjamin's surprise, a sensation akin to jealousy burned within his breast, tart and bilious. He'd *never* been clever enough to earn her laughter; not unless it was at his own expense.

Embittered, Benjamin took a swallow of wine and ignored Amos's gleeful jab against his ribs.

"I think the womenfolk should retire," Jedediah announced, sending Clara a pointed look. "Why don't you three head into the sitting room?"

"Oh yes, I'm certain we have *much* to discuss," the redhead agreed, her tone smug as everyone rose from the table. "Thank you for the entertainment, gentlemen." To Benjamin, she curtsied. "Perhaps you should listen to your cousin, Philip. He seems far more worldly."

Again, a sickening sensation flooded Benjamin's gut, and after bowing, he flushed as one by one, the women filed from the dining room.

Downing the remainder of his drink in one large, triumphant swallow, Amos slammed his glass onto the table. "Now, then!" he exclaimed. "Who wants to hear about the time I slew a group o' rebels, hmm?"

Jedediah appeared intrigued, but all Benjamin offered was a weakened smile.

ONCE JEDEDIAH RETIRED for the evening, the womenfolk continued their embroidery and chatted in the sitting room. Benjamin and Amos said their goodnights, but the former didn't return to his bedroom. No, he was presently searching through Clara's bedchambers. It was foolish—dangerous—and yet he knew that for the sake of the colonies, he needed to finally glean that dreaded bodice pin. He'd wasted far too much time as it was.

Exhaling, he assessed the room with a quick, calculating eye. Despite the poor lighting, he could see a nightstand, a desk by the window, and parallel to his left was a vanity with several jars and a jewelry box. Interest piqued, he appraised the area more closely and realized a small pin holder sat alongside Clara's washbowl.

There you are, he gleefully thought. But that was when he heard it: the soft, feminine tread of footsteps, followed by the *click* of an opening door.

Benjamin frantically blew out his candle and Clara entered the room, shutting the door behind her as he stood frozen in terror. Backlit by the faint glow from her hearth, his heart stuttered as the redhead briskly moved past him, clearly intent on the dying fire. She pushed and prodded at the kindling, and then, after the flames came back to life, she set aside the poker and rose, stifling a scream once she realized just who was inside her bedroom.

"You!" she exclaimed.

"Er...me," Benjamin weakly affirmed. "I'm sorry, I—"

"What are you doing here?"

"Books...ah...I'm searching," he quickly lied. "You seem the most well-versed in regards to...i-in regards to *certain subjects,* so I wished to investigate."

Clara scoffed, irritably folding her arms. "And you couldn't think to ask? Nor check the library?"

"What I'm researching is a delicate matter," Benjamin continued to fumble. "The truth is, Charlotte thinks I lack experience, so...I was hoping you might have some books to reference."

Finally, there was a softening in Clara's stance—had she truly accepted that hogwash?—yet her expression remained skeptical. "Lottie wishes for you to do...what, exactly? Brush up on the art of feminine pleasure?"

Good God...

Squirming with disquiet, Benjamin nodded. "Yes," he lied. "I beg your pardon for stealing into your room like this, but surely, you can understand why I felt the need for secrecy?"

Clara hummed. "There is no shame in inexperience, Philip. But unfortunately, when it comes to our dear Lottie, you are right: She's a rather demanding sort. And if this is what she wants, you won't hear the end of it until she gets her way." Sighing, she gestured him forward. "Have a seat. I can gather some books for you...and perhaps you can show me the precise issue?"

A spike of heat flared up beneath his collar, and swallowing, Benjamin choked, "*Show* you?"

"Of course." Clara shrugged, taking the candlestick from his hand and setting it aside. "If you don't know how to please, then if I am to help, I must at the very least know what to fix. Wouldn't you agree?"

"W-well..."

She gestured toward her bed. "Go on. Sit. Evidently, we have much to discuss."

Benjamin hesitated, then slowly did as she asked. This woman was confounding. Had she not sniped at him for such topics mere hours ago?

After gathering a few books, Clara approached with growing amusement. "Why are you acting like this is your execution?" she teased. "The thought of kissing isn't that abhorrent, is it?"

Anxious, Benjamin darted his eyes in between her face and the floor, perplexed. "Kissing?"

"Yes." She nodded. "We'll discuss other things first, of course, but being a good kisser is essential to the art of lovemaking. I figured that's where we should start. Charlotte will surely appreciate it."

Heat pooled within Benjamin's stomach and he looked away, swallowing sharply. "I don't need to learn how to kiss," he said.

"Oh, no?" Unconvinced, Clara prodded, "Does Lottie agree?"

"Yes," he coolly assured her, "Lottie does." His only experience was a quick, dry peck on the lips during his formative years, but she didn't need to know that one small detail.

"How wonderful!" Clara exclaimed. "I can't wait for you to prove me wrong." With a look that suggested she did not, in fact believe him, she took a seat alongside him near the head of her bed. "Here you are," she declared, setting the tomes into his lap. "I want you to read these over the next few days. Some have diagrams, like with Rueff's book on midwifery, but most are vital life lessons."

Bewildered, Benjamin lifted the top book and scoffed. "*Hamlet*? What does *this* have to do with intimacy?"

"The fact you have to ask tells me all I need to know, Philip." Gesturing to the book, Clara explained, "In Act 3, Scene 2, Hamlet asks Ophelia if he should lay his head upon her lap—if she thinks he is alluding to 'country matters.'"

Benjamin shrugged. "And?"

"Goodness, do I have to sound it out for you? *Country* matters. He is quite literally speaking of her private parts." Catching his alarm, she simpered. "It's a clever pun, wouldn't you agree? I love a good innuendo, and most especially whenever said innuendo is geared toward a woman's pleasure."

Benjamin squirmed, embarrassed. "How is referring to her...*carvel's ring* an allusion to female pleasure?"

"Because, Philip, the act alluded to is what you could and should do for our Lottie—preferably, with your mouth."

The heat in Benjamin's stomach spread, his hands tensing as he set aside the stack of books. "I've heard talk of such things, but...I-I wasn't quite sure what to make of it."

Clara laughed, the sound soft and airy. "Most men don't," she assured him, "so I expected as much. But I can assure you, women do enjoy a nice, fervent surprise as much as menfolk."

He drew a breath. "Then you...?"

"Yes." She nodded. "I must admit, it's very unusual to come across a man who does it well, but practice makes perfect." Noting his horror, she laughed brightly. "Fear not! I don't intend to make you do anything of that sort." Tapping his knee, she said, "First thing's first. I want you to kiss me. And not in some dry, platonic way you'd kiss a cousin."

Benjamin's chest quivered. "I...uh..."

"What? Haven't you and Charlotte kissed?"

"Well yes, but—"

"Do what you did then," she said, curling her fingers through his shirt collar. "If I am to salvage your upcoming marriage, I must find out precisely what to fix." Gaze flickering between his eyes and mouth, she commanded, "Kiss me, Philip."

He breathed out as though winded. Clara was soft and warm and confident, and when he cupped her face between his hands, he grew wholly ensnared by the jade fire of her eyes.

Throat dry, Benjamin brushed his lips over hers, trembling as he angled in for a light, careful kiss. It was quick and close-mouthed, chaste, and when he pulled back, he grew intimidated by the scornful look in Clara's eyes.

"Does Lottie not inspire passion?"

He balked. "W-what?"

"If *this* is how you kiss my sister, then I understand why she is so concerned." With a pointed look, Clara took his face between her hands and dragged his mouth firmly into her own.

Benjamin's breath hitched, and his hands fell to her waist, his grip tightening as their kiss grew fiercely enthusiastic. Helpless and touch-starved, he met her tongue with his and fed the growing need for distraction—for feeling *good* instead of the pain, the hurt, the suffering—and he groaned into her mouth once her fingers snagged through his hair and pulled. A warm, pleasant heat rippled through Benjamin's limbs, and clumsily, he tried to mimic her passion. That was when she broke the kiss.

Humming in thought, Clara pressed a hand to her lips and cleared her throat, a pretty pink staining her cheeks. "That was…adequate," she decided. "I've certainly had worse, but I've also had better." Raising her eyes, she instructed, "When you try again, please don't lap at my mouth like a dog."

Embarrassed, Benjamin swallowed and looked away. "That was new to me, I must confess."

"You don't say?" Grinning, Clara lifted a hand and tapped below his chin. "Kissing with tongue is an acquired taste, but if done properly, can make one wholly weak in the knees." Amused, she tucked a loosened lock of hair behind his ear. "This time, I want you to envision those 'country matters' we discussed."

Benjamin frowned. "Why?"

"Because, if you picture how you would perform orally between Lottie's legs, you might actually do well with the kissing aspect."

Benjamin's face flooded scarlet, but he nodded in response, dumbfounded.

"Show some initiative," she continued. "Lottie loves confidence, so that will get you far in her good graces." Scooting forward, Clara encouraged, "Try again."

By this point, it felt as if he were floating. Overwhelmed by the huskiness of her voice, the scent of her rose water, her very presence, Benjamin cupped her face and crashed his mouth into hers, emulating her assertiveness. Clara's soft gasp caught between their lips, and emboldened, Benjamin glossed their tongues and tilted her head back, devouring her whimper once her hand fell to his lap. Her palm pressed downward and he made a small, helpless noise, his breeches tightening as he rocked up into her touch. He attempted to deepen the kiss, but she pulled away, pink cheeked and astonished.

"That was better," Clara allowed, shakily pushing back a wayward curl. "I'm...I-I am actually a little besotted after that, so you are an exceptionally fast study."

Heart pounding, Benjamin took her hand. "I apologize," he choked. "It wasn't my intention to become so...enthused."

"Nor was mine," Clara whispered, lowering her gaze to his mouth. "Perhaps we should postpone areas of stimulation for another day."

Benjamin attempted to calm his breath, perplexed. "Areas of stimulation?"

"Yes..." Glassy-eyed, she tugged down his collar and cravat and pressed a deep, open-mouthed kiss against the side of his neck. Her lips were warm and wet, and an immediate shiver lanced up his spine. When she withdrew, she explained, "That was an area of interest. You felt added pleasure, did you not?"

Trying to ignore the hard, throbbing ache tenting his breeches, Benjamin nodded, mortified. "I...think I should return to my room," he stammered. Fumblingly, he grabbed the books at his side and rose, unable to meet her gaze. "I'm appreciative of your expertise, but to delve further would be inappropriate."

Clara snorted, a wry smile curling her mouth. "Yes, well most men are appreciative," she teased. "I love Lottie and want what's best for her...but you're right. This *is* a little inappropriate."

Very, very inappropriate.

Clearing her throat, Clara rose and clasped her hands, her eyes darting between Benjamin and his books. "I hope you've learned something today, Philip. If you need more instruction..."

"I'll come find you," Benjamin said, nodding. "Thank you for helping me and Lottie."

Silence burned between them, thick and palpable, and as he gazed upon Clara's upturned face, Benjamin was stricken by how small she looked...defenseless. As much as she tried to hide behind bluster, every now and then, he could see little cracks in her armor.

Why had she agreed to their intimacy in the first place? Did she only feel valuable whenever touched?

"Philip?"

Benjamin blinked away his internal fog, then forced a melancholy smile to his lips. "Forgive me," he murmured. "Good night, Clara...I hope you sleep well." Tentative, he lifted a hand and cupped the side of her face. Clara peered at him in confusion, then tensed when he leaned down and pressed his lips to hers.

"For Charlotte," Benjamin whispered into their kiss.

"For Charlotte," Clara whispered back, dazed.

He withdrew and she wobbled, folding her hands as though in prayer.

"Good night," Benjamin murmured again. He opened the door and stepped out into the hallway, reeling from both the desire and danger he'd narrowly escaped.

WITH THE ARRIVAL of morning's light, the lambent sunshine streaming in through Clara's curtains did little to conceal her sin. She wasn't cleansed nor unashamed. In fact, while she lay there, the first thing that came to mind was Philip's eyes—his hands on her face, firm and steadfast, and the way he'd kissed her with both aggression and a lingering sweetness. And his parting touch... It was the softest, gentlest kiss she'd ever received, and something deep inside of her fractured at the realization. While most men leered at or groped her, this man, this Philip Ashby, held her with the utmost care as if she were precious, worthy, and not just some desirable plaything. For the first time in her life, she felt wanted.

"Oh, tar and sugar," Clara muttered under her breath.

Knock. Knock. Knock.

Bolting upright, she gasped and drew up her quilt. "Yes?" she called, cursing the slight break in her voice.

"Mademoiselle, it's Angélique," the servant replied. "You have a letter. May I come in?"

Exhaling in a slow rush of air, Clara straightened and agreed, "You may."

There came a pause, then the door clicked open, and the young woman entered. She held out the letter. "I didn't open it, mademoiselle, but I recognize the hand…it's from your sister."

"Oh! Charlotte!" Clara exclaimed, delighted. She pushed back her partially closed bed curtains to get a better view. Though once she accepted the letter, that same rush of staggering guilt slammed between her ribs. She winced and chewed her lip. "Thank you, Angélique. That will be all."

Her servant curtsied and left the room.

Alone, Clara tore open the seal and instantly felt warmed by the sight of her sister's careful, practiced hand. Though as she continued to read, that smile wiped from her face.

With an unsettled gasp, Clara dropped the letter and drew a hand over her mouth. The gleeful message was forever seared into her mind with those six little words:

Philip cannot wait to meet you!

CHAPTER TEN

Betrayed

A T BREAKFAST LATER that morning, Benjamin was surprised to find the entire Boyd family present. While soft-boiled eggs were served upon pewter cups, Deborah prattled on about how a Mrs. Whose-It was planning on suing a Mr. What's-It, and how she desired the proper counsel.

Jedediah seemed mildly interested in this case, so he, too, jabbered on about dull legal jargon while the rest of the room ate in silence—a true feat for Amos, who gleefully shoveled morsel after morsel into his mouth.

Cracking his egg with a silver spoon, Benjamin glanced across the table at Clara and frowned, concerned to see her so quiet. It wasn't like her... Could she be regretting their tryst? She ate in quick, angry little bites, her mouth pinched as she kept her gaze focused on her plate.

Before Benjamin could engage her, a frantic, pounding knock came at the front of the house, and once William went to intercept their caller, the door burst open and Major Markham came barreling in through the foyer.

"Jedediah?" he called. "Jed! Forgive the intrusion, but I'm afraid it's quite urgent."

Beneath the table, Benjamin grabbed Amos's elbow, silently pleading with him not to make a sound.

Adam, fortunately, only had eyes for their host. Breathless, he explained, "I've just ridden over from Mr. Collins's farm. There was a fire in the middle of the night, and it seems everything is lost."

Deborah gasped. "Everything? You mean…?"

"Yes, madam: the food, the livestock…all of it." With wet eyes, the major doffed his hat. "My men no longer have a secured source of produce and meat. I hate to come to you like this, Jed, but I am afraid the Crown must lean on you now more than ever. And I offer my protection, if desired, to watch over your home in case those…those *rebels* come here next."

Catherine and Deborah both cried out, but Clara barely lifted her head.

Jaw tightening, Jedediah set down his fork with a nod. "I appreciate you warning me, Major, and any and all protection you are willing to lend. To be frank, I am amazed we're only receiving threats of this nature now."

Adam's throat bobbed with emotion. He briefly glanced toward Amos, but didn't seem concerned, nor surprised to see another redcoat at the Boyds' breakfast table. Exhaling, he continued, "Ensign Thomas will be court-martialed for this. It was *his* responsibility to gather the produce, and given how loud and boisterous he's been, I imagine he inadvertently tipped off a rebel sympathizer."

Benjamin felt Amos's pleased nudge beneath the table, but didn't dare glance at his friend. They'd done it. If nothing else, they had *stopped* Eleazor, and thus, stripped him of his power.

"Ashby?"

Benjamin jerked, realizing that all eyes were on him. "Yes, Major?"

"Would you mind if we spoke?" Looking to Jedediah, Adam explained, "Forgive me, but I really must insist upon borrowing your guest."

"No, no, please," Jedediah encouraged. "Take him into the drawing room, if you must."

"Thank you, Jed." With a frail smile, Adam nodded farewell

to the group, then encouraged Benjamin to follow for more privacy.

Flexing and curling his hands, Benjamin tried to calm himself as they entered the drawing room. Clearly, he was needed for his alleged shipbuilding business. There was no reason for him to be suspected over the fire, and enough time hadn't passed for Mr. Collins to know his tampered goods were undelivered.

Once he'd shut the door, the major shakily drew a hand to his chest. "Apologies for any alarm, but I didn't wish to speak candidly in front of the womenfolk...not even Jed. He is a practical sort, but unaccustomed to hard times." With a weary smile, Adam amended, "I suppose you aren't so dissimilar in that regard—begging your pardon, of course—but you seem far kinder, so I was hoping you'd be the best to whom I could appeal."

"Of course," Benjamin agreed, encouraging him to continue. "I am at your service."

Shoulders drooping, Adam tucked his chin and exhaled. "It's gone," he whispered.

"Yes, sir, you've already—"

"No, Ashby, that's it. It's *all* gone," Adam said. "We've enough rations to last us 'til the end of the month, but my goal was *never* to impose upon innocent families. The colonists are not our enemy. Surely, you know this?"

Befuddled, Benjamin opened his mouth to reply, but the major was already barreling onward.

"My dear sister, Mathilda, is a colonial," he explained. "I support our king whole-heartedly, but I never wanted to enter this war—not when it's brother against brother. But in the end, I chose my country...because without the Crown, how can my family survive?" Adam laughed weakly. "You must find me despicable."

Benjamin gaped at him, genuinely stunned. "No, I...I do not," he offered. "I, too, am fighting for family." He flashed a feeble smile. "Whatever you require, sir, it will be done."

Adam's eyes welled up and he clasped Benjamin's hand. "Thank you, Ashby, *thank you*," he gushed. "I pray it won't be an imposition, but I was hoping you could reach out to your men—the ones in Philadelphia?—and ask them to send donations to His Majesty's 17th Regiment of Foot." Expression stern, he instructed, "'Tis only to be donations, mind you. I won't take anything that hasn't been offered."

"You are too kind, sir," Benjamin replied, baffled. "If only all men were much like yourself."

Adam drew away with a huff. "You flatter me, sir. *You* are the true hero, transporting goods and doing your part." He sighed and thumped Benjamin's shoulder. "You are a good man, Ashby."

No, Benjamin sorrowfully thought, *I am not...* How could he be? This major was trying to protect and *save* his men—all of whom were God's creatures—and Benjamin now had a hand in their potential deaths. He didn't believe they wouldn't find food, but with the general lack of sustenance amongst the very citizens of New York, he wondered if he and Amos had acted in haste. Was vengeance worth this much hardship?

He opened his mouth to speak, but Adam stepped forward and inclined his head.

"That man out there...from whose regiment does he belong?" he asked. "Although there are far too many soldiers to keep track of, any friend of Jed's is assuredly a friend of mine."

Benjamin's heart stammered. "Oh, uh...I don't know, sir," he said. "That private is my cousin, Reginald Ashby, and I believe he's only just arrived from Hempstead. He was transferred and stopped for a visit."

Adam hummed. "I'll have to introduce myself at some point," he said. "Alas, today is not that day. I've a lot of damage control to do, so you must forgive my abridged visit."

"Of course," Benjamin agreed, slumping in relief. "I appreciate you giving me the opportunity to serve you, Major. And if there's anything else I can do..."

"Pray," Adam entreated, reaching out and shaking the other

man's hand. "Pray for us and our sons, brothers, and fathers, and a safe return to our homes. Pray for the womenfolk and our children, and that they never bear witness to the ugliness we've seen." He smiled, though the expression was threadbare. "And above all, pray for this senseless war to end, Ashby. That our king and the colonists alike will see reason and reach an agreement."

Relinquishing his grip, Adam returned his hat to his head. "I must take my leave. Send my regards to Jed and the others, won't you? And please..." Here, he smiled more genuinely. "Allow me to write you and your cousin a pass to come visit sometime, and we'll all get acquainted over a nice game of Brag. Though I must warn you: I always win."

Benjamin mirrored the other man's smile, a peculiar knot forming deep in his throat. "Thank you, Major. Though I must warn *you*: Reggie cheats."

Adam laughed, delighted by the candor. "Well, in that case, both of our skills will be put to the test. Until then, sir."

Both men bowed, and then the major briskly left the room, each urgent thud of his boots stomping against Benjamin's heart.

AFTER JEDEDIAH EXCUSED himself for a day of court proceedings, the womenfolk retired to the sitting room, and Benjamin dragged Amos outdoors to speak more privately. Standing inside the stockade, both men were speaking in fierce, frustrated whispers.

"Whaddaya mean, you're gettin' second thoughts?" Amos seethed. "Y'can't give up now! What about Dan?"

"Don't," Benjamin pleaded. "Don't you dare."

"I can and I will," the cabinetmaker snarled. "And need I remind'ja that you enlisted before comin' out this way? That'cha promised to serve once this stint was through?" He scoffed, puffing out his chest. "Are y'plannin' on defectin'? 'Cause I'll drag ya in for reprisal me'self!"

"You don't understand!" Benjamin cried. "You weren't there, Amos. You didn't see the pain in Major Markham's eyes, nor how much he cares for his men—the very *sister* he's forced to fight against, just as *I* am my own! I'm convinced the majority of these redcoats are like you and me...that they must be decent people! Surely, the ones responsible for Daniel are in the minority!"

Amos's upper lip curled. "Aye, and it's either you choose those 'decent men' or your family! I'll tell y'this much, lad: Were your roles reversed, Markham'd have y'hanged without a second thought."

Benjamin flinched, a sour sensation taking root in his heart. He knew Amos was right. He knew it. But why did he feel no less aggrieved?

"War is sacrifice, Moony," the cabinetmaker continued. "Everyone's gotta give somethin' up, even if it don't feel right."

A twinge of fury lanced through Benjamin's chest, and lifting his chin, he hissed, "My brother is *dead,* Amos. I gave up everything to be here. *Everything!* So if I can keep others from enduring that same pain, I am going to do so!"

Amos cuffed him soundly against the ear. "Would'ja listen to yourself?" he growled. "Aye, y'*did* give up everything, so why don'tcha make that sacrifice worth it, uh? Finish what'cha started! Finish what *Dan* started! This *is* the way to end our sufferin'!"

Benjamin's chin wobbled, and he covered his ringing ear, miserably resigned.

"I'll break into Boyd's desk," Amos continued. "Clearly, you're compromised. Not just in terms o' the mission, but your heart. So this ends today. Did'ja get the pin like I asked?"

Ashamed, Benjamin shook his head. "No...but Clara has a pin jar on her vanity. Her room is the farthermost one on the left side of the hall."

Amos nodded. "Good. I'll get one. While I'm doin' that, I want'cha to play lookout." His expression hardened. "Y'think you can manage that, or are y'gonna get soft again?"

Benjamin winced. "Of course not," he murmured. "First and foremost, my allegiance is to you and Father—to Danny. Whatever you need, it will be done."

Amos's expression softened, then he thumped the other man's chest. "Go to the sittin' room and make sure none o' the lasses leave. If a servant walks in on me, I've already got a plan in mind, so I only need to make sure the Boyd women don't go walkin' about."

Benjamin exhaled. "All right. And when you're finished?"

"Grab your things, and we'll sneak off to the stables. I mean it, Ben. We're done here. There've been too many close calls."

Benjamin nodded and headed for the house. Although he knew this was for the best—*of course it was*—a chasm split within his chest, deep and cavernous, at the thought of never again seeing Clara Boyd. Just like with Daniel, he wouldn't be granted the chance to say goodbye…

TO BENJAMIN'S ALARM, when he found the womenfolk in the sitting room, Clara was nowhere to be seen. No one knew where she was. Deborah assured him she was off grabbing a book from the library, but once he'd checked for himself, the beguiling redhead proved absent from that room, as well.

Blood and thunder…

With restless agitation creeping up his spine, Benjamin checked her bedchamber, and then each consecutive room until all that remained was his very own. *Surely not…?*

Steeling himself, Benjamin stepped inside and scanned the area, so engrossed that he nearly missed the click at his temple. Tensing, he registered the cold pressure and glanced to his right, his eyes round once he beheld Clara with a Queen Anne flintlock pistol.

Tears streamed down her face and she drew a breath, her chest trembling as her aim grew more resolute. She looked wild—*betrayed*—and with a seething voice that punctured directly through his heart, she demanded, "Who *are* you?"

CHAPTER ELEVEN

Out in the Open

THE AIR WAS thick and stagnant, making it difficult to breathe. Benjamin lifted his hands in submission. The hard glint to Clara's eyes lanced across his heart like tiny, hacking pickaxes, and her scowl remained despite the contrition on his face.

"Clara…"

"Who *are* you?" she demanded again, her voice wobbly.

"I…I-I am—"

"I *know* you're not Philip Ashby," she hissed, "so I am only going to ask you once more: Who are you?"

"Benjamin Cartwright," he blurted. "I am a loyalist sympathizer, and I *do* own a shipbuilding business in Philadelphia. That was the Lord's truth."

"Then why did you lie?" Clara demanded. "Why did you pose as Charlotte's betrothed?"

"You didn't give me much choice, if you'll recall," Benjamin said. Slowly, he took a step toward her, but when Clara fiercely re-aimed the pistol, he stumbled back and raised his arms higher. "You were so eager for me to be Ashby, so I grossly misconducted myself and aided in a ruse I deeply regret. I wanted to tell you sooner, but…by that point, I'd muddled everything beyond repair."

Clara snorted. Tears sparkled in her eyes and her chin trembled. "You wanted to tell me, but didn't," she accused. "What are you, a thief? Do you want money?"

"No." Benjamin shook his head. "I wanted to lend my aid to the cause—to assist your father in any way I could. Regrettably, I believed that if I backtracked on the Philip Ashby assumption, none of you would accept my help." His mouth quirked. "Truth be told, this all felt like a sign from Providence. Ashby's city matched my own, and I knew enough about your family to aid in the fabrication."

Clara stiffened. "You may know about *us*, but we don't know about you," she coolly observed. "I've never heard of any Cartwrights in Philadelphia. Are you certain that's your true name, or do you need a moment to come up with a new lie?"

Benjamin flinched, and out of the corner of his peripheral, he spotted movement.

Unfortunately, Clara spotted it too. She jerked toward the doorway and raised her flintlock, but not in time to fend off Amos's attack. He tackled her and hurtled them both to the ground, the redhead crying out once she misfired into the wall.

Benjamin ducked and staggered back, wide-eyed as Amos ripped the weapon from Clara's hand and curled an arm around her throat.

"Don't!" Benjamin pleaded.

The cabinetmaker ignored him and squeezed. Clara choked and squirmed, clawing at his forearm while tears of exertion streamed down her cheeks. Harder and harder he tightened his grip, closing off her airway.

"Amos, that's *enough*!" Benjamin thundered.

"We can't have 'er warnin' the others!" he volleyed. "D'ya really think she'll stay quiet? You've really done it now, Moony-boy!"

Clara wheezed and slackened her hold, her eyes rolling back as she sagged from the effort of trying to breathe.

Furious, Benjamin grabbed Amos and yanked him off of her, fearful as he dropped to his knees and gathered her into his arms. Tasting bile, he cupped Clara's face and urgently tapped her cheek. She was unresponsive but still breathing. He could already see light bruising along her throat.

"You bastard," he growled. "Why did you have to be so rough? You could have *killed* her!"

"Y'mean as *she* woulda killed *you*?" Amos refuted. "You're welcome, by the way."

Benjamin scoffed. "She wasn't going to harm me. She was bluffing!"

"Oh, really? The blasted thing was loaded, Moony. She had every intention of usin' that pistol!"

He swallowed. "Be that as it may—"

"We have to go," Amos cut in, vaulting to his feet. "I got the paperwork outta Boyd's desk, so grab your shite an' anything else we might need."

Benjamin paled. "We can't just leave her…"

"We *can* and *will*," Amos hissed, rounding on his friend in an instant. "Now ain't the time for chivalry! She's a bloody Tory, Ben. Or have ya forgotten that while gettin' inside 'er mutton?"

Face burning scarlet, Benjamin's upper lip curled, but he grudgingly knew his friend was right. They didn't have time to waste.

Torn, Benjamin looked at Clara, then hoisted her into his arms.

"Oi!" Amos growled. "Put that doxy-dell down!"

"I intend to," Benjamin snapped, his eyes blazing. Carefully, he laid Clara across his bed and adjusted her so she'd be comfortable. With a knot in his throat, he curled his hands over hers and gave them a gentle squeeze. "I'm sorry," he whispered.

He was. Oh, God, he was! If there was one thing he wished had turned out differently in this venture, *this* was assuredly it.

"Let's go!" Amos clapped a hand onto Benjamin's shoulder and roughly ripped him back, causing him to stumble.

Benjamin was tempted to get into another argument, perhaps even throw a punch or two, but instead, he tamped down his anger and grabbed his valise and a couple books from his nightstand. "Let's go," he gruffly agreed.

CLARA AWOKE AFTER a splash of water shocked her into con-sciousness.

"She's coming to!" a girl—Catherine?—exclaimed.

Groggy, Clara blinked the fog from her eyes and groaned, only to wince at the tender pain in her throat. "Where...? W-where...?"

"You're in Mr. Ashby's room," Catherine said, concerned as she looked to Angélique. The servant was wide-eyed and clutching a water pitcher. "Do you remember what happened?"

"Philip..."

No, not Philip, she realized. *Benjamin Cartwright.*

Furious, Clara rocketed upwards, only to instantly regret it when she fell back onto her elbows.

"Easy, darling!" Catherine exclaimed. "Are you hurt? Your neck is...i-it's bruised." Gray eyes turning to flint, she demanded, "Did Mr. Ashby do this? Did he...take liberties?"

"No..." Clara swallowed past her nausea. "No, no, he didn't take any liberties." Extending a hand, she gently pushed Cathe-rine away. "I'm soaking wet."

"We had to wake you, mademoiselle," Angélique said, shift-ing guiltily. "I apologize."

"It's no matter," Clara grumbled, brushing a soaked curl from her face. "Have either of you seen the Ashbys?" When both women shook their heads, she cursed. "Of course not. Of bloody *course* not."

"What's going on?" Catherine demanded.

With an embittered sneer, Clara said, "It would seem my earlier suspicions were correct, my darling. We have been duped."

DUE TO THEIR limited time to escape, Benjamin and Amos took a dory boat up the Hudson. The Continental encampment in Middlebrook, New Jersey, wasn't so far away, so they could easily make it by water, and then by land within a few hours, if conditions remained favorable.

"I'm sorry."

Amos glanced at Benjamin, his brow puckering as he continued rowing. "For what?"

"For everything...and wanting to hit you." Here, Benjamin offered a weak smile, though it never quite reached his eyes.

Amos cackled. "I'd like to see ya bloody *try,* lad! You Hoskinses are all bark an' no bite. There's never any follow-through."

"Dan followed through," Benjamin softly said.

Amos's smile faded. "Aye," he agreed. "That he did."

Exhaling, Benjamin dragged a hand over his face. "I was foolish to think this could've worked. I'm no spy, and you know it. I've ruined everything."

Amos frowned. "Y'protected our ranks from tampered goods, so it wasn't a complete waste o' time. Speakin' o' which..." He gestured. "Quit slackin', will ya? We'll get to camp faster if you actually row."

Jerking upright, Benjamin mechanically moved his arms. "Sorry," he apologized again. "I'm a bit distracted."

Amos snorted. "She got to ya, did she?"

"Who?"

"The Boyd girl. I may be a lot o' things, but blind ain't one of 'em."

Looking away, Benjamin muttered, "I don't know…I never thought I'd see the enemy as human. This entire time, it's been easy to label them as scum—*monsters*—but the more I got to know the Boyd girls, and Major Markham, in particular, the more I realized they have hopes, dreams, and fears like the rest of us. We all bleed the same."

"Not quite," Amos said. "I may've only spent one night with 'em, but they'll never be like us. The rich don't have the same fears as the rest o' the world."

"Poverty's befallen many affluent families," Benjamin reminded him, rowing with languid strokes.

"Ah. So you're *pityin'* 'em, are ya?" Frowning, Amos scolded, "Viewin' the enemy as human is only gonna get'cha killed. From here on out, I want'cha to look at each redcoat an' Tory as a movin' target. Y'get me?"

"That's horrible," Benjamin whispered.

"Horrible, but the only way to survive," Amos said. "Y'think I *like* killin' people? It rankles somethin' fierce, Moony, but it's sure better than bein' dead." Huffing, he groused, "Oi! Row in time with me, eh? Clara may've made'ja into a loggerhead, but she ain't worth a capsized boat!"

Clenching his teeth, Benjamin corrected his stance. "What am I going to tell Bishop?" he asked. "He took a chance on me, and I failed…"

Expression softening, Amos shrugged. "Y'weren't even gone a full week, so I doubt he'll be too upset. Zounds, Moony, you're only one man. It's better to be safe than rush your work."

As if aiding in testament, Benjamin's healing knife wound throbbed and he winced, nodding. "Right. Still, I wish I had more to offer than an oral report. Bishop's not one to act on hearsay. He needs physical proof…proof I don't currently have."

"Y'mean the proof I swiped from Boyd's desk?" Amos asked, smugly waggling his brows. He reached inside his inner coat pocket, then tossed the leatherbound book into Benjamin's lap. "I didn't get much time to look it over, but the second I saw Tryon's name, I snatched it up an' made a run for it."

"Major General Tryon?" Ebullient, Benjamin stopped rowing and opened the book, scanning the pages with an eagerness that soon turned to dread. "Amos…"

"Aye?"

"These are battle plans—*Continental* tactics." With horror gripping him by the throat, Benjamin perused the notations and said, "Somehow, someone got these to Boyd—undoubtedly, because he has Tryon's ear—to provide the major general with options that'll make it easier to attack our lines in New York and Connecticut."

In a clumsy rush, Amos vaulted forward and peered at the pages, causing the dory to rock wildly before righting itself. "Zounds," he hissed. "Y'think this is all they got on us?"

"I don't know," Benjamin said. "Clearly, someone's trading our secrets…someone who knows the ins and outs of our camp."

"A right-hand man?"

"Not necessarily. However, I'm not ruling anything out, so I suspect there will be a lot of sleepless nights in our future. I intend to keep my eyes and ears open."

Slowly, a soft smile filled Amos's face. "Not cut out for bein' a spy, eh? It's good to have y'back, Yale-man."

Benjamin snorted. "How come? Because I'm giving you orders to spy on our own men? Clara was right: You *do* live for discord and mayhem."

Amos's smile stretched into a grin. "Aye, to the highest degree. But jus' so y'know, it'll be *me* givin' *you* the orders now." He proudly tapped his chest. "Bishop promoted me to corporal before I came out this-a-way."

"Corporal?" Benjamin echoed, amused. "How in God's name did you pull *that* one off? You can barely wipe your own arse."

"Oi!" Amos snatched the book. "Can'tcha ever jus' say 'congratulations,' y'barmy hob?"

The two shared a good laugh, warm and cathartic.

"THAT DEGENERATE! I'LL kill him. I will *kill* him!"

In a rage, Jedediah seized a vase and hurled it hard across the sitting room, the Boyd women flinching once it shattered across the floor. Without provocation, two servants rushed forward to clean the mess.

While they picked up the shards, Jedediah furiously started to pace.

"What was he doing here?" he demanded. "*Who* was he? I don't know any bloody Cartwrights!"

"I don't know, Father, but—"

"You keep quiet!" he growled at Clara. "As I recall, his staying here was *your* doing, so you're the least qualified to offer your opinions!"

Clara's chin jutted. "I wasn't aware I was *ever* qualified, given your refusal to listen."

Enraged, Jedediah grabbed a candelabra and threw it against the adjacent wall. The unlit candles popped free and rolled across the floor.

Wincing, Deborah offered, "Perhaps Mr. Cartwright was hoping to marry our Charlotte. Surely—"

"*You* keep quiet, as well!" Jedediah thundered. "Ever since that jolter-head arrived, you have done nothing but preen and flirt, you…you insatiable *harlot!*"

Catherine gasped and burst into tears.

Infuriated, Clara curled an arm around her sister. "Don't you worry, Father," she seethed. "No man in his right mind would *ever* saddle himself to this family—or at the very least, not to *you.*"

The room fell silent. Even the servants faltered in their clean-up, their eyes nervously darting between their enraged employer and his daughter.

"Get out." Despite the boiling anger within Jedediah's bulging eyes, his voice was deathly low.

Clara's brow creased. "I—"

"Get *out!*" he growled, knocking a small table onto its side. "You are not worthy of the Boyd name. You are not worthy of this *family*. So you are to leave at *once!*"

Jerking at the thunderous quality of his voice, Clara shook herself free of Catherine's grip and coolly agreed, "I thought you'd never ask."

The other women wept, and as she drew up her skirts and stormed from the room, Clara forced herself to keep moving without looking back.

WHEN BENJAMIN EMERGED from his assigned tent, freshly changed and out of his prior disguise, he found Amos there waiting for him.

"Well, look at that!" the cabinetmaker crowed. "At long last, the stick's been removed from your arse!" Laughing, he playfully punched the other man's shoulder. "You all settled in?"

Benjamin huffed, a lopsided smile filling his face. "I certainly won't miss dressing like the upper class," he agreed. "And I've settled in fine, thank you. Bishop did a marvelous job with planning ahead."

Amos nodded. "Who they gotcha quarterin' with?"

"Uhh, I didn't catch all the names, but one was Frederick Anderson, I believe?"

"Anderson? Oof, he smells worse than he looks! Might wanna stick close to the soap in your valise."

Chuckling, Benjamin promised, "I'll keep that in mind. How are you faring?"

"Weeell, red suited me quite nicely, but I'll be all right now that I'm back in blue. How 'bout yourself?" Amos appraised him. "You puttin' off the inevitable?"

Benjamin sighed. "If you mean talking to Bishop, yes *and* no. He's currently indisposed, so I haven't had a chance to discuss the specifics—or rather, the *failures*—of our mission."

"We'll get past it," Amos assured him. "We've faced far worse than this, y'know."

Benjamin spared him a cynical glance, yet knew he was right. "Where are you headed?"

"I'm stickin' 'round for a bit, actually…jus' to make sure things go well," Amos said. "You've had quite a day, so I'd hate to see y'crumble under pressure."

Benjamin snorted. "Thanks for the confidence."

"Oi, quit bein' such a looby," Amos admonished, elbowing him. "Y'know I trust ya."

They turned and started walking.

"I'm not sure I trust myself," Benjamin softly admitted.

"Meanin'?"

"Meaning, my track record has been less than exemplary as of late." He thought of Clara, and frowned when he realized that after everything, *he* was the one who'd been manipulated. His fieldwork pushed his heart straight into the snares of the enemy.

Shaking his head, Benjamin jolted once he spotted a figure in the distance. The man's face was obscured by several thin, dirty bandages wrapped around his head, but there was a dark slant to his mouth that Benjamin immediately disliked.

Nudging Amos, he asked, "Who is that?"

"Hmm?" Following Benjamin's gaze, he supplied, "Oh, jus' some newcomer. Haven't had a chance to speak with 'im, but the name's Elijah Brooks. He's a defector."

Benjamin scoffed. "And you trust him?"

"I trust no one, Moony-boy, but Major Yates vouched for 'im. Brooks is healin' from burns all over his face, 'cause some Tories tried to tar an' feather 'im while he was out o' uniform. Changed his allegiance right then an' there."

"I see..." Tensing his hands, a cold, sickening sensation churned through his gut, and when he and Amos passed by, Benjamin was overcome by a low tremor at the sight of the man's sharp, wolfish grin.

CLARA WAS UNCERTAIN if Jedediah meant what he said. If she was unwelcome to return, that put her in considerable danger. Despite her bravado, she didn't actually feel safe in the streets of Lower Manhattan, and especially with so many lonely, leering soldiers that dotted the streets. This was why, for now, she was taking the back roads along the upper part of the island to try and clear her head. Perhaps after an hour or two, she could return, and her father would finally see reason.

Drawing her shawl in around her shoulders, she kept her eyes on the road while she traveled on horseback. Her mount's trot was aimless, and fretful, she wondered if she had enough coin to stay at a tavern, should worse come to worse.

That was when a stagecoach appeared in the distance.

Skeptical, Clara slowed her horse's tread and pulled the reins, frowning as the coach rolled to a stop, and a well-worn, friendly face peered back at her from the passenger window.

"Apologies, Miss," he said. "Do you happen to be Clara Boyd?"

All at once, her defenses went up. "Who wants to know?"

Doffing his hat, the man revealed a head of dark, wavy hair and bright, twinkling brown eyes. "Mr. Oliver Yates, at your service. I was actually on my way to visit your family."

Offering a brief nod, Clara frowned and looked away. "I'm afraid you won't find my father in a pleasant humor, Mr. Yates. A rather…*tense* situation has arisen."

"I'm sorry to hear that," Oliver said. "But if it eases your mind at all, I actually came with the intention of speaking with *you,* and not Jedediah."

Clara blinked in open bafflement. *"Me?* With all due respect, sir, I have no idea who you are. What could you possibly wish to discuss with a perfect stranger?"

"Forgive me," Oliver said, "but I cannot speak plainly in these woods. If you'll accompany me, I can have your horse tethered to my own. I will tell you everything you wish to know, starting with the alleged Philip Ashby."

Clara bristled at the mention of Benjamin. Despite the hollow, lurching sensation in her breast, she offered a tight nod. "Very well, Mr. Yates," she agreed. "Please tend to my horse."

CHAPTER TWELVE
Baiting the Hook

NERVOUSLY FIDDLING WITH her shawl, Clara stared out the coach window as the afternoon sun blazed overhead. Her new acquaintance, Oliver Yates, sat across from her jotting notes into a leatherbound journal. Once she'd informed him of Benjamin's escape, he'd become agitated, *furious,* and was still muttering to himself while writing in his book.

"You're *sure* he's not coming back?" Oliver pressed. "There is no chance of him returning?"

Perplexed, Clara shook her head. "Are you finally able to speak freely?" she demanded. "Can you *please* tell me what's going on?"

Closing his journal, Oliver sighed and clasped his hands. "Yes, forgive me, Miss Boyd," he said. "My name is Major Oliver Yates, and I am an officer in the Continental Army. However, I'm aiding the British head of intelligence along the side. I don't feel the colonials can win this war, and thus wish to restore order as soon as possible." His dark eyes flashed with displeasure. "For the past several weeks, I've been feeding information to the British and certain loyalists, one of whom is your father." When Clara tried to interject, Oliver held up a hand. "Since I cannot be in two places at once, as soon as the rebel spy plot enacted itself about a sennight ago, I enlisted my own blackguard to keep an eye on things. Specifically, on *your* side of town."

"But why?" Clara asked, puzzled. "How did you know to watch out for us, in particular?"

"Because in camp, I aid Major General Edwin Bishop with his intelligence gathering. I know all about your Philip Ashby—or Benjamin Hoskin, as he's truly known—and how he was dispatched to observe you and your family."

With her pulse spiking, a lump formed in Clara's throat. "But…why would this man, this *Benjamin Hoskin,* want anything to do with my family?"

"You're influential loyalists with prominent British ties," Oliver reminded her. "If he could immerse himself into your conversations, it was likely he'd acquire intelligence to bring back to Washington's camp."

Nettled, Clara demanded, "And if you knew of his intentions, why did you wait until now to say something?"

Oliver leaned back in his seat. "Because, Miss Boyd, without true proof of spy work, we cannot charge him for treason. I couldn't just steal Bishop's reports without it being obvious, so I had to wait. As of this morning, I received word that a shipment 'Ashby' was supposed to deliver never made it to its destination. We finally have the proof we need, which is why I was hoping…" He laughed, the sound a snarl. "Well, clearly the Lord has other plans."

A sharp, shuddering breath rolled through Clara. "But he seemed so sincere."

"Blackguards often do," Oliver replied. "My loyalist spy, Kit Donnelly—or Elijah Brooks, as he's known amongst rebels— undoubtedly seemed sincere to you, as well."

"Kit *Donnelly?* The man who hosted Father's cockfight?" Clara asked, astounded. "Why didn't you inform the officers? Surely, they could've played along and helped!"

"Not necessarily," Oliver replied. "For these delicate matters, it's best to keep only a few people involved. That way, the likelihood of things getting bungled is far smaller." He sighed. "There *was* the issue of Donnelly and Hoskin getting into a scuffle, but that all worked out in the end."

Clara blinked in alarm. "Does that mean *your* man murdered George Stewart?"

Oliver shrugged, unrepentant. "Alas, the cause requires sacrifice. Stewart was in league with Hoskin, and I wanted Donnelly to question him. Unfortunately, his efforts got a bit spirited."

Clara bristled. "I'd hardly call what happened 'a bit spirited.' As for Phil—ah…*Mr. Hoskin,* he was in a poor state when he returned."

"He was believed dead," Oliver agreed, "but not long after, was spotted with your father, so we knew we still had a job to do."

"And you need me to do what, exactly?"

"Pose as bait," he said. "If I offer you to my rebel superiors, my loyalty will be secured."

Clara shook her head, not understanding. "Meaning what? You *already* serve under the Continentals, so why would you need me to prove your valor?"

"Because," Oliver replied, "with my allegiance clear, Donnelly and I can get Hoskin to the King's Men without rousing suspicion. If he's captured in plainclothes with incriminating documents, he can be hanged as a spy."

The words sent a quiver of horror through Clara's throat, but she swallowed it back like bile. Benjamin brought this on himself. It was assuredly what he deserved. "Why are you so concerned with this man?" she wanted to know. "With all due respect, Major, your plot seems a little over the top for one rebel."

Oliver frowned. "Isn't it obvious? In the art of war, appearances are important," he said. "Hoskin's brother is a folk hero amongst the rebels, so if we string up Benjamin, it'll harm their morale. The objective here is to make an example of those who enact treason; and rather than hang the entire operation of blackguards, especially since it'd be difficult to find and apprehend them all, we've opted for mercy by singling out one man." He crossed his legs. "I've not yet told the British head of intelligence about Hoskin's identity, but that's because I need a clear advantage, something to offer, should everything go south before my plans are enacted."

Clara laced her hands, her head spinning with all of this troubling information. "All right," she cautiously began, "but why would the rebels want me? You mentioned needing my help, so how am *I* to play into this?"

Oliver smiled. "By having you under rebel control, they'll be able to put pressure on your father."

Clara laughed, the sound harsh and scornful. "With all due respect, sir, my father doesn't give a single fig about me."

"Perhaps not, but *they* don't know that," Oliver said slyly. "So long as they believe they'll have the upper hand over Jedediah, and by proxy, several British and loyalist connections, we'll be in business."

Clara chewed her lip. "But what am I to do once I'm their captive? If you think I'll let those vile, reprehensible rebels lay one hand on me—"

"I'll ensure you're protected," Oliver promised. "As long as you do exactly what I say, you'll be safe."

Slowly, the rigidness faded from Clara's shoulders, and the ocean of hurt crashing against her heart stilled at the thought of having peace. She held out a hand in agreement. "I accept your terms, Major. I pray the hangman's noose finds Benjamin Hoskin with swift alacrity."

WITH EDWIN AVAILABLE to speak at long last, Benjamin stood inside the man's tent, anxiously waiting while the major general perused Boyd's book. Glancing over his shoulder at Amos, Benjamin tried not to wince when his friend nodded in encouragement.

"This is insufficient."

With a startled jerk, Benjamin turned back around. "But, sir!"

"I cannot move forward with hearsay," Edwin spat. "Our internal relations are strained enough without muddying the waters. This 'proof' doesn't mean we have double agents in our ranks. Were this to be a false report, we could do irreparable—"

"We have *already* caused irreparable damage!" Benjamin thundered. "By ignoring intelligence such as this, we've allowed Boyd to aid in slaughtering our men! Why is this book written in his *own hand* considered hearsay?" Furious, he jabbed his finger forward. "Did you not see his entries from last year? He was given vital intelligence on how to disrupt supply lines in Fairfield and Norwalk! If we didn't have an insider, how else could he have known?" Catching himself, he reined in his temper. "If we ignore this lead, if we ignore that someone is feeding Tories and the British alike with our strategies, we'll never win another battle. Do the lives of your men mean nothing?"

"You will watch your tone when speaking to your superior, Hoskin!" Edwin growled. "I know full bloody well what is at stake here!" He slammed down his fist. "And to think, I was just about to promote you to captain!"

Benjamin faltered. "Captain, sir? But…I have no true field experience. The first and last battle I've endured was—"

"For Daniel," Edwin supplied, his features earnest. "Yes, I am aware. But the fact remains that even with your botched mission, you've shown true resilience and passion, something these men could use for their morale." Looking to Amos, he asked, "What say you, McQuinn?"

Amos brightened. "In terms o' leadership, Moony'll be a sound choice," he said, his eyes sparkling with pride. "But if y'mean the book, he has a point, sir. Even if Jedediah was just blowin' smoke out his arse, it can't be denied these *are* our plans. Someone gave 'em to 'im, someone with connections to our officers."

Edwin opened his mouth to reply, but the tent flap opened and his aide, Francis Holmes, stepped inside.

"Major General, Major Yates wishes to see you…says he's got someone you'll want to meet." Eyes shifting toward Benjamin, he added, "I think her name's Tara Boyd."

"Clara," Benjamin whispered, startled. "But how…?"

"Is the girl with him?" Edwin cut in, rising from his seat. "Has she been questioned?"

Francis nodded. "Yates said she'll give us leverage against the Boyd family. He claims they have new information that could sway our strategy."

"And the girl," Benjamin cut in, "is she hurt?"

Francis shrugged. "Seemed fine to me, sir."

"Bring them to me," Edwin agreed. "If I deem the major's plot suitable, we will move forward with his request."

The young aide bowed, then stepped back outside the tent.

WHEN THE TENT flaps opened again, two men entered, one being Francis Holmes, and the other Oliver Yates, both of whom flanked a very peevish Clara Boyd.

Her eyes cut toward Benjamin, and his heart plummeted, throbbing with a harsh, fearful ache as she was dragged before Edwin.

"This is her, Major General," Oliver crowed. "What do you think, sir?"

Edwin appraised all present company with an unreadable frown. "What were you doing beyond our campgrounds?" he demanded.

"I intercepted a letter from one of our couriers," Oliver explained. "The note said Miss Boyd was unattended in Lower

Manhattan, and that this might lead to a good opportunity. So I intervened and promptly grabbed her. I know I should've come to you first, sir, but I decided to take matters into my own hands. She was quite the fighter at first, but now she's docile as a lamb. See?" As if to demonstrate, he pinched Clara's cheek.

Putting on a show for their ruse, which, admittedly, wasn't too difficult, she jerked and bit his fingers. He howled and retracted with a snarl. "You...you doggess!"

"Keep your filthy rebel hands off me!" she seethed. "*All* of you!" Furious, she spat at their feet.

Francis clocked her across the face, her body hurtling to the ground from the mighty blow.

Benjamin moved to assist, but Amos caught his arm. It wasn't wise to show his feelings toward an enemy had changed. He *knew* that, yet rage simmered beneath Benjamin's skin as he watched Clara snivel and curl against the grass.

"There will be no striking the prisoner," Edwin barked. Nodding to Oliver, he added, "You may escort her to the stockade. Once we're ready to contact the Boyds, I will send for your assistance."

Oliver bowed. "Thank you for entrusting me with her welfare, sir."

Edwin offered a bow in reply, then both Francis and Oliver gathered up Clara's weeping form. As she was escorted from the tent, she didn't so much as glance in Benjamin's direction. Her revulsion stung.

Ignoring Amos's eyes on him, Benjamin reeled with the new flood of information and exhaled. If Clara was being held in camp, then as a mere private, he wouldn't be permitted to speak with her, nor oversee her care. He *couldn't* let Clara face this alone, not when he was the direct cause of her torment. For this reason, he announced, "Major General, sir? I...I would like to accept your commission. That is, if I am still welcome to be captain?"

Bemused, Edwin's stern expression softened into pleased acquiescence. "Of course, Hoskin," he agreed. "You'll be given a troop under the command of Colonel Travers. He'll see about your uniform." As Benjamin bowed and turned to leave, he added, "Oh, and Hoskin? You were right. Thus far, your reports have been sound, and I'd be a fool to ignore this lead. Just remember, we can't save everyone."

With a tight smile, Benjamin offered another bow, then excused himself into the early evening sun.

CLARA'S NEW LODGINGS were nothing short of hell itself. She was being kept in a barn, of all places, manacled to a post while she sat amongst nickering horses.

This was all Oliver's fault. Despite his vow of protection, he didn't once intervene and keep that vile aide from striking her. Now that it was mid-evening, the lump on her cheek had faded to a tender bruise.

"You comfortable there, Miss?"

Glowering at the soldier on guard, Clara curled her lip before turning to face the front.

"You too good to talk to me?" he asked, approaching with a threatening swagger. "I asked you a question."

Clara swallowed, her heart pounding.

"Listen here, you rich, Tory doggess. I'll—!"

The stockade door opened, and Clara and the soldier jerked before glancing toward the intrusion. A man with a tray stepped inside, and despite her rage and frustration toward him, Clara was never more relieved to see Benjamin in all her life. Bedecked in a blue coat with buff facings and a gold epaulet on his right shoulder, a pristine white waistcoat, red wool officer's sash, and buff breeches with a saber at his hip, he cut quite the formidable figure.

"Er…Captain Hoskin!" the soldier spluttered. "Wasn't expectin' you here. I was told—"

"You were told to obey orders," Benjamin snapped, "so kindly obey mine. You are dismissed."

Leery of the fiery look in the other man's eyes, the soldier nodded, then sidestepped him to make his leave.

Once the barn door slid shut, the tension in Benjamin's posture softened, and he looked toward Clara with glassy, mournful eyes. "I'm so sorry." When all she did was glare at him, he sighed and stepped forward. "May we speak candidly?"

She scoffed, resentful as the urge to weep welled within her throat. "You lied to me," she accused. "You lied to my family. We took you in, and cared for and trusted you, and yet all you have to say is you are 'so sorry?'" She laughed, the sound sharp and derisive. "Is that 'candid' enough for you, Captain?"

Benjamin winced. "I deserve that," he murmured. "You've no reason to trust, nor even *like* me, but I swear to you, Clara, my feelings for you and your family, or at least, *you*, were completely genuine."

Clara snorted. "How can I believe that? Everything I knew about you has turned out to be a lie, *Captain Benjamin Hoskin.*" Upper lip curling, she looked him over in disdain. "If nothing else, that traitorous uniform becomes you."

Benjamin swallowed, approaching with the tray of food. "I didn't intend for you to find out this way. Had I been given more time…"

"You would've told me the truth? Just like the first two times you were given the opportunity?"

Avoiding her gaze, Benjamin gestured to the tray in his hands. "You should eat," he deflected. "I was hard-pressed in gathering something for you, so these are my personal rations."

Clara glowered at him. "Those are yours?"

"Yes."

"They are no one else's?"

"No, of course not."

Grudgingly acquiescent, Clara held out her hands and Benjamin smiled, sinking to his left knee. Though once he held out the food in offering, Clara furiously smacked the tray from his grasp, sending the stew splattering across the dirt.

"I hope you starve," she seethed. "If you think for one minute that I will *ever* accept anything from you, even something that will save my very life, you are sadly mistaken!"

Rattled, Benjamin gathered the discarded wooden bowl and returned it to its tray. "Clara, you must eat."

"Miss Boyd."

He squinted. "I'm sorry?"

"Miss Boyd," she coolly reminded him. "You are not my familiar. You are not my *equal*. Therefore, you must address me with the proper respect."

Benjamin's heart lanced painfully at the contradiction, and gritting his teeth, he wobbled while rising from the ground. "Very well," he agreed. "My apologies, Miss Boyd."

"Don't act like you're the victim here," Clara hissed. "You came into my life under false pretenses, so you have no right to behave as though I owe you anything."

Benjamin winced. "I am aware of this, but—"

"There is no 'but!' You destroyed what we could've been the moment you decided to pose as Lottie's betrothed!"

"Then…you *do* admit there could've been something?" Benjamin regarded her through wide, hopeful eyes, and Clara gaped at him in shock.

A tension throbbed between them, long and silent, before she furiously spat onto his boots. "Get out," she growled at him. "Out, and go to the devil! If Providence is kind, I will never have to see your face again!"

Benjamin dizzily stepped backward, each barbed arrow slinging from the bow of her lips leaving him wounded and reeling. "Very well," he choked. "I'll have someone bring your food in the morning." He bowed his head. "Good day to you, Miss Boyd."

He hesitated as though he wished to say more, hunched his shoulders, and then promptly left Clara to cry into her hands.

CHAPTER THIRTEEN
Testing Boundaries

CLARA ENDURED A full week of negligence and subpar conditions, or at least, subpar compared to what she was accustomed. Meals were delivered by surly, not to mention rude men with clear disdain toward her political leanings, and to her great displeasure, she was always left alone with one of these clotpoles keeping guard.

On top of bland, and sometimes nonexistent, meals, a lack of privacy, and overall discomfort, one notable change was Benjamin kept his word. Not once did he set foot into that barn, and it bothered Clara that she was disappointed. Even after everything he'd done, she still held an inkling of affection for him. He was a patriot, a liar, and didn't deserve one ounce of her sympathies.

"Rebel scum," she muttered.

That was when the door opened. Looking up, Clara groaned when Oliver stepped in with her tray. He dismissed the guard on duty, then approached with a chipper swagger.

"Good morning!" he chirped.

"I am not speaking to you," Clara spat.

"Truly? Because you're speaking right now." When she shot him a withering glare, Oliver chuckled and set the tray alongside her. "Why are you being so sour? Things are going well!"

"For *you,* maybe," she hissed. "For days, I haven't heard a single word from you, Major. What's going on?"

"So good of you to ask!" Gesturing to the tray, he encouraged, "Eat. Drink. You'll need your strength for what I'm about to ask of you."

Skeptical, Clara pulled the tray into her lap. "What are you proposing?"

"I'm not proposing anything. I am *telling* you to get friendly with Captain Hoskin."

Choking on the sour ale she'd sipped, she placed a hand over her heart and shook her head. "No. Absolutely not."

"But Miss Boyd—"

"Do you truly expect me to behave as though we're friends after everything he's done? You are mad, Major! Even if I agreed, the captain isn't stupid. He'd grow suspicious, were I to suddenly welcome him with open arms!"

Oliver sighed. "You make a fair point… However, it's been a sennight without seeing one another. And if you were as fond of him, as *he* clearly is of *you,* he might be hopeful enough to believe it."

Clara blinked at him. "Fond of me? How do you mean? Has he said something to give this impression?"

Oliver grinned. "My, my! If I didn't know any better, I'd say you actually sounded eager."

Scowling, she looked away and picked at her bread. "I'm just curious, is all. I need to assess his temperament before I enact my so-called groveling."

"Whatever you say." Catching her lip curl, he commanded, "Eat your fill. I'll send word that you wish to speak with Hoskin. The minute he receives my message, I'm sure he'll come tripping over here like the mealy-mouthed, lovelorn puppy he is."

In spite of herself, Clara flushed. "Two people can be friendly without romantic aspirations. Why, I have zero interest in your dog-like appearance, so I think I make a fair and valid point."

Oliver's chin tensed. "You wound me, Miss Boyd."

"And I'll gladly do so again, you cad. Perhaps if you actually saw to it that I was treated like a lady, I'd be far more ingratiated."

"I'm working on it."

"So you've said!"

"Look, my dear, you are not *nearly* as important to the rebels as you are the elite," he said. "This is war. You won't see anyone tripping over themselves to save an attractive girl with bleating lungs."

Holding her bread, Clara sneered. "Weren't you just going, Major? I prefer not to eat when men, or rather, *things,* that churn my stomach are present."

Oliver offered a stiff bow, then left her to her racing thoughts.

REGRETTABLY, OLIVER WASN'T far off in his assumptions. It barely took an hour before Benjamin was pushing open the door, his face such a sickening mask of hope that she immediately looked away.

"Good morning, Miss Boyd," he greeted. "You asked to see me?"

Clara drew her knees toward her chest and shrugged. "I was bored, yes. It gets tiresome seeing the same three chubs day in and day out."

Though she was supposed to be friendly, it seemed unwise to behave as though she'd missed him. Benjamin was no fool. Bored indifference, she decided, was her best tactic.

With his eyes cutting toward the guard on duty, Benjamin nodded to the man, indicating that he was relieved of his post. The soldier left without so much as a questioning look.

Once they were alone, Benjamin stepped forward and appraised Clara with genuine concern. "How are you faring?"

"'Endure it, heart! Thou didst bear worse than this,'" Clara quoted, her intonation filled with mocking zeal.

Benjamin's brow creased. "I'm sorry?"

"*The Odyssey*," she explained. "You've read it, have you not?" Without waiting for a reply, Clara continued on, "I'm rather partial to that quote as of late. I'm not so certain I have borne worse than this, but I'll manage."

Clearing his throat, Benjamin fidgeted beneath her gaze. "I recall it, yes... Though lately, I've been reading the copy of *Hamlet* you gave me."

Clara scoffed. "Why? You don't actually believe we'll be continuing our *lessons,* do you? Now that you're no longer Charlotte's betrothed, that offer is completely off the table."

Benjamin burned a brilliant shade of scarlet. "N-no, uh...of course not. I just thought you'd be happy to hear I've taken your advice to heart."

"Yes, well if only you'd taken my love of honesty to heart, as well," she groused.

Benjamin ducked his eyes, ruefully shaking his head. "I apologized," he reminded her. "I promise you, I will always be sorry for what I've done."

"Not sorry enough, apparently." Folding her hands, Clara lifted her arms. "You could at least unshackle me while we're talking. I am a lady, not some common criminal."

Benjamin glanced around them, torn. "I'm not supposed to."

She scoffed. "Who says? You're some fancy captain, are you not? Aren't you the one telling everyone else what to do?"

"Within reason," he snapped. "You're a prisoner of war and must be treated accordingly."

"In what way? Being caged like a common animal?" Eyes alight with fury, Clara hissed, "I've done nothing to you, Captain Hoskin. *Nothing!* And yet you persist in punishing me for the sins of my father. I don't care about this horrid war! I just want it to be over!"

Regret colored Benjamin's face and he frowned, rubbing his fingers together in a nervous tic. "I know you must think me cruel, but—"

"I don't think you cruel," she cut in. "Which is precisely why I am asking, nay, begging you, to treat me like a human being." Clara's eyes grew wet, and she held out her hands to him. "Please, Ben. My shackles are chafing my wrists."

A seedling of hope bloomed within Benjamin's chest and he swallowed, curious as to why she'd addressed him as a familiar. Did she consider them friends again?

Avoiding her gaze, Benjamin knelt and retrieved the key from his pocket. Keeping his eyes focused on the task at hand, he unfastened her manacles and freed Clara's wrists. A stab of guilt throbbed between his ribs once he brushed his thumb over the red, angry-looking abrasions on her skin.

"Thank you," she murmured.

Against his better judgment, Benjamin stooped to press an apologetic kiss to her inner wrist, his pulse thrumming once her fingertips brushed the expanse of his jawline in a slow, careful caress. Did she forgive him? Did she still hate him?

Lifting his head, Benjamin tried to speak, but his words were devoured by the harsh press of Clara's mouth. She was passionate in her movements, painful almost, and when she snagged her fingers through his hair and yanked, he melted into her touch and kissed her back with equal enthusiasm.

Both of Clara's hands moved to his lapels, and then she was dragging him down over top of her. While their tongues tangled, she wrapped a leg around his waist and started grinding into his growing arousal. A muffled cry caught in his throat each time she bucked against him just right.

Dizzy from sensation, Benjamin pressed his mouth strongly into hers and cupped her face, his own hips rolling downward as she bit back a gasp. Her soft sounds made his breeches tighten. Impatient, Benjamin tugged her petticoats up over her legs, their kiss wet and needy and escalating in aggression as he increased the incessant rocking between her thighs.

That was when he felt it: a knuckle of pain in his sternum,

stabbing and white-hot, followed by Clara's knee to his groin. Benjamin yelped and barely resisted once she shoved him aside.

A look of disgust bled across her face as he reached for her, and she struck his hand in revulsion. "Do not touch me," she seethed.

Benjamin tried to get to his feet, but in his present predicament, Clara was much faster.

Scrambling upright, Clara raced toward the barn door and ripped it open with shaking, eager fingers. Sunlight assaulted her senses, but she didn't recoil. No, she rejoiced in the discomfort, an unshakable grin touching her lips as she dashed into the campgrounds.

While she darted through the grassy, tent-filled area, avoiding milling and drilling soldiers alike, nobody paid her any mind. Or at least, nobody did until a surprised Amos McQuinn was there to cut her off.

Equally astonished, Clara skidded to a halt. "You," she growled. "You're the miserable cur who tried to kill me!"

In a rage, she turned toward a campfire and snatched an unmanned musket. Clumsily, she whipped it in Amos's direction, praying the weapon was loaded.

"Whoa, whoa, hey," Amos coaxed, "steady now, Miss. I really don't think y'wanna do that."

"Why not?" Clara spat. "You've deprived me of my every freedom, so *I* will be more than happy to deprive you of *yours!*"

Cocking the hammer, she gave a start once Benjamin caught her elbow and jerked her back against him. He ripped the musket free from her hands and immediately disarmed her.

"You rebel scum," she seethed, bucking against him. "You...you treasonous hob!"

Amos snorted. "Ah. Well, now I see why she's found such a deep place in your heart, Moony-boy."

Ignoring him, Benjamin set aside the musket and took Clara's shoulders. "Miss Boyd, I know you have no reason to trust, nor even listen to me, but you've just needlessly endangered yourself."

Clara scoffed. "Well! Acquainting myself with you was surely the start of that!"

Frustrated, Benjamin tightened his hold. "Please listen!" he begged. "Now that you've exposed yourself to the camp, none of whom knew you existed prior to this moment, might I add, you've brought yourself into potential contempt. You stand out far too much in that gown, so we need to get you some new clothes." Gaze soft and pleading, he explained, "A Tory, and most especially one of the elite, is bound to be of interest to a vengeful patriot."

Upper lip curling, Clara glanced around them and decided that yes, he unfortunately was correct. She was the only one dressed for high society. Everyone else looked as if they'd taken a roll through the dirt. Eyes narrowing, she proposed, "If you wish to protect me, you should let me go."

"You know I can't do that."

Sending her sharp glare in Amos's direction, she amended, "Then at the very least, keep *him* away from me."

"I'll see to it," Benjamin promised, sparing his friend an apologetic glance. "For now, please come with me. We'll discuss what to do once we're safely back in the stockade."

As Clara was escorted in the direction she'd fled, neither took notice of the defector, Elijah Brooks, sour and calculating as he watched them from a nearby tent.

CHAPTER FOURTEEN
A Truce

When Benjamin returned to Clara later that afternoon, he was carrying a valise practically overflowing with garments. He checked over his shoulder, secured the barn door, and then strode toward her with purpose. "Put these on," he instructed. "A camp follower agreed to lend you some clothes. Naturally, she's unaware of the specifics and thinks she is aiding a general's wife."

Arching a brow, Clara grew snide. "A camp follower? Well! I should've known you were friends with a doxy, given how well you can kiss."

Flustered, Benjamin snapped, "The woman is not a doxy. She's married."

"Even worse!"

Agitated, he tossed the valise into the dirt. "Put these on," he said again, but with far more conviction.

Clara scoffed. "With *you* here?"

"W-well…"

"I require privacy, Captain."

"Of course." Embarrassed, Benjamin turned and faced the opposite direction, sighing as he dragged a hand over his face. "All the necessary garments should be in that bag, though I haven't checked myself."

Opening the valise, Clara peered inside and grimaced while

unearthing the stained raiment. "This woman has jumps instead of stays? How slatternly!"

Benjamin rolled his eyes. "I apologize for not meeting your standards, Miss Boyd, but this isn't a bloody draper shop. You must take what you can get."

Clara curled her lip. "Is that your motto in life? Because truly, your allegiance to the patriot cause is finally starting to make sense!"

Benjamin stiffened but didn't take the bait. "Let me know when you're finished," he said.

There came a pause, then Clara ventured a soft, "Um…Captain Hoskin?"

He sighed. "Yes?"

"I know this may come as a shock, but…I don't truly know how to put these on."

"What?" Horrified, he remained frozen in place. "How do you mean?"

"Well, I know the basics, like slipping into a shift, but my lady's maid always helped me get dressed. Could you…? Possibly…?"

Benjamin scoffed, completely mortified. "I am *not* helping you get dressed."

"Whyever not?"

"Are you seriously asking me why? You don't see anything wrong with that request?"

Clara huffed, placing a hand on her hip. "Not when it's a matter of life and death, I don't!"

Benjamin sourly appraised the wall, hating how she'd thrown that back in his face. "I don't know what you expect me to do… I had a mother, but did not help her get dressed, nor was I privy to her morning and evening routine."

Clara pouted. "Yes, but surely the two of us can figure something out?" Coming up from behind, she shoved his shoulder. "Turn around! I'm tired of shouting at the back of your head like some noddy!"

Benjamin tensed, flexing and curling his hands. "Are you decent?"

"Yes. I haven't taken anything off yet."

Turning to face her, he was relieved to find she was telling the truth. Gnawing on the inside of his cheek, Benjamin appraised Clara from top to bottom. "Let's start with…uh…taking everything off? I-I mean! Not your shift, but your jacket, and…" He gestured lower. "Skirts?"

Clara snorted. "Although I cannot get dressed, I assure you, I *can* take everything off."

Eyes narrowing, Benjamin accused, "Do you mean to tell me you've…y-you have been intimate with men, and yet don't know how to get dressed?"

She shrugged, unimpressed. "You needn't disrobe to shag, Captain Hoskin. And if I did, the man fixed my clothing since he was the one to disrupt it in the first place."

Benjamin winced. "I wish you wouldn't speak like—"

"You wish I wouldn't speak like what?" she seethed. "A common strumpet?"

Lowering his eyes, he murmured, "No… I wish you wouldn't speak as if you aren't of value. I have told you before: I don't think you're a trollop."

Pressing her lips together, Clara ignored the buoyant leap in her chest. Affecting indifference, she raised her hands and pointedly unfastened her green caraco jacket and stomacher. Benjamin's eyes remained fixated on the ground, though a part of her wished he'd stop being so gentlemanly, that he would look, so that for once during their acquaintance, she could actually understand the kind of man he was. She'd never met someone who showed her respect and meant it.

Shrugging out of her jacket, Clara unwound her petticoats and untied her pockets and panniers. Out of the corner of her eye, Benjamin started to fidget, his hands clenching and releasing. His discomfort made her smile. After sparing him a sly glance, which he didn't see, she struggled out of her stays and tossed them to the ground, leaving herself in only her shift, stockings, and shoes. She turned to face him.

"You may assist me now," Clara said.

Benjamin shook his head, still keeping his eyes on the ground. "Are you sure you can't figure this out? You just did a remarkable job removing your clothes, so—"

"I am *not* lower class," she coolly reminded him. "There are certain rules that must be upkept, so please, just help me into my jumps, apply my pockets, and tie up my petticoats. The back ties are first, and then the front, and that should be that."

Benjamin scoffed. "'That should be that?'" he echoed, annoyed. "If it's so simple, perhaps you should allow yourself the adventure of trying new things."

Clara simpered. "Oh, I think not, Captain. I believe it is your turn to be adventurous."

Rolling his eyes, Benjamin fetched the yellow silk jumps from the valise, unwilling to keep arguing. "Hold still," he muttered. Easing her arms through the garment, he tugged the front together, and then fumbled with the ties. "Uh…" Heat prickled beneath his collar, and he looked shyly at Clara. "Is this correct?"

Clara sneered. "I'd suggest lacing it first," she cooed. "Unless, of course, you'd prefer that these slatternly jumps hang wide open?"

Benjamin flushed. Pulling away to a more appropriate distance, his fingers grew jittery while he laced up the front. The positioning of his hands was *far* too intimate for comfort.

"See? You're a natural," Clara teased him, batting her lashes. "Are you certain you've never dressed a lady before?"

Benjamin huffed. "Maybe we should try this in complete silence."

"Why? Am I making you uncomfortable, Captain? You kill men for a living, and yet it's my indecency that's such a bother?"

Benjamin's stance grew rigid. "I do not kill people for a living," he snapped. "What I do…it's for the glory of the cause. And for God."

"But how do you know?" Clara countered. Lifting her arms while he applied her pockets, she continued, "The loyalists believe themselves to be in the right as well, and God is aligned with the just and true. What if it's *my* side He favors?"

Benjamin was silent for a long while. Frowning, he helped her slip into her underpetticoat and fumbled with the front and back fastenings. "Your side is oppressive and cruel."

"So is yours," Clara hissed. "Don't think I don't know what goes on in these camps. To be frank, I am amazed I haven't been ravished by one of your guards."

Flushing at the stinging force behind her words, he tied her garment and drew a breath. "Can't you see why patriots wish to be free of tyranny? Why they wish to control their own fates, with the king so very far away?"

Clara shrugged. "I can, but my family would be affected, should the king abandon us. Our livelihood rests upon trade with Great Britain."

Benjamin chose not to say anything, since that was something that he, too, heard as a common reason amongst his Tory friends. Frowning, he helped Clara into the outer petticoat, then fastened the back and front ties.

Touching his hands, Clara halted his gruff movements. "I'll handle the rest," she murmured. When he stepped away from her, embarrassed by his frustration, she probed, "Can I ask you another question?"

Sighing, Benjamin handed her an apron. "That depends on the inquiry," he replied. "Though if it has to do with women, or my love life, I am going to have to respectfully decline."

Clara sneered. "All right, Captain Clodpate. I actually *do* have a mind outside of carnality, you realize." Applying her—or rather, some *doxy's* apron—she asked, "If you are not a shipbuilding merchant from Philadelphia, where are you from, and what is it you do?"

Benjamin straightened with a hint of relief. "I am a preacher's son from Long Island. I really did study at Yale, but I became a bookkeeper."

She gasped, amusement lighting up her eyes. "A preacher's son?" she echoed, a laugh bubbling in her throat. "That explains the prudishness…"

Benjamin soured. "I am not a prude."

"Oh, no?"

"You said so yourself that I…th-that I am an exceptional study."

She scoffed. "Yes, but that doesn't mean you're not prudish, Captain. There is no need to be ashamed. Why, it's incredibly rare to find a man who is disinterested in sniffing about between a woman's—"

"Is that all you wanted to know?" Benjamin cut in, his cheeks warm.

Chewing her lip, Clara sidled closer with a twinkle to her eye. "I have many questions. One of which being how a preacher's son pulled off being a rich, distinguished businessman, but I digress. My true concern is apologizing for earlier. I'm sorry for kneeing you in the gingambobs."

Benjamin snorted. "No, you're not."

"You're right," she agreed, "I'm not, but I am sorry it had to come to that."

It took Clara a moment to remember she was angry with him, that she was supposed to dislike him. Smothering her coyness, she said, "Either way, we both have worn masks with one another. You may consider us even, if it pleases you."

Benjamin arched a brow. "Then…does that mean you forgive me?"

"I'm uncertain if forgiveness is the right word, but I am amenable to being on speaking terms again." She extended her hand. "Truce?"

Benjamin glanced at her physical peace offering, hesitant, before wrapping his hand around her fingers in a gentle squeeze. "Truce," he agreed. "Though this means what, exactly?"

"That you're allowed to speak to me, within reason, and help me blend in with these…" Clara curled her lip, looking around them in contempt. "These rebels."

A touch smug, Benjamin grinned. "Perhaps you'll find you rather like our side of things."

"Ah, yes. About as much as a bayonet to the skull, I'm sure." Her lips quirked and she mirrored his smile, albeit grudgingly. "Go on, then. Show me how to be rebel scum."

Benjamin rolled his eyes. "As much as I'd love to stay and do precisely that, I have plans for a raid."

Clara's smirk faded. "A raid? Where?"

"Never you mind. I'll have someone come by with your dinner." Realizing that he was still holding her hand, Benjamin parted their fingers as if she'd burned him, his own digits twitching before he curled them into a fist. "From here on out, so long as you remain cooperative, you can keep your shackles off. Good day to you, Miss Boyd."

She nodded, but was no longer in high spirits. Something about his announcement gave her a dark, sinking feeling in the pit of her stomach…

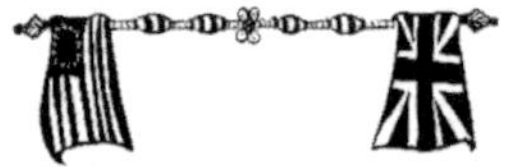

BENJAMIN KNEW EVERYTHING was time sensitive. Although this intelligence had been gleaned at the last minute, their source said they needed to act now in order to stay ahead of the game. According to Yates, an insider swore that a local cabin was the headquarters for some prominent Tories, and that if Benjamin and his scouts were to come by, they could potentially find and steal future plans. But as far as Benjamin could see, the cabin he and his men had just entered hadn't been used for years.

"This doesn't feel right," he muttered. Eyes scanning the filthy, leaf-littered floor, he frowned. Why would Yates send them here? Hadn't he been smart enough to investigate the claim first?

"We should search anyway," Elijah Brooks insisted. A few others nodded. "It's what we came to do, right?"

Benjamin nodded in return, but he wasn't convinced. He still had an unsettled feeling in his stomach…

Inspecting an empty table and ransacked desk, he only halted when he heard a twig snap. He turned, but lurched once the sound of gunfire rang through the air, and a line of poorly aimed musket shot pockmarked the wood.

Blood and thunder…

Falling to his knees, Benjamin banged his shins against the floor and rolled onto his side, fumbling for his flintlock.

"Tories?" he asked, straining to see through the broken windows. *Who tipped them off?*

"Tough to say," someone shouted.

Lifting his voice above the din, Benjamin called to the other men, "Everyone all right?"

A few affirmatives followed, and he crept toward the front door.

"Where you goin'?" one of the scouts asked. "We need to stay together!"

"Actually, I think Captain Hoskin has the right idea," Elijah spoke. "To divide and conquer should be our best bet." Looking to Benjamin, he asked, "Might I have the honor of guarding your attack?"

Benjamin frowned, skeptical, before agreeing, "As you wish, Brooks. Be sure to stay close."

"Of course, sir."

Benjamin lingered by the door, then rushed over the threshold before diving around the side. He could hear shouts in the distance, but no further gunfire as he raced to a proper hiding spot.

"Over here!" he hissed to Elijah. "I think they might be reloading." When he received no response, he glanced over his shoulder and scanned the area. "Brooks?"

A sharp, painful *thwack* rattled through his head, and Benjamin swayed, stunned, before dropping to his knees. Wet warmth followed, and when he touched the spot of pain radiating beneath his cocked hat, he realized he was bleeding.

"Careful, there," he heard behind him. "That looks like it might hurt."

Benjamin turned his head and squinted at Elijah, his vision tilting in a sickening blur of color. "You...y-you...?"

Elijah sneered. "Me," he affirmed, then lifted his foot and struck it soundly into the captain's face.

CHAPTER FIFTEEN

Ghosts from the Past

WATER SLUICED OVER Benjamin's face, cold and stinging, and he lurched upright with a gasp. Blinking the stunned fog from his eyes, he leaned over and retched, faintly nauseous as his head throbbed in a dull, staccato rhythm.

"Ah! So good of you to join me!" a voice exclaimed.

Whipping his head in that direction, and instantly regretting it once his vision wavered, Benjamin coughed and squinted. "Who…? W-what…?"

"Easy, Captain," Elijah mocked. "Try not to hurt yourself with all these questions!"

Gaping in bemusement, Benjamin's brow creased as the man crouched in front of him. Within the light from the campfire, he could make out Elijah's dark, glittering eyes beneath all the bandages and a sharp, wolfish smile. A shiver of recognition tore through him and his teeth gnashed. "You're…y-you're the man from the pier!"

"And the man from the party, too! Kit Donnelly, at your service," he said, grinning. "This must be why you're part of the intelligence team, eh? Though it's too bad you didn't use that savvy of yours beforehand."

He nudged Benjamin with his boot. "I took a knife to my own face so I could wear these bandages. I didn't want anyone recognizing me. Speaking of which…" Pulling a patch knife from his belt, he gestured toward Benjamin's middle. "Let's take a look at that wound, shall we?"

Benjamin's eyes sparked with panic, though once he struggled, he discovered that his hands and feet were bound with rope. Writhing, he growled as Donnelly grabbed his throat and squeezed.

"Hold still," Donnelly barked, his vitriol surprising Benjamin. When he grudgingly obeyed, his assailant slashed the buttons to his waistcoat, and cut through his shirt until he bared the pink, healing injury. A sneer twisted Donnelly's mouth. "That's a mighty shoddy job there, Captain. I think we need to fix that right up."

Benjamin resisted, but Donnelly sliced his blade across the stitchwork. Panting and twisting in pain, Benjamin cried out while his reopened wound stung and bled. "Go ahead and kill me," he rasped. "I won't tell you anything."

Donnelly licked the blood from his blade, then spat as though the taste repulsed him. "I don't give a whit about your intelligence," he hissed. "It'd certainly be a perk, but I'm more concerned with your clear memory problem."

Benjamin gawped. "Are you saying you aren't a double agent?"

Donnelly giggled. "Oh, I am a spy," he assured him, "but I didn't join the cause for our glorious king. In fact, I'll bet the man who hired me is mighty miffed, seeing how I disobeyed direct orders." He waved a hand. "You were supposed to be captured at the raid and taken to the nearest British encampment, but clearly I had other plans."

Benjamin grimaced, squirming as his wound continued to pulse. "Who *are* you?"

Lips curling, Donnelly leaned toward him and snarled, "'My name is *Legion*, for we are many.' All the men you've wronged are here to stand trial for your sins!"

Benjamin blanched at the declaration, all too familiar with that Bible verse. "You're mad…"

"Oh, yes," Donnelly agreed, "I am quite mad—with the need for justice." Seizing Benjamin by the coat, he hefted him upright and dragged him toward a wooden bucket.

Struggling against the other man, Benjamin yelped once he was shoved onto his knees, his vision spinning while both his head and middle throbbed. "I already told you, I won't talk," he spat. "This won't bring you anything."

"Other than immense satisfaction, you mean?" Giggling, Donnelly took Benjamin's neck, then forced his head into the bucket.

Due to shock, Benjamin inhaled a sharp gasp of water and choked, struggling against his assailant's grip until he pushed up enough to breathe. Donnelly tightened his hold, then shoved the captain's face back into the water. Benjamin gurgled and writhed until, at long last, Donnelly jerked him upright.

Benjamin sucked a frantic breath, his lungs burning as he dizzily blinked water from his eyes.

"Do you remember yet?" Donnelly barked.

"Remember what?" Benjamin gritted, feeling queasy.

"How about a certain *Freyview skirmish* after a rebel hanging?" Grip tightening around the captain's nape, Donnelly hissed, "You all ambushed those loyalists and redcoats, slaughtered them, and you ran my brother through with your own blade."

Slowly, a prickle of unease raised the hairs on Benjamin's body. "You were at the ambush?"

"I saw you kill him with my own eyes," Donnelly snarled. "You might've been masked, but your kerchief slipped and I saw you. I know who you are, and I know what you did!"

"No..." Benjamin fiercely shook his head. *No, no, it wasn't true!* "I...I didn't stab him hard enough to kill... I saw him run away!"

With a fierce growl, Donnelly slammed Benjamin into the water, pushing with renewed force. "Liar!" he seethed. "Tell that to my brother's grave!"

Benjamin flailed with all his might, clenching his teeth as

water sluiced up his nose and into his ears. He knew it was pointless. He knew it was smarter to remain calm, but with this newfound information, he sensed the danger he was in and could only focus on his fight or flight instinct.

Donnelly dragged him up and Benjamin coughed, spluttering the water from his lungs. Between every sodden gasp, he wheezed, "I was just…d-doing…my duty."

"And I'm doing mine," Donnelly snapped. "Horace was my only brother, my *friend*, and you're going to pay for taking him from me!"

"I lost…my brother…that day too," Benjamin choked. "Daniel…"

"Don't you dare," Donnelly roared, spinning him about. "Don't you dare try and compare us!" Furious, he smashed his fist into Benjamin's nose, satisfied once a thick, crimson gush of blood flowed from his nostrils. Again and again, he struck the captain's face until, finally having grown weary, he shook out his stinging knuckles and dunked Benjamin back into the bucket.

IT WAS WELL into the evening hours when the barn door opened, and Clara groggily lifted her head. "Captain Hoskin?"

The figure in the doorway was clearly not Benjamin. He was shorter, and his sneaky stance instantly gave her pause. Rocketing into a sitting position, she blinked the sleepy fog from her eyes as the figure approached.

"Miss Boyd, it's me," the voice whispered. "Y'know me as Reginald Ashby, but me real name is Amos McQ—"

"I don't care who you are, you miserable cur!" she spat. "I told you, and I told Captain Hoskin that I never wanted to see your craggy face again!" Furious, she scrambled to her feet.

Amos kept walking toward her. "Put aside your grudges for a second, will ya? I need'jer help."

Clara scoffed, indignant. "If you think for one minute that I'll ever help you—"

"Ben's missing," Amos cut in, his tone earnest and pleading. "He's been taken, an' I can't trust nobody else in camp. I thought'cha might know by who."

All at once, it felt as though someone had reached inside her chest and squeezed. "The captain is…missing?"

"Aye. Ben took a few men on a raid this afternoon, but he an' that Elijah Brooks fella disappeared."

Clara's blood ran cold. "The man who killed George Stewart…"

"What?"

"His real name is Kit Donnelly. He's working for a man in this camp and was also the one who attacked Benjamin."

Amos snorted. "And'ja didn't think to tell us this why?"

"Because I wanted you both to suffer!" Clara shouted. "Only now, I…!" What? Had she truly changed her mind? Benjamin and Amos were no different, just as she hadn't changed; their sides were far too polarized to ever get along, and yet she didn't believe Benjamin deserved to die.

Impatient, Amos grabbed her shoulders. "Who's Donnelly's contact? Who told 'im to do this?"

Covering her face, Clara drew a breath and closed her eyes. Could she commit such a betrayal? Could she truly aid the enemy just to save Benjamin's life?

"Major Oliver Yates," she blurted.

Amos's brow scrunched. "You're lyin'…"

Clara shook her head, affronted. "No, sir, I most certainly am not. He's the man who brought me into camp."

Amos's face darkened with understanding. "That wily ol' son of a gun."

"What are you going to do?" Clara asked. "You can't just walk into his tent demanding answers."

The cabinetmaker scoffed. "Oh, no?"

"Not if Captain Hoskin is missing," she reminded him. "Major Yates might know where Donnelly's taken him, so you'll need a trade."

Amos chuckled. "Perhaps you Tory hobs are smarter than I gave y'credit for." Taking her arm, he agreed, "I think I'll use *you* as bait."

"I was hoping you'd say that," Clara said, surprising him. "He thinks I'm an asset in swaying both the captain and major general, so he won't wish me harmed."

"Good to know…" Gesturing at the barn doors, Amos encouraged, "Well, let's jus' hope the ol' lobcock hasn't already wandered off. C'mon."

Nodding, Clara followed after, her heart in her throat as she prayed she'd made the right decision.

PACKING HIS PISTOLS, Oliver slung a leather satchel over his shoulder and turned as Amos burst in through the tent flaps, a belt knife pressed beneath Clara's chin, and his flintlock aimed at Oliver's head.

"What is the meaning of this?" the major demanded.

"Oh, I think y'know what," Amos growled. "Go on, step back. An' don't even think o' whippin' out those pistols."

Grudgingly, Oliver held up his hands.

Amos entered and held Clara securely against his chest, his eyes fiery and full of warning. "Where's Cap'n Hoskin?"

"Haven't the foggiest," Oliver replied.

"Aye? Perhaps y'know where your boy Elijah Brooks went off to then, eh?"

A brief look of alarm crossed the major's face, but otherwise, he remained impassive. "If I knew that, I would've let you know at once."

Amos chuckled. "Well, that's a bit funny, seein' how your girl here sang like a lark an' told me aaaall about your lil' plans."

Oliver's eyes widened, and he looked to Clara for confirmation.

"I'm so sorry, Major!" she faux-sobbed. "He...h-he threatened to kill my family!"

"Quiet!" Oliver seethed. "You shut your mouth, girl!"

Holding out his flintlock with more aggression, Amos snapped, "All right, this is what's gonna happen: You're gonna tell me where Benjamin is, an' I jus' might let'cha live."

Oliver sneered. "I'd rather die for my king and country than aid in ruining our nation."

"Maybe so," Amos agreed, "but'cha can't do much without your bargainin' piece, now can ya? Without Clara Boyd, you've got no leverage."

Oliver flinched. "You wouldn't dare."

"Wouldn't I?" Taking his knife, the cabinetmaker drew the blade across Clara's collarbone in a shallow, stinging stroke. This time when she cried out, her sob was genuine. "I'll only ask y'once more," Amos said. "Where? Is? Ben?"

"I-I don't know!" Oliver blurted. "But...I do have an idea of where Donnelly's taken him. I was actually about to head there myself."

Amos grinned, his dark eyes glittering. "Looks like we'll all be takin' a lil' trip then." He aimed his flintlock between Oliver's eyes and fiercely gestured toward the tent flaps.

BENJAMIN JERKED AWAKE, his vision swirling with spots as he

struggled to focus on his surroundings. In his mouth was the tang of iron—*blood?* He winced once he lifted a bound hand to his throbbing nose. His reopened stomach wound strained with the movement and he gasped, collapsing against the earth.

"Hmph. It wasn't very nice of you to faint while we were talking," Donnelly admonished, nursing a tin cup of ale. "Ready for round two?"

Swallowing back his nausea, Benjamin exhaled and closed his eyes before opening them again. "What do you want from me?"

Donnelly feigned offense. "What do I want from you?" he echoed, a snort catching in his throat. "Why, if our talk didn't make that obvious, I'm not sure what else to tell you, Captain."

Benjamin blinked in confusion. While before, Donnelly had been angry, murderous, his present state was giddy…like something else entirely. As the man rose and approached, he was reminiscent of a cat gleefully going in for the kill.

"Your brother wasn't personal," Benjamin rasped. "In war, there are casualties. We all knew the risks when we signed up."

"Not all!" Donnelly barked, immediately losing his smile. "Horace never wanted to go to war. He was a peacemaker, a good man, and let you run him through rather than defend himself! Father made us go to war, lest we lose our inheritance!"

The hollow of Benjamin's cheek twitched. "That is not my fault."

"You killed him!" Donnelly shouted. "You! Killed! Him! It is your fault!" He withdrew a flintlock and aimed it at Benjamin with a shaking, jittery hand.

That was when they heard voices.

Both men looked toward the commotion, startled by the sight of lamplights.

"Kit!" Oliver shouted. "Donnelly, you must stop this. The rebels know our plans!"

Mouth dropping, Donnelly shook his head and fiercely raised his flintlock. "Stay back!" he warned. "I'm not leaving 'til I get what I came for!"

"It's over!" Oliver called in return. "At the very least, if we have Captain Hoskin alive, we can make a trade with Washington!"

While the two squabbled, Benjamin discreetly rolled onto his side and eased up onto his knees. Panting, he grimaced and broke into a cold sweat, his wounds throbbing with each painful breath. Withdrawing a folding knife from his right boot, he held it between his bound hands and hacked at the restraints hitching his feet together. After several desperate sawing motions, the rope frayed and gave way.

Donnelly glanced toward him, and with a sudden burst of adrenaline, Benjamin staggered to his feet and took off running.

"Hey!" Donnelly shouted. "Halt, you rebel coward!"

Wind whipped through his wet hair and Benjamin tasted bile, nearly tripping while attempting to keep his balance. His hands were still tied and did little to aid in his frantic escape.

Benjamin could hear footsteps clambering behind him, but still he ran, refusing to look and potentially lose purchase on the muddy ground.

Bang!

The pain was what hit Benjamin first, followed by his spine bending at an awkward angle before he collapsed into the dirt. He tried to get up, but couldn't. Only a numb, tingling sensation raged throughout his limbs, leaving him frozen with shock. There was a ringing in his ears from the gunshot, and he desperately willed his body to rise, only to find no response…no collaboration between his thoughts and limbs.

The sound of brisk footfalls rushed across the forest floor, and as Benjamin lay there motionless, he screamed once he realized he couldn't move his legs.

CHAPTER SIXTEEN

Bruised and Broken

T HE SOUND OF clinking tools roused Benjamin from his slumber. Groggy and head pounding, he squinted through the morning sunlight and swallowed.

At his side, Dr. Elliott Weston organized his box of medical tools, pausing every so often to wipe the blood from an instrument. All around them, other injured men lay in bed, some asleep while others moaned in anguish. Benjamin's eyes opened more fully. The camp's medical tent was no place any man wished to awaken, and the longer he gaped at Dr. Weston's tools, the more he realized the blood might possibly be his own.

Squeamish, Benjamin groaned and closed his eyes.

That drew Elliott's attention. Raising a bushy gray eyebrow, he peered at his patient and hooted. "Finally!" he exclaimed. "I was beginning to think you'd never wake up, boy."

"How…h-how long was I out?" Benjamin croaked.

"Long enough to cause a stir." Heading over with a flask, Elliott indicated that he lift his head. "Drink up, y'hear? You're gonna be parched."

Grateful, Benjamin clasped his hands around the flask and drank. After he'd had his fill, he sank against the bedding and shivered. "What's become of my assailant?"

"Dead," Elliott muttered. "So's that other traitor…Yates, I think his name was? That loose cannon, McQuinn shot 'em both up. He claimed self-defense. Though from the looks of it, he couldn't be that far off, seein' how banged up you are."

Benjamin swallowed. A sense of panic speared through him, and when he tried to sit up, he cried out before collapsing against the cot. "My legs…"

"What about 'em?"

"I can't move them."

Pushing his spectacles up the bridge of his thin nose, Elliott lifted the sheets. He peered at Benjamin's stockinged feet, then prodded both with his finger. "Y'feel that?"

"I-I think so? I don't know…" Voice choking with terror, Benjamin pressed his palms over his eyes. "I feel something, but any time I will myself to move…"

"You can't," Elliott supplied, concerned. "I was afraid this might happen."

Benjamin immediately lowered his hands. "Why?"

"You had some musket shot in your lower back, and I removed it," he said. "If I hadn't, it might've killed you."

The terror within Benjamin's chest spread. "But…if you hadn't, would I be able to move my legs?"

"That's tough to say, Captain."

Sagging against his pillow, Benjamin drew in several shallow, panicked breaths, his head feeling floaty and detached from his body. "I…I-I can't breathe…"

"Yes, you can, boy. You can't talk without breath," Elliott admonished. Nevertheless, he took Benjamin's hand. "Just give 'er a squeeze. There now…good. That's it. Breathe in, squeeze, then breathe out."

Benjamin obeyed, tears stinging his eyes as he choked on his own air. Why couldn't he calm down? Why couldn't he focus?

A dry sob caught in his throat and he squeezed harder, clutching desperately until Elliott pulled back with a curse.

"Christ Almighty, you've got a strong grip," he muttered. "When I said to squeeze, I didn't mean shatter every bone in my hand!"

"S-sorry." Shuddering, Benjamin finally felt a semblance of calm. If Dr. Weston was unbothered by his condition, shouldn't he be, as well?

"Why don'tcha describe your legs for me?" the surgeon suggested. "What do they feel like?"

"Strange...heavy. And numb."

"Hmm." Pursing his mouth, Elliott instructed, "Cover your eyes. I wanna test somethin'."

Doing as he asked, Benjamin blacked out his vision with his palms.

"D'you feel that?"

Below, there was a very faint, but unmistakable pressure against the arch of his foot. "Yes," Benjamin said, trying not to get too excited, "yes, I feel it! You're touching the middle of my foot...the underside."

"Very good," Elliott commended. "How 'bout this?"

There came an odd sensation from his pinky toe, and it took Benjamin a moment to realize the doctor was wiggling it. "You're moving my little toe," he said, "yet...I don't think I can move it on my own."

"Try."

"I *am*," Benjamin hissed, uncovering his eyes. "Any time I think to move, I can't."

"Hmph. Well, maybe—"

"Might you clarify Captain Hoskin's condition?"

Both men jerked, and Dr. Weston turned toward the intrusion. "Major General!" he cried. "It's good to see you, sir." Fumblingly, he grabbed a chair, then dragged it over by Benjamin's bedside. "Please sit!"

Edwin acquiesced. His curious, analytical stare brought Benjamin great shame, and he could no longer hold his superior's gaze. Not like this. Not when he was broken and useless.

"Can you feel your legs?" Edwin asked.

Still looking anyplace else, Benjamin nodded. "Yes, sir...very faintly, but I can feel something."

"And you can't move them, you said?"

Reluctant, he swallowed before nodding again. "That's right."

Dark eyes filling with pity, Edwin shook his head. "Hmm. Then this will be very difficult, indeed."

A spark of panic blitzed through Benjamin's veins. "What will, sir? Because if this is about the breach, I know who was involved! It would seem—"

Edwin laid a hand over his wrist, silencing Benjamin's excitable ramble. "I'm afraid that is no longer your concern. After much deliberation, I have decided to relieve you of your post."

"What?" Alarm filled Benjamin's gut, sharp and piercing. "But, sir! I told you I can feel my legs!" Edwin tried to speak, but Benjamin cut him off. "The fact I still have sensation proves I can get better! Please! You mustn't do anything rash. There is still so much more I can do for the cause!" Here, he looked desperately to Dr. Weston. "Tell him I can recover," he begged. "Tell him!"

Elliott's upper lip twitched in sympathy. "I can't promise any such thing, Captain. Injuries like yours take time to heal and are all different…there's no tellin' what'll come of this."

Benjamin's throat prickled. "You're lying," he hissed. "You're lying! I know I can get well!"

Edwin remained impassive. "You will get better, yes. Of course, you shall," he agreed, "but you'll do your healing back in Freyview with your father."

Benjamin's mouth dropped. "Freyview? But—"

"Arrangements have already been made," Edwin cut in. "McQuinn will take you back, and Colonel Travers will continue your intelligence report."

"No! I can serve just fine in my state," Benjamin spat, his shoulders quivering. "I am not an invalid, sir. I didn't lose my mind! I can still think. I can still act. I can still create all the bloody plans it takes to service this army!"

"Comport yourself!" Edwin thundered. "I know you are angry, Hoskin, and I know you're hurt. But you will not take this out on me, nor anyone else! We are doing what is best for your health!"

"But this isn't what's best, sir! My heart and soul are in this mission—in this cause! Please…" Tears welled up in Benjamin's eyes. "Please don't take this away from me."

Silence followed, long and thick, before Edwin commanded, "Ready your reports for Colonel Travers. If you fail to do this, if you deliberately disobey me, you will be court-martialed." Benjamin opened his mouth to speak, but the major general cut him off. "Now," he continued, "about that girl… If your intelligence report doesn't include Miss Boyd, I must insist upon an addendum."

Benjamin's brow creased. He was so overwhelmed, so distraught, that he could scarcely figure out which topic to focus on. He couldn't lose the intelligence. He couldn't lose the operation. But the mention of Clara brought a stab of disquiet between his ribs. "Miss Boyd, sir? Is there a reason she's of interest to you?"

"She might've been involved in the breach," Edwin said. "Those mutineers brought her into camp, and therefore, she cannot be trusted."

Benjamin shook his head. "No. She was not part of that coup. Miss Boyd's here against her will, and for the sake of fairness, should be returned to her family."

Edwin drew up in his seat. "Absolutely not! She is a potential link to Tory information, and therefore, must remain here!"

"But—"

"Clearly, you are in no position to be making any judgment calls, Captain. The girl stays."

Benjamin pressed his lips together into a tight, grim line. "Yes, sir."

Edwin rose from his seat. "Dr. Weston will help ready your things, and McQuinn will take you home. Are we understood?"

Benjamin sneered. He felt like a child, the very invalid he'd claimed he was not. "Yes, sir," he gritted again. A painful lump formed in his throat. "It would seem I can't take up Daniel's mantle, after all."

Edwin's face fell. "This wasn't what I wanted for you, Captain. Remember that." Before the younger man could respond, he turned and whisked from the tent.

"Easy does it…"

"No, no, support his *back*, you arsehole!"

Benjamin stared at the tent ceiling, expression blank while Amos and a handful of men argued about how to properly lift him onto a stretcher. At long last, they reached an agreement, and while Amos supported his arms, two other men took his middle, and the remaining two grabbed his feet.

"On the count o' three!" Amos exclaimed. "One…two…"

Barely listening, Benjamin gaped listlessly while they lowered him onto the wicker structure on the floor. Once there, the men started squabbling—again—about how to lift the stretcher.

This was humiliating. Unable to fend for himself, all Benjamin could do was listen in mounting agitation as everyone sniped about how to proceed and fought about what was best for *him*.

"Oi, you'll be all right, Moony," he heard Amos reassure. "We've got the cart waitin' 'round front."

A cart? So, he was going to be shipped off like a bloody sack of potatoes?

Embittered, Benjamin lowered his eyes and swallowed, gesturing for Amos to come closer. When his friend knelt, Benjamin asked, "What's to become of Clara? Bishop said—"

"She's stayin' here," Amos cut in, his voice equally hushed. "He already told me."

"Amos, you know it can't come to that," Benjamin said. Glancing toward the other men, who were still squabbling, he implored, "You have to help her escape."

"Escape? But—"

"Get her out of here. Anywhere is safer than this camp. I realize that now."

Withdrawing, Amos looked to Benjamin with sad eyes. "I know this'll be lonely for you, but—"

"Just do it, Amos! This isn't about me!"

The two men stared at one another, silent and pleading, before the cabinetmaker sighed. "I'll see what I can do, all right? Jus' know that if I succeed, someone else'll hafta take y'home."

Benjamin nodded, relief settling across his face. "Whatever it takes," he agreed. "As I said, this isn't about me."

The sadness in Amos's eyes deepened. "It never is, is it? Even when you're like…"

This. The word hung between them, harsh and unspoken, and Benjamin stubbornly looked away. "Perhaps I'll see you soon. If you'd be kind enough to fill me in on…events, I'd appreciate it."

Amos nodded, then rose before gesturing for the men to head out.

Gritting his teeth, Benjamin curled his hands and closed his eyes while they finally, *finally* lifted him akin to a helpless newborn.

The stretcher swayed back and forth, handled as gently as possible, but the motion still sent shockwaves of discomfort throughout Benjamin's body. His bruised face ached, his head pounded, and his legs were disconcertingly numb, and while he was carried toward the cart like living waste, he swallowed the screaming sob that yearned to burst from his chest.

THIS TIME WHEN Amos called on Clara, she was relieved to see him. "How's Captain Hoskin?" she asked, approaching with clasped hands. "I've heard the guards whispering, but never loudly enough to create a sound picture."

Amos shook his head, his eyes devoid of their typical mischief. "He's real bad, Miss Boyd. Can't even get up."

"What?" Paling, Clara blinked at him in shock, her head swimming as she struggled to process this terrible news. "Is he…c-can he…?"

"Seems he can move every part but his legs," Amos clarified, nodding. "The doc ain't willin' to give promises, but he said Ben might be able to walk someday…an' even then, it's doubtful it'd be without a cane."

"Oh…" Drawing a hand to her breast, Clara closed her eyes and wavered. Bile burned the back of her throat, and she swallowed around it, suppressing the guilt for not saying anything, for not warning Benjamin in time. "Where is he?" she asked. "Can I see him?"

Amos shook his head. "'fraid not. He's already on his way home to Freyview." Catching her shock, the cabinetmaker continued, "He sent me to come get'cha. With the mutineers dead, the first place Bishop's gonna look is here…with you."

Clara's mouth dropped. "Me?" she squeaked. "He doesn't actually think I had a hand in this?"

"Maybe not as a ringleader, no, but certainly a key player," Amos affirmed. "It'd be your word—nay, a Tory's word—against everyone else's, so things ain't lookin' good. That's why I've come to take y'home."

"No." Defiant, Clara shook her head. "Absolutely not. If I'm deemed a traitor, I won't bring that down upon my family, or more specifically, my sisters. Benjamin's being taken to…Freyview, you said?"

"Aye."

"Then that's where I'm going, too."

Amos's eyes widened. "Now hold on—"

"Take me there, or I'll find a way myself!" she spat. "I don't hail from some lowly town, so it would be the perfect hiding place."

"But—"

"Ever since I arrived, all I've done is listen to you. Correction, listen to blithering fools. Thus far, all it's accomplished is crippling Captain Hoskin! So you're going to listen to *me* for once."

Amos huffed, rolling his eyes.

"And this…" Furiously, Clara balled up her fist and struck Amos soundly, causing him to cry out and stumble back.

"Jesus!" he exclaimed, clutching his throbbing nose. "What was that for?"

"That was for cutting me, you sniveling cur! It had better not scar!"

Scoffing, he withdrew his hand and squinted at the smear of red. "You…ya actually made me bleed."

"The sooner you realize we all bleed red instead of blue, the better," she spat. Nodding to the stockade door, Clara commanded, "Go on then. Find me a way out of here."

Sneering, Amos wiped his bloody nose against his sleeve. "Very well. But if you're thinkin' o' livin' with Moony, I hope y'realize his father's a reverend."

"Men find me delightful," Clara said, matching his sneer. "Even the holy ones." With a wince, she looked at her hand and gave it a shake. "Your hard head hurt my knuckles…"

Finally, a hint of amused disbelief touched Amos's eyes and he chuckled, taking her elbow. "C'mon then, bruiser. Let's find you a way outta this 'ere camp."

CHAPTER SEVENTEEN
Shamed and Blamed

WITH A HOOD pulled over her head, and her valise with borrowed clothing in hand, Clara followed Amos through the campgrounds. If anyone paid them any mind, she couldn't be certain. She'd been far too afraid to look, but given how very few knew of her arrival, it had been relatively seamless getting from the stockade to Amos's dory. Or rather, it was seamless until she needed to get *on board* said dory.

"I am not riding in that," Clara said.

Amos huffed. "With all due respect, it's either that or swim."

"But...! I have never been in a boat," she said, dismayed. "How am I to navigate?"

Rolling his eyes, Amos took her valise, stepped into the dory, and then held out his hand. "I'm navigatin'. You jus' sit there and do nothin'...somethin' I'm sure you're mighty accustomed to."

Clara harrumphed, not appreciating the barb. Nevertheless, she knew it was either this or stay and face treason charges, so after taking his hand, she lifted her leg and fell into the small vessel.

"Whoa, there!" Amos exclaimed, dropping the bag to catch her waist. "Lord above, have y'never walked before?"

"Not on water," she seethed, furiously shoving him away. The momentum made her totter, and, lacking all poise, she stumbled and landed upon a bow seat. Face coloring, she straightened her skirts and checked the pins in her hair. "How long will it be?"

"Not long," Amos assured her. "An hour or two, give or take. With as careful as Moony's accommodations haf'ta be, we might make it there before 'im."

"Oh." Clara nodded, though her features melded into remorseful sadness. She didn't want to think about Benjamin. Somehow, with her own possible sentence on the horizon, she'd been able to ignore the inevitable and pretend he was still well, that he was still unharmed, and that her actions hadn't been the ones to unravel him.

"You all right?"

Clara looked up from the water, troubled, before offering Amos a tight smile. "If you persist in the gallantry, this is going to be a long ride."

Amos huffed. "I think the whole 'this is gonna be a long ride' bit is *my* line, but you're right...I'll stop."

His expression shifted to something melancholy, and Clara realized he must be thinking of Benjamin. They were close friends, far closer than she'd ever been with any woman, and a sting of envy unfurled within her breast. No one beyond her sisters gave a flying fig about her, and as she watched Amos stew in silence, that truth never rang clearer.

Drawing her cloak beneath her chin, Clara closed her eyes and attempted to calm her racing thoughts.

UNFORTUNATELY, AMOS WAS right. When they arrived via horseback at a saltbox house, which was nowhere near the opulence Clara was accustomed, she was disappointed to find Benjamin hadn't yet been delivered to the Hoskin residence. That meant she'd have to meet his father, nay, a reverend, with no one but Amos as a shield. With a shuddery breath, she clutched her valise as Amos escorted her up the long, dirt pathway to the door.

"C'mon now," he coaxed. "What're you all tongue-tied for, uh? What happened to that speech about holy men?"

"Those holy men weren't fathers of rebels. Correction, enemy soldiers I've led into harm's way," Clara sharply replied. "Although I don't believe you've told him the truth, I cannot imagine it'll stay a secret for long."

Amos whistled. "By St. George…didn't think about that."

"Nor did I," Clara admitted. "Men of the cloth are often impersonal, supercilious, and cold, but Benjamin is none of those things…and surely, he inherited some of his father's traits? Reverend Hoskin must be a kind man, a fair man, but regardless, he'll hate whoever wronged his son."

"Hate's a mighty strong word for a man o' God," Amos reminded her. "Two years ago, while fetchin' supplies for a trade, I accidentally set Josiah's stockade on fire. If he forgave me for nearly costin' 'im an entire winter's worth o' supplies, he can forgive *you* for doin' what'cha thought was necessary."

Clara's gaze hardened. "Do you forgive me?"

Amos appraised her, perplexed. "I never thought to blame you…"

"I blame me," she softly said. "Major Yates asked for my help, and I gave it without hesitation."

The cabinetmaker moved to reply, but the front door opened and a tall, robust man with graying, light-brown hair and kind, penetrating blue eyes stepped over the threshold. Clara drew to a stop.

"Amos McQuinn!" the man crowed, relief alighting his weary features. "Thank you for sending word of Benjamin's condition. Is he close by?"

"Aye, shouldn't be long," Amos assured him. Approaching the older man, he drew him down for a tight embrace. "You all right then?" When Josiah nodded, Amos explained, "That young lass back there is Clara Boyd. She's a camp follower, an' gifted with medicine. I think she'll do a fine job helpin' Moony get acclimated, if y'wouldn't mind the assistance."

The man hummed. "That would be wonderful, yes. Thank you both for being so considerate."

Clara balked, blinking between them in shock. She was not proficient in medicine, and she certainly wasn't gifted beyond holding court. A faint bloom of red stained her cheeks once she realized Benjamin's father was appraising her. Awkwardly, she dipped into a curtsy. "Clara Boyd, sir," she greeted.

"Reverend Josiah Hoskin," he replied, offering a deep bow. "It's a pleasure to make your acquaintance, Miss Boyd. Won't you come in? I'll show you to your room."

Finally, Clara's self-assurance returned and she brightened. "Charmed, Reverend. I see now where your son gets his unshakable charisma."

Fortunately for her, Josiah seemed pleased by her demeanor. That was when Amos cleared his throat.

"I'mma head out an' see if I can find Ben's caravan," he said. "That way, I might be able to help."

Clara's eyes widened in alarm. "You're leaving?"

"Aye, jus' for a bit. I trust they're not too far behind. Besides…" he spared her a brief once-over, "this'll give you two a chance to get acquainted, eh?"

Perhaps Amos wasn't nearly as forgiving as he'd claimed. Pursing her mouth, Clara nodded in faux acquiescence. "As you wish, Corporal. Thank you for accompanying me."

"Corporal," Josiah echoed, a fond pride brimming within his gaze. "It's incredible how my two favorite people have now been promoted."

Amos flashed a smile that never reached his eyes.

Once they'd all said a proper farewell, the cabinetmaker rode off, and Josiah led Clara inside the cozy clapboard saltbox.

"I haven't housed a woman since my wife's passing," he said, "so my apologies if the arrangements aren't to your standards."

Clara took in the modest living room. A fowling piece hung on the wall over the fireplace, and two rocking chairs were seated across from the hearth. Other than these and a small dining room table set, there was very little to be found. The spartan furnishings proved the Hoskin residence was lacking a woman's touch, and unbidden, a pang of pity swelled within her breast. Had Benjamin grown up without his mother? He'd mentioned Mrs. Hoskin briefly during their last talk, but Clara hadn't thought to ask.

Josiah seemed embarrassed as he showed her around. The expression was one she'd seen on Benjamin many a time, and Clara promised, "This is more than sufficient, Reverend. Thank you for your hospitality."

On this matter, she was truthful. He was far more gracious than many of the wealthy hosts she'd endured over the years, and his eagerness to please was genuine, as opposed to the cloying, infernal bottom kissers her father brought into her life.

"Well…" Josiah gestured toward the guest bedroom. "This was my son's room, and now it's yours."

Clara frowned. "Won't Benjamin need it himself?"

A morose smile touched the reverend's mouth and he shook his head, placing his hand fondly against the entryway. "No," he murmured. "No, this was not Benjamin's…though he and his brother shared it for a time." Josiah's gaze grew wet within the candlelight, yet Clara decided she was mistaken once he chuckled and waved a hand. "As I said, it's yours now. And if you need any additional clothing, you may also borrow from my late wife's belongings." He cleared his throat. "Supper is at six, so I hope you will join us."

Clara nodded. "Yes, of course…thank you, sir." They shared a brief bow and curtsy, and Josiah left her to her business.

WITH THE HOSKIN residence ahead, a sour, churning sensation overtook Benjamin's gut. The sky blurred in and out of focus, and remaining on his back, the cart tossed him about with each dip in terrain. Amos was sitting alongside him and glanced down with concern.

"You all right there, Moony?"

"Never better," he muttered.

"Oi, no need to be an arsehole," Amos grumbled. "Clara's fine, y'know. I did everything ya asked. Try showin' a bit o' gratitude, aye? You're alive. That's far more than others can say."

Benjamin's eyes welled up, and a painful lump formed in his throat. He was alive. He was alive, while other men—Daniel—were dead. Life truly wasn't fair. In his instance, the second chance was wasted. He could do nothing in his present state.

The cart rolled to a halt, and the men transporting him started to argue, specifically, about where to carry his stretcher. That was when a new voice entered the fray.

"Thank you, gentlemen, but all that fussing won't be necessary," Josiah called to them. "One of my neighbors, Mrs. Harriet Finch, has been kind enough to lend me her late husband's bath chair. Bring Benjamin inside, and we'll see that he's comfortable."

Benjamin drew a sharp breath. Just the sound of his father's voice, of his kindness and patience, and everything he did *not* deserve, caused his composure to weaken. And when Josiah climbed into the cart and entered his line of sight, Benjamin crumpled and burst into tears, quivering as he covered his face in grief-stricken shame. All the sorrow he'd been withholding came pouring forth, and with several sharp, shuddering sobs, he choked, "I'm…I-I'm so sorry, Father. Daniel…I-I should've…I shouldn't be the one who…"

I'm so sorry God chose me, and not him. I'm sorry. I'm sorry!

"Hush, now," Josiah soothed. Cupping his son's face, he forced Benjamin's hands away and kissed the younger man's brow, his eyes both soft and mournful in their affection. "It's good to have you home," he whispered. "I've missed you terribly."

Not like this, Benjamin thought. *Not like* this! And as he spotted Clara lingering in the doorway of his childhood home, his shame and self-revulsion reached a boiling point.

Kill me, he pleaded to God. *Let me die.* Please, *let me die!*

What could be worse than this? What could be worse than letting down the father he loved and revered so much? To come across as nothing more than a battered, broken invalid to the woman of his secret, innermost affections? How could she want to be around him? Stand him? Surely, she was only there because of her plight at camp…

"Can you sit on your own?"

Josiah's query broke through his self-pitying thoughts, and trembling, Benjamin shook his head. "N-no, not entirely, sir…only a little."

Josiah nodded, his chin tense with emotion. "I see." Turning toward the other men, he pressed, "Well, don't just stand there. Someone, help me lift him up! I deserve to hug my son, do I not?"

Amos was the first to reach him, and then someone else grabbed Benjamin's other side, and carefully, they tugged him upward until it was safe enough for Josiah to draw him into his arms.

The reverend embraced his son with a quiet sob, his comforting strength no longer impenetrable. Nudging his cheek into Benjamin's crown, he smoothed a shaky, soothing hand along the captain's hair.

Benjamin hadn't realized how badly he needed his father until his arms were wrapped around him. Throat raw, he wept into Josiah's shoulder, gripping the reverend's dark wool overcoat, that familiarness, much as he had as a small boy; much as he had after his mother died, and he'd been forced to understand so young that the world was not kind. Josiah always assured Benjamin that despite the world's cruelty, everything happened for a reason.

Did that mean he was being punished for failing Daniel?

ONCE BENJAMIN WAS loaded onto the bath chair, a slightly reclined, wicker seat with two back wheels and one in front, and an axle for steering, Clara noted the shame on his face while Josiah rolled him in for supper.

Already standing at the table, she offered both men a curtsy.

"Mrs. Finch was kind enough to make supper," Josiah announced, interrupting her disquiet. "All I had to do was reheat everything!" Pleased, he pushed Benjamin's chair into place at the table and seated himself alongside his son.

Clara hesitated, then awkwardly slid into the ladderback chair across from both men. "The stew smells very..." She lifted her spoon and prodded at the meaty substance. Her forced smile faltered, and she concluded, "Interesting. You must thank Mrs. Finch for me, Reverend."

"Please, call me Josiah," he entreated. "You are a friend of Benjamin's, and the patriot cause, so therefore, you are a friend of mine."

Clara glanced at Benjamin, but his eyes were focused anywhere but on her. "Of course, Josiah. Thank you, sir."

After the reverend led them in prayer, a thick, disagreeable silence followed, and Clara finally grew brave enough to sample her meal. To her pleasant surprise, it wasn't terrible at all; in fact, it was rather good, and the vegetables and unidentified meat warmed her stomach in a full, hearty way she'd never experienced at her family's dinner table.

When Josiah used a piece of bread to sop up his stew, Clara mimicked him to get the full effect. It was only Benjamin who wasn't eating. His gaze remained sorrowful and downcast, and after cleansing her palate with a sip of ale, she lowered her tin cup and offered, "I could help you, Captain Hoskin? If you'd like?"

Horrified, Benjamin lifted his head. "Help me?"

"Why, yes," Clara replied, gesturing to his bowl. "I'm unaware of the specifics of your condition, but if you are unable to feed yourself—"

"I can feed myself," Benjamin hissed, his vitriol startling her. "Just because I am confined to this…this vile *chair* doesn't mean I can't take care of myself!"

"Benjamin Ezekiel Hoskin!" Josiah thundered. "You are not to speak to Miss Boyd in that fashion. As your caretaker, she is only trying to help!"

"Caretaker?" Eyes flashing, Benjamin looked to her in mortification. "Is *that* what she told you?"

"Amos explained her role in this, yes," Josiah replied. "There is no need to be ashamed, son. We all need help from time to time."

With a scoff, Benjamin shoved away his bowl. "I'd rather starve than ask for help. Bishop no longer believes in me, and it's so comforting to know my own father thinks me an invalid, as well!" Tears shone in his eyes, but he did not cry. "I'd like to be excused, sir."

All at once, Clara shot up on unsteady legs. "*I* will leave," she choked, flushing from both hurt and humility. "I am the guest here, and clearly, I have upset my hosts." She looked to Josiah. "Thank you again for your hospitality, Reverend." Her gaze drifted to Benjamin, who was scowling down at his lap. "Good day to you, Captain. I pray the morning finds you in a better humor."

Before anyone could change her mind, Clara drew up her skirts and rushed from the room.

CHAPTER EIGHTEEN
Crossing Swords

WHEN CLARA AWOKE the next morning, it was to the shrill, unpleasant crow of a rooster. She yanked her pillow over her head and pushed downward, attempting to block out the horrid noise.

"Rebel scum," she muttered. Even their *animals* were a nuisance.

Unfortunately, the bothersome bird did not let up in its crowing, so Clara ripped the pillow from her head and grudgingly rose. Despite the comfortable bed, she'd barely slept a wink. In between acclimating to her new surroundings, fearing for her sisters in New York City—surely, Charlotte was home by now?—and stewing over her latest encounter with Benjamin, she'd had more than enough to occupy her mind.

Grumbling to herself, Clara fetched her clothes. She didn't have Benjamin's help this time, a thought that both distressed and guilted her, and deflating, she set to work on laying out her garments.

A FEW FAILED attempts and one success later, Clara emerged in search of her host. She hadn't noticed any servants the day prior, so she imagined Josiah would be making breakfast. The thought was…perplexing, if she was being honest. She'd never known a man who could cook before, not beyond one's servants.

After a bit of searching, she found him in the outdoor kitchen, tending to a fire in the stone hearth.

"Ah! Good morning!" he crowed. "How did you sleep?"

"Very well, thank you," Clara lied. "Are you…?" She gestured, and he chuckled.

"I am making breakfast, yes. Why don't you give me a hand?"

"Me?" Clara squeaked, horrified. "But sir, I don't—"

"Please," Josiah entreated. "I'd very much enjoy the company."

Oh, tar and sugar.

Clara forced a smile and agreed, "I'd be delighted, sir. Thank you."

"What's with all the formalities?" he asked. "Please! I've told you before, call me Josiah, not sir. My father, a regular ol' blaggard, if you want the truth, made me call him sir. I don't much care for it."

"Your son calls you sir," Clara pointed out.

"Yes, well…Benjamin's rather fond of the conventional."

Unable to help herself, she grinned. "He does seem a bit stiff…begging your pardon, sir—ah…Josiah."

He mirrored her grin, though it never quite reached his eyes. "You are a camp follower then?" he asked, straightening from the hearth. "Is that how you met my Benjamin?"

Smile fading, Clara shifted in place. "Er…yes. I did his laundry. Many of the soldiers' laundry, in fact." Falling silent again, she watched Josiah rake a bunch of coals toward the front of the hearth. "What are you making?"

"*We* are making buttered eggs," Josiah corrected. "Why don't you hand me that skillet?"

"The, um…skillet?" Glancing around, she only relaxed when

he gestured at a cast iron pan with three legs.

Lifting it in bemusement, she brought the skillet over and extended it in offering, watching Josiah set it over the raked coals. In front of the hearth, there was a cast iron rack already toasting bread. Josiah rotated it with a handle, then removed the bread to inspect both browned sides before placing them onto a trencher.

"Benjamin likes two," he explained. "Buttered eggs are his favorite."

"I didn't know," Clara murmured, idly fiddling with the lacing on her red, quilted jumps. "I don't know much about him at all, truth be told... We've only been acquainted for a short while."

"Yes, well..." Josiah rose with a grunt, his joints popping. "My Benjamin's a bit on the quiet side. He's friendly and fond of conversation, whenever the situation calls for it, but it takes a bit of coaxing to get him to be forthright."

"So I'm starting to learn," Clara muttered.

Josiah headed to the kitchen table. "Might you grate some nutmeg for me?"

Oh, botheration... What did nutmeg even look like?

Agape, Clara looked from one item on the table to the next, her head spinning. "Forgive me, Josiah, but I do not see it..."

With a helpful tap, Josiah indicated a bowl filled with nutmeg seeds.

Good gracious, how was she supposed to grate them? Catching her bottom lip between her teeth, Clara retrieved a knife, which seemed far too dull for grating. She laid out one of the seeds. Josiah was busy cracking eggs into a bowl, so he wasn't aware of her distress.

Dear God, she prayed, *I know I haven't asked anything of You in quite a while, haven't even spoken, for that matter, but* please *do not make me look like a fool!*

Lifting the knife into the air, Clara brought down the handle with a dull *thwack.* Her blow shot the seed straight across the room, making it skitter along the stone floor and spin to a stop.

Dismayed, she lifted her wall-eyed stare to Josiah, who regarded her curiously.

He broke into a grin and laughed, his eyes twinkling in perplexed fascination. "Where do you hail from, Miss Boyd?"

"Uh…New York City."

"And do city folk *smash* their nutmeg?" he asked, chuckling. "Good heavens, what a pointless method! Here…" Lifting a grater from alongside the mixing bowl, he placed it in front of her. "Try this. Drag the seeds across the grates and scrape everything into this bowl."

Pink-cheeked, Clara accepted the grater and did as instructed. She wasn't stupid, but she was assuredly spoiled, and she felt awkward and clumsy while dragging a seed across the grooves. To her delight, the grating soon yielded a powder. A warm, pleasant smell filled the air, reminiscent of the jumble cookies prepared by the Boyds' cook. With a pleased smile, she dusted the spice inside the bowl.

"Perfect!" Josiah commended. "Now grab the cream and butter."

This time, he was sure to point out the ingredients, and Clara lifted both the creamer and blob of butter before following him to the hearth. While Josiah poured his egg mixture into the skillet, she fidgeted with discomfort.

"Josiah?"

He hummed, gesturing for her to pour in the cream.

As she did so, Clara asked, "With all due respect, how did Captain Hoskin take up a musket? Given your faith, I would've thought you'd both believe in turning the other cheek."

A slight shadow overcame Josiah's eyes. "Normally we do, yes," he allowed, "but not when our very God-given liberties are at stake."

"But what if you're wrong?" she pressed. "The other side believes they have a God-given right to the colonies as well, and they are far stronger."

Josiah inclined his head. "True, but the strong and plentiful are not necessarily victorious. Were it not for David's unshakable faith, his story with Goliath might've turned out far differently." He gestured for her to put the butter into the pan. "I, myself, took up a musket in the French and Indian War, but have since sworn to never again take a life. Not all things done for survival are beautiful, you know."

"I suppose I don't know," Clara replied. "Though I appreciate the sacrifices made in war, this all affects me so very little. This is the only time I've known someone hurt during battle. And given the captain's pain and anger, his sacrifice hardly seems worth it."

"That is not for us to decide," Josiah countered. "There is a plan for all of us in this life, and I'm confident Benjamin will find his path."

"I wish I could share in that sentiment," Clara muttered. "God can be vengeful...perhaps Captain Hoskin is being punished, rather than rewarded."

Josiah didn't respond right away. He scraped at the egg mixture with his wrought iron spatula, the furrow between his brows deepening. "Do you believe my son a bad man?"

Clara blinked. "W-well, no, but he's..." *A spy. A blackguard! The very lowest of the low.* Shaking her head, she amended, "Of course not, Josiah. Benjamin may be stubborn, but he's a good man."

"Then you have your answer," Josiah replied. "Being human is filled with pain and suffering and grief...if mankind were truly being punished, would we also have been gifted the joys of love and friendship, and the support of those who care?"

A flash of skepticism lit up Clara's features, but she bowed her head by way of answer.

Here, he gently squeezed her arm before scraping the cooked eggs onto each piece of toast. "These are done," he said. "Why don't you bring them to Benjamin?"

"I..." A shiver of unease formed between her ribs, recalling how poorly he'd reacted to her yesterday. "Of course, Josiah. I'd be delighted."

She lifted the trencher, then left the kitchen with dread curdling inside her stomach.

WHEN BENJAMIN AWOKE, it took him a moment to remember where he was. The planked ceiling overhead was familiar, *home*, yet he blinked around him in confusion. In the distance, he could hear a cow lowing. Squinting through the sunlight pouring in through his window, he realized he needed to relieve himself. Thank God Clara hadn't volunteered for *that* task too.

Nettled, he tried to rise and his back seized up, a sharp cry catching in his throat before he collapsed onto the bedding.

Oh.

Panic settled over him in waves, and suppressing a whimper, Benjamin reached over the side of his bed. His upper body movement wasn't too affected, not beyond where he'd been shot, yet his legs remained heavy and numb as he fumbled in search of his chamber pot.

Perspiration formed along his brow, and clenching his teeth, he groped at the vessel before lifting it off the floor. Unfortunately, he lost his grip, and the empty chamber pot overturned and rolled a short distance across the floor. It was now out of reach, taunting him, and with a frustrated growl, Benjamin tensed his jaw.

You must fetch it, he thought. *You cannot become* anyone's *burden!*

Ever determined, he pushed himself up with his arms while keeping his back straight, his muscles straining until he was in a sitting position. Huffing and puffing, Benjamin drew back his covers and used his upper body strength to turn the dead weight of his legs over the side of the bed. Still trying to keep his back straight, Benjamin slowly lowered himself down with his arms. Once he was nearly upon the floor, his muscles gave out and he dropped onto his side.

"Rot it all," he snarled.

Attempting to crawl—he would *never* cry for help—Benjamin put all his weight onto his forearms and dragged himself belly-down across the wooden flooring, much like a floundering snake. With each drag, an intense stinging sensation whipped up his spine. It was painful, debilitating, and with a furious sob, he collapsed facedown and screamed into the wooden planks.

Rot this injury. God rot his ineptitude! How could he ever hope to function if he couldn't even *relieve* himself?

Alit with frustration, Benjamin struck his nearby washstand and overturned it, sending the washbowl and pitcher on top hurtling to the floor before they shattered. With his breath burning like fire through his lungs, he grabbed whatever was within reach and chucked the items as far as he could throw them.

That was when Clara entered the room.

Nearly dropping her tray, she fumblingly set aside Benjamin's breakfast and rushed over to his prostrate form. "Oh! Oh goodness, are you all right?" she asked. "What on earth happened?"

When her hand curled beneath his elbow, Benjamin shook her off. "Leave me be," he growled. "I can take care of myself!"

Eyes sparking like flint, Clara snapped, "Ah yes, clearly! Thank you for reminding me that normal people wallow about on the floor!"

"I am *not* normal," Benjamin seethed. "Not anymore." Attempting to roll over onto his back, he gave a pained hiss, and tears of anger and exertion leaked from his eyes. "Just go," he pleaded. "Leave me here."

"I will not."

Careful in her movements, Clara assisted Benjamin in lying flat on his back. "There now," she soothed. "See? That wasn't so bad."

"Not so bad?" Benjamin echoed, incredulous. "I just needed help rolling over like an infant. How in God's name can that not be 'so bad?'"

"You have all your limbs and your health," Clara coolly said. "In your line of work, I don't think I need to remind you how lucky you are." Chin tensing, she picked up stray pieces of ceramic. "Although it may be unconventional, men have functioned with far less than their legs."

"And what would you know of it?" Benjamin spat. "From that very little time spent in camp, what could you have possibly learned about injury and self-efficiency?"

Clara scowled at him. "I don't need to see in order to understand," she retorted. "Why, isn't that the very basis of your religion? Having faith in the unseen? Ben, God—"

"Is laughing at me! He gave me all these ideas, yet I am powerless to enact them! While Washington and his men are out there fighting for our freedom, I am stuck here licking my wounds like some sniveling dog!" Quivering, Benjamin's throat seized up. "You don't understand," he choked. "If I can't fight, I am nothing."

"That's not true," Clara argued. "Ben, as loath as I am to admit it, you are smart. Cunning, too."

He scoffed. "That's high praise, coming from some Tory doll."

"Now see here!" Clara snarled. "You're not the only one to have a hard life, you miserable lobcock! I hurt, too. I bleed, too. But you don't see me falling apart and taking it out on those offering a helping hand!" She jabbed a finger against her chest. "Who even says I want to be here? There's nothing I'd rather do less than aid a traitor to the Crown!"

"Then leave," Benjamin hissed, his chin quivering. "Go! Since I didn't ask for this, and you clearly despise it, do us both a favor and return to your precious city!"

"With pleasure!" Making a show of dropping the gathered shards onto the floor, she dusted off her hands, lifted up her skirts, and tearfully tore from the room.

CHAPTER NINETEEN

Losing Faith

WHEN JOSIAH FOUND Benjamin later that morning, he balked at the sight of his son half-draped over his bed, struggling vainly to pull himself onto the mattress.

"Benjamin!" Josiah exclaimed, rushing forward. "Where is Miss Boyd?"

"It doesn't matter. I can take care of myself!" Benjamin growled. Face pink with exertion, he gnashed his teeth and pulled himself upright. As his father reached to help, he gave a fierce, "*No!*" and slipped, swearing sharply once he collapsed hard onto his side. Hissing in pain, Benjamin grimaced and swallowed back his nausea. "Please," he begged, "please, just go. I can't bear for you to see me this way."

Josiah harrumphed. "You are my son. If you cannot allow me into the darkest depths of your despair, then whom will you allow?"

The piercing edge to Benjamin's gaze faded. "You know I trust you implicitly."

"Then why are you shutting me out? 'As iron sharpens iron, so one person sharpens another.'" Expression softening, he persisted, "Even the best and most useful blade cannot sharpen itself, Benjamin. We were created to help one another." Extending his hand, Josiah entreated, "Allow me."

This time, Benjamin acquiesced and took his father's hand,

clenching his jaw as together, they hefted his weight up onto the mattress. Benjamin fell face-first onto the bed, and after a bit of huffing and puffing, he rolled onto his back with Josiah's help.

"Christ," Benjamin swore. Catching his father's admonishing look, he amended, "Sorry, sir... Camp life has spoiled my tongue."

"Among other things," Josiah muttered. "Your manners could use some work."

"With all due respect, sir, my deportment is the absolute last thing on my mind."

Sighing, Josiah sank onto the bed and patted Benjamin's wrist. "This isn't the end of the world. God has shown you much kindness in your plight."

"Kindness?" Benjamin echoed. "You have lost two sons in this war, one to execution, and the other to lameness, yet you consider my plight a kindness?"

"You don't know the ending of your story," Josiah reminded him. "Perhaps this hindrance is exactly what you'll need."

Benjamin's temper flared. "Wars have never been won fighting on one's back. I am utterly useless this way—to myself, to you, *and* the cause."

Josiah's own temper sparked in his eyes.

"Sir, if I may..."

"No, you may not," he snapped. "I know you are hurting, Benjamin, but you would do well to remember your teachings. Surely, you know you are never abandoned; not whenever you are so deeply surrounded by love." When Benjamin shook his head, Josiah growled, "Are you so blinded by discontent, so consumed by arrogance that you believe yourself above all healing?"

"Sir—"

"You are *not* being punished, Benjamin, nor are you the first to experience a trial of this magnitude. You must keep the faith! You must hold on to those who love you!"

Benjamin flinched as though struck. "I'm trying," he gritted.

"Ever since this horrid war started, I have tried keeping my head above water. But the truth is, I don't know what I believe in anymore." He laughed wearily. "I am not Daniel."

A thick silence followed, and Josiah rose from the bed. "I will leave you to your rest," he murmured. "In a little while, I'll have Miss Boyd come in with your dinner."

Benjamin winced. "Don't bother. She's not staying."

"Whyever not?"

"I kind of…told her to leave. And she agreed."

Spearing his son with an admonishing look, Josiah finally noticed the scattered ceramic shards and items strewn across the floor. "I'll tend to this in a few minutes," he muttered. "If I find Miss Boyd and she still intends to help, I expect you to swallow your pride and apologize."

Benjamin said nothing, so Josiah turned and left.

NOT WISHING TO alert anyone to her departure, Clara escaped via window and started up the beaten path toward town. Eyes swollen and heart heavy, she debated on how to proceed. Did she truly wish to run? Why had she let Benjamin, a rebel who'd made her question her very stance on the wickedness of man, make her feel ugly, when all she'd wanted was to help?

"Miss?"

Hastily wiping her tears, Clara turned to discover a woman with deep brown eyes, dark hair, and pleasant smile lines.

"Apologies, ma'am," she said, "but I thought I'd pop in and check on Josiah and his boy. Are you the caretaker Reverend Hoskin's spoken so much about? Miss Boyd?"

Paling, Clara prayed she didn't look upset as she replied, "I…am she, yes. Are you Mrs. Harriet Finch?"

The woman laughed in delight. "Oh, goodness, I'm so glad my reputation precedes me! Makes things easier that way, don't you think?" Warmly, she lifted the tureen in her hands. "If you're going to market, would you postpone? I made dinner for the Hoskinses, and I'd be honored if you joined us."

"Thank you, Mrs. Finch, but I'm not hungry." Clara's voice came out far sharper than she intended, and her chin wobbled.

"What's this then?" the woman asked, her eyes soft and probing. "You all right there?"

"No," she whispered. *I haven't been all right for a long, long time.*

"No?" Harriet echoed. "Well, that won't do! Why don't you walk with me, uh? I've got a good ear, and a sound mind. Honest! I can try and cure whatever ails ya…though this stew is a mighty good start." She winked. "Take me up on my offer, Miss. Please."

Clara sniffed, her shoulders sagging. She didn't truly wish to leave—*couldn't*—so she agreed, "Oh, very well. The Hoskinses just had breakfast, so you're rather early for dinner."

"I'm always early," Harriet said. "That way, I can never be late."

Clara hummed. "I suppose I cannot argue with such logic…" She waited for Harriet to take the lead. "How long have you known the Hoskinses?"

"Oh, goodness. My whole life! But that's rather easy, when we all live in the same town." Harriet smiled. "Is it like that where you hail from?"

"No." Clara's expression grew bitter. "New York City's bustling with opportunity, so people are always coming and going. I've lived in the same house my entire life, but…it's not the same. I didn't have the stability you seem to possess."

Harriet snorted. "Who said anything about stability? We're all dicked in the knob 'round here!" With a bright guffaw, she nudged Clara's arm. "City life can't be so bad, right? I imagine it must be mighty exciting."

Clara snorted. "Yes, of course…if you enjoy being paraded about in society, always expected to put on a show for every fool desiring your dowry."

Harriet looked her over with interest. "Society, eh? Are we talking high society? What on earth are you doing out here with the likes of—?"

"All girls enter society," Clara quickly reminded her. "I wasn't suggesting I am rich; I merely don't like being put on display. And in the city, it's difficult to find a moment's rest. Out here, however…" She shrugged. "I imagine it's quite easy to hide."

Harriet squinted at the odd phrasing. "Yes, I reckon so. We've some peculiar folks out in these parts, but no one's hiding from anything. Not to my knowledge, of course. And I make it my business to know." She hummed. "What made you think of that, anyway?"

The unspoken *are* you *hiding from something?* lingered between them, and flustered, Clara said, "Oh, no reason. I've been reading a lot of literature lately, all featuring heroines hiding dark, tragic pasts. It's merely colored my thoughts, I suppose." She forced a laugh. "I really must learn to amend myself!"

Harriet grinned. "Sounds thrilling! Though it's mighty sad whenever we have to read about other people, especially fictional people, to get some excitement." She winked. "Fortunately, that's never the case with me. I wouldn't say I'm a busybody, but I get involved in the community. That's why I've called in a physician for the Hoskinses. He should be arriving soon, so I hope they'll be pleased!"

Clara frowned. "A physician? What is his specialty?"

"Not invalids, if that's what you're asking, but he knows how to cure the mind. After I gave birth to a stillborn many years ago—many, *many* years ago, so there's no need to look at me like that, dear—Dr. Wagner's father, Dr. Wagner, Sr., took away my hysteria and kept it away."

"With what?"

"Tinctures, mostly. I'm not sure what'll work for Benjamin, but I've the utmost faith in Dr. Wagner. Despite neither hailing from Freyview, both've proved competent."

Clara looked away. "Yes, well…it seems we all could use a bit of faith these days."

Ignoring Harriet's questioning look, she quickened her pace.

WHEN CLARA RETURNED with Harriet, Benjamin was far from receptive toward having guests. He sat by the fire, resigned and scowling while the women and his father chatted about a Mrs. Whose-Its being *most uncouth* at market.

Benjamin hated gossip. He always had, and now that it was likely himself at the forefront of these wagging tongues, his temper kept waxing and waning with each ill-intentioned word. And Clara…why had she stayed? Surely, it was a decision borne of pride; surely, it was only to torment him.

Every now and then, he caught his father's gaze. It was evident Josiah wished for him to apologize, but Benjamin was nothing if not consistently stubborn. If Clara desired an apology, she could ask for one herself. He would never apologize for speaking his mind. Daniel certainly hadn't.

"When Benjamin was about this tall," Harriet declared, dragging him from his self-pitying thoughts, "he was the naughtiest little boy on this side of the Sound!"

Clara laughed, wrinkling her nose. "Captain Hoskin? Naughty? What did he do, steal from the rich and give to the poor?"

"Why, no!" Harriet exclaimed, bemused. "Back then, he was a bit of a brat—begging your pardon, Josiah—and I caught him stomping through my vegetable garden with his friends on more than one occasion. But that's beside the point…"

Clara looked Benjamin's way with a sneer, only to falter at his sour, stony expression. Glancing back at Harriet, she urged, "Go on. You have me so curious!"

Josiah sighed. "I have a feeling I know which story this is."

Harriet huffed. "Yes, well, I wouldn't imagine you'd soon forget! On the week of my late husband's fortieth birthday, God rest his soul, I hosted teatime for our friends. Josiah and his wife were invited, naturally…" She nodded at the reverend. "But I had a strict 'no children' policy. I didn't even want them in the back parlor, as is customary. Benjamin must've taken offense, because when my guests and I sat down for tea, the little monster had urinated in every single cup!"

Clara burst into surprised laughter, her brows knitting skeptically. "But how do you know it was him?"

"He confessed! And quite proudly, too!" Harriet tried to continue, but a series of knocks interrupted. "Oh!" Rising from her seat, she gleefully announced, "That must be my surprise!"

Bemused, Benjamin lifted his head. "A surprise?" It was the first time he'd spoken that afternoon, and a seedling of dread sprouted within his stomach when Harriet winked. That meddlesome woman! He didn't need nor want anything from her.

Bustling over to the door, Harriet opened it with a flourish. On the other side stood a proud, sharp-nosed man with a supercilious smirk and long, dark hair pulled into a ponytail.

"Dr. Wagner!" she exclaimed. "Come in! These are—"

"The Hoskinses," he said, nodding. "Oh, believe me, I know." He cut his hazel eyes toward Benjamin. "And look at you, you son of a bitch!"

Harriet paled at his language. "Y-you…?"

"Know Benjamin Hoskin? Why, of course! We went to Yale together," Dr. Wagner explained. "Once my path as a clergyman didn't pan out, I decided to become a physician like my old man." Entering with his medical bag, he assessed Benjamin with a sneer. "I should've known you'd end up like this. You were always too mischievous for your own good."

Benjamin scowled at the physician. Deep inside, a tendril of resentment unfurled within his chest and he clenched his hands.

John Wagner was the absolute last person he wanted to see. As he fumed over his misfortune, John turned to Clara with an appreciative once-over.

"And you must be Hoskin's lovely caretaker," he crowed.

Eyes cutting to Benjamin, Clara offered, "Yes, but perhaps not for long. I'm afraid I am much more welcome by some than others."

"I couldn't imagine that being the case," John replied. "You are much how I always envisioned Helen of Troy."

Suppressing scornful laughter, Clara lifted a hand to hide her smile. "You and Captain Hoskin went to school together?"

John's smile dimmed. "We did, yes. The bugger pulled a rather unfunny trick on me, but now that I'm older, I can at least acknowledge its cleverness."

Harriet whooped. "More pranks? Goodness, Benjamin, did you ever grow up?"

Red-faced and eyes hard as flint, Benjamin's mouth screwed downward as he looked away.

"He's not much of a talker, is he?" John observed. "Back at Yale, we could scarcely get this cur to shut his yapper." He bowed to Josiah. "Begging your pardon, Reverend."

"And your purpose here is, sir?" Josiah coolly asked. "Mrs. Finch said you were a surprise?"

"Evidently, yes! I was told to offer my medical expertise," John said. "I promise you, I can curb, if not completely cure whatever is ailing your son."

Benjamin straightened at once. "No," he hissed. "Absolutely not."

"Whyever not?" John asked, bemused. "My laudanum treatment is quite effective!"

"Laudanum?" Blinking rapidly, Benjamin shook his head. "Oh no, I don't think so...I've heard it's quite expensive."

"Not to worry, Hoskin. You're getting a friend's discount, if only for Mrs. Finch's sake," John said. "And laudanum is scarce these days, yes, but I've been hoarding it long since before the war. I'm also friends with a French surgeon, who brought plenty from overseas and allowed me a small cut of his shipment."

Josiah frowned. "And how much of this *treatment* do you intend to give?" he interjected. "During my military service, some of our men happened to die from these tinctures."

John puffed up, affronted for being questioned. "I can assure you, Reverend, that those men were not taking the proper dosage. I have everything completely under control. You have my word as a gentleman."

While the two men discussed, Benjamin started wondering if Wagner was right. Benjamin was emotionally in pain, so didn't he deserve a semblance of relief, given how he may never again be happy? It was far better to be numb than made constantly aware of his present hell. That much he *did* know.

Swallowing, Benjamin exhaled. "Yes, well…I suppose you have a point," he decided. "I'll take your so-called medicine."

"Benjamin!" Josiah exclaimed. "Are you sure?"

Benjamin didn't lift his head, his features somber as he nodded. "Yes, sir. If I cannot get better, I wish to *feel* better."

John clapped his hands, smug in his triumph. "Splendid! I knew the ol' Wagner charm would eventually wear you down!" Retrieving a bottle filled with reddish-brown liquid, he set it onto the table by Benjamin's side. "Mix a few drops of this with alcohol whenever needed. And by that, I mean whenever you're in pain."

Benjamin frowned. "I don't feel much of anything at all, truth be told…nothing beyond an occasional burning in my spine."

"Laudanum is for the weary in spirit, too," John assured him. "Take it whenever you're not feeling your best."

Benjamin deflated. At this point, he couldn't remember the last time he'd felt his best, and bitterly, he glanced down at the bottle, resigned.

"Alas, I must be off," John announced. "I have another engagement. However…!" He turned to Clara. "Would you care to accompany me, Miss Boyd? There is the loveliest public assembly a few towns over, and I'd be delighted if you joined me." He looked to Harriet with a grin. "Mrs. Finch informed me she's already attending, so she can serve as our chaperone."

Clara blinked in shock. "Oh! Well...I don't really have an appropriate dress for a dance, Doctor."

"Balderdash!" he exclaimed. "You look gorgeous as is. Doesn't she, Hoskin?"

Benjamin gripped his armrests, overwhelmed by the sudden stinging slice between his ribs. "She is *not* available," he growled. "As my..." Swallowing, he gritted, "As my caretaker, she can't just come and go as she pleases."

"Oh, really?" Clara snapped. "This morning, you told me I should return home. I assumed my services were no longer desired." She turned back to John. "I would be honored to accompany you, Dr. Wagner."

John looked at Benjamin with a wink. "To the winner goes all the spoils, eh, Hoskin? Don't look so glum. Have some laudanum!"

Benjamin moved to snipe at him, but Harriet laid a hand on his shoulder. "Now, now," she admonished, "why don't we get you into bed?"

"It's not even dark out," he spat.

"Well yes, but—"

"For God's sake, I am not a child!" Furiously, he shook her off. "I'm only an invalid because you are refusing to treat me as a man—a *whole* man!"

"Benjamin!" Josiah thundered. "You will apologize to Mrs. Finch at once!"

"No, sir, I won't. Not when for the past few months, I have sacrificed *everything* for the greater good of the colonies, for others who don't even *appreciate* it." He quivered. "I am no longer that man, so I will do whatever I please for myself and no one else!"

The room fell silent and Benjamin drew a breath, shaking and humiliated. Pointedly, he swiped the laudanum and placed it into his lap, then tried to wheel himself around in a clumsy arc.

Unfortunately, due to the cumbersome nature of his bath chair, he was unable to self-propel and steer without the mercy of a willing individual.

Josiah stepped forward. "Benjamin—"

"I'm going to bed," he snarled, hot tears of frustration filling his eyes. "If anyone is in need of me, do not bother."

Wordless, his father stepped behind him and aided in his plight.

While Benjamin was wheeled away, his chin tucked toward his chest and his shoulders shaking, John looked to Clara with a snort. "I'm so sorry you had to see that, Miss Boyd. The man is a scoundrel."

Clara didn't answer. Her eyes watered and she touched the shawl at her neck, her gaze never straying from where Benjamin sat only moments before.

CHAPTER TWENTY
Hide and Seek

THE CARRIAGE RIDE was wholly abysmal. Although Clara prided in being able to talk to absolutely anyone, she couldn't bring herself to listen, engage, nor flirt as John prattled on about the dull trappings of his life. He claimed brilliance since boyhood. Did all men have to be so heinously full of themselves? By the time she'd started listening again, he was talking about fowl in spirited distaste.

Clara stifled a groan. Oh, what a fool she'd been! She only came because she'd wanted to punish Benjamin for his cruelty, as if he even cared whether or not she was interested in John! And for whatever harsh reason, Harriet was choosing to read rather than engage, so she wasn't even granted the reprieve of a female buffer.

Scowling, Clara folded her arms. She needed to shut him up. She needed to hear something, *anything* other than what a "wonder" John was, and how he'd been a "godsend" to the medical field.

"That prank you mentioned earlier," she spoke, "what was it?"

John frowned at the interruption. "You really want to know?"

"Why, yes!" Clara said. "Although many feign interest, I assure you I am a woman who only speaks whenever invested."

John's brow furrowed. "Am I to take your prior silence as a

bad sign?" When she smirked, he laughed. "You're quite right, my apologies. Of course, you are interested!" He cleared his throat, his face taking on the dramatic expression she'd grown to loathe. "I was just starting at Yale," he began. "The other boys were nice enough, even Hoskin, but I was somewhat of a recluse and preferred the company of books. That's why I decided to host a Latin club."

Clara arched a brow. "Wouldn't the obvious alternative be a book club?"

"I suppose, but I loved Latin and enjoyed speaking and reading it at any given opportunity," John said. "I tried getting my entire class involved and put up a few broadsides to earn their interest."

"Did you get it?"

John snorted. "Ah, yes. I most certainly did receive attention. Hoskin replaced my broadsides with counterfeits. Little did I know, he'd completely changed the verbiage. The irksome prat encouraged everyone attending to bring a chicken. I am *horribly* allergic, so by the end of it all, I was sneezing to high heaven since I was dealing with ten fowls!"

Clara clapped a hand over her mouth, her eyes sparkling with amusement. "Oh! Oh, goodness," she breathed, trying to sound scandalized. "Was Captain Hoskin disciplined?"

"No," John grumbled. "It was done off school grounds, and I was far too humiliated to take my shame public, or rather, *more* public. So he never received comeuppance." Slowly, his face melded into smug satisfaction. "Then again, our Lord and Savior saw to it that Hoskin was punished. Just look at the man!"

Clara's sneer wiped from her face. "You believe God is punishing Benjamin for a silly little trick? And one that didn't even harm you?"

John drew up, affronted. "It did harm me! I was ill for days!"

Ill in the head, perhaps, she thought. "Nevertheless, it's rather harsh to wish lameness upon a man because of one small, inconsequential prank."

John's upper lip curled. "With all due respect, Miss Boyd, you don't know Hoskin as I do. His intentions were malicious."

"I'm beginning to see why," she muttered.

"What was that?"

"I'm afraid I might cry," she amended. "Oh goodness, Doctor, your plight has moved me in ways I cannot express!"

Softening, John patted her hand. "There now, what's done is done. I am quite all right, I promise. And once you've given me the honor of a dance, I shall be all the hale and heartier!"

"And thank heaven for it!" Clara exclaimed. As John squeezed her hand, she lost her smile and bitterly locked eyes with Harriet's amused gaze.

BENJAMIN REMAINED UPON the thin divide between wakefulness and sleep. All around him, sounds wobbled and reverberated akin to a coin descending a well, yet none were enough to rouse him.

"Moony-boy, you awake?"

Shifting beneath his quilt, Benjamin hummed, comfortably swaddled as if relaxing in a warm bath.

"Moony? Ben?! C'mon, please... For Chrissake, open your eyes!"

The sensation of being shaken, and quite vigorously, brought Benjamin into a state of consciousness. Bleary-eyed, his gaze settled upon a concerned face. "Amos?" he slurred. "When'd you get in?"

Amos blinked in shock. "Oi, have you been drinkin'?"

"*Sleeping,* if you must know," Benjamin grumbled. A painful *thrum-thrum-thrum* formed around his temples in direct contrast to the warm, pleasant euphoria settling within his bones. "Could you lower your voice, please? You're so loud..."

"By St. George," Amos growled. "What've you been doin',

uh?" His gaze settled upon the laudanum by his bedside. "This?" he demanded. "Is *that* what you've been takin'?" Furious, he snatched the bottle. "How much did'ja have?" When Benjamin groaned, Amos grew more persistent. "I mean it, arsehole. How much did'ja take?"

"I dunno," he mumbled. "Maybe three drops? It's what was advised."

Amos gritted his teeth. "Laudanum's for men in pain."

I am, Benjamin thought, his anger instantly sobering him. *This is who I am now, so I need it. I need this!*

But rather than reveal such desperation, he replied, "As I've said, this is what the doctor prescribed. If he believes it'll help, then I am willing to see it through."

Amos scoffed. "Oi, at what cost? I've seen how men react to this poison! You really wanna open yourself up to that world o' hurt?"

Benjamin sniffed, his nose oddly blocked up. "I feel fine," he promised. "I'm confident I'll only need a few doses. That, at the very least, should be enough to make me better."

Amos grimaced. "Well, only if you're sure…"

"Positive." Benjamin forced a smile.

And as the cabinetmaker forced one of his own, Benjamin realized this was the first time he'd ever truly lied to his friend. A sensation akin to a writhing, restless snake coiled within his stomach, and eager to deflect, he asked, "Why have you come? Did you receive word from camp?"

Amos squinted. "Moony, you've only been home one day… I may be an arsehole, but I wasn't gonna skip town with you still settlin' in."

"What?" Blinking in shock, he groaned before sinking more fully into his pillow. "Blood and thunder, this truly is imprisonment."

Sighing, Amos lowered onto the bed and removed his hat. "If it makes y'feel any better, Bishop feels badly 'bout this whole thing."

Benjamin snorted. "Oh, yes. He feels badly, but not enough to keep me in the operation. I feel so much better."

Amos huffed. "Your sarcasm's noted and not appreciated. A bit o' faith would do ya good."

"Faith?" Benjamin echoed, trying not to raise his voice. "I am trapped here in my bed, unable to help with the most important task of my life, and yet you have the gall to scold me on my lack of faith? Amos, I'm positively unmanned. Where Father would've once denied the assistance of a female caretaker, he agrees because nothing physically untoward can happen between Clara and myself. It's humiliating, degrading, so answer me this: What more harm can befall me? What can this laudanum do that God has not? Are you truly going to deny me my right to aid in this cause? My final obligation to Daniel?"

Amos's face softened. "But why d'ya need to do more, uh? You've already done your part, and it's been a mighty good one."

"This is for the people I love," Benjamin choked. "I am merely a flame, helpless but to burn until I fulfill my purpose. And until this war is through, it hasn't been fulfilled." His gaze grew wet. "Please, let me help. Lie to Bishop, if you must. I need to be involved!"

Amos sighed, his eyes shining with pity. "Look, Moony, no matter what we do, I jus' don't think it'll ever be good enough for ya. Your obsession's makin' y'reckless. We can't rush any o' this."

Benjamin swallowed. "Just keep me in the loop," he pleaded. "Don't make any major decisions without me. That's all I ask."

Gently squeezing Benjamin's shoulder, Amos agreed, "Consider it done."

THE PUBLIC ASSEMBLY was held at the Green Turtle Tavern, a

moderately sized establishment with low-hanging lanterns, stuffy portraits of the owners, and a large wooden floor that was perfect for festivity.

Despite Clara's love of dancing, she grew disdainful once she entered the room, arm in arm with John as he preened beneath everyone's gaze. Just like in the carriage, Harriet was of absolutely no help. She was off gossiping rather than serving as a chaperone.

Oblivious to Clara's torment, John whispered, "Just look at this crowd. They can't take their eyes off us! They must not be accustomed to seeing such a handsome couple."

Couple?

Repulsed, Clara painted on her typical smirk, the faux coyness lightening her expression. This was what she deserved, was it not? No decent man would ever want her…

"Come now, don't be so modest," she cooed, playing up to his vanity. "You know this venue, so they must be staring at *you*. I trust they're looking for someone to lead by example."

"Then allow us both to lead," John coaxed. "Despite the stringed music, no one has yet ventured onto the dance floor. Shall we show them a thing or two?"

Clara stiffened at his sudden nearness but lifted her chin to draw toward his inappropriately close mouth. "Of course, Doctor," she purred. "I am at your disposal."

And she did, in fact, feel disposable. Despite John's constant flattery, he never once made her feel wanted nor desirable, not in the way Benjamin had each time he'd kissed her with that reverent, painful shyness… And yet, that hadn't been Benjamin Hoskin at all. No, that was Benjamin pretending to be Philip Ashby, a man who at this point was nothing more than a distant dream.

Throat stinging at the memory, Clara allowed John to lead her onto the dance floor. As they got into position, a pompous voice crowed, "John Wagner? *The* John Wagner? C'mere, you ol' son of a gun!"

A tall, heavy-set man with a periwig emerged from the throng of partygoers, clearly well in his cups if his ruddy cheeks—not to mention, incredibly loud voice—were any indicator. A thin, tiny woman with powdered hair, powdered breasts, and a flouncy, elegant gown was practically glued to his side. Clara appraised them with distaste but was grateful for the interruption. She'd nearly had to dance with the clotpole.

"…I tell you, those rebels are far more formidable than they let on!"

The petite woman huffed, waving her fan beneath her pointed chin. "Oh, honestly, Isaac, must you always speak of war? We already know the King's Men shall succeed."

Isaac's eyes were glittering with passion. "I wouldn't expect you to understand, Lenora," he snidely said. Turning to Clara, he exclaimed, "You, there! Surely, you can speak some sense into my nubby-headed wife?"

Clara jerked, not expecting the attention. "Oh, I don't presume to know anything about war," she said. In her experience, men preferred being humored rather than engaged in debate. "But you're right, sir…we must stay alert, what with these vile Continentals being absolutely everywhere!"

"Well, this *is* the United States of North America," John pointed out. "It's only natural that it'll be overrun by Continentals."

Clara didn't appreciate his tone but maintained her naïve expression. "Why, of course, Doctor," she agreed, "but how can we determine who is friend or foe?"

"Precisely!" Isaac exclaimed, jabbing a finger in her direction. "There, you see, Lenora? While you prattle on about gowns and teacakes, this woman actually sees what's underneath our very noses!"

Lenora huffed, turning said nose into the air. "Well, I hardly think—"

"Yes, my dear, and that's precisely your problem! Were you to realize Our Majesty's forces don't have nearly as good a handle on things as they'd like us to believe, then perhaps you wouldn't be so quick to roll your eyes. As Miss, uh…" Isaac pointed to Clara again. "What is your name, dear?"

"Clara Boyd," John supplied, much to her annoyance.

"Yes, yes, of course," Isaac said, waving a hand. "As Miss Boyd said, these rebellious Continentals are everywhere! Fortunately, my nephew is aiding the cause. He reports to the British head of intelligence, himself! But, alas, this whole town's crawling with those traitorous cowards. Why, just last week, they pillaged and ransacked Harold Stubbs's manor, and then drove him out into the street before giving him a sound beating. We can no longer trust even our neighbors!"

Clara gasped, her pity genuine. "Oh, the poor man!" she exclaimed. "And you say your nephew reports to the British head of intelligence?"

Brimming with pride, Isaac nodded. "Indeed! Peter's a useless cur, but he counts where it matters. I daresay it's his uselessness that makes him such a fine informant, because nobody gives the blithering fool a second glance."

Clara moved to reply, but Lenora snapped her fan shut with an air of finality. "All this talk of war is putting me in poor spirits," she complained. Eyes cutting toward John, she asked, "Would you care to dance, Doctor? Someone needs to lead the festivities, so it might as well be us."

John hesitated. "As honored as I am, Mrs. Richardson, I am afraid I've already promised my first dance t—"

"Oh, please don't refrain on my account!" Clara exclaimed. "We can dance later, Doctor."

A bit put out, he ultimately bowed in acquiescence, then turned to Lenora. "I would be honored, Mrs. Richardson."

Accepting his hand, Lenora's expression grew snide as she told Clara, "Dear Isaac seems most charmed by you, Miss Boyd. Why don't the two of you share a dance?"

Clara frowned. Lenora's intentions weren't entirely clear, but they also weren't obscure either. She wanted John alone. She wanted to punish her husband, too, and by God, Clara wished she could thank this woman for the opportunity to get away from Dr. Wagner for a while. "I'd love to," she said, feigning joviality.

As Clara took Isaac's hand, she cursed her thoughts for drifting back to Benjamin with his tired eyes and world-weary smile…

BY THE TIME Clara returned to the Hoskin residence, it was well into the late hours of the evening. She was greeted by Josiah, who flashed a pleasant grin while reading by the fire.

"Oh! Good evening, Reverend…" She curtsied. "I wasn't expecting you to still be awake."

Josiah chuckled and set aside his book. "You didn't think I'd retire until I knew you had made it in safely, did you?"

Clara balked at that, startled. Her own parents didn't concern themselves with her whereabouts, so long as it didn't ruin their precious reputation, so his kindness was wholly inconceivable to her. "I appreciate your concern…thank you."

He inclined his head. "How was your evening?"

"Uneventful, truth be told. I found myself eager to return here." It bothered Clara that this wasn't a lie. Chewing her lip, she added, "And how is Benjamin? He seemed…distraught, for lack of a better word, and I cannot help but feel partly responsible."

Josiah sighed. "I got him to eat, if that's what you're worried about, but not much else. He kept feigning sleep."

Clara arched a brow. "But suppose he was asleep?"

"No, he assuredly was not. A father knows these things." He gestured to the back quarters. "I trust he's still awake. I doubt he's hungry, but perhaps he is in need of assistance?"

A sinking feeling formed in the pit of Clara's stomach, yet she curtsied and turned to oblige.

Heading to Benjamin's bedroom, she waited a beat, then knocked on his door. "Captain Hoskin? Ben, may I come in?"

Nothing but silence greeted her, so with a pinch of alarm in her chest, Clara twisted the knob and pushed through the entryway. There, in the far corner was Benjamin, still sitting in his bath chair, but this time with his face freshly soaped while he gathered his shaving utensils from a table. His broken washbowl and pitcher had recently been replaced.

All at once, their eyes met, and he scoffed.

Nettled by his scorn, Clara frowned and closed the door behind her. She couldn't believe she'd actually missed him. "Am I interrupting something?" she asked. "Other than your pity party, of course."

Expression sharp, Benjamin's gaze raked across her frame with clear contempt. "I wasn't expecting you back so soon," he said. "Given your eagerness to leave, I assumed John would've taken you to bed by now."

The room fell deathly silent, hurt and resentment simmering hotly beneath the surface.

"How dare you?" Clara snarled. "Just because I enjoy the company of men, you think you can address me as if I am some cheap, common harlot? Whatever happened to the man who said I wasn't a trollop? Who supposedly respected me?" Her chin quivered. "I don't care that you're an invalid; if you *ever* speak to me that way again, I'll knock your headrails right down your throat!"

She didn't need this kind of abuse. Not from him, too.

Benjamin was quick to lose his sourness, and a look of genuine remorse flooded his face. "I'm so sorry," he choked. "I-I didn't mean..." Swallowing, he lowered his gaze and nodded to the shaving utensils in his lap. "I am just upset. I can't see into the looking glass on the wall, and I am not yet capable of fetching the one from my valise." He indicated the bag under his bed. "I know it's no excuse, but...I am sorry. I've been a total arsehole."

"Yes," Clara agreed, "you most certainly have." Her expression softened. "However, I'd rather not add to your distress by reciprocating." She approached his chair. "I may not know much about shaving, but perhaps I could help?" Catching the leeriness in his expression, she laughed. "What? How hard could it be?"

"Well, you could cut me," Benjamin pointed out, "and given my comportment, I'm expecting plenty of nicks."

"Nonsense." Taking note of the straight razor in his hand, she asked, "Your soap's already been applied, so what comes next?"

He laughed incredulously. "Though I appreciate the offer, it takes years of practice," Benjamin said. "If you could just fetch my looking glass, that's all I'll need."

"Hmph, suit yourself," Clara said. "I wasn't too keen on shaving you anyway." Trying not to smile—why did she feel affection for this noddy?—she moved over and grabbed his valise. After rummaging through the small bag, she plucked the mirror free and straightened. "Would you like me to hold it for you?"

When she glanced back at him, she noted the way Benjamin's features warmed, and a painful shyness flooded across his gaze.

"I don't need you to do that," he assured her, "but…I would enjoy the company…if you wouldn't mind?"

Clara smiled. "Truth be told, I think that's the first thing you've said today that I haven't minded at all." After grabbing a small cloth, she returned to his side and pulled up a chair, sitting alongside him and lifting the looking glass.

"I've never watched a man shave before," she said. "It seems…intimate, for lack of a better word."

Benjamin caught her gaze, flushed, and then promptly looked away again. "I've never been watched, if it makes you feel any better."

Clara snorted. "I wasn't bothered in the slightest, but I appreciate the concern." Angling the mirror when he peered into the glass, she admired the way his biceps bunched beneath his rolled-up, loosely fitted linen sleeves, his lashes low as he dragged the blade across his skin. A few long, golden-brown strands of hair loosened from his queue and hung alongside his cheeks, swaying with each movement and dragging her eyes toward his proud chin, the distinct dip of his Adam's apple, and the narrow, open shirt collar framing a smattering of dark curls. Her thighs tensed, and an intense heat pooled within her lower belly.

"Did you enjoy your night with John?" he asked.

Clara jerked, guilted by her staring. "No," she said. "He was a complete doddypole, and only half as charming as a dirt clod."

Benjamin laughed. "Come now, there's no need to insult dirt clods."

Clara fought a smile of her own, and once their eyes locked, a deeper warmth settled in her stomach. "You make that look so easy," she said, indicating his blade. "Are you certain I can't help?"

A wry smile tipped the corner of Benjamin's mouth. "*Very* certain. Thank you." Cleaning the straight razor in his shaving bowl, he smoothed the blade over his other cheek. "What about Dr. Wagner reminded you of a dirt clod?"

This time, Clara's smile blossomed unfettered. "You're really enjoying this, aren't you?"

"What? Am I not allowed?" An embittered quality overtook his face, stark and filled with shadows. "I enjoy so very little as of late."

Clara softened. "You may not want to hear it, Ben, but you're very lucky." When he curled his lip at her, she argued, "No, you really are. Your father...he is so warm and loving and kind. You may lack the ability to stand, but you have no shortage of love in this house. I confess I envy you."

Incredulous, Benjamin stopped shaving. "Why? Are you saying you'd wish for my life over yours?"

"Yes...I daresay I would." Shoulders slouching, she amended, "I know you do not have it easy, and I do love my sisters more than anything, but...until tonight, I'd never known what it was like to have a paternal figure care about me as a person, and without an ulterior motive." She shrugged. "Wouldn't you agree that love is more important than mobility?"

Benjamin frowned. "That's easy for you to say. *You* can still walk."

"Yes, I can," Clara agreed, "but being able to walk, being just like all the rest, is hardly a consolation, Ben. Being loved and cared for and respected is what matters."

Avoiding her gaze, Benjamin continued dragging his straight razor across his face, his movements sharp and stilted.

"You disagree," she accused. His face soured, and she sighed. "You only disagree because we are never appreciative of what we have."

"No," Benjamin coolly said. "I disagree because my father, my best friend, and a socialite are all waiting on me hand and foot, as though I am some life-sucking leech! Ever since my affliction started, I have brought nothing to the table."

"Well, you're not completely useless...you are an excellent paperweight," Clara teased. When he didn't crack a smile, she sighed and lowered the mirror. "I don't know why I bothered coming back here."

"Why did you come back?" Benjamin agreed, taking the cloth and wiping his face. "For someone who hates 'rebel scum' so much, you're certainly quick to horn in on my affairs."

Clara bristled. "After all that's happened, after everything we've been through together, can you truly believe I'd be so callous as to disregard your feelings? I am a loyalist, but I'm not a monster, Ben. I had hoped that by this point, you could see that."

Benjamin faltered, setting aside the cloth.

When he did so, Clara noted the bloom of red on his cheek and winced, her hand instinctively drawing to his face. "Oh," she breathed. "Oh, goodness, you've cut yourself..." Snatching the cloth from his lap, she took his chin and dabbed at the bleeding cut. Benjamin jerked at her sudden closeness, his eyes averting as she applied pressure to the wound.

"I am not an invalid," he groused. Wincing at the tragic irony, he amended, "That is to say, I can take care of myself."

"Of course, you can," Clara agreed. "But you don't have to be so stubborn all the time, you know. You are *allowed* to ask for help."

Hesitant, Benjamin slid his hand up her arm and encircled her wrist, anchoring her palm against his cheek. His eyes grew despairing as he appraised her face. "I need your help," he whispered.

Help me forget. Help me stop feeling so worthless, so empty...

With a shivering breath, he leaned forward and pressed into the giving rush of her mouth, his free hand tangling through her hair and drawing her lips into his more strongly. Clara stiffened against him, but then both of her hands gripped his shirt, and she angled into his kiss, drinking of him with such ardor that his head spun.

Tugging and pulling and yanking, he attempted to get closer still. Opening his mouth beneath hers, he cradled her face between his hands and devoured her every breath, a stab of elation swelling between his ribs once he realized he was wanted. He would never give up in battle, but this? *This,* he wished to succumb to completely—his very own personal surrender.

Her touch lit through his bloodstream like a bonfire, and once he deepened the kiss with an explorative roll of his tongue, her palm struck harshly against his cheek. An explosion of pain followed, and she jerked back in a fury.

"Don't you dare," Clara seethed at him. "Don't you dare confuse me like this! I've been used, abused by enough men in my life, so don't you add to it just because you're in pain! You either care for me or you don't! And by God, if the answer is no, I don't want you *ever* touching me again!"

Benjamin quivered. "Clara..."

She shoved herself free of his hold, then threw the bloodied cloth into his lap. Tears sprang from her eyes, and as he fumblingly reached for her hand, she smacked him away. "I said no!" she warned. "If you think I'll allow myself to be whipped back and forth, you are sadly mistaken!"

"I'm sorry," Benjamin choked. "Please, Clara..." His vision

blurred with tears. *Please, don't leave me. Please, please don't.*

Clara faltered, genuine pity flooding across her features, but then she spun about and rushed for the safety of the hall. The door slamming shut reverberated like a gunshot through his chest, and with a feeble cry, Benjamin tugged on his hair and gave in to all the sorrow, the hurt that had consumed him ever since the start of this reprehensible war.

CHAPTER TWENTY-ONE
Trials of the Heart

WHY DID HE destroy everything he touched? Was it because he, himself, was broken? Benjamin hadn't meant to hurt her; he hadn't meant to wound Clara, yet the moment she'd drawn away from him, he'd seen all the anguish in the world welling within her bright eyes. He'd recognized it and empathized with it, because he, too, saw that very same pain in his own gaze each time he peered into a looking glass.

Was it wrong of him to kiss her? Yes, it was, because Benjamin could no longer do for Clara what men like John Wagner could. He couldn't take her dancing, nor go arm in arm for a stroll, nor sneak off at night for a lover's assignation. The thought nearly wounded him more than the injury itself. All he could offer was his intellect, his heart, and Benjamin knew Clara would never be content with limitations.

Embittered, he remained in bed bearing the sting of yesterday's cut—the wound she'd tended to—while drinking today's laudanum. The taste was as bitter as his mood, and Benjamin devoured the tincture in three eager swallows.

That was when the door opened. Nearly choking into the wooden cup, he set it aside with a graceless fumble. Clara entered with a tray of food in hand, her eyes downcast while her mouth remained pinched and sour. Her entire demeanor screamed of disagreement, so Benjamin chose not to speak. He'd already done more than enough damage.

"Good morning," Clara muttered. "Your father and I made buttered eggs."

Benjamin flashed a doubting smile. "*You* made buttered eggs?"

"All right, so I only grated the nutmeg," she replied, still unsmiling. "You would've known I helped with yesterday's batch too, had you not been so cross with me."

Benjamin winced. "I know I deserve that…and I'm sorry."

Wordless, Clara came over and set the tray into his lap. "I trust you don't need anything else?"

He hesitated, torn, before suggesting, "Just your forgiveness."

"For what?" Her gaze grew sharp and piercing.

"For everything…but for last night, in particular."

Her mouth twisted. "Ah. So you are sorry for kissing me?"

"What? No!" Benjamin earnestly shook his head. "No, no, never that, but…I am sorry I hurt you." Expression doleful, he explained, "In case it isn't obvious, I am rather terrible at expressing how I feel."

Clara's gaze remained frigid, but there was a slight softening around her mouth. "I'm going for a walk with your father," she deflected. "If something comes up between now and the time we return, it will have to wait." Glancing toward the whiskey bottle on his nightstand, she coolly added, "Then again, you might not remember what you need."

Benjamin flushed. "That's part of my tincture regimen."

"Yes, well, Mother's physician prescribes much the same." Clara shrugged. "Sometimes, I daresay she doesn't remember she even *has* a family, let alone obligations beyond her drunken stupors." Turning on her heel, she muttered, "Good day to you, Captain."

Benjamin tried to reply, to stop her and further explain himself, but she'd already stepped into the hallway and shut the door.

THE ROLLING HILLS overlooking placid, endless blue instilled in Clara a peace she'd never before experienced. Though she also lived by the water, there wasn't the same urgency here in Freyview. She could pretend this was her life. She could pretend she was *free*. And while strolling alongside Josiah Hoskin, she almost believed it.

"What do you think?" Josiah asked, nudging her to attention.

Clara shaded her eyes beneath her hand and smiled, stepping along the grassy knoll overlooking the gleaming sea. "I adore it," she told him. "I think you're lucky to have such a closeknit community. Where I am from, we had friends growing up, but we live primarily in seclusion. So many have moved in and out of the city that it never felt safe to grow attached."

"Attachments are hard," Josiah agreed, "especially with houses divided over war. Sometimes, it seems human connection isn't worth it, that we're better off alone and safeguarding our hearts. But God didn't create us to be solitary beings. We all find one another for a reason."

Clara blinked at him, amazed. "You really think so? You believe I was intentionally brought into your world?"

"Of course! You may not feel your worth, but I promise your influence has been felt, and most especially by my son."

All at once, Clara stiffened. "Yes, I agree. I've pushed him toward an increasingly foul temperament."

"Nonsense!" Josiah cried. "He is certainly disagreeable. Many men in his position would be. But I know my son, and had you not intervened, he would be far, *far* worse. He doesn't like to appear weak, so having an audience adds to his stubbornness."

Clara looked away, electing to ignore the dull, cutting ache across her heart. "What was he like before the war?" she asked.

Embarrassed, she quickly amended, "If you don't mind my asking, of course."

"Why would I? We men of the cloth are supposed to be open books, so you can ask me absolutely anything…within reason." Josiah chuckled. "Benjamin before the war, though…" He hesitated, his eyes instantly losing their pleasant twinkle. "It was a simpler time. He was quiet, but mischievous, introspective and eager for knowledge. One afternoon, he caused an uproar by taking several books up to his favorite reading spot. He completely lost track of time, not realizing that his friend's father had reported them stolen."

Masking her smile, Clara said, "I am not surprised. Although Benjamin acts ignorant about certain topics, he is very keen to learn." All at once, memories of his hands on her waist and his mouth on hers, clumsy and eager while she gave clear, equally enthusiastic instruction, caused her cheeks to flood pink, and an intense, unmistakable heat to flare up beneath her fichu.

Unaware of her yearning, Josiah continued, "Benjamin loves just about any book! Nature, too. Even when he was older, I'd catch him tending to the garden out back, simply because roses were his mother's favorite."

Clara sobered at that, her blush fading. "You have a garden?"

"Only the best in Freyview! I wouldn't expect you to have noticed, given how it's a bit off to the side," Josiah replied. "The garden's my domain, admittedly, but whenever he can, Benjamin insists upon caring for the roses." He spared Clara a sad smile. "Don't tell him I told you, but I believe he tends them to keep his mother alive…as if she is still here. I've overheard him talking to her many a time." Chin quivering, he confessed, "I talk to her sometimes myself. I've God to guide my path, but things would be far simpler, were she here by my side. Lorraine would know how to help our Benjamin."

"I'm so sorry," Clara murmured. "If it eases your mind at all, I think you are a wonderful father. My parents…w-well…" She winced, feeling selfish. "Sometimes, it's as if they might as well be dead. They don't care about me. Not really."

When Josiah grunted in disbelief, Clara agreed, "I'd like to think my parents love me, but you know what they say: Actions speak louder than words."

"Indeed, they do," Josiah allowed, "but whether or not your parents love you is irrelevant. God loves you. *We* love you. And our home will always be yours for as long as you need." He touched her shoulder. "I pray it isn't selfish to hope it'll be for a long, long time."

Clara's eyes welled up and she drew a breath, overcome by his devotion. This wasn't right... As much as it pained her, he deserved to know the truth.

"Josiah..." With a shaking swallow, she tried again, "There is something you should know..."

"Traitors!"

Whirling about, Clara gasped as three men descended upon the scene. In a rush, Josiah cut in front of her, protectively drawing her behind.

"What seems to be the trouble here, gentlemen?" he asked. Despite the fierce look to these reprobates, his tone remained unshaken.

The ringleader, a farmer named Randolph Fritz, fiercely spat at their feet. "Nothin' at'tall, Reverend. Just takin' a walk."

"As are we," Josiah replied, "so I'd suggest you be on your way."

"And why's that?" he pressed. "In'nit true you're no longer wieldin' a musket? Seems a lil' unwise to threaten us." Gaze sliding toward Clara, he added, "We just wanna welcome the new rebel to the community."

Clara paled. "Rebel? But...b-but I am not a patriot!"

A second man spat on the grass. "You're livin' with the Hoskinses," he growled. "You're no loyalist!"

All at once, two of the men swarmed upon Josiah and rendered him incapacitated, holding his arms while Randolph swung his fist into the older man's gut. Josiah cried out and doubled over, winded, and the men laughed while Clara screamed at them to stop.

When they ignored her, a fury licked across her heart unlike any other. Josiah wasn't meant to be treated as a traitor; he had the heart of a rebel, but he was not deserving of punishment!

Blinded by emotion, Clara rushed forward and threw herself onto the back of the nearest man, shrieking while scratching at his neck, face, and shoulders, and whatever stray inch of him she could manage. "Let go of him, you cur!" she snarled. "Let go!"

Unfortunately, Randolph had his arms free and easily wrenched her to the ground. Clara yelped once he trapped her beneath his boot.

"Please!" Josiah cried. "Do whatever you wish to me, but have mercy on the girl!"

Randolph bared his crooked teeth. "What, y'mean the way you rebels had mercy on my wife?"

Josiah closed his eyes, consumed by pity. "Randolph, what happened was an atrocity. An anomaly, I assure you, because most patriots are good people who—"

"Deserve to *die,* that's what!" Furious, he seized a hunting knife from his belt. "I'mma do to this rebel doggess what they did to my Molly!"

With furious tears in his eyes, he returned his attention to Clara, whose shoulder he kept pinned beneath his boot. She swung with one arm while the other went to his ankle, and once he knelt with the glimmering knife, she tipped back her head and screamed.

AMOS HAD BEEN heading toward the Hoskin residence when he heard the cry. Alarmed, he spun around and around before settling on the direction, then took off into a sprint.

The screaming continued at a frantic decibel, and removing his dirk from its scabbard, he dodged errant tree roots and unstable terrain before staggering into the fray.

"Fritz!" he called, beckoning to the ringleader.

The farmer halted, lifting his head while Clara sobbed and struggled. Curling his upper lip, he spat, "This don't concern you, McQuinn! Get along!"

Hefting the weight of his blade, Amos replied, "See, that's the trouble: You're hurtin' a mighty nice lass, *and* our good ol' friend, the reverend. That wholly makes it me concern."

The two men restraining Josiah exchanged glances but didn't make a move to attack.

"I don't wanna hurt'cha," Amos continued, "but if y'don't let 'er go, I'mma cut your knob off."

Randolph laughed in disbelief. The distraction was enough for Clara to slam her knee against his groin. He doubled over with a howl, and she crawled free of his hold.

"You doggess!" he snarled.

Amos raced forward with his dirk. Randolph clumsily rose and lifted his knife, but wasn't fast enough. Amos's boot connected square against his chest, and the man jerked with a stunned *oof!*, barely able to fend off the following uppercut across his chin.

"Clara," Amos called to her, "run!"

Frantic, she staggered to her feet but didn't obey his order. She couldn't with Josiah still entrapped. Dismayed by the swelling bruise on his cheek and faintly bleeding cut beneath his left eye, she realized it must have occurred during her scuffle with Randolph. Josiah had sworn to never harm another soul, so rather than fight, he had shouted to the high heavens, struggling against Fritz's men and begging for her life to be spared.

Tears nipped at her eyes and she drew a breath. Her life was far from exemplary, and in that moment, Clara wished she was worthy of the woman he perceived her to be.

"Clara!" Amos called again, side-stepping Randolph's punch. "Get out of here!"

"I…I-I can't!" she cried. Drawing a hand to her throat, Clara realized with increasing dizziness that she was finding it difficult to breathe. Her garments felt as though they were squeezing her ribs, and as she attempted to take deeper, calmer breaths, she only succeeded in hyperventilating.

They're going to die, she fearfully thought. *They are going to die, and it's all my fault!*

Swallowing a scream, her vision dipped and spun, and staggering as though drunk, Clara collapsed before her world bled into shadow.

BENJAMIN SLEPT AWAY most of the morning. His buttered eggs lay untouched on his nightstand, and groggy, he fumblingly reached for his bath chair, which sat waiting for him flush against his bed. In some ways, the laudanum worked a little too well. His mind was hazy, yet he felt calm, peaceful, and his limbs were loose as he struggled to heft himself into the seat. Using his arms to support himself, Benjamin dragged the dead weight of his legs out of bed and nearly lost his balance once he collapsed into the chair.

Huffing and puffing from exertion, he clenched his teeth and closed his eyes. That was when he heard the commotion out front.

Alarmed, Benjamin grabbed the large wheels at the back and attempted to push himself forward, but it was no use. The chair could not be self-propelled. While he struggled, the frantic shouts out front continued. "Father?" he called. *"Father?"*

He heard a sob, and with a spike of panic in his breast, Benjamin sobered enough to grab the bell at his bedside and ring it with fierce impatience.

That was when Amos appeared in the doorway.

"What's going on?" Benjamin demanded, tasting bile. "What happened?"

Expression grave, Amos crossed the room and grabbed the handles on his chair, pushing him toward the door. "Tories," he explained. "They got the drop on Clara an' your father, but I got to 'em before they...b-before she..." He grimaced, shaking his head. "The important thing is, Miss Boyd's unharmed. Her sensibilities, on the other hand..."

Horrified by this flood of news, Benjamin jerked as though struck in the chest. Despite his gratitude toward Amos, a wave of hopelessness crashed over him, harsh and all-consuming. He couldn't have saved Clara even if he wanted to. He was immobile, helpless, and left to the mercy of every man, woman, and even child in town.

Overcome, he tightened his hold on the armrests and swallowed, his heart jangling between his ribs. Amos rolled him toward the front of the house, where they found Josiah cradling Clara protectively beneath his chin.

An instant spike of fury charged through Benjamin's frame. "Where are the assailants?" he demanded. "The constable should know of this!"

Amos's mouth bitterly quirked. "Y'know there's no law now," he said, guiding him to a stop. "None that people are willin' to listen to, anyway. It's brother versus brother, an' neighbor versus neighbor. I jus' took me fist to three men I normally get along with jus' fine. Thankfully, a group o' hunters came along an' scared 'em off."

Rageful fear coiled within his stomach like a viper, and looking beseechingly at Josiah, Benjamin asked, "Are you all right? Your face...it's—"

"I'm fine," the reverend cut in, soothingly brushing his hand over Clara's mussed hair. "I wasn't their intended target."

Appraising Clara more fully, Benjamin took note of her grass-stained clothes, and the wrath within his gut ignited from a spark to a blaze. "I want names," he commanded. "Give me their names, and I'll—"

"Do *nothing*," Clara cut in, her voice wobbly. Wiping a hand over her eyes, she withdrew from Josiah's embrace and turned to Benjamin. Despite her trembling chin, there was a fiery resolve to her gaze. "It's finally time to act. Not you, not Corporal McQuinn, but *me*. I never want to feel that helpless again."

Benjamin blinked at her, astonished. "B-but—"

"Whatever you're doing, I want to help," she continued. "You may have your flaws, but you have never once stooped to what my own side has just done. At heart, I will remain supportive of the Crown, but at the end of the day, all I want is to protect my sisters. And I truly believe that men of your caliber will be the ones to save this land from ruin." Shoulders curling, she drew a breath and looked to Josiah. "In short, I have not been truthful with you," she confessed. "I am not a patriot. My father is one of the most influential, staunch loyalists in all the colonies."

The tragic fondness in Josiah's eyes remained. "I didn't imagine so," he softly said. "Whenever we first cooked together, you could scarcely figure out my utensils. No caretaker, or at least, no good one, can't at the very least figure out how to grate nutmeg."

A tearful laugh bubbled in Clara's throat. "Then…you are not angry?"

"Of course not." He gently pressed her arm. "Some of my dearest friends are staunch Tories. I'd never turn you away over the convictions in your heart. As long as you are praying for guidance, that's all we can do. It isn't my place to say whether or not you're right or wrong. And besides…" He looked to Benjamin. "You are being harbored under the protection of my son. I trust his judgment implicitly."

Benjamin locked eyes with his father, and a painful lump swelled in his throat. He knew then that he could potentially fix his wrongs and use Clara, just as she requested.

"If you're serious about assisting me, I have an idea, Miss

Boyd," he spoke. "I was wrong to think you would be safest here. Clearly, there isn't a place anyone can be wholly protected, not in this unholy war. But at home with your family, where you belong, is inevitably the best path moving forward." He nodded to her. "By morning's light, Amos will escort you home."

Clara jerked. "But...b-but I am not welcome there. My father—"

"Will take you back," Benjamin assured her, "because I am going to give you false information."

Here, a frayed smile lifted the corners of his mouth, and Clara realized this was the first time that light, *true* light, had entered his eyes since his paralysis. "How do you mean?"

Nodding toward Amos, Benjamin said, "I'll falsify a letter, one that includes regimental statistics, a ledger on weaponry, and general information regarding Washington's next move. If you take it to your father and claim you were held captive by rebels, spied on them before your escape, and stole a Continental missive, I can guarantee he'll not only take you back, but pass that information along to British officers."

A stab of unease swelled through Clara's breast. "But...what happens to me when that information proves false?"

"Nothing," he assured her. "In war, plans change. They are forced to change, in fact, so no one will think ill of your source. Not when my name is on the dotted line."

"Your name?" she echoed, aghast. "Captain, if my father sees your name on our correspondence, he'll ensure you're hunted down and strung up for treason."

Benjamin shook his head. "Not if he believes he can get information," he insisted. "As far as I am aware, he never learned my true surname. Still, you make a valid point... Perhaps we should amend your story to this: Major Yates abducted you for ransom purposes, and during your imprisonment at camp, a young captain grew fond of you and helped with your escape. Unfortunately for him, you did not share in his affections but allowed him to believe as such to glean information and earn your freedom."

Clara hummed, still skeptical. "And this captain's name will be?"

"You can tell your father whatever name you wish, but I plan on signing my name as Apollo," he said. "Back in college, my classmates teased me for being proficient at everything thrown my way; and seeing how Apollo is the Greek god of so many of my interests—music, poetry, archery, you name it—that became my moniker. This will make it seem like you have a secret admirer, *and* it'll protect my identity. What do you think?"

Clara held up a hand. "I cannot be a blackguard," she said. "Spies are scum—cowards. I'm only betraying my values for the sake of ending this war, and I was hoping you would have something far less repugnant for me to do."

Bewildered, Benjamin shook his head. "But this is the way to end the war, and I promise your side is doing the very same. It's why Bishop enacted this operation in the first place."

She looked between him and Amos. "Operation?"

"It's a whole network," Benjamin explained. "Bishop's the head of intelligence, Amos and I are two of his agents, and there are a handful of couriers who forward our information. And you will be part of that group as well, should you accept."

Glancing at Josiah, who offered her an encouraging smile, Clara nervously twisted her hands. She'd known Benjamin was a rebel spy but hadn't realized how deeply entrenched this whole scheme was.

"How is my role to remain secret?" she asked. "The British officers had knowledge of you beforehand."

Benjamin faltered, considerably thrown. "Officers have my name? As in, associated with a spy mission?"

She shook her head. "Not quite. The man Corporal McQuinn killed, the man who..." Awkwardly, Clara gestured to his bath chair, then continued, "Yates is the one who aided your head of intelligence, and passed along tactical plans to the British."

Swearing under his breath, Benjamin pressed, "Are you sure?

They know my identity?"

"No." Clara shook her head. "What I meant was, Yates gave the British tactical plans and made mention of you, but *without* your name. To my understanding, he was hoping to offer you as some sort of trade. It was better for him to keep an advantage, should things go wrong."

Relief flooded Benjamin's features. "Good," he said, nodding. "It's not ideal, but we'll still have an edge since Bishop relieved me of my post. No one will suspect us."

Amos hummed. "I haven't yet received word from Bishop, but I'm sure he'll still wanna use me for intelligence gatherin'."

"So let him use you," Benjamin agreed, "but in the meantime, try to be there for Clara and myself, too. Write Bishop and let him know our intentions. He needs to be aware that she's on our side." He looked at the redhead, who'd grown increasingly pale during this exchange. "Don't fret. Since our methods of communication are too complex to learn overnight, we will be using invisible ink and mask letters."

Blinking rapidly, Clara echoed, "Invisible…? Uh?"

"I'll give a demonstration after dinner," he promised. "With the latter method, you hold the mask over the letter you've written, and a cut-out reveals the true message. Again, that might be too complex for you, so we'll begin our correspondence with the ink. We'll write something trivial to one another. I'll occasionally feed you false information, since I imagine your father will want our correspondence to continue. Underneath the regular message, we will write our intended updates in the invisible formula. These letters will be placed into a dead drop in the woods. You and Amos will work this out together, so that way, nothing can ever get intercepted."

Clara opened and closed her mouth, overwhelmed.

Sensing her distress, Benjamin said, "I know it's a lot to take in, but—"

"It's far more than just 'a lot,'" she said. "You are talking sheer fiddle-faddle! Masks and falsehoods, and invisible ink? What kind of sorcery are you enacting for this cause?"

"Oi, it's no sorcery," Amos assured her. "It's the work o' chemistry! That means—"

"I know what chemistry is, you loggerhead." Glancing toward Josiah, Clara flushed and amended, "My apologies. I am just so terribly overwhelmed…"

"As I said, I'll walk you through it," Benjamin promised. "It's not just the cause that's on the line, but your safety."

His eyes took on an earnest, pleading sheen that left her reeling, and Clara jumped when Josiah's hand came upon her shoulder.

"I'll tend to dinner," he announced. "Why don't the three of your keep discussing your new venture?" Gently squeezing her against his side, he added, "I'm so glad you're all right, Miss Boyd. So wholly, utterly glad."

Josiah hugged her once more, and as he headed off to the outdoor kitchen, Clara's heart shattered and reassembled from his affections, affections she assuredly did *not* deserve.

Amos cleared his throat. "Weeeell, I'mma head out me'self," he said. "If I'm takin' Miss Boyd back tomorrow, I'd like to prepare."

Benjamin nodded. "Very well. When should we expect you?"

"Bright an' early, so be up an' at 'em." He pointed a finger at Clara in warning, then grinned before making his departure.

The silence that followed was heavy, suffocating, and with a sliver of nerves roiling within her breast, Clara turned to Benjamin and blurted, "I actually have to leave, as well. Ah…to help your father."

Benjamin's hand shot out and clasped firmly around her wrist, halting her frantic escape. His gaze was soft and plaintive, and as they locked eyes, his grip loosened and he gently stroked her wrist. "I'm so glad you're all right," he murmured. "And I thank you…for being willing to help, even if you don't believe in our cause."

Clara remained stock-still, hating how she wanted, no, needed the torment of his hands on her skin. With her pulse thrumming wildly in her throat, she managed a soft, "I may not believe in your cause, Ben, but I do believe in you."

Benjamin's features warmed at her words, clearly touched. "Clara, I...I-I don't know what to say..."

With his eyes glowing akin to fireflies at dusk, he squeezed her hand, but she jerked herself free of his grip. "I'll see you after dinner, Captain," she said. "Please be patient with me...I imagine I'll need extensive instruction."

When his gaze remained yearnful, incendiary, she drew a breath and quickly broke away from him, rushing to the kitchen to escape this cursed snare of her own making.

CHAPTER TWENTY-TWO

Letters

14 June 1779

Dear Captain,

I apologize for the delayed response, but my life has been a whirlwind this past fortnight. I've reunited with my beloved sisters, and they are understandably fraught with worry. I have also met Charlotte's fiancé, Philip Ashby. You will be delighted to know you are (surprisingly) more personable. Your backside is far more appealing, as well.

Now that I've properly scandalized you, I can move on to the heart of the matter. We parted on rather abrupt terms, so I am writing to see how you are faring. Despite our differing loyalties, I do enjoy your company.

Sincerely,
Clara

[Hidden correspondence]

Forgive the short letter, but I didn't feel safe speaking candidly. You were right. Father did accept my story and has encouraged me to write under the guise of friendship. He wished to proofread my letter to ensure I am not being too transparent, which is why I hid this one and created a false version. From here on out, I will write two letters: one for you, and one for his approval.

I'm afraid nothing of import has occurred since my

departure, but that may actually be a godsend. I'll let you know if anything changes.

-CB

23 June 1779

Dear Miss Boyd,

Thank you for inquiring about my health. I've been a little unwell, but the doctor's regimen has raised my spirits. As for the rest of your letter, I know you are trying to shock me, so I am returning the favor by not taking the bait.

I, too, enjoy our unorthodox talks, so I hope you'll allow me the pleasure of a continued correspondence.

Sincerely,
Apollo

[Hidden correspondence]

A decoy would be perfect. The only problem is, what I state here might not coincide with your false letter, so it would behoove you to warn me of any major discrepancies. In fact, since my letters are being placed into the dead drop, and thus, shouldn't fall into his hands, it might be best if you forge a letter that coincides with yours, and then burn my own. Either that, or pretend we haven't corresponded until I have something worthy to share.

Although I've already briefed you on what you need to search for, please heed this reminder for your safety: While keeping watch in the city, do not needlessly endanger yourself. You are smart and capable, and I have the utmost confidence you'll thrive in this position.

-BH

2 July 1779

Dear Captain,

It would seem my father's favor with the British has officially dissolved. As of last week, we've been forced to billet like every other unlucky cur in town. Some soldiers chose not to stay, and instead have taken our hay, wheat, rye, and other provisions under a requisition order. Our animals—including my favorite horse, rot them!—were taken as well, while we've been forced into the servants' quarters to make room for the King's Men. Father claims he'd give his very life for our king, yet I can tell he is displeased by the inconvenience. It's quite different from donating of our own accord.

Sincerely,
Clara

[Hidden correspondence]

I felt no need to hide my feelings, seeing how Father's too distracted to be bothered with our letters. Still, I have taken all your suggestions to heart and will abide by them. Furthermore, I've made it my mission to listen in on every conversation in which these soldiers partake.

According to one of the officers, a man named Peter Richardson, someone who's been spying for the British head of intelligence, is serving in a New Jersey loyalist militia. I must confess, I've known about him ever since the public assembly I attended with Dr. Wagner. I did not, however, realize the extent of his involvement, nor his importance. As I'm sure you can guess, Richardson is pretending to be a patriot sympathizer, and thus, is feeding rebels false information. From what I've gathered, he will be traveling to New Windsor, New York, near your commander's headquarters, so I pray you make haste. I know not of his intentions, just that he is gathering intelligence and planting lies into the mouths of whomever will listen.

-CB

10 July 1779

Dear Miss Boyd,

I am happy to hear your present situation is treating you well. Despite our political disagreements, I find it honorable that you stick to your principles, something that these days, many assuredly fail to do.

My courier is headed for Fairfield tomorrow. He is to meet with a Connecticut platoon that plans to attack, and hopefully recapture, Fort Black Rock from the British. It pains me that I can't join him. Although I am unable to be in the thick of battle, he informed me that our troop numbers are low. The hope is the British will be weakened from their prior skirmish earlier this month.

Forgive me for going on about this, as I am certain a lady of your position has no interest. Thank you for indulging me. Say a prayer for their safe venture, won't you?

Sincerely,
Apollo

[Hidden correspondence]

I didn't feel it wise to respond to your plight in the open, because I need you to inform your father of the Fairfield attack. This is a decoy so they will hopefully send reinforcements elsewhere. Instead of Fairfield, Amos revealed that Washington intends to attack Stony Point, New York, under the guise of night.

In regards to Peter Richardson, why didn't you tell me sooner? I'm concerned that he, too, might know of Washington's plans for Stony Point, but given his location, I am cautiously optimistic. This decoy should at the very least put a stop to that concern, should it arise.

-BH

23 July 1779

Dear Captain,

You're too kind to hold me in such high regard. Either way, you are right. As a woman of society, I do not wish to dwell upon war. Instead, I hope you'll allow me to regale you with much happier news.

Earlier this week, Mr. Ashby returned to Philadelphia, so I took Charlotte to a local bookseller for a distraction. She was rather unbearable, you see, given how deeply she's grown to adore him, so I purchased her John Cleland's *Memoirs of a Woman of Pleasure* to serve as a distraction. I must confess, I thought of you. Charlotte's blush was reminiscent of the time I gave you Jacob Rueff's *The Expert Midwife*. Tell me, Captain, have you any news on that front? Do you have complete, unbridled knowledge of the female body? Or are you to disappoint me yet again, and confess you never truly gave it a read?

With all these avenues of excitement, I suppose I'll leave you to your thoughts. I imagine you have much to reflect upon.

Complacent and Unashamed,
Clara

[Hidden correspondence]

Forgive me if I spoke out of turn. You surely understand how darling I find your embarrassment, and I wasn't lying when I said I am tired of war discussion. At the very least, I'd prefer to only speak of the cause in our hidden correspondence, as opposed to focusing solely on it throughout these letters. If I am only to speak of war, I'll go mad.

In regards to Peter Richardson, when would I have told you? Should I have brought it up after you implied I was a harlot, perhaps? Or maybe after you kissed me? Either way, I was never beholden to you, nor your cause, and I'm still not. To be frank, my allegiance lies with my sisters and the assurance of their safety. Alas, protection under the King's Men no longer seems to be that path.

I've heard about the patriot victory at Stony Point. Despite the fact it gives me no pleasure to hear of the Crown's loss, you have my congratulations, Captain. It seems your plan worked. Admittedly, I feel guilty... Is the blood of those men on my hands since I, myself, am the one who delivered the fatal misinformation? Major Markham and his men were involved, you realize. He is alive, but...what of the others he undoubtedly loved? What of those I've met in passing?

I don't know how you can stand it, Ben. Does it not haunt you? Do you not feel bad, knowing how the victims of that attack will never return to their homes and families? Because I mind. I mind very much, indeed.

-CB

3 August 1779

Dear Miss Boyd,

I must confess, for the longest time, I was at a loss on how to address your filthy talk. I imagine your parents never speak that way, so the mind wonders where you've acquired such behavior. Regardless, I cannot claim innocence in light of my eagerness for knowledge, and inexplicably, I'm starting to view your commentary as charming...a charm that's very much an acquired taste, but a charm, nevertheless.

I've a considerable amount of time on my hands

these days, so I will read any and all recommendations you have. Please don't make me regret this decision.

Sincerely,
Apollo

[Hidden correspondence]

I apologized before, so all I can do is echo my shame. I was cruel and unkind, and I hate how I spoke to you that night. I enjoy your company, Clara, and our lives in Freyview are quite bleak without you. Before your stay, I cannot recall the last time Father was so warm and free of spirit. I'm of the firm belief that you have saved him—the both of us.

Although I'm horrified to learn of Major Markham's misfortune, I am equally relieved of his safety. Regardless of our differing sides, he is a good man. I'm not so blinded that I cannot see that.

In the way of guilt, I doubt this will be of any comfort, but it does get easier. I'm certain you were hoping for a more concrete answer, but the truth is, I cannot give you that. What I can give is the assurance that you don't have to fight this alone. But with that said, if you are having second thoughts, I need to know immediately. Please don't shield me from your feelings.

-BH

18 August 1779

Dear Apollo,

Apologies for the delayed letter. I've been absolutely distraught by the disarray in town, and needed time to process.

Earlier this week, I happened upon a crowd gathered on Chatham Row. A man was being flogged. His crime, I learned, was for being out past curfew the night prior,

and several officers were making an example of his disobedience. I left soon after, seeing how I couldn't bear the
sight of those deep, grotesque stripes upon his back.

As if that were not enough, I later heard about a merchant being murdered right in his shop, simply for asking
a royal officer to pay what he was owed. It is intolerable,
Captain! Have things always been so cruel, or had I purposely put on blinders to avoid seeing the king's cause as
anything but exemplary? Mind you, patriots are no saints.
There is plenty of violence from their end, as well, but
seeing how I am in a loyalist area, the hatred against
rebels is far more rampant.

Thank you for the much-needed distraction of discussing books. I assure you, I'll be happy to compile a list
for your perusal. Give me some time. I want to ensure
you receive the very best!

Affectionately Yours,
Clara

[Hidden correspondence]

I've realized this evil is normal now, and the only way to
combat it, to stop it, is to aid in your fight. So yes, as
much as it pains me, I will continue helping you. Ending
this bloodshed is far more important than my discomfort.

In regards to events worthy of note, the British are
searching every man, woman, and child leaving Manhattan. I've heard talk amongst the officers that there is
suspicion of espionage on the route your courier(s?) take,
though it's unclear how this information has been ob-
tained. It seems some redcoats found critical evidence
during a raid, but to what extent, I cannot be sure. Because of this, I implore your couriers to use caution. If
they are apprehended in the city, they'd assuredly hang.
Just so you know, I have still been burning your letters
and creating decoys, just in case Father needs to see

them.

Please take care of yourself, Ben. Stay safe.

P.S. Against my better judgment, I must reciprocate your sentiments. Please be sure to pass on my affections to your father. I miss him terribly.
-CB

29 August 1779

Dear Clara,

I'll never gloat, nor rub your face into what I have already known. If nothing else, this war has despaired me to the human condition, of what evils we are capable…myself included. I've harmed, maimed, stolen, and killed in this battle for our nation's independence, and I pray I will be forgiven my trespasses. I once told you I am doing this for God's glory, but now I'm not sure. What if I am doing it for my own? For vengeance?

With that said, I am aggrieved you've discovered this truth so harshly. It seems that man, no matter how bolstered by the will of God, can still be prone to evil. I pray this is not the case for myself.

In the way of books, I love to read. I always have, and I always will. Though when it comes to your selection, I trust you can understand my reluctance. At least try and throw in something scholarly, if you wouldn't mind?

Most Affectionately Yours,
Apollo

[Hidden correspondence]

Just to be wise, I implore you to wait at least one month to write. Hopefully by then, the British checkpoints will be far less aggressive. On the positive side of matters, that should give you ample time to create a list of books.

I also intend to stay safe. I need to prove once and for

all that I am not a prude, and in order to do that, I need to be alive. Although it may not be of any real comfort, the British won't come for me here in Freyview. Even if they discovered I am your source, and not "Apollo" from the Continental encampment, they would need me to stay in the field, seeing how I'm more likely to give away valuable intelligence unawares, rather than by force. The true man in danger would be your father since it'd appear he is shielding me. For his sake (and my couriers'), I will exercise more caution.

This is our final correspondence, at least for now. Despite my better judgment, I am going to miss you.

-BH

16 December 1779

Dear Apollo,

I wanted to write you in time for the holiday. Seeing how you are a preacher's boy, I imagine your home must be teeming with visitors. How is your father? He never got to show me his garden, and from time to time, I find myself daydreaming about how it must look. Before Mother became a drunken stain on society, she tended to a garden of her very own. I believe it granted her a sense of purpose, because once Father demanded our servants take over—he deemed it *improper* for a lady—she withered away and became a shell of the woman she once was. I used to help her with the planting, if you could believe it. I didn't tell your father, for fear of overstepping, but should he ever need a hand, I can lend my aid quite well. I've heard you are rather gifted with gardening, yourself, and with roses, specifically.

Although I don't wish to dwell upon sad things this holiday season, something you wrote stood out to me: vengeance. Vengeance for what? Who has wronged you?

Donnelly and Major Yates are dead, so surely you are not still thinking of them?

Forgive the aforementioned. I know I can be meddlesome, but hopefully that won't sour you to my recommended books list. Yes, I finally compiled it! And I included a book in this very parcel. Do you like it? Charlotte refused her copy of *Memoirs of a Woman of Pleasure,* so I am sending it to you. Here's your chance to prove once and for all that you are not a prude. Merry Christmas!

Recommended Books for a Prude:

- *The School of Venus* by Michel Millot
- *Thérèse the Philosopher* by Jean-Baptiste de Boyer d'Argens
- *Moll Flanders* by Daniel Defoe
- *The Decameron* by Giovanni Boccaccio
- *The Libertine Parnassus,* an anthology by multiple authors

I hope you will enjoy these erotic glimpses into the human condition. You requested something scholarly, but truly, what is more educational than sex, the very act that fuels us into existence? Fear not, Apollo! It's not all debauchery…depending upon whom you ask.

Affectionately Yours,
Clara

[Hidden correspondence]

Although I still don't feel safe writing to you, I couldn't hold off any longer. Not only because I miss your bumbling letters (and I mean that with the sincerest of affection), but because within these past few weeks, I've befriended a young captain who's divulged some unsettling news.

Apparently, the British believe you rebels cannot

withstand another campaign; not just because of your small troop numbers, but because American currency will soon be entirely depreciated. He bragged how the British have procured the same paper used by the Continental Congress. As of now, they are counterfeiting our money and spreading it en masse with the hopes of economic collapse. I must confess, I am not well-versed in monetary issues, but I know enough to realize this is a dangerous and ingenious plot. I pray you'll alert your superiors in time.

In spite of all this bleakness, I hope you and your father have a merry Christmas. Hug Josiah for me, won't you?

-CB

2 January 1780

Dear Clara,

Thank you for the book…even if the book, itself, is far from appropriate. I actually took so long because I wished to finish the novel and give a sound report. Although it wouldn't normally take me a sennight (and then some) to read this, I had to keep hiding it to spare Father, and myself, the embarrassment.

Despite my shock, I found myself sympathizing, and even empathizing with Fanny Hill. She valued her virtue and didn't wish to give it to just anyone. I imagine you're laughing at me as you read this, but I very much believe the same. I know we've had our lapses in the past, and that I allowed you to introduce me to bodily pleasure, but in spite of my prior claim, I do not regret a single moment. I trust you. I admire and respect and hold the highest of affections for you, and therefore, couldn't think of anyone more worthy of my desires.

Forgive me for speaking out of turn. Evidently, it

seems my innermost thoughts have become loosened, much like poor Fanny Hill's morals.

In the way of Christmas, I am afraid there isn't much to report. With funds tight and provisions tighter still, we did very little other than worship. Regardless, I thank you for thinking of us. Feel free to regale me with your own holiday.

Devotedly Yours,
Apollo

[Hidden correspondence]

Thank you for the report. I've since forwarded this information along through Amos, who has informed me that Washington is aware and has written Congress. Whether or not they act is in God's hands. I know you'll be scornful, but you are assuredly a patriot at heart. I thank you with my entire soul for thinking of the colonies.

P.S. Father was delighted to receive your hug. He hopes you will accept this written phrase as one of his own.
-BH

11 January 1780

Dear Apollo,

I am delighted you read my gift! However, regrettably, it would seem we have vastly different interpretations of the source. While Fanny started out wishing to secure her virtue, she soon realized sex can be had for pleasure and not love. Are you sure you are so similar? As I'm certain you read it through a biblical lens, I, myself, read it through the experiences I have endured. Love is almost never involved in sex. A man may proclaim it while you squeeze his gingambobs, but there's little meaning behind the sentiment. That is why I must reject your affections.

Not because I do not reciprocate them, but because all men are liars.

Three years ago, I fell in love with a sailor. That alone should've been my warning, because a sailor's mistress will always be the sea. Alas, love makes us wholly asinine. I did not wish to see the signs. I didn't care that he was barely around, because he told me he was in love with me…that he wished to wed and have a brood of children. But once he'd made off with my virtue, the scoundrel disappeared into the night, and I received a letter announcing his departure for England. That was the last I heard from him. I wanted to die. I nearly took my own life, in fact, and once I got a firm grip on my self-worth, I resolved to never again give away my heart so freely. Lust and sex are safe, meaningless ways to feel the sweet sting of human contact…the illusion of being loved, but without the crushing pain that follows attachment. All my life, I have been made to feel cheap and unworthy, and when I thought my Timothy was different, that I finally was worthy, he proved I was right all along. Nobody cares, and I am merely a means to an end.

Perhaps for a time, I felt you were unique, but distance has fortunately allowed me the opportunity to reclaim my wits. Even if we had fully succumbed, I never would've allowed our relationship to progress beyond the physical.

If you were not, in fact, claiming your affections for me, then please forgive my lapse and accept my apology. I had been hoping to discuss more books with you, but this opened wounds I never wished to debate…but since I do care for you, I felt it necessary to explain myself in full. I'm not some harlot, sir. I am a woman who feels far, far too deeply, and the fact you were able to lie to me about your true identity not once, but twice proves I cannot trust that you have my best interests at heart. I'm sorry it had to come to this.

Farewell,
Clara

[Hidden correspondence]

I am relieved to hear Washington has written Congress. However, I must argue with one claim you made: I'm not a patriot. I am choosing to give up my role in this operation, because I know you have many devoted, able-bodied men who'd carry out this mission far better than I. Please do not contact me about my decision. If, for whatever reason, I decide I wish to assist your cause again, I will reach out to you.

P.S. Tell Josiah I'm sorry. His hug was beyond sufficient, and far more than I deserve. In many ways, he is more a father to me than my very own, and our separation doesn't reflect my feelings for him. Take care of yourself, Ben. You know this is for the best.
-CB

20 January 1780

Dearest Clara,

I must admit, words fail me. I've so much I wish to tell you, to confess, but all I can focus on is the damage I have caused. I never meant to hurt you. I'm uncertain if I wrote my last letter with the intent of proclaiming my affections, but I can no longer deny that I do, in fact, have deep, irreversible feelings for you, and all I can do is lay my heart at the altar of your feet.

You say that men are liars. This is factual. Men do lie, but for every scoundrel, there's a man who is genuine in his affections. I couldn't tell you my true identity, because this cause is so much more than me, more than my feelings for you. But please: Allow me to welcome you deeper into my heart by admitting one small, festering truth. Earlier, you asked why I desired vengeance. My answer is I once had a brother, and I viewed him as the very light unto my feet. He was so pure and kind and good, unbelievably good, and it's this goodness that got him killed. In daily life, he made certain to share his meals and the very clothes off his back; he sang songs and recited prayers to boost morale; but ultimately, nobody saved *him*. And I regret not being there. I regret not dying in his place, and every day I ask God why such a pure, devout soul was sent unto Heaven, while I remain here, a mere shadow in comparison.

I am not asking for your pity. I'm not even asking you to reconsider, although I sincerely wish you would. Rather, I'm seeking to share my soul, just as you have so kindly done. Although I admired and respected you before, your candid confession endeared you to me unlike any other. I do not care about your past, because it doesn't define you.

With that said, your rejection doesn't surprise me. I am a cripple. I am useless, and therefore, no one you could ever love. Although it aggrieves me, I'm capable of letting you go. I only wish for your happiness.

Forever Yours,
Apollo

[Hidden correspondence]

Although I understand your romantic rejection, I beg you to reconsider giving up the cause. You're wrong. We do need you. *I* need you. Your intelligence has been valuable and pleasing to our commander. I know this means little to you, but we are forever in your debt.

P.S. Father would never be upset with you. He knows, just as I do, that you are at the very center of our hearts. We'll protect you until our dying breath.
-BH

15 February 1780

Apollo,

I needed time to compose myself, for your letter upended me in mind, body, and spirit. First, I cried. Not just because of what I perceived to be sincerity, but because of your brother. My heart aches on your behalf, and I thank you for sharing that with me. However, the more I read on, the angrier I became.

Do you think so little of me that you believe your disability is what inspired my rejection? How dare you act as though I cannot make up my own mind, and that I'm only choosing this path because of your injury? It's an insult to both me and yourself! While you may think you were showering me with compliments, your conjecture was nothing short of degrading.

The true irony here is that as a preacher's son, you are blind to your own self-worth. I mean, by God! Do you think yourself beyond mercy? The Lord forgives all, and thus, you're absolved for not being there when your brother needed you most. Pull the scales from your eyes! You are not beyond love, and you are not beyond forgiveness, and you certainly aren't defined by your injury. My one true regret is I cannot be the one to prove this to you. Although I wish you the very best, I'm asking you to never contact me again.

-Clara

[Hidden correspondence]

When Father inquires, I will tell him you were seriously injured, and thus, no longer of any help to the loyalist cause. Please accept this as my official resignation.

-CB

29 March 1780

Dear Miss Boyd,

I know you asked me to never write you again, but I request most humbly to be able to check in on you from time to time. Despite my prior words, I meant no offense; you are assuredly a permanent fixture of my heart. It pained me to have to wait so long to send this, but I owed you the time and distance you so sorely deserve.

Please tell me how you are faring. I promise I'm content to remain only your friend.

Your Most Humble and Obedient Servant,
Apollo

[Hidden correspondence]

I'm aware you no longer have any interest in espionage, but I wanted to thank you for your efforts. As of 18 March, the Continental Congress recalled all of the currency in circulation. This means the British scheme has been thwarted, and it's largely thanks to you.

Your nation is forever in your debt. And so am I.

-BH

27 April 1780

Dear Miss Boyd,

I hope you can forgive the second letter. I suppose it's asinine of me to believe—or rather, hope—that the post rider misplaced my correspondence, but I cannot help but be a fool. Could you please write me? If not to let me know I have your forgiveness, then to tell me how you are? I would've undoubtedly heard word, had you fallen into any harm, but I still wish to see it confirmed by your hand.

I hope you are well. Father sends his love.

Still Devotedly Yours,
Apollo

16 May 1780

Apollo,

I thought long and hard on whether or not to humor you. Clearly, my meddlesome affections won out, though I wouldn't take it to heart. I don't intend to write beyond proving my safety.

You are a good man, assuredly too good for me, and I refuse to let you burrow beneath my defenses. You may be excellent at scaling walls and burning down encampments in raids, but the fortress of my heart is one you will never vanquish. Goodbye, Captain. And I mean that sincerely this time.

-Clara

20 July 1780

Apollo,

I thank you for adhering to my request. I know this may come as a shock, but I wish to check in on your behalf. Catherine brought home a suitor last week, and he had the bluest eyes…and yet somehow, they were not nearly as blue as your own. I felt a stab of guilt within my breast and was compelled to reach out to ensure you are all right. I hope you can forgive how cold I've been toward you. This is by no means an invitation to correspond regularly, but I do give you permission to write me just this once.

Reluctantly Yours,
Clara

[Hidden correspondence]

Although I am genuinely interested in learning of your condition, I must confess this is the true reason I am writing. Although I care little for your cause, my heart froze once I heard talk of 8,000 British troops embarking at Whitestone in Queens with the aim of Newport, Rhode Island. Meanwhile, Admiral Graves, with 11 ships, has already been sailing there to thwart a French fleet. I feel this is something your commander should know about.

Although I'm unsure you can win this war, I at the very least wish to give you a fighting chance. You and your friends deserve to live, Ben. Pass this along as soon as you can.

-CB

25 September 1780

Dear Apollo,

Your failure to respond has me concerned. While you were once so desperate for my letters, you are now content to ignore them? Although I can understand, seeing how your heart must surely be bruised, I implore you to write a small word or two stating you are well.

Yours,
Clara

[Hidden correspondence]

Seeing how the British plan was upended, I am going to assume you received my letter and passed it along. Nevertheless, I'm relieved the matter with the French fleet didn't end poorly.

This is, however, my final correspondence. That turncoat, General Benedict Arnold, has entered New

York City, and is having suspected blackguards (patriots) arrested for espionage. A tailor named Hercules Mulligan was among those arrested. Do you know him? Regardless, I pray Arnold's search doesn't extend to other areas. I fear for my family and for you, which is why I will no longer write beyond this message. I'd hate for our correspondence to fall into his hands.

-CB

1 October 1780

Dear Miss Boyd,

Forgive me this letter, but I must entreat you most humbly on behalf of my son. Benjamin is unwell. He's fallen into some sort of despairing stupor, and I believe you are the only one who can help. Please, if you have any affection for us at all, will you not return to us? I believe the very sight of you, no matter how brief, will restore him to the vitality he once possessed. He is so pale and weak and miserable… I can barely get him to eat.

I feel selfish asking this of you, and most especially when you have your own family to concern yourself with, but Benjamin is all I have. Will you not help me save his life?

Your Most Humble and Admiring Friend,
Rev. Josiah Hoskin

One week later

BENJAMIN JERKED AWAKE, gasping as a cold sweat overtook his

entire frame. He'd been like this for several months, and the severity of his symptoms depended upon how much laudanum he ingested. And Clara... He closed his eyes. His addiction became *worse* once she'd written him off, and despite her recent correspondence, he had been far too disoriented to properly respond. She surely hated him anyway...

A shiver tore through Benjamin and he gnashed his teeth, his mouth dry as he beheld his father sleeping fitfully at his side. In one hand was an open Bible, and the other was curled beseechingly around his wrist.

Retracting himself from Josiah's grip, Benjamin cleared his throat. "Father?" he croaked. "Are you awake?"

Josiah stirred, then opened his bleary eyes. "Benjamin?"

"Please..." Benjamin swallowed, that all-too familiar panic settling within his bones. "My laudanum..."

"Is gone," Josiah replied sternly. "I threw it out this morning."

"W-what?" Chest heaving in alarm, Benjamin's breath grew shallow as a rope of terror squeezed around his lungs. "I...I need that for my condition," he rasped. "It helps me."

"How is *this*—" Josiah gestured to his son "—a blessing of any true merit? You are unwell, Benjamin, and I wish I'd realized the cause far sooner."

His dread turned to rage, and curling his upper lip, Benjamin smashed his fist against the nightstand. The washbowl on top rattled in warning. "I need my medicine, goddamn you!" he hissed. "I need it! I *need* it! Give it to me!"

"I told you, it is gone," Josiah replied, his tone even despite the tears in his eyes.

"No..." Frantic, Benjamin shook his head. "No, no, I had enough to last me another sennight! Please..." He reached out a despairing hand. "You must send for Dr. Wagner."

Josiah's eyes narrowed. "I am never allowing that infernal man into my house again. From here on out, we are going to look to God for guidance, we are going to pray, and we will finally get you well again."

"I *am* well!" Benjamin screamed, a low sob catching in his throat. "Can't you see that it's *you* who is making me this way?" Manic, he tore at his bedding until he'd thrown the blankets to the floor, his body overcome by the agonizing, ever-present restlessness that accompanied his need. "Give me my laudanum! Please, I know you have it somewhere!"

"Benjamin, you must calm yourself!" Leaping up to still his son's desperate thrashing, Josiah clasped Benjamin's wildly jerking arms while shouting above the din, "'I can do everything through Him who gives me strength!'"

"God did nothing for me," Benjamin sobbed. "Nothing! He allowed this to happen!"

"'No temptation has overtaken you that is not common to man,'" Josiah recited. With tears spilling freely down his cheeks, Josiah pleadingly squeezed his son's hands. "You will vanquish this demon, Benjamin. You will. There is always a way out."

Benjamin's face crumpled and he bit back another sob. "You hate me," he accused. "You wish me to fail!"

"Benjamin…"

A thick, suffocating quiet overcame the room, and bewildered, he beheld his father's face, which was ash-white as he gaped toward the foot of his bed.

Following Josiah's shocked gaze, Benjamin's heart leapt once he spotted his left foot. His toes were slightly elevated. They had *arched*. Quivering, he dared to wiggle them once more, testing the uncomfortable, numbing stretch. The sensation was akin to pins-and-needles.

"My God," Josiah whispered, his voice choking up with tears. "Benjamin…you moved."

CHAPTER TWENTY-THREE
The Sweet Sting of Poison

SENSATION WAS THE first thing he gained back. Although Benjamin noticed a slight change in his legs over the past few weeks, it had been so subtle that he hardly paid it any mind. Now, however, everything overwhelmed him. Any brush against skin surged through him, prickly and uncomfortable in its intensity. Had he always felt so strongly?

"It's a true miracle," Josiah said, beaming while Benjamin flexed his feet. "You were at your lowest, and then a sign presented itself!"

Benjamin snorted, dark scorn dancing behind his eyes. "Far be it for me to dismiss your claim, Father, but I imagine Dr. Wagner's technique is responsible." For several months, John came by once a week and moved Benjamin's limbs, if only to ensure his muscles didn't completely atrophy. *That* was surely why he'd regained some mobility.

Josiah frowned. "I know that is your withdrawal speaking, so I'll forgive the offense." Extending a tray of stew, he added, "I've brought your dinner, and I expect you to pray before eating. The two of us have much to be thankful for."

"What do *I* have to be thankful for?" Benjamin hissed. "I am in pain. I am suffering, and yet you don't even seem to care."

Offering the bowl of stew, Josiah's sternness softened once his son promptly turned his head. "No matter how you feel toward me, Benjamin, you must eat."

"I'm not eating until you fetch my laudanum."

"You know I can't," Josiah replied. "As I've already told you, I got rid of the tincture. I drained the contents into the grass."

An electric bolt of fury blitzed across Benjamin's eyes, and gnashing his teeth, he seized the stew before fiercely hurling it across the room. The wooden bowl clipped the wall and rolled across the floor, food remnants dashing haphazardly along the paneling.

Holding tightly onto the empty tray, Josiah remained unmoving despite the tremor in his hands. "Benjamin…"

"To the devil with you," he seethed. "You have the key to get me well again, the very *solution!* Yet here you stand refusing me the cure. It is you who's delivered me unto this purgatory!"

Josiah's eyes grew wet, and he set aside the tray. "I am doing this because I love you. You can't see it now, but you will."

With a guttural cry, Benjamin embraced himself once a violent chill rolled through his frame. Restless, his legs weakly moved beneath the blankets, his head turning as a pang of nausea overcame him in unrelenting waves. "Please," he begged, tears filling his eyes. "Papa, *please…*"

Josiah jerked. Benjamin hadn't called him "Papa" since he was very young. The last time, in fact, was before they'd discovered Mrs. Hoskin in her sickbed.

Weeping piteously, Benjamin's face scrunched and he screamed into his shoulder, his hands clawing at his chest while he writhed and shuddered. The nausea increased, and the all-too-familiar taste of bile nipped at the back of his throat.

"Papa," he choked, his voice drowning in tears, "*help* me…"

Benjamin vaulted forward and retched, emptying the very little in his stomach across the floor.

Josiah moved his son's chamber pot over, just in case there was more sickness to catch, and carefully aided Benjamin in lying against his bedding. Trembling, he smoothed the matted, sweat-slicked hair from his son's eyes. "I'm here," he whispered. "'I have chosen and not rejected you. Do not fear—'"

"'—for I am with you,'" Benjamin choked, tears spilling heavily into the corners of his mouth.

Josiah's chin quivered and he nodded. A look of pleading understanding passed between them, and then he gathered Benjamin fiercely into his arms and held on tight. The younger man wept into the crook of his neck with a harsh, choking wail, needy and small, and a frightened boy of nine all over again.

"We'll get through this," Josiah whispered into Benjamin's hair. "We will. We *will*. Together."

Teeth chattering, all Benjamin could offer was a feeble whimper.

Three Days Later

AT THIS POINT in her life, lying to her family had become an art form. After giving the excuse of visiting her cousin in Oyster Bay, and that her cousin's servants would be assigned to her travel and care, Clara met Amos in town. Together, they started the journey to Freyview, the place for which she oddly yearned.

"I used to think home was where you were born," she told the cabinetmaker conversationally, her fingers toying with the lace on her fichu. "But now, I realize it's where you feel safest...the most loved. Is Freyview that place for you?"

"Aye," Amos agreed. The cart wobbled a bit, and the two horses in front nickered. "Why d'ya ask, hmm? Don't tell me you're gettin' all soft on us patriots."

She snorted. "Not hardly...though I suppose I'm warming up to one or two of you."

"One in particular, eh?"

She shot him a warning look. "Well, it certainly wouldn't be you," she agreed. "You're still not forgiven for cutting me with that knife."

"Oi!" Amos exclaimed. "That was over a year ago!"

"I'm a Boyd," Clara replied. "We can hold grudges for centuries, and *have*. To this day, our bloodline won't speak to anyone with the surname Walsh, and all because my great-great-grandfather insulted some Walsh fellow's manhood. In retaliation, that Walsh slept with my ancestor's wife, and ever since, we've had this odd rivalry where we shag each other's spouses and fight…and not necessarily in that order."

Amos whistled. "How do I become a Boyd then, uh? Sounds like a mighty nice feud to be havin', 'specially if those Walsh wives are lookers."

Clara snorted, though she was smiling. "You're an utter arse, Corporal. How you've gleaned a promotion is beyond me, given your complete lack of decorum."

"All right, all right. Easy on me pride there, will ya? Sometimes, it's all a man's got!"

Smile fading, Clara lowered her eyes and laced her hands, thinking of Benjamin and how he was assuredly in a similar position. "Thank you for doing this," she murmured. "It wasn't wise to bring my lady's maid, so…thank you. I imagine you didn't wish to serve as a chaperone."

"This is for Moony too," Amos said. "I haven't been able to stop by an' visit much, but I know my friend, Clara, and he's in trouble. And if cartin' your spoiled arse all over God's creation is the way to help 'im? Well…I guess I'll endure a bit o' your jawin'."

To his alarm, Clara burst into tears, her hands sweeping toward her mouth.

"Zounds," he swore. "Aw, no…I didn't mean nothin' by it! I thought I was bein' roguishly charming!"

"It's not…i-it's not you," Clara sniveled. "I cannot help but feel responsible for this… Ben begged me to write him, and yet I cast him aside. What if I've killed him? C-condemned him to an early grave?"

Amos snorted. "Well, someone thinks a mighty lot o' herself!" When she sobbed anew, he swore again. "Jesus, c'mon. I was jus' havin' a bit o' fun! Oi!"

Wiping a finger beneath her eyes, Clara swallowed and drew a breath. "I'm sorry, Corporal. It's just...Ben scares me. Not because he's cruel or overbearing, but because he is neither of those things. I don't know how to handle a man of that sort."

Amos huffed. "Far be it for me to disagree with ya, but Moony's plenty overbearin'. Why, jus' the other week—"

"I was unfair to him," Clara continued, "and if I can't save him...if I cannot help, I'm unsure my heart will ever recover."

"He ain't dead," Amos argued, his features growing sharp. "Ben won't die, 'cause he's a strong ol' son of a gun, and *you* won't let 'im die, 'cause you're a decent chit. Keep the faith."

Clara withdrew her handkerchief and nodded. "I suppose I'll have to," she agreed, dabbing her eyes. "These days, I don't have much else..."

WHEN THE HOSKINS' weathered saltbox came into view, Clara felt an immediate leap in her chest. She nervously rubbed her hands over her skirts, grateful for the outer petticoat for absorbing the sudden sweat on her palms.

"You want me to wait here?" Amos asked. "I figured I'd stop in at some point, an'—"

"I'd rather you didn't," Clara said. Catching the look on his face, she winced and amended, "I'm sorry, Corporal, but I haven't seen Ben in a little over a year, so I'd prefer to do this on my own. Do you have someplace you can get settled?"

Amos nodded. "Aye. Unlike you, people in these parts actually seem to like me."

Slowly, the corner of her mouth quirked. "Thank you, Corporal. If I wish to find you, where should I send word?"

"For now, the MacPhersons'. I plan on bouncin' between here an' camp during Moony's recovery, so at least in this way, I'll be outta your hair." Pulling the cart to a halt, Amos sighed and nodded at the house. "Well, go on then. Give 'em me best."

Clara nodded, then grabbed her valise and unsteadily lowered herself into the grass. Had this been any other situation, she would've sniped at him for not being a gentleman and assisting, but with the prospect of seeing Benjamin, of discovering him unwell, her stomach churned as she made her way across the grounds.

To her surprise, the door opened not long after.

Josiah's mouth dropped and his eyes brightened. "Miss Boyd!" he exclaimed. "Oh, good God in Heaven. My prayers have been answered!"

He rushed across the grass and drew Clara into his embrace, crushing her against him as she squeaked in surprise. "I heard the cart, but didn't realize it was you," he continued, holding her tighter still. "How was your trip? Are you in need of rest?"

Overwhelmed by his enthusiasm, Clara laughed before extricating herself and peering into his kind blue eyes. "It's so good to see you," she told him truthfully. "I would've come the moment I received your letter, but I needed to find a ride into town."

"Of course," Josiah agreed, nodding. "I am so very glad you did." With a wave to Amos, who waved back once he started driving up the beaten path, he added, "How long do you intend to stay? All withdrawals are different, but—"

"For as long as it takes," Clara assured him. "My family thinks I'm visiting my cousin, and it's never unusual for us to stay a fortnight or so. If I am needed beyond that, I'll write to them." Lifting her valise, she added, "Am I to stay in my old room?"

Josiah smiled and gestured for her to accompany him. "You

will, indeed. Once you get settled in, I'm sure Benjamin would delight in a visit."

With a soft intake of breath, Clara nodded and followed after.

TEETERING UPON THE thin divide between mania and clarity, Benjamin's eyelids fluttered and he groaned, shivering violently while a restless wave crashed over him. Feeling the need to move, he weakly managed to roll onto his side, his body quivering from the strain, before he ultimately slumped onto his back again.

Help me, Father in Heaven. Help me, help me. I want to die. I want to die!

All he could think of was his laudanum, of how he'd be overcome by warmth, much like the sweet relief of easing into a pleasant bath. He needed it, he *needed* that, and with a low growl, he wrapped his arms around himself and gnashed his teeth in despair.

That was when the door opened.

Amidst his sleep-deprived delirium, for just one moment, Benjamin genuinely believed he was hallucinating. The stunning green eyes, delicate nose, and ripe, rosy lips belonged to a sweet, heart-shaped face he would know blind. Clutching himself more strongly, a full-body shudder rolled through him as the woman carefully closed the door.

"Clara," he choked.

"Rebel scum," she greeted, unmistakable tears sparkling in her eyes. She came toward him, untying her bergère hat and casting it carelessly to the floor. She sank into the chair at his side and took one of his clenched hands, smoothing her fingers over his fist before stroking his brow. "Oh, Ben," she whispered.

"What have you done to yourself?"

Unable to resist, he leaned into her touch like a bloom seeking sunlight, his cheek nuzzling into her palm as he shivered harder. "W-what are you doing here?" he demanded. "You…y-you came back to us."

"I did," she agreed, sounding surprised herself. "I've come to realize you are more important than my pride…than my heart. I couldn't live with myself, were I to find out…th-that you'd…" Unable to speak the fateful words, she exhaled and brushed back his sweat-matted hair. "It doesn't matter. We are going to get you well again, and you'll be able to return to your duty. You'll see."

Chin tensing, Benjamin's nostrils flared and he seized her wrist, making her cry out. "Do you have it?" he demanded, his voice pitching in desperation. "You've met Dr. Wagner…do you have my laudanum?"

Bemused, Clara shook her head. "No, Ben, of course not. No one has your laudanum, because it is making you ill."

"No, it's making me better!" he snarled, causing her to draw back in alarm. "When I don't take it, I am sick. When I do take it, I feel good. There's a clear path here, yet both you and Father refuse to see it!"

Gnashing his teeth, Benjamin whimpered as the restlessness returned full force. His irritation spiked, and he shoved Clara's hand away from his face, his body squirming as the nausea returned. "Please," he rasped, "I'm getting worse…I need my laudanum!"

Unsure of what to do, Clara fetched the pitcher of water on his nightstand and poured him a drink. "Here, take this," she entreated. "You look feverish." Extending the wooden cup, she yelped once Benjamin furiously knocked it from her grasp, sending a sluice of water across the floor.

"You *know* what I need!" he screamed at her. "You know it, you know it!"

He bucked and feebly kicked beneath his blankets, and Clara gasped before drawing a hand to her breast. "Ben," she choked, "you…you can move."

"What of it?" he snarled.

"What of it?" she echoed, stunned. "Why, a mere year ago, mobility was all you yearned for, and now you don't even care?" He groaned and weakly rolled onto his side, and with tears blurring her vision, Clara hesitated before crawling over him onto the bed. Had this been a normal situation, Benjamin would've halted at once, perhaps even blushed in that sweet, endearing way she loved. But that Benjamin was gone. In his place was a hurt, fearful animal, and as she lay alongside him and the wall, she wrapped her arms around his waist and nudged her face between his shoulder blades. Each time he screamed and thrashed, she embraced him more strongly, pinning his arms as she tried not to cry.

"I've got you," she whispered into his sweat-drenched shirt. "Just hold on…"

Please hold on.

WHEN CLARA CAME out to supper that evening, her eyes were bloodshot, and she was pale with exhaustion. Despite Benjamin having fallen asleep, she could still hear his screams while she'd desperately held on to keep him from hurting himself.

Josiah looked up from setting the table. "Miss Boyd? Are you all right?"

"No," she whispered, not feeling the need to lie. "Ben is…h-he's so lost and cruel, and angry. I barely recognize him."

"It's the laudanum," Josiah assured her. "It can destroy even the best of us. Believe me, I've seen its effects. When I served in the French and Indian War, some of the soldiers became dependent upon their tinctures. The recovery was nearly as dreadful as the addiction, itself."

Clara shivered. "For how long?"

"It varies," he said, "and Benjamin only stopped receiving the tincture as of three days ago. He's going to be at his very worst, but the most harmful of his symptoms will taper off with time."

Nodding, Clara touched a hand to her throat. "And his legs…you didn't mention he could walk."

"I'm not sure he can," Josiah admitted. "That, too, happened a few days ago, a complete miracle." With a tearful smile, he gestured for her to join him at the table. "We were arguing, and suddenly his toes moved…and before we knew it, he had limited mobility in his feet, his ankles, and later on, the entirety of both his legs. I didn't wish to rush him, especially in light of his situation, so he hasn't yet attempted to get out of bed. I think he's too unwell to try, truth be told."

Clara nodded, sinking into the chair across from him. "Before this moment, I never thought Ben capable of violence. He grabbed me, and…attacked me several times."

Closing his eyes, Josiah nodded before filling her cup with ale. "I know he'd never hurt you," he replied, "though I also know this is of very little consolation. The man he was—*is*—won't be showing his face for quite some time."

Gripping the edge of the table, Clara gaped at the chicken and potatoes on her plate and exhaled. "They say you don't understand true helplessness until you see someone you care for at their very worst," she agreed. "I hope and pray this is his poorest state, Josiah, because I'm not sure I can bear much worse. If anything, my presence is doing very little."

"He asked for you every day," Josiah replied. "Perhaps not always by name, but the moment I entered his room each morning, he would inquire if I'd received a letter in your hand." His lips quirked and he lowered his eyes. "I assure you, Miss Boyd, you are the absolute best person to be here."

Tears sprang to Clara's eyes, but she didn't cry. Swallowing around the knot in her throat, a swell of emotion churned within her breast. "I won't leave him," she promised. "And I won't leave *you,* either."

She reached across the table and Josiah took her hand, squeezing gently as he murmured, "Let us pray."

OVER THE NEXT several days, Benjamin was unbearable to be around. He'd curse and spit, throw whatever was within reach, and sometimes attempt to physically lash out at whomever was in the room. Clara reminded herself this wasn't personal, that this wasn't *him* attacking her, and yet it still stung. It hurt, and as she lay awake that night, listening to his moans of pain and restless agony through the wall, she could stand it no longer.

Ripping back her covers, Clara swung her legs over the side of the bed and fetched her candle, foregoing her dressing gown as she padded into the hall on quiet feet. Benjamin wailed again and she winced.

With a sharp, fluttering stab of nerves, Clara lifted her arm, then rapped against his door with purpose. The moaning stopped, and she quietly pushed her way into his room. "Ben?"

He panted in response, covered in sweat as he lay there in bed, his limbs tangled within his sheets. With her heart plummeting at the sight, Clara set aside her candle and came over to him, already trembling as she reached out a hand. These days, she never knew if concern would enchant or infuriate him, and as her fingers brushed through his loosened locks, a twinge of relief unfurled within her breast as he leaned into her palm. Her fingertips were cool against his feverish skin, and as they locked eyes within the dancing candleflame, she asked, "How are you feeling?"

He shook his head. "I-I don't feel very..." With a queasy

retch, Benjamin broke away and dove toward the side of his bed, grasping his chamber pot before hurling unceremoniously into the earthenware vessel.

Wincing, Clara fiddled with her braid slung over her shoulder, only halting once he ceased being sick. She approached and sat alongside him, ignoring the sickly sweet odor of vomit as she wrapped an arm around his waist. Benjamin's teeth chattered and she stroked her fingertips through his hair, her voice low as she asked, "May I do something for you?"

Benjamin choked back his nausea and peered at her through the sallow lighting. "Like what?" he rasped. For a moment, his eyes flickered with hope, and he clamped his hand around her wrist. "My laudanum? Do you have it?"

With a pained cry, Clara yanked herself free and rubbed the affliction. A hot, nettled ribbon of agitation stitched through her heart, but that quickly dissolved into guilt as she looked away. "No," she murmured. "No, of course not, but I do have something to offer that's always helped." She looked to him in earnest. "May I?"

Benjamin gazed at her distrustfully, then offered a slow nod. He appeared so lost, so helpless, and the sight of his mussed and sweaty queue, small, constricted pupils, and overgrown stubble left a dip in her stomach.

With a rush of breath, Clara turned toward him and crossed her legs, indicating that he pivot. "Sit here," she entreated. "When my sisters and I were younger, we would braid each other's hair before bed every night. It might seem silly to you, but it always made me feel safe and loved."

Benjamin snorted. "You mean to tell me a *servant* didn't braid your hair?"

Ignoring his scorn, she agreed, "Perhaps at first, yes, but that was one thing my sisters and I wished to learn for ourselves. Angélique taught us. She was only a child, herself, at the time."

Expression softening in defeat, Benjamin shivered and turned toward the neighboring wall.

With careful, gentle passes of her fingers through his hair, Clara undid his queue and attempted to remove the mass of tangles by hand. "Where is your comb?" she asked.

"Over there," he grumbled. "By my washbowl."

Rising to fetch it, Clara grabbed the wooden comb and returned to his side, her pulse quickening as she seated herself behind him. There was something intimate about viewing Benjamin in this way. He was defenseless here, unguarded, and Clara took the utmost care as she drew the comb through his knotted strands. Benjamin flinched every so often, but as the tangles became few and far between, his posture relaxed, and the tension in his shoulders lessened.

Rolling his head toward his chest, he hummed softly, and Clara felt a twinge of fulfillment since it was a sound of pleasure and not pain.

Chewing her lip, she rebraided his hair with practiced, tightly-woven overlaps. "I was thinking we could go for a walk tomorrow… Perhaps in the afternoon?" she asked.

Benjamin's spine went rigid. "You know I can't walk."

"No, I don't," she countered. "All I do know is you have a sort of mobility, and the potential to care for yourself." Frowning, she continued plaiting his hair. "Have you tried?"

"No…" Agitation evident, Benjamin mumbled, "My fear is that after all this time, I won't be able to."

Clara huffed. "So you'd rather not try at all, and ensure you won't ever walk again, as opposed to taking a chance?"

"I don't want to build myself up for that kind of disappointment," he growled. "I don't expect you, a woman who's always been given whatever her heart desires, to understand."

Clara flinched. "Since you are in pain, I'm going to ignore that asinine remark," she said. "Ben, you don't understand. I—"

"No, *you* don't understand!" he thundered. Shaking her off, Benjamin snapped his head in her direction and nailed her in place with his wild, desperate eyes. "It's so easy for you to speak your thoughts, to give your unwanted opinions when you, yourself, have never hurt this way!" He heaved a dry, unfeeling laugh. "What, so you think that after all this time, I can just get up and walk? Run? Kick my heels and dance around the room?"

Clara drew back, her eyes glassy with hurt. "No, of course not," she said. "But Ben, surely you—"

"Surely, *you* aren't so ignorant that you believe you can help me!" he snarled. "Unless you have a tincture in your hands, I don't want to hear another word!"

"Ben..."

"Get out," he growled. "Out, damn you!" Snatching his comb off the bed, he fiercely lobbed it across the room.

As it struck the wall, Clara recoiled and staggered to her feet. "You can't drive me away, Captain Hoskin," she choked. Chin quivering, she curled her hands into fists. "You can maim me, call me names, spit at me, but I am not leaving this house. Not until you're well again!" Drawing a shuddery breath, she swept a hand toward her chest. "You should know you've changed me. Being away from my home, being out here with a bunch of rebels...I quickly realized I can be so much more than who I am, who I *was*. That even a woman can raze the walls that bind her and be whomever she wishes to be...that the fight for independence isn't just for men. It's for me, too." She blinked back tears. "Granted, I am not fighting against my king and country, but I still feel as though I am fighting—to be seen, to be heard, to be *respected*. And somehow, someway, I've found all of that here in this sleepy, inconsequential little town by your side. And maybe I'm wrong, but I think that makes you far from useless."

Benjamin's molten gaze turned wet and he leaned onto his palms, clawing at his bedding with quivering, talon-like fingers. "You're wrong," he hissed. "If I was so useful, Bishop would've requested I return to the field."

"Your self-worth does not hinge upon your superior," Clara snapped. "Hasn't it ever occurred to you that true merit isn't determined through perception, but how you help people? How you touch their lives?" She breathed a maudlin laugh. "Ben, you may not realize it, but you have saved me; and with God as my witness, I am not leaving this house until I save you, too."

With tears spilling freely down her cheeks, she grabbed her candle and stormed from the room, leaving Benjamin sitting there in stunned disbelief.

CHAPTER TWENTY-FOUR
Lifting the Veil

AFTER THE FIRST two-and-a-half weeks of Benjamin's withdrawal, Clara wrote to her family announcing an extended stay. Although she knew her parents wouldn't care in the slightest, her sisters, assuredly, were concerned about how she was faring. It was quite easy to lie and speak of drama performances, handsome suitors, and other gaieties, when in reality, she was constantly covered in sweat, whether it be Benjamin's or her own, and her clothes reeked of bile from tending to his vomit spells.

With her hair precariously pinned in place, Clara stumbled outdoors for some much-needed fresh air, her exhaustion evident as she moved toward a fence and leaned miserably against the wooden supports.

"You all right there, Miss Boyd?"

Jerking in surprise, she glanced over her shoulder and balked, not having expected Mrs. Harriet Finch.

"Oh, don't mind me," the older woman said. "I heard about Benjamin's state and felt the need to stop by. The whole town's been talking about it."

Mopping the sweat from her brow, Clara sighed and pushed herself away from the fence. "Captain Hoskin's as well as any man in his situation can be," she replied. "Reverend Hoskin gave him two canes, so we haven't lost hope."

"Oh?" Harriet strode forward. "How's that going?"

"I don't know," Clara bitterly said. "The captain won't try walking around me…I suppose he is embarrassed."

"Men are funny like that," Harriet agreed. "Their pride's both a blessing and a curse." The older woman's stance became conspiratorial, and she lowered her voice. "Do you mind if I ask a personal question?"

Clara's expression turned withering, but she nodded. This woman said whatever she pleased, so it would be pointless to try and divert.

Harriet leaned closer still. "Why are you doing this, Miss Boyd?" she whispered. "You're devoting your young, lovely life to a man who is far too broken, or at least, for whatever it is you are assuredly seeking."

Clara frowned. "And what is it I am seeking, Mrs. Finch?"

"Why, marriage, of course! You're of a certain age, and so is Benjamin. But Miss Boyd, he is a cripple." She shook her head. "It's doubtful he can give you children in his present state."

A burst of hot, untamed fury blazed within Clara's breast, and she dug her nails so deeply into her palms that they bled. She wasn't sure why she did it. Perhaps it was the days upon weeks of physical and emotional torment, but with a feline-like growl, she wound back her arm and struck the older woman harshly across the face.

Harriet yelped, lifting a hand to her stinging cheek. "You…y-you hit me!" she cried.

"Ben is far more than his body, and children are not the be all, end all," Clara seethed. "I care not for my father's legacy. His very bloodline can die with me, for all I care, but Ben? He is good and kind and deserving of our respect. He nearly *died*, Mrs. Finch. He became crippled to bring better lives to people like you and me, and yet here you stand degrading his efforts? I'll damn well hit you again, you…you fatheaded doggess!"

Still clutching her cheek, Harriet's expression grew snide. "And how long have you been in love with him, Miss Boyd?"

Clara's composure faltered, and her chin stiffened with defiance. "I'm going inside now, Mrs. Finch. Don't let me catch you on these premises again."

Spinning about on her heel, she stormed toward the Hoskin residence, her heart pounding as she desperately tried to ignore the memory of Harriet's skeptical, all-knowing eyes.

"TRY IT ONCE more."

Benjamin grimaced, his limbs trembling as he clutched his two canes. He was presently seated on his bed, panting while resting from his latest stumble around the room. "No more," he pleaded. "Father, walking requires strength, a strength I barely possess."

"Mere weeks ago, you couldn't walk," Josiah pointed out, "and yet here you are, granted the gift of sensation returning to your limbs. Who knows what more can happen, should you put your mind to it?"

Benjamin groaned, dropping his head forward in acquiescence. With a slow, puffing intake of breath, he clenched his teeth before drawing up to his feet with considerable strain. His knees wobbled violently from the effort, and leaning his weight against the canes, he dragged his right foot forward, and then his left, before sluggishly moving across the hardwood floor. His injury gave him a crooked, lumbering gait, which made it all the more difficult to maintain his balance.

The chills of withdrawal still occasionally gripped him as he moved, and a sore, uncomfortable ache whipped through his back each time he took a staggering step.

"That's it," Josiah encouraged. "You've nearly got it!"

A feeble smile touched Benjamin's mouth, but that was when

his knees buckled. He collapsed to the floor with a great cry, his shins banging painfully against the hard wood while he quivered from overexertion. Hot tears burned his eyes, and snarling, he struck his fist against the floor.

Rushing to his fallen son, Josiah helped him to his knees and declared, "You did so well, son…so very, very well."

Finally, the tears fell, and Benjamin sagged onto Josiah's chest, weeping pitifully against his waistcoat. "No more," he begged. "Please, Father, I can't…"

"You can," he soothed. "You are strong and capable, and even if this is as good as it ever gets, you need to keep your constitution fit."

"But what if I never fully walk again?" Benjamin weakly asked.

Josiah gently brushed his fingers through his son's hair. "Then we will love you regardless," he asserted. "You are not broken, Benjamin. You are whole. I am only pushing you because I know you, and I know you will regret not having at least tried." His expression softened. "A dear friend of mine from college was in a similar state such as yours. Did you know that?" When Benjamin shook his head, he continued, "Gregory had very little function in his left arm and leg due to a carriage accident, but none of us ever considered him to be any less of a man. And if anyone truly did…well…clearly, they were a horse's arse."

Benjamin balked, unaccustomed to hearing his father swear.

"The point is," Josiah continued, "you *will* get beyond this, especially with me and Clara here to help."

Benjamin winced. "Miss Boyd isn't beholden to me," he miserably replied. "She should return to her family."

Josiah drew back in concern. "Why are you so despondent? Has something happened?"

Shaking his head, Benjamin avoided his father's gaze. "No…I-I just feel she'd be far happier, were she not having to look after me like some wretched invalid. I am not her responsibility."

Josiah frowned. "It's not considered a hardship when you care for someone, Benjamin. She is here of her own free will."

"But how much of that free will is tainted by guilt?" Benjamin prodded. "Despite her snobbery, she has a good heart, Father. She wouldn't leave me here, and that's precisely the problem. I need to convince her I am well again."

"But why are you trying to drive her away?" Josiah pressed. "What if she *wants* to stay with us?"

"She doesn't," Benjamin snarled. "No one would ever condemn themselves to this life, no matter how much affection they claim to have." He chuckled bleakly. "I cannot stand the man I've become. With the gradual clarity from my past fog, I am so ashamed of how I've treated you both."

Passing a hand through his son's hair, Josiah squeezed his shoulder. "Nobody thinks of you as that man anymore, Benjamin. That was the devil."

Benjamin sniffed and ran his sleeve beneath his nose, exhaling in frustration. "I just want to be well again…to return to my duties."

"I know," Josiah allowed, "but regardless of what happens, you must be open to a helping hand. And if Miss Boyd's the one reaching out for you, why not reach back? Perhaps she needs you as much as you need her."

Benjamin lifted his head, perplexed. "What do you mean by that?"

Stooping to kiss his brow, Josiah murmured, "I'll tend to dinner. Do you need help getting into bed?"

It wasn't lost on Benjamin how his father purposely ignored his question. But rather than press the subject—surely, he was mistaken—he accepted Josiah's aid, and clumsily rose with his canes.

THE WEEKS THAT followed were filled with trials and tribulations, yet Clara withstood them with dogged resolve. She remained by Benjamin's side as little by little his foul temper abated until he could go a full day without begging for laudanum. He could finally hold down a meal. He could smile and laugh, and by God, he could blush in that shy, charmingly embarrassed way he had whenever they first met all those months ago.

Benjamin seemed healthy. He seemed like *Benjamin* again. With a song in her heart, Clara was thrilled when he invited her to join him in the garden that afternoon. She'd heard he was able to walk with one cane now as opposed to two, but she was unsurprised when he did not rise to greet her. Instead, he remained sitting by a rose bush reading.

He didn't yet seem comfortable trying to walk around her. She wasn't sure why; perhaps he feared she would see a weakness in him…something unsightly and unwelcome. Didn't he realize that any progress, any moment with him, no matter how small or insignificant, instilled in her the greatest joy? Clara had never felt that before, the sheer bliss of being around another human being, and delighting in their companionship without the need for words, touch, nor reason. Not once had she possessed a true friend, which made her assume, nay, deny it could be anything but platonic affection within her breast; so much so that she ignored her pounding heart as she approached.

"Reading, are you?" Clara asked. She leaned over his shoulder and scoffed. "And *scripture*? Goodness, I should have known! You're a true preacher's son until the very end."

"I've needed to brush up on my behavior," Benjamin replied, his tone defensive.

She snorted. "Indeed? Is there anything in there that instructs kindness toward smart, completely delightful young loyalist women, by chance?"

Benjamin hummed, though he was smiling. "I suppose 'love thy neighbor' covers that one…but just barely."

Seating herself on the bench alongside him, she flashed a grin.

"Despite the barb, I am not going to let you sour this for me," she said. "I've been waiting for months, nay, over a year, to see this garden, and I'm honored you finally allowed me the pleasure."

"You could've come out here while I was ill," Benjamin reminded her, perplexed.

She faltered. "Well yes, I could have," she agreed, "but it wouldn't have been the same. This place is special to you…and I wished to see it through your eyes, rather than my own."

He studied her a moment, the cool breeze loosening a few long, golden-brown strands from his queue. "You once said your mother had a garden. Was it anything like this?"

Looking around at the beautiful array of red roses, pink chrysanthemums, and white asters, a melancholy smile lifted Clara's mouth and she shook her head. "No," she murmured, lacing her hands, "no, not at all. Mother's garden was grand and ostentatious, and a front to hide the ugliness within. But this…" She lifted her shoulders. "It feels *real*, somehow, beautiful in its simplicity. I can tell a lot of love was put into each seedling."

Benjamin swallowed, his bare throat bobbing. "Mother arguably loved *too* much," he agreed. "She died because she didn't want to trouble us with her condition…to worry us and make us sad." With a sorrowful laugh, he looked away. "She used to call me her 'little bumblebee,' because I was noisy, energetic, and really loved flowers…or rather, *her* flowers. I liked watching her while she gardened. Some days, I'd read while she tended to her rose bushes, or we'd pull out weeds together and recite scripture."

Hesitant, Clara laid her hand over his and gave it a gentle squeeze. "Far be it for me to detract from this moment, but I genuinely thought she might've called you 'little bumblebee' because you are a pest."

Startled by this declaration, Benjamin laughed, his brows lifting incredulously. "That's a bit pot-meet-kettle, don't you think?"

Clara giggled. "I only meant when you get all holier-than-thou, of course!" Nudging him, she gazed out over the horizon. "Thank you," she softly said. "I really am glad you shared this with me. It means a lot."

"I couldn't imagine sharing this with anyone else," he replied just as softly. Reaching for her hand again, Benjamin entwined their fingers and met her gaze with his pleading, yearnful eyes of periwinkle. "I'm glad you decided to stay. For a long while, I assumed you were doing this out of guilt, but...I'd like to think I was wrong."

Clara paused, her heart stammering in her chest. "I was doing it out of guilt," she admitted. "Or at least...I was at first."

"And now?" Benjamin asked, the heartbreaking need in his voice lancing through her chest.

Opening her mouth, she moved to offer him a reply, but the crunch of twigs underfoot jolted them apart and she turned, both relieved and nettled at the sight of Josiah ambling toward them.

"Such a perfect afternoon for a read!" he called. "I hope you don't mind if I join you for my daily reflection?"

Clara forced a smile and shook her head. "Why no, Josiah, of course not. Please, join us." Moving over so he could sit beside his son, she ignored Benjamin's eyes on her, knowing how his deep anguish and desire would be gazing back at her, should she choose to succumb and reflect his yearning with that of her own.

As THE SUN sank below the horizon, much like paint dripping over a still-wet canvas, Clara was unable to calm her racing mind. Her thoughts kept circling back to Benjamin, of how he'd practically begged and pleaded with her to want him, need him, *love* him without so much as a word. He deserved an answer, did he not?

That was why, she supposed, she found herself heading to his room. She tucked a copy of Voltaire's *Candide* under her arm as a feasible excuse (who would question being given a book?), and hesitated once she found his door ajar. Usually, it was completely closed…was this an unspoken invitation?

Despite her better judgment, Clara leaned forward and peered through the slat of light. There, standing alongside his bed was Benjamin, his back facing her as he fussed with the front of his breeches, shirtless and with his cane propped against his nightstand.

Unbidden, a sting of pride swelled within her breast. Although she could see him limping around with a slow, lumbering gait, he had done it—he *had!* In spite of all his negative naysaying, Benjamin not only regained a decent amount of mobility, but he'd progressed to the point where he could stand on his own two feet. Why hadn't he wished to share that with her? Was he ashamed, or did he not find her deserving of applauding in his triumphs?

Pushing the door open, she moved to announce herself when Benjamin slid his breeches over his backside. Wide-eyed and with her heart in her throat, Clara swallowed as he bent to unfasten the buttons at his knees, almost naked and oblivious to her presence as her pulse drummed throughout her entire frame. This was wrong. *Wrong!* Why couldn't she speak? Why couldn't she move? She'd seen plenty of men in a state of undress—far, far too many, in fact, and yet somehow, this was different. This was Benjamin, a man she both valued and respected, and also ached for despite the constant warning bells inside her mind.

Feeling dizzy, Clara gripped the doorway to support herself, somehow unable to tear her eyes from him as he stepped free of the garment and tended to his stockings.

From this angle, Clara could see the faded, slightly smooth scar from where he'd been shot in the spine. Although it should've been a simple circle, it was somewhat of a starburst due to Dr. Weston's slapdash surgery.

Overwhelmed, Clara fanned herself with her book. It was of little help, but Lord above, she couldn't figure out how she *should* feel, what with the constant tug-of-war between guilt and lust and pity and longing.

Unable to stand it, she quipped, "You know, I once told Catherine you have the backside of a Greek god. How fortunate that some things never change."

Benjamin cried out, whirling so quickly that he was knocked off balance. He stumbled forward, stunned, and Clara dropped her book before rushing forward to catch him. Unfortunately, she miscalculated his body weight, and the two went crashing to the hardwood floor, sprawling haphazardly with their limbs entangled.

It was inappropriate, beyond improper, and yet as they both lay there panting, their lips mere inches apart, Clara felt a throb between her legs as Benjamin shifted above her, his body bunching up her skirts between the hot apex of her thighs. With this position, she was granted a thrillingly close look into his eyes, both of which were heavy-lidded and deep and blue, much like the sapphire shade within a burning candleflame.

Heart pounding, Clara lifted a hand and cupped his cheek, her thumb tracing the curve of his mouth. His breath fanned over her face and she closed her eyes, a whimper catching in her throat once an undeniable prodding pushed between her thighs. Parting her legs in surrender, she framed his bare hips between her knees and trembled, edging his cheek into her own before his lips grazed the curve of her neck. It all felt so good, so raw, and tangling her fingers through his queue, she displayed her throat to him as his mouth opened white-hot against her skin.

"Benjamin?"

Gasping, Clara jolted and Benjamin lurched upright, clumsily rolling onto his side as Josiah's voice carried from down the hall.

"Benjamin?" he called again. "Did you fall? I thought I heard a noise…"

"Uh…" Swallowing, Benjamin shook his head and hoarsely

shouted, "N-no, Father! It's all right. I can manage myself!"

As the sound of Josiah's footsteps faded, Clara realized with increasing embarrassment that she'd interrupted Benjamin's evening bath. Pink-cheeked, she rolled into a sitting position and smoothed a hand down the front of her apron, spluttering her apologies while avoiding his gaze. Though once she tried to rise, Benjamin seized her wrist, anchoring her there while he beseechingly sought her attention.

"Don't be sorry," he entreated. Gently, he entwined their fingers and drew her hand to rest over his heart. "You never have to be sorry. Not with me." Here, he smiled in that boyish, shy manner that was so distinctly *him* before drawing her hand to his lips. Her stomach fluttered and a responding throb pulsed between her thighs, leaving her increasingly lightheaded.

"I…I-I have to go," Clara choked. Extricating herself from his grip, she dizzily launched herself to her feet and ignored the hurt in his eyes, a stab of dismay burning through her breast once she fled from the room, from her heart, and out into the safety of the empty hall.

LATER THAT NIGHT, a knock cut through the air, and Clara jerked awake. Upon realizing it was coming from the front door, she groggily rose, slipped into a dressing gown, and stepped out into the hall.

While creeping toward the living room, she heard Josiah's hushed, but diplomatic voice. Though once she spotted him, she realized his posture was rigid as he spoke to a shadowed group of redcoats holding torches and lanterns.

"Benjamin's sleeping," he said more sternly. "Unless you have actual proof of these accusations, I am going to ask you gentlemen to leave."

"Oh, we most certainly have proof!" a familiar voice spat.

Clara watched Dr. John Wagner step forward, his scornful features twisting as he stopped directly before Josiah. "These letters," he said, holding them up. "Whenever I assisted in Hoskin's regimen, he was sometimes so horribly ill that he'd leave these out for *anyone* to see."

Despite Josiah's back facing her, Clara saw his spine stiffen. "How dare you go through my son's belongings? Why, I could see to it that you—"

"Are hanged for treason!" John growled, thrusting the letters beneath the reverend's nose. "These show precisely how your son was conspiring against the Crown! General Arnold's been searching for spies and traitors, and once I heard of his intentions, I immediately knew who to add to his list!"

"These prove nothing!" Josiah hotly argued. "They are signed by someone named Apollo!"

"Apollo was your son's moniker in college!" John thundered. "I have many colleagues who'd be willing to attest!"

The British officer leading the charge held up a hand, indicating silence. "Thank you, Doctor, that will be all," he coolly said. To Josiah, he continued, "By order of the king, I hereby declare we are to make an arrest against your son, Captain Benjamin Hoskin of the Continental Army."

"Insanity!" Josiah exclaimed. "My boy was discharged due to lameness!"

"And you have my condolences," the officer replied, "but alas, he is not only lame, but a blackguard. The Crown doesn't take kindly to traitors, Reverend." He turned toward his men. "Seize them."

The soldiers pushed their way into the house, and Clara gasped as two men overpowered Josiah and forced him to his knees.

"Benjamin!" Josiah shouted. "If you can hear me, you must run! Run!"

Spinning about, Clara took off down the hall in pursuit of Benjamin's room. Behind her, she could hear the sound of boots slapping heavily against the flooring, and a sob caught in her throat as she pushed open his bedroom door and burst over the threshold. Benjamin was unsteadily rising from his bed, dressed in his nightclothes as he blinked the sleep from his eyes.

"Clara?" he croaked. "W-what...?"

"Come quickly," she pleaded. "Your efforts have been discovered, and there are soldiers here to take you into custody." Rushing to his side, she urgently tugged on his elbow. "Please...you must hurry! Do you think you can pull yourself through the window?"

Mouth open and eyes glassy with shock, Benjamin shook his head, then jerked once a group of soldiers filed in through the doorway.

"Stand down!" one of them shouted, to which Benjamin lifted his hands. Clara tried to remain by his side, but was jostled away once three soldiers restrained, searched, and wrenched Benjamin toward the hall.

"Don't!" she cried. "Please, there is no need for such roughness!"

She stumbled after them, tears stinging her eyes as she reached for Benjamin's elbow, but one of the soldiers harshly shoved her. She toppled and clipped her shoulder against the wall, her chest shivering with sobs as Benjamin was dragged to the front door.

Josiah begged and pleaded as they passed, but no man paid him any mind as he followed them outdoors. John, smug in playing his part, was the very last to approach the door, which was why Clara sought him with outstretched hands.

"John!" she called. "Dr. Wagner, please!" Racing to his side, she took his arm and peered up at him with bright, watery eyes. "You must tell them this was a mistake! It's completely cruel and cowardly to attack a man in Ben's condition!"

"You have no right to accuse anyone of being cowardly, Miss

Boyd," he hissed. "They might not know who 'CB' is, but *I* certainly do."

She flinched, her mouth falling agape. "If you know, then why haven't you reported me?"

"Because of leverage against Hoskin, just in case there are any complications with his execution," he said, smiling wider still. "I copied the letters so that they no longer have your name. Instead, the King's Men are on the lookout for some made-up chit named Isabella Greene. I'd suggest holding your tongue, lest you bring your family's reputation into question."

Clara's chin trembled. "You truly are a monster...how can you be so unfeeling, and all because of some ridiculous, trivial prank from years past?"

"You listen to me," he snarled, leaning in close. "This is about doing what's right for my country, for our king. I would've thought that as a loyalist, you would understand."

"I understand plenty," Clara sniped, her eyes sparkling with tears. "I may be loyal to our king at heart, but I make certain to never align myself with lobcocks."

Side-stepping him, she rushed through the open door and out into the vengeful night, desperation welling within as she found Josiah standing there in mournful disbelief. Coming up alongside him, she leaned into his flank and he wrapped an arm around her, both weeping as Benjamin's shivering, submissive form was hauled into the back of a prisoner's cart.

CHAPTER TWENTY-FIVE

But Once to Serve

THE NEXT MORNING, Amos sat on the MacPherson's property, whittling while he chewed a piece of grass between his teeth. That was when frantic shouts arose.

Spitting the grass, he abandoned the stick and leapt to his feet, still holding his knife as a young boy came clambering up the hill.

"Oi!" Amos exclaimed. "What's all this, uh?"

The boy came to a stop, struggling for breath as he held up a small scrap of paper. "I…I-I was paid to…t-to bring you this…a-as fast as…as I could."

"Zounds, I can see that," Amos said, taking the letter. "Y'might wanna sit down a sec, lad." When the boy did as recommended, the cabinetmaker looked at the message. The words *"He's in trouble. Come quickly. -CB"* were scrawled hastily across the parchment.

Swearing, Amos knelt alongside the boy with dark determination. "Anyone see you take this?"

The boy shook his head, still panting. "N-no, sir…no one. Just the pretty lady who…w-who paid me."

"I'll pay y'one shillin' more to keep your mouth shut about this. Y'get me?"

Eyes brightening, the boy nodded. "I won't say a peep!"

"Good lad." While Amos reached for his coin purse, he

peered out toward the skyline at the gray, foreboding bleakness creeping along the horizon.

"TELL ME THE truth!"

Benjamin panted, his nose dribbling blood as he remained bound and hunkered inside a makeshift prison cell.

Snarling, the appointed man for his torture, a loyalist named O'Grady, harshly clocked his face. "Listen here, y'hulver-headed arse," he hissed, "you're a dead man, so make nice with the Lord and tell me where Isabella Greene is!"

Benjamin lifted his gaze, confusion blitzing across his eyes. *Isabella Greene?* "I…I don't know who that is…"

O'Grady struck him and Benjamin yelped, crashing painfully onto his side.

"We've got your letters, y'sniveling codshead, so there's no use denying it!" the balding man barked. "We need to know who she is to you, and *where* she is!"

Despite the pain throbbing through every nerve ending, Benjamin was overcome by a wave of relief. They didn't know about Clara. Somehow, by some miracle, they didn't know she was involved. A grateful smile stretched Benjamin's mouth, aggravating the cut on his upper cheek.

"Oh, so y'think this is funny, do you?" O'Grady growled. "I'll teach y'true comedy!"

Snagging Benjamin's collar, he dragged the younger man across the dirty cellar floor until he reached a wooden bucket. All at once, panic burst within Benjamin and he squirmed, a shudder ripping through him as it became difficult to breathe. Images of that night flashed behind his eyes: memories of inhaling water while Donnelly laughed and jeered his cruel incitements.

"Please," Benjamin begged, terror ringing in his voice, "I...I-I can't breathe..."

"Aye, that's the point," O'Grady snapped. "Unless you've got information for me, in y'go!"

Lips flapping soundlessly, Benjamin yelped as the man seized the back of the neck and dunked his head into the bucket with a forceful, aggressive shove.

BY THE TIME Amos arrived at the Hoskin residence, everyone was waiting for him at the dining room table. Clara stood and twisted her hands, her face pale as Josiah gestured for Amos to join them.

"What's this about, uh?" he asked. "What happened to Moony?"

"Sit down," Josiah entreated, to which Amos shook his head.

"Nuh-uh, too glimflashy to sit. Jus' tell me what's goin' on."

"General Arnold," Clara choked. "He...h-he's been sending out groups of soldiers to arrest potential blackguards. I'm unsure how many others were targeted, but Benjamin's involvement was leaked by his physician."

Amos's eyes blazed. "Why that back-bitin' sonofa—"

"He's not the point of this," she interjected. "Seeing how they have proof of Ben's espionage, he'll be executed. That doesn't leave us much time to plan."

"Long enough," Amos said. "Is he bein' held prisoner here?"

Josiah nodded. "They wanted to take him to New York City, but I bribed them with coin, livestock, and wheat to keep him here. Once I reminded them that Benjamin would be made an example of amongst his own people, as well as other potential blackguards, they agreed and dispatched a message for Arnold's approval. Once they receive word, the execution will begin...or postpone, depending upon whether or not he agrees to the terms."

"So, we might have more than a few days," Amos surmised, his brow creasing. "No matter. I've got an idea."

"What are you proposing?" Clara asked.

"Never you mind. The less y'know, the safer you'll be. Jus' be assured I'll be scopin' the area."

She frowned, nervously fiddling with her fichu. "And do you need a map for this excursion?"

He shook his head. "I know this place like the back o' me hand, all the surroundin' areas, too."

"And what if you don't return in time?" Josiah pressed.

"We'll have a backup plan. For now, I need you—" Amos pointed at Clara. "—to visit with Moony. As his caretaker, you can request a moment alone with your patient."

Pulse leaping, Clara flushed and looked between both men. "I imagine I'll need a bribe for this…"

"Only with coin," Josiah cut in, expression stern. "If they demand more, I'll be there to help barter."

Releasing a breath, she smoothed her hands over her jumps and nodded. "What do you need me to do?"

Finally, Amos's mouth quirked into a grin. "How d'ya feel about carryin' a knife?"

WITH HIS ARMS tied around a support beam, Benjamin squirmed against the cellar floor, feeling as if there were a sharp blade in his lungs. He didn't dare think of Josiah nor Clara, of what would become of his body. Would he be delivered home? Would his bones entwine with the tall, gnarled trees he and Daniel played in during their youth? Or would he be cast aside in some nameless, forgotten grave?

The tavern cellar doors opened, and then blinding light filtered in over the hay-strewn floor. The sound of boots slapping against steps roused Benjamin's attention, and he winced once a guard, Stevens, strode forward with a sneer.

"Hoskin! You've got yourself a visitor, so you'd better look alive."

Benjamin remained unmoving, his lent clothing still soaked from earlier.

"Hoskin!" The guard snapped his fingers. "We don't got all day! Well..." He chuckled. "*You* don't got all day."

"Will you leave us, please?" a familiar voice asked—*Clara*—and his heart leapt once she came into view. "I paid quite a bit of coin to see my charge, so I demand some privacy."

Stevens grunted. "Sorry, but that's not happenin'. I'm feelin' generous, so I'll stand over here so you two can jaw."

"But sir!"

"Take it or leave it."

Stevens walked off to the far corner of the room, and Benjamin sluggishly rose. When he staggered against his supportive post, Clara gasped. His right cheek was cut and swollen, and in addition to the rope tying his wrists, he bore pink, chafed rings from being so tightly restrained.

Trembling, Clara reached forward and took his bound hands. She shook in his grip and it pained him to see, to feel, how little comfort he could provide.

"Oh, Ben..." With tears in her eyes, Clara wove her arms around him and the obstructive post, fiercely embracing him. Her breath dissolved into soft, shuddery sobs, and her fingers gripped his soaked shirt while he willed the post and shackles to disappear. His bindings kept them from truly embracing, from holding one another as tightly as he wished. Once Benjamin nudged his cheek into her hair, her sobs tore through him akin to a dull blade.

"It's all right," he soothed, his lips brushing her crown.

"No," Clara choked, "it's not. You look…y-you look dreadful, and you're here all alone, and…and you've clearly been tortured, and I'm not even able to help you shoulder this pain!"

"As it should be," Benjamin sternly replied. "This is what I deserve."

"How?" Clara demanded.

"Because I've hurt people," he whispered.

She shook her head. "Ben, nearly every soldier has hurt people," she dismissed. "This is *war,* and—"

"No, no, you don't understand," he cut in, his voice raw. "I never told anyone this, but…I am so much worse." She withdrew then, meeting his eyes as a silent plea to continue. He shivered, and his bottom lip quivered in shame. "When Donnelly held me hostage, he revealed that on the day of my brother's execution, I killed a man…his own brother." Benjamin's eyes grew glassy, and he tensed his jaw.

Clara touched his hands. "What happened?"

He swallowed, no longer able to hold her gaze. "Some patriots and I staged a rescue for Daniel. Amidst the confusion, I stabbed a man to defend myself. I didn't realize he died." Benjamin exhaled, long and tremulous. "Losing Daniel was the worst pain imaginable, so I empathize with what Donnelly endured. I am responsible for his loss, Clara—*me*—which is why I must willingly accept this sentence. This is my atonement. I deserve to hurt, to suffer, to die for taking a life."

Clara's gaze sharpened. "You are not going to die, Benjamin Hoskin, and you don't deserve to hurt, suffer, or hang because a grown man enlisted of his own accord. Sacrifices are made in war; I am learning that every passing day, and I imagine Donnelly's brother knew this, as well." She lifted a hand, and his heart stuttered as she stroked his bruised cheek. "In the end, all we can do is pray we'll make the right choices and be the very best version of ourselves we can. And Ben, you have taught me to be better…to be kinder, and more accepting. I may not know what lay in that man's heart, but I know what lies in mine." Here, she flashed a tearful smile. "You've opened my eyes to a world I never thought possible: to admiring, supporting, and even *caring* for people I once viewed as the enemy. I have nothing but the deepest respect and affection for you."

Benjamin's gaze softened. "Clara..."

She framed his face and rose on tiptoe, joining her mouth fervently with his. Benjamin angled into her kiss as though starved, melting into her touch while fumbling in boyish, clumsy desperation at whatever part of her his bound hands could reach. Her lips edged more strongly into his, and he kissed her back with equal need, both helpless and eager to forget, to postpone, to ignore his pending fate.

Discreetly, Clara lowered a folded pocketknife beneath the waistband of Benjamin's breeches. He broke the kiss, baffled, before she edged her cheek into his and whispered, "Only use that if necessary. We don't know when we'll be able to help you, so it is imperative that you keep that hidden."

He nodded against her cheek.

"All right, time's up!" Stevens gruffly cut in. "The deal was ten minutes, but I'd say I've given you more than enough time. I'm about ready to cast up my accounts with all this lovers' claptrap!"

With her hands on Benjamin's, Clara mournfully drew back. "Take care," she whispered. A lone tear trailed into her mouth, and when he entwined their fingers, she whimpered. "Please, Ben. I have to go..."

Wordless, Benjamin drew his lips to the softness of her palms, nuzzling her as his heart dropped. This wasn't fair. It wasn't! Now that he'd found someone to love, he would never experience the joys of being Clara's husband, of holding their firstborn in the crook of his elbow, beaming with fatherly pride at the perfection they'd created. If there was any remaining kindness in this world, his father and Clara would live on. Benjamin would miss their birthdays, their achievements, and their losses; he would fail to be there when they needed him most, just as he'd failed them here in the land of the living.

"I'm sorry," he choked.

Wiping the tears from her cheeks, Clara winced when Stevens impatiently flanked her side.

"Come along," he grumbled. "I'll be in trouble if you stay much longer!"

Clara lifted her chin. "Yes, very well," she agreed. "You may escort me outside, sir." As Stevens led the way back to the cellar steps, she glanced at Benjamin over her shoulder.

Benjamin flashed an encouraging smile. He wished to ingrain her in his memory, his heart, and as they locked eyes that final moment, he felt oddly reassured by the fond smile on her lips.

IT TOOK FOUR days for Benjamin's execution, four whole days of sitting about in limbo, unallowed to visit, nor send notes to the prison. A part of Clara wondered if she and Jedediah were on better terms, if he might've been able to break the pending noose. Loyalists and redcoats looked up to him, revered her father, and she supposed this was why she, herself, hadn't been troubled, not beyond being questioned for her infatuation with a "loathsome rebel." But she wasn't just infatuated. By some cruel, unlucky twist of fate, Clara had fallen in love with Benjamin Hoskin. She was uncertain of when and how…whether it was during their private, increasingly fervent letters, or being there at his most vulnerable, or seeing him overwhelm, overcome, and conquer all odds, but she did love him. Tragically, she did, and as she stood amidst the crowd gathering at the gallows, it felt as if her very heart were tattooing the beat of the executioner's drum.

Behind them, Benjamin was being led toward the quickly erected gibbet; and despite the bruising on his face and heavy, twisting gait to his step, there was a certain pride, a spiteful fire in his eyes as he limped toward his fate. All eyes were on him. Even with the King's Men flanking his sides in their bright, magnificent regalia, no one turned their heads from Benjamin as the redcoats helped him along.

Nervously, Clara searched the crowd. Amos was nowhere to be found, and yet he'd promised he had everything under control. How was this adhering to his promise? The proposed backup plan was for Josiah to use a flintlock, to potentially sacrifice himself, and the thought of losing not just Benjamin, but the both of them burned agonizingly within her stomach.

At her side, Josiah lightly touched her hand. He'd grown intuitive to her moods over the past month, and grateful, she interlaced their fingers.

"It will be all right," Josiah whispered to her. "God will provide."

Clara's eyes stung and her chin wobbled. Would He? God gave her Timothy, but He'd also taken him away… What if that same agonizing fate befell her with Benjamin? Amos had sworn that during the night, he'd tampered with the rope so that it was likely to weaken and snap, but what if that wasn't enough?

The echo of snare drums throbbed painfully within her breast, and each step Benjamin took left Clara increasingly lightheaded. "Josiah," she pleaded.

He held her hand tighter. All around them, everyone remained deathly still, watching Benjamin get corralled to his doom. When he was helped onto a wooden crate, the executioner rose with him and slid a noose around his neck. And as their eyes locked from across the crowd, when she saw Benjamin's shame, his sorrow, his affection, she suddenly forgot how to breathe. She squeezed Josiah's hand so tightly that her bones ached.

A gruff, no-nonsense provost marshal stepped forward, and he opened a scroll once the drumming stopped. Clearing his throat, he shouted above the silence, "The accused, Captain

Benjamin Hoskin of the Continental Army, having been found guilty of espionage and treasonous conspiracy against the Crown, and therefore God, shall hereby be executed as a blackguard on this day in the year of our Lord, 1780. If the condemned has any last words, let him speak now, lest he carry that burden to the grave!"

Fumbling at her fichu, Clara quivered as Benjamin continued facing her. Though rather than cry or spit or curse, he remained composed as a faint smile touched his mouth. And then he raised his voice and proudly proclaimed, "'How beautiful is death, when earned by virtue? Though you ensnare my life, my country will be free!'"

A flurry of startled voices arose, and Clara's mouth dropped once she realized just *who* Benjamin's brother was. The death of Daniel Hoskin had made him a folk hero of sorts, scorned by loyalists and martyred by patriots, alike, and here Benjamin was, honoring his brother by reciting his infamous last words. Tears blurred Clara's vision, and when the executioner shoved Benjamin fiercely from the crate, she screamed once the rope caught his fall in a harsh, taut swing.

CHAPTER TWENTY-SIX
Mr. and Mrs. Smith

BENJAMIN'S VISION PITCHED and wavered along with the treacherous swing, the noose catching his fall so jarringly that he almost lost consciousness. He heard a scream—*Clara?*—and kicking his legs, he gritted his teeth while searching with his feet for land.

Amidst the crowd, a familiar figure materialized and he halted, the fight in him draining once a pair of bright, mischievous brown eyes and a crooked grin greeted him amidst the jeering spectators. All at once, tears swam across his vision and Benjamin trembled, bright spots of light dotting his peripheral as he met Daniel's gaze.

"I'm…sorry," he rasped. He was. By God, he was! Nearly every night, Benjamin prayed his brother would somehow know how deeply he was mourned, his counsel yearned for, his companionship missed; and above all, he prayed Daniel knew how remorseful he was that he'd failed to be there when he needed him most.

A lone tear trickled down Benjamin's cheek, uncomfortably warm as he struggled to breathe. Daniel's impish expression changed and became austere amidst the heckling crowd.

"You can't give up, Moony," he spoke, his words a disconcerting rasp amidst the ringing in Benjamin's ears. "Live for them, for *her*, and achieve what I failed to do."

Failure was too harsh a word. And when Benjamin moved to reply, all that came out was a strangled rush of air, his face turning blue as his lungs quivered and burned from lack of breath. Daniel disappeared and a newfound burst of resolve enveloped him. Gritting his teeth, Benjamin dipped his bound hands inside his breeches and grabbed Amos's pocketknife. Withdrawing it and flicking open the blade, he thrust up his arms and hacked at the rope, his limbs feeling heavy and numb as the bright spots in his vision worsened.

A gunshot tore through the air, and he flinched, awaiting the inevitable embrace of his Savior. But when death didn't come, when he realized he was still alive, Benjamin brightened at the sight of Amos on horseback, aiming his second flintlock at a charging soldier before squeezing off another shot. The redcoat jolted, stunned, before plummeting to the ground. From all angles, a small group of patriot militiamen descended upon the enemy, following Amos's lead. Screams and shouts arose from civilians, and each spectator took off in a different direction, leaving the scene in complete and utter chaos.

Amidst his sawing, Benjamin scanned the crowd for Clara. She was nowhere to be found... Was she safe? Had she been accosted as vengeance toward *himself*?

Panicking at the thought, Benjamin sliced through the rope and dropped heavily onto his side. He throbbed and ached all over, and gasping for breath, he coughed as four horse hooves stomped alongside his peripheral.

"Oi!" Amos called. "You all right there, Moony?"

"It's...i-it's about...time," Benjamin rasped, the ache in his throat growing raw.

Amos huffed. "No need for the sass, ya ingrate!" Hopping down from his mount, he took Benjamin's elbows and helped him to his feet, using his shoulder to support the other man's weight while unfastening his restraints. "Clara an' your father are at the wharf," he explained. "I've got a dory set up for ya. The others an' I can hold everyone off 'til you get outta here." When

Benjamin gaped at him, he growled, "Go on, get to 'em. *Go!*"

Not needing to be told twice, Benjamin accepted the horse's reins and allowed Amos to swing his leg up until he was seated. The cabinetmaker gave the horse's rump a sound smack, and the steed took off in a bolt, giving Benjamin little time to prepare as he held on for all he was worth. A musket ball whizzed overhead, barely missing his ear.

"He's getting away! Don't let him leave!"

Feeling sick, Benjamin desperately nudged his heels into the horse's flanks. From this vantage point, he could see a slew of dead redcoats dotting the ground like drops of blood. There was no one there to stop him…

Still struggling to breathe, Benjamin panted while leaning in toward the horse's head, hoping this newfound angle would allow him greater speed. Despite his vision tunneling, he was able to hone in on Clara and his father, both of whom were huddled inside a dory along the docks.

Almost there…

Digging his heels in harder, Benjamin released a triumphant breath once the horse tore up alongside them, and he tugged on the reins, drawing the snorting beast to a stop. Though once he dismounted, he doubled over and coughed, his knees giving out as Clara climbed onto the pier and raced to his side.

"Ben?" she coaxed, taking his elbow. "Ben, we have to go…"

Josiah was at his other side in an instant, and weakly, he let his father heft him up and drag him toward the boat. Clara rushed over to hold the vessel still before he was clumsily placed inside. The craft rocked and Benjamin collapsed to his knees, sucking the salty air into his lungs as Josiah helped Clara in alongside him.

"You must go," he told them. "I imagine McQuinn and the others won't serve as a distraction for long."

Perplexed, Benjamin lifted his head, his breath still wheezing in his lungs. "W-what…? Aren't you…coming with us?"

"No." Josiah shook his head. "I must stay here."

"But—!"

"I'd only slow you down," he continued. "A party of two is much better at evading danger than three."

Curling her arm around Benjamin's shoulders, Clara looked to him with tears in her eyes. "You *have* to come with us," she pleaded. "It's too dangerous here!"

"I'm not the one they're after," he reminded them. "And besides, once McQuinn finishes up, he'll come back for me. The moment it's safe to do so, I'll find you and make contact."

"Write to…t-to the troops in Morristown," Benjamin agreed. "I have friends there."

Josiah nodded, tearful as he knelt and held out a hand. Tremblingly, Benjamin clasped his father's hand in return, then fell into Josiah's embrace as the older man fiercely drew him into his arms. "Be safe, Benjamin," he whispered, "and take care of her."

Gripping his father's coat, the unspoken *always* filled the air between them, and Benjamin sank onto his haunches with a lump in his bruised throat. Retrieving the oars, he never took his eyes off his father while Josiah pushed them away from the docks.

PROLONGED OCEAN TRAVEL was dangerous with so many enemy vessels, so they steered up an estuary that would lead to Union Wharf. Amidst this time, Clara had been aiding in the rowing but finally needed a moment to rest, so Benjamin continued on without her help.

"He'll be fine, you know." Clara's voice was gentle as it carried over the breeze. "Your father's a remarkable man, and Corporal McQuinn knows his way around a weapon. I'm sure they've escaped by now."

Benjamin hummed in agreement, though there was clear melancholy in his eyes. "I never thanked him," he murmured.

"Father sacrificed so much for me, and yet I never told him how grateful I am…"

"He knows," Clara assured. Expression fond, she watched Benjamin row to correct their course, all the while assessing his condition. There was a stark, rope-shaped bruise and abrasion from where the noose dug mercilessly into his skin, and his eyes were bloodshot from the strain of staying alive. Despite their need to remain on their respective sides, Clara felt a strong urge to go to him, to cup his face and kiss those harsh, ugly marks, and praise the God she barely spoke to for sparing his life. But instead, she ventured a weak, "Are you all right?"

It wasn't like Clara to be timorous, but what if Benjamin wasn't all right? What if he'd been injured so grievously that he was dying, and didn't know it?

Benjamin lifted his gaze and smiled. "I've been better," he rasped. Even with the direness of their predicament, he chuckled, the sound pained before he broke into a coughing fit.

Anxious, Clara asked, "Do you need water?"

He shook his head, and the hacking slowly subsided. "No. We've been traveling for a couple hours, so it should only take two or three more to get to New Haven. I can refresh myself then."

Stunned, Clara hissed, "It's only been two hours?" When he nodded, she groaned and dropped her chin into her hands. "Why New Haven? Do you have family there?"

"I went to school there," Benjamin reminded her. "I know the area well and feel we can blend in until I figure out how to get us back to camp."

Clara grimaced. "So, we *are* heading to Morristown?"

"Eventually, yes. It's what's safest." Clearing his sore throat, he explained, "If we headed there straightaway, our pursuers might expect it and cut us off."

"You think we're being pursued?" Shivering, Clara wrapped her cloak around her shoulders. It was cold and bleak and the beginning of December. She couldn't imagine anyone pursuing a rebel spy in such conditions, regardless of the reward.

Benjamin met her eyes, and a new shiver passed through her, but this time due to the tender warmth that burned within his kind, all-encompassing gaze. "Are *you* all right?" he gently asked.

A knot formed in her throat and she exhaled. It was so like him to deflect and only be concerned with *her*. "I am," she assured him. "Other than being scared half to death, I didn't sustain harm." Slowly, a mischievous smirk curved her lips. "Alas, it also seems my bottom is numb from this uncomfortable wooden seat."

Benjamin blinked, startled by her candor, before he broke into a wide grin. "Believe me, there are far worse things that can go numb down there."

Clara laughed. "If you're referring to what I think you are, then yes, I can't say I disagree…though I am surprised I've so deeply influenced your ribald sense of humor."

"Of course you have," Benjamin replied. His voice became low and fervent. "You've been an imprint on my heart for over a year now, Clara…that kind of affection doesn't go away."

With a tremulous breath, she squirmed and fended off a blush. "Ben, I hope you realize I very much wish to kiss you…but since I also fear we might capsize amidst my ardor, you'll have to wait until we make it to land." Here, her gaze grew pointed. "Row faster."

With a bashful smile, Benjamin acquiesced.

UNFORTUNATELY, BY THE time they moored against Union Wharf, the weather was far too severe for any romantic dalliances. The sky had darkened, and with a shriek, Clara covered her head while thick, heavy droplets of sleet pelted them relentlessly from above. The precipitation started long before their arrival, so both Benjamin and Clara were drenched as they stumbled along the pier.

"We need a horse!" he shouted over to her.

"An inn, more like!" she volleyed. "We can't possibly travel like this!" Nearly tripping over her skirts, she reached for Benjamin's hand, and the two staggered half blind as the chilly wind whipped and whistled from all sides.

Along the wharf, anchored ships rocked precariously atop the waves, and the constant motion made Clara's stomach turn. Her breath burned like icy fire in her lungs, and squinting at the row of closely knit buildings they stumbled past, she wondered if any of them could provide refuge. "Ben?"

"Just a little farther!" he called back. "There's an inn right off Water Street!"

Unfortunately, Benjamin's heavy limp was finally starting to take its toll. Amidst his efforts at getting his legs to cooperate, he tripped and fell harshly to his knees, panting as Clara frantically stooped to assist.

"You need to find shelter!" he shouted over the rain. "I can't...I-I can't keep going..."

"I'm *not* leaving you behind!" she scolded. "Come...surely, we can find a horse or coach!" Leaning down to shoulder his weight, she helped him rise on wobbly legs.

Being only early evening, there was still enough light to guide their way, and yet the bleak sky and blinding sleet made it difficult as they searched. Benjamin and Clara limped past another row of ghostly buildings, each only coming alive with the flicker of candleflame within their windows. Most citizens were smart and remained indoors. Those in the streets were either taking it in stride, or stumbling along the slick path, much as Benjamin and Clara were.

"Look!" the latter exclaimed, nearly giving a sob of relief. Pointing up ahead, she indicated the lumbering stagecoach headed their way.

Eager, she waved a hand while she supported Benjamin's weight with the other, her arm squeezing him more securely as the horse-drawn carriage crawled to a stop.

"The inn off Water Street, please!" she called to the grave-faced driver.

He appeared put out since that was in the complete opposite direction he was facing, yet he nodded and indicated that they climb inside.

THE CARRIAGE RIDE was quick. After paying their driver, Clara and Benjamin practically threw the door to the Mulford Inn off its hinges, dripping wet and shaking as they crossed the threshold. They both knew they must look a fright: Clara, sodden and pale, and Benjamin, inappropriately dressed without a waistcoat, nor jacket to cover his shame.

The innkeeper, however, seemed wholly indifferent. The old man looked up from his book with a pout, clearly bothered by the intrusion. "Just a moment," he said with a sigh.

Being indoors made it all the more apparent of how miserable it was outside, and with the warmer air upon her skin, Clara shivered harder. Benjamin hobbled toward the front desk and she followed, watching the innkeeper retrieve a leatherbound book.

"Wanna room?" he asked, sounding bored.

Benjamin cleared his throat. "Uh…yes, please. For me and my wife."

A jolt rushed through Clara at the declaration, her eyes wide and cheeks warm. Naturally, it made perfect sense to create such a lie, given how scandal would follow an unwed couple, but that didn't keep the giddiness from flooding her veins.

"Name?" the innkeeper asked, impatient.

"John Smith," Benjamin lied.

Sloppily scratching out the alias, the innkeeper muttered, "Mr. and Mrs. Smith," before turning to the key rack. He wiggled his fingers, then plucked a key that read 7 in chalk above the hook.

The old man handed Benjamin the key, and Clara offered her coin purse, seeing how he was still wearing his lent raiment. Benjamin was embarrassed by the gesture but accepted since there was no other choice.

"Your room comes with a meal," the innkeeper announced, already reaching for his book again. "I can take everything up to you."

From this angle, the title was revealed as *A Treatise of the Use of Flogging in Venereal Affairs*. Clara's interest was instantly piqued, but Benjamin grew flustered, his eyes snapping toward the wall. "Uh…thank you. That would be wonderful."

"I'll see to it," the man muttered, never lifting his eyes from the text.

Benjamin touched her arm, and Clara followed toward the staircase behind the desk. Once they were safely out of earshot, he muttered, "I suppose we won't be getting supper for a while."

"Definitely not," Clara agreed.

Guided by candlelit sconces alongside each closed door, they found the seventh room, and Benjamin inserted the key into the lock. "I hope there's at least a bed warmer," he said.

"Why? *I'm* here, aren't I?" Catching the spark of boyish panic in his eyes, Clara laughed while he fumbled with the key. "You do realize there will only be one bed, yes?"

The lock gave way, and Benjamin stumbled in through the door, rattled as he placed the key onto a wash table by the window. Across from him was a banked fire, two ladderback chairs, and pressed against the wall was the promised bed with a frayed, but serviceable quilt possessing tremendous character—perhaps a little too much, given the wear and tear.

Outside, the icy rain continued beating steadily and Clara

shivered, closing the door and rubbing her arms for warmth. Now that they were stationary, it was getting increasingly difficult to ignore the uncomfortable chill.

Seeing her distress, Benjamin limped over to the hearth and grabbed a fireplace bellows, pumping air onto the embers while a few soaked, bedraggled locks of hair bobbed in his face. The fabric of his borrowed shirt stuck to his broad shoulders, and his shoes squelched as he knelt, trembling in front of the flickering flames.

Clara softened. Approaching him, she laid a hand on his shoulder and squeezed, encouraging him to stop.

Bewildered, he looked up at her questioningly. "Is something wrong?" he asked.

Wordless, she brushed the backs of her fingers against his cheek, studying his weary fatigue, the bruising along his face and neck, and overall masculine beauty. His eyes tilted to hers more directly, and a lump bobbed in her throat. It was painful to think how those eyes had nearly been closed to her forever.

Benjamin moved to speak, but she tucked her fingers beneath his shirt collar and tugged, the fabric stubbornly catching against his skin.

"Clara? W-what...?"

"I'm taking off your clothes," she replied sternly. "If I don't, you'll catch your death of cold."

Unnerved, he reluctantly lifted his arms to aid in his disrobement. With this preferred angle, Clara got a better grip, and little by little, she peeled the waterlogged fabric from his skin. Benjamin staggered to his feet, self-conscious as she laid out his garment to dry.

"You don't have to keep helping," he said, his voice filled with shame. "Over the past several weeks, you've done more than enough to take care of me."

Unruffled, Clara corrected, "I took care of you because I *wanted* to. Believe me, Ben, you would know if this were all against my will." She frowned at the water droplets clinging to his torso, each catching the firelight with a warm, ethereal glow. "I suppose that'll have to do until we receive a towel…"

"*If* we receive one," Benjamin corrected.

"Right. If." Stepping forward, Clara reached for his breeches, but Benjamin's hand came around her wrist. She jerked at the contact, startled.

When she lifted her eyes to his face, a stinging heat filled her as his other hand cupped her cheek, his thumb skimming the full, parted curve of her lips. "You're wet too," he observed.

Clara wished to make a joke, but the vulgar quip died in her throat as his fingertips drifted downward, hesitant and unsure as he traced her quilted jumps. His cheeks grew charmingly pink as he asked, "May I…?"

Wordless, Clara nodded.

Expression focused and determined, Benjamin struggled with her lacing before finding success, a shyness glowing in his eyes as the garment loosened.

Untying her cloak from her neck, Clara let the raiment fall in a drenched, graceless heap. She reached for Benjamin's breeches once more, but this time, he didn't stop her. While he worked on her jumps, she unfastened the double buttons along his waist. With each newly freed clasp, she could see his eyes darting nervously in between his breeches and the task at hand, sweetly bashful despite having nothing to be embarrassed about.

Once her jumps were hanging open, Clara shrugged the garment from her lithe frame, then returned her focus to his fall front. Benjamin hesitated, his gaze low while fumbling along her outer petticoats. Upon finding the ties, he ducked to unfasten the ribbons, the motion drawing his cheek nearly flush against her own.

Unable to resist teasing him, Clara lifted her mouth and whispered in his ear, "See? I *knew* you were a natural at disrobing women."

Despite being unable to see Benjamin's face, she could feel the hot warmth emanating from his skin. Her outer skirts slipped to the floor, wet and cumbersome, just as she finished unfastening his fall flap. It dropped downward, and she moved to tug his breeches beneath his hips.

"W-wait," he pleaded, catching her arms.

"Why?" she pressed. "Ben, you have nothing to be ashamed of."

Gaze pointing toward the floor, he stepped back and unfastened the buttons around his knees, allowing his breeches the room for proper removal. Clara, in turn, tended to her under petticoats, shoes, and clocked stockings, and discarded them atop her other clothing. Left in only her shift and lace cap, she watched as Benjamin awkwardly stepped out of his shoes and breeches. After he'd removed his stockings, he swallowed once he caught her eyes on him.

He was beautiful in his shyness. Tense and unable to keep his eyes on her, Benjamin looked between her face and the floor in rapid succession, his hands curling as he uncomfortably shifted from side to side. Although Clara briefly saw him during their candlelit fumbling, this felt more genuine…intimate, and her breath hitched at the sight of corded muscle, bruises, and various scarring.

Closing the distance between them, Clara lifted a hand and laid her fingertips against the harsh, uneven mark above his hip bone. Although Benjamin never told her directly, Amos once relayed how Donnelly sliced open Benjamin's wound, which meant he'd been stabbed, stitched up, reopened, and resewn all in a matter of weeks. With a painful swell of emotion, Clara brushed her thumb across the scar and spread her free hand over his chest, his true frailty reflecting in the sharp, staccato rhythm of his heart.

Tears sparkled in her eyes, and Clara leaned forward to brush a soft, barely there kiss against the rope burn on his neck. Benjamin flinched, perhaps pained, before ultimately relaxing into her touch. Cupping his cheeks between her palms, Clara rose on tiptoe and opened her mouth against his pulse, wet and warm before he shivered beneath her ministrations. Earnest in her ardor, she seared her lips along the stark bruising, her tongue darting out against his skin as his hands fell to her waist.

"Y-you're still dressed," Benjamin choked. She pressed a placating kiss to his chin and stepped back.

Removing the cap from her hair, Clara unpinned her long, curly locks until they came cascading over her shoulders. Benjamin clearly wished to help. His face was an open mask of desire, and his palms lifted, but she denied the assistance and unlaced the collar of her shift. The neckline loosened, and the garment slipped from her lissome curves before puddling around her feet, leaving her bare and practically glowing within the firelight.

Benjamin breathed out as though winded. His eyes widened, and his pupils became blown, his mouth opening and closing as he appraised her in wordless wonder. When she stepped toward him, he grew endearingly flushed, the healthy pink flooding from his face to his chest.

"I…I-I have to sit down," he stammered.

"Why?" Clara asked, concerned. "Because of your condition?"

Benjamin blushed further. "N-no, uh…because of *you*."

She laughed, a warmth fluttering within her breast. When men told her she was beautiful, she considered it a ploy, a way to ensure she gave up her body to their forceful, pawing hands. But when Benjamin implied her beauty, Clara couldn't help but believe him…couldn't help but feel that she was, in fact, beautiful.

Taking his hand, she lowered to kiss his knuckles, her touch soft and fond as she murmured, "All right then. Have a seat."

Stumbling toward the chair by the hearth, Benjamin sank upon it as she joined him. Clara drew between his legs, and his hands fell to her waist. Her wet mouth urged into his, deep and slow, and with a roll of his tongue, he tasted the headiness of their kiss, his fingers knotting through her hair as he melted into the needy slant of her mouth. To his surprise, Clara was the first to break away.

"Wait a moment," she pleaded, breathless as she cupped his face. "What are we doing, Ben?"

Swallowing, he turned his head and pressed a kiss to her palm. "Tonight, you are my wife," he reminded her. "I…I want you, all of you…if you will have me."

Clara quivered, brushing her thumb over his lips. "And you're sure you wish to give up your virtue? To damn yourself for me?"

A molten look overcame his eyes within the firelight, and curling his hand around her wrist, Benjamin whispered, "I'm *already* damned without you." Chasing her mouth with his, he snagged his fingers through her hair and gathered her into his arms, angling into their heated kiss as Clara framed his hips between her thighs. The silent plea of *moremoremore* burst through his veins, and trembling all over, he smoothed his hands from her waist to her breasts, inflamed by her soft moan once his thumbs rolled over her nipples in careful, hesitant circles. He didn't know where this confidence was coming from, this want, this need, this desperation, but with Clara grinding herself against his swelling hardness, he wished to do nothing but succumb.

While her fingers unraveled his queue, Clara pressed more urgently into their kiss, her lips crashing strongly into Benjamin's as he traced his fingertips along her skin. His touch was reverent and oh-so-careful, his worshipful behavior nearly bringing tears to her eyes. When had a man taken this much care? She couldn't recall anyone ever being so cautious in the way they handled her. Breaking the kiss to nudge their foreheads together, she panted against his lips, overwhelmed and shaking while his tentative touch trailed between her thighs. Clara gasped, her head tipping back as Benjamin prodded at her entrance. That was when he pushed two fingers inside her. Once he flexed and curled them between her walls, she started to writhe, whimper, and curse, her nails digging pleadingly into his shoulders while she bucked her hips.

Benjamin's expression grew sweetly awestruck, his eyes heavy-lidded, and his mouth slack as he rocked his hand between her legs. He was enraptured by Clara's sudden desperation, his cock becoming painfully hard beneath her bottom as she squirmed and grasped his wrist.

"Rub me," she pleaded.

Bemused, Benjamin allowed her to guide his thumb until it was placed over her clit, then he followed her lead, clumsy at first as he mimicked the brisk, fervent little circles she encouraged him to rub across her bud. All at once, her breathing grew labored. Her eyelids fluttered closed, and while rolling into the assault between her legs, Clara mewled and yanked on his loosened queue, desperate as she started to twitch and spasm around his thrusting fingers. She didn't wish to come undone…not yet.

"Wait, wait," she entreated, forcing them both to stop. Lips brushing his, she informed him, "I want to ride you."

Benjamin drew a hitched breath, his limbs quivering as he nodded. The unspoken *anything for you* filled the space between them, and helping her get more comfortable in his lap, his lashes went half-mast as she rolled her soaked entrance along his tip, testing the feel of him before they locked eyes.

"Is this all right?" she asked.

He nodded again, squeezing desperately at her waist.

Curling her arms around his shoulders, Clara pressed an assuaging kiss to his mouth, hoping to calm him as slowly she eased herself down around his length, his body tensing beneath her as a deep, throaty groan rumbled inside his chest. Trailing kisses from his cheek to his neck, Clara spread her legs farther and rolled her hips, taking him down to the hilt as he cried out and clutched her shaking frame. They both grew needy, frantic, and then his mouth was clumsily seeking hers once more, her hands yanking on his undone hair as she began to rise and fall against him.

Benjamin shuddered, and Clara licked into his mouth, devouring his low groans as he arched into her rocking hips. He'd always heard stories growing up, specifically, about kissing and sex itself, but nothing could've possibly prepared him for the warm, thrilling pleasure that coursed throughout his limbs, his cock throbbing each time her heat clenched tightly around him.

With their lips brushing amidst each thrust, Clara gasped as Benjamin drove between her legs whenever she sank down, the act leaving her dazed and her knees wobbly as his thumb returned to rubbing her clit. Though unexpected, it was Benjamin who stopped this time, his chest heaving as he shook his head.

"It's too much," he rasped. "I…I don't think…I-I can't…" Desperate, he took Clara's waist and hefted her upward, disengaging while pressing a kiss over her heart. "Please," he begged her. "I…I-I want to try something…"

Beholden to his every whim and fancy, Clara slid off the chair and allowed him to guide her onto the floor, where they both lay out amidst the flickering firelight. Amidst his clumsy crawl, it was clear to her that he wished to love her as though unencumbered, that he wished to give *her* pleasure as opposed to himself.

Lifting a hand to curl over his cheek, Clara spread her legs, and then Benjamin was covering her mouth with kisses, deep and passionate, as he drew her thighs up to lock around his waist. Cupping his face, Clara angled more fiercely into his lips, frantic as her heels pressed into his bottom and pulled him upward, attempting to gather him back inside her.

Benjamin didn't need any provocation. Dizzy and eager, he drove inside her warmth and growled into her mouth, their tongues tangling as with slow, decidedly awkward thrusts, he attempted to find his rhythm. Benjamin's inexperience was overshadowed by his desire to learn, to delight, to please, and he was rewarded once Clara shivered and arched with impatience. Determined to deepen her pleasure, Benjamin broke their kiss and laid his forearms flat against the floor, their eyes locking as he rolled more persistently between her thighs. At this angle, there wasn't quite so much strain on his spine.

Clara's legs cramped up each time his hardness rubbed and stroked her bud, and with her mouth falling agape, she panted as their noses brushed along with the firm, steady pounding between her legs. She felt weightless, overstimulated, and once he reached between them and circled her clit, Clara practically sobbed as she snagged her nails across his broad shoulders, her heat gripping around him as Benjamin lurched at the sensation.

It was too much, it was too much, it was *much too much*.

Thrusting into her with a renewed force, Benjamin kept his eyes on hers as he fell apart, a guttural cry catching in his throat once he spilled between her trembling thighs. Desperate to join him, Clara rocked into his fingers when they returned to her clit, her eyes fluttering shut when finally, *finally*, her walls clenched hard around his softening arousal.

Their shared breathing filled the air, hushed and labored as both gradually came down from their high. Benjamin withdrew enough to cup her flushed face, wearing a bright, decidedly dazzled smile from seeing Clara so beautiful, sated, and dare he think it, happy. She was the moon, and he the helpless wave lured in by her gravitational pull. He never wished to be parted from her ever again.

"Are you all right?" he asked, gently brushing a thumb across her lips.

Mirroring his fond smile, Clara laughed and ran her fingers through his hair. "Shouldn't I be asking *you* that? Though for what it's worth, I'm very impressed. This *was* your first time, was it not?"

Her fingers traced his cheek, and Benjamin chuckled, brushing his nose against hers. "I had a bit of literary help, if you'll recall."

"The books I recommended?"

He nodded, sheepish.

"Hmm. I'll have to send Jacob Rueff and Fanny Hill a gift basket." Benjamin pulled out from between her legs and Clara gasped, still sensitive. "My God, Ben…"

"No need for the blasphemous moniker," Benjamin quipped. He lowered and pressed a kiss to her neck, humming against her skin. "When can we do this again?"

Clara laughed, her nose crinkling in amusement. "You enjoyed yourself, did you? I should've known; even the devout Benjamin Hoskin isn't immune to carnal stirrings."

"Not where you're concerned," he agreed, propping his chin onto her shoulder. "Am I going to get a real answer?"

Expression tender, she edged her forehead into his, lightly tracing a finger over his lips. "We can do it again whenever you wish…even now."

"Now?"

She nodded. "Well yes, if you can get aroused again. I've never met a man who can, but I would thrill in being proven wrong." Nuzzling him, she teased, "Just think of this as your own little personal challenge."

With an impish glimmer to his eyes, Benjamin lifted to capture her mouth with his but was thwarted when a knock came at the door.

"I've got your supper!" the innkeeper shouted, sounding impatient as ever.

Clara snorted. "I suppose he finished flogging those *venereal affairs* of his."

Rolling up into a sitting position, Benjamin assured her, "I'll get our food and send him away."

"What?" she squeaked. "Like *this*? Ben, you're not wearing a stitch!"

"Yes, and that'll definitely get rid of him, will it not?" Flashing a wry grin, he rose on unsteady legs and limped for the door.

Clara clapped a hand over her mouth, biting her lip to keep from giggling. And as Benjamin opened the door, obscuring his nakedness from the other man, she heard the innkeeper gripe about "noise complaints," and she buried her face into her palms, collapsing against the floor as she dissolved into a fit of laughter.

SEVERAL HOURS LATER, the icy rain was still coming down steadily against the streets of New Haven, thundering against the windowpane as Benjamin lay in bed wide awake, his fingers stroking Clara's hair while she remained pressed into his side. The gentle rise and fall of her breast brought him comfort, of knowing she was safe, alive, and finally his to hold.

Rolling onto his flank, Benjamin watched her longingly from across their shared pillow. Tracing the slope of her cheek, he leaned forward and pressed a kiss to her brow, feeling her stir as his fingertips grazed her shoulder and traveled down, down, to glide over her hip.

"Are you studying to be an anatomist?" Clara quipped, her voice heavy with sleep. Slowly, her lashes fluttered and she lifted her eyes to his, the verdant green startling him from this close. Benjamin felt overwhelmed, reborn gazing into them, and with a lopsided smile, he drew their foreheads together.

"More like I'm trying to figure out how I got so lucky," he murmured. "I keep expecting you to come to your senses."

Groggy, Clara teased him, "Worry not, I'm sure that will come sooner rather than later. You *are* a man. I've seen what they have to offer, and I am not terribly impressed."

Benjamin grinned. Even with the playful belittlement, he felt as if he couldn't stop smiling. Tenderly tracing her spine, he asked, "Have you thought about what you'd like to do once we arrive at camp?"

Nose wrinkling, Clara regarded him incredulously. "Not really…I'm still processing today's events, truth be told. It's overwhelming getting used to the idea that we are both still alive."

The warmth in Benjamin's eyes dulled, and he nodded. "Fair

enough," he agreed. "But in our present situation, we can't afford to let our guard down…and I must admit, our marriage ruse gave me an idea." Edging his forehead back into hers, he asked, "How would you feel about aiding in my espionage again, but this time as my wife?"

Clara drew a hitching breath, stunned. "Are you asking…? D-do you mean as a pretend wife, or…?"

Benjamin hesitated at her query, for he'd initially only meant marriage as a cover. But the longer he gazed into her wide, crystalline eyes, the more he realized that yes, he did want her as his wife, and that he had for a long, long time.

Stroking his fingertips against her cheek, Benjamin's eyes colored with adoration as he murmured, "Clara, I know I can't provide for you in the way you deserve, but you have never once abandoned me…not even when I was sick and cruel and hopeless. For that reason, and many, countless others, I wish to remain by your side for the rest of my days." He cupped her cheek. "I may not have been your first, but I pray to God I'll be your last."

A swell of emotion swept Clara out into the sea of her heart, wild and tumultuous as a disbelieving laugh caught in her throat. Cradling his face, a shuddery sob rattled within her chest once she realized she was truly loved…that she was finally wanted.

Crashing her mouth into his, Clara tasted their mingled tears as she wrapped her arms around him, giving him her resounding *yes* through her lips and heart. She felt so warm, so full that she was close to bursting.

Benjamin broke the kiss and nuzzled her temple. "Clara, I—"

"Love you," she finished for him, nodding tearfully. "Me too." Wiping his damp cheeks, she added, "I suppose we should get out of bed and celebrate? There should still be a little ale leftover from supper…"

A mischievous shine came to Benjamin's eyes, and he took her hand, pressing a kiss to her knuckles. "You're not going anywhere."

He playfully rolled her underneath him and Clara laughed,

their lips joining fiercely as she parted her legs, drew him down into her arms, and then succumbed to the very fire in her soul.

EPILOGUE

25 December 1784

CHRISTMAS IN FREYVIEW was always a joyous occasion, but with the war for independence won and everyone home again, spirits seemed far brighter, and hearts all the warmer.

With Clara's help, Josiah actually decorated that year. Small evergreen tree branches were hung on the walls, wax ornaments were placed upon the dining room table, and a simple evergreen wreath graced the front door. The reverend was never much for decorating, and even less so after Daniel's death, yet with all his dearest loved ones under the same roof, it had been easy for Clara to convince him.

Bustling about in the dining room, Josiah, Amos, and Clara prepared for their evening meal. The latter set two plates in honor of her sisters, neither of whom could join them since after England's loss, the Boyds packed up and moved to London. Clara missed her sisters terribly, yet only Catherine wrote her. Charlotte very much disapproved of her elopement. Despite her heartache over the rebuff, she had faith her sister would one day forgive her.

In the way of her parents, they also objected and wrote her out of the will. She didn't want their riches anyway. For the first time in her life, she had everything she needed right within her very heart.

Speaking of which… With a frown, Clara realized two very important people were missing.

"Excuse me a moment," she said, gathering up her skirts and

leaving the room. All around the house, she began her search, first on one side of the old saltbox, and then the other, before she heard her husband's playful, singsong voice coming from his old bedroom.

Clara moved to the door and poked her head inside. There, creeping throughout the space was Benjamin, the cozy, flickering dance of firelight illuminating his path as he heavily limped along. His cane was propped in the corner, just in case he tired out.

"Now where could he be?" Benjamin asked, feigning exasperation. "I can't seem to find him…"

A giggle arose from underneath the bed, and grinning, Benjamin limped toward the noise with the pretense of searching. Once he stopped, he slowly, carefully lowered himself to the floor.

"That's funny," he said, "I could've *sworn* Daniel was here somewhere…" The giggling started up again, and with a playful growl, Benjamin swooped underneath the bed and grabbed his son, who screamed in delight and burst into spritely, unrestrained laughter.

"Papa, no!" he cried.

Dragging the three-year-old from his hiding spot, Benjamin lifted him to perch onto his hip, then warmly tapped his nose. "I think you mean, 'Papa, please, please take me to supper so I can spend time with my wonderful family.'" When his son pouted, he reminded him, "If we don't eat, I'll be forced to sup upon your fingers…and I'm very hungry."

Without warning, he nibbled on Daniel's hand, who shrieked and pushed at Benjamin's face.

"Don't eat!" he scolded. "Don't!"

"Don't?" Benjamin echoed, chuckling. "Now you sound like your mother…" Setting Daniel onto the floor, he encouraged, "Come along then. Help me find the most beautiful woman in all the world."

A clearing throat came from the doorway, and both turned to find Clara wearing a bright, tender smile.

With a chipper gasp, Daniel rushed forward and latched onto her skirts, exclaiming, "I found her, I found her!"

"Who, the most beautiful woman in all the world?" Benjamin asked, straightening to behold his wife. When she met his gaze and that smile was suddenly all for him, a strong flutter bloomed within his chest. "You most certainly did," he whispered.

Pressing a hand to her swollen belly, Clara simpered. "And is all this flattery genuine, or a deflection for keeping everyone waiting?"

"You've never kept anyone waiting?" Benjamin challenged.

"Women are expected to, because the visual feast is always worth it. Men, on the other hand…" Here, she fondly lifted Daniel into her arms, kissing his cheek while stroking his strawberry-blond curls. "They are only forgiven the offense when very young."

"And as your obedient husband, I will keep that in mind," Benjamin replied, his smile lopsided and warm. "Am I allowed a kiss, or am I still in trouble?"

Clara laughed, her eyes shining with the firelight. "When has flattery ever worked on me?"

"Never, but I am still willing to try." Lifting a hand, Benjamin brushed his fingertips against her cheek. "Was that a yes or a no?"

"What do *you* think?"

Beaming, Benjamin leaned down to kiss her, but Daniel gasped and quickly thrust up his hands, placing his chubby fingers over Benjamin's mouth and shoving. "No!" he whined. "Nooo."

Laughing, Benjamin pulled back with a faux pout. "You wound me, Danny. Don't you like seeing your parents in love?"

"Yuck!"

Sharing a conspiratorial grin, Benjamin and Clara dove in and kissed the boy's cheeks, poor Daniel squealing as he squirmed between his parents' affectionate assault.

"Down!" he pleaded. "Down!"

Avoiding his flailing limbs, Clara acquiesced and urged, "Run along then, you little beast. Grandpapa Hoskin has a special dessert for you, and a few hugs, so be sure to say thank you."

Eager for the promised treat, though perhaps not so much for the hugs, Daniel scurried off, leaving Benjamin and Clara alone in his bedroom.

"That's *your* influence, you know," he teased.

"*Me?* I'm the more insatiable of us, so I hardly ever say no," Clara countered, adjusting his cravat. "In fact..." Here, she reached into her side seam pocket, then withdrew a sprig of mistletoe. "Your father wouldn't let me hang this up. I suppose he wasn't keen on the possibility of kissing Amos. I held onto it in case of an emergency."

"How thoughtful of you," Benjamin quipped, coiling a loosened lock of her hair around his finger. "Unfortunately, you're not quite tall enough to make this work." Taking the sprig from her outstretched hand, he held it above their heads with a smirk, his nose brushing hers as he whispered, "Merry Christmas, Mrs. Hoskin."

Mirroring his bright smile, Clara lifted on tiptoe and edged her mouth into his, gripping his lapels as he deepened their kiss with a slow, fervent roll of his tongue.

He moved to properly embrace her, but Clara laughed and withdrew, breathless and pink cheeked. "What are you trying to do to me, darling? I am *already* with child."

"Perhaps I want to make sure of it," Benjamin murmured, edging his forehead into hers. "Should we join everyone before they start to talk?"

She snorted. "Is it truly a party unless at least one rumor is started?"

He chuckled, moving to shut the door. "You're right," he agreed. "We can surely delay things a few minutes more."

"I'll bet you can even finish in two," Clara replied, her eyes twinkling.

Ignoring the playful barb, Benjamin grinned and pulled her into his arms, muffling her shriek with a kiss as they stumbled and fell upon his bed.

APPROXIMATELY TWO MINUTES and thirty seconds later, they waited a few minutes more before returning to the dining area, where Josiah and Amos were entertaining Daniel with a game.

"C'mon, lad," the latter coaxed. "Which hand'll it be?"

The boy stuck out his tongue in thought, his pretty, large, hazel eyes shining before he pointed to his left.

"Right'cha are, lad!" Amos exclaimed, opening his hand to reveal a couple shillings. "Save these for when you're older, Danny-boy, 'cause you'll get swept up by some sweet young thing, and she'll bleed'ja dry."

Handing the coins to the eager child, Amos glanced at Benjamin and Clara with a smirk. "And how was the bed, eh? Still as sturdy as y'both remember?"

Josiah cleared his throat, unamused.

"Oi! I meant to *sit* upon! Whaddaya take me for, Reverend?"

Benjamin's cheeks grew bright pink, but Clara, unruffled as ever, sat across from Josiah while Benjamin took the chair to her right. Scooping up Daniel, she placed him into her lap and brushed her fingers through his soft, unruly curls. "We were looking for one of Daniel's toys," she replied, her knack for deception perfect as always. "He was playing in Benjamin's room earlier this afternoon."

Amos flashed them a knowing sneer. "Uh-huh. And did'ja find it?"

"Yes," she replied. "We put it in Benjamin's valise."

"I'll bet'cha Moony filled up *your* valise, as well."

Josiah cleared his throat again, yet far more loudly this time. "Shall we offer a few words before we say grace?"

"Good thinkin', Reverend," Amos agreed. "This house definitely needs the Lord after dealin' with these two."

Despite his friend's playful ribbing, Benjamin rose and commanded their attention. "I, uh…I'd like to say something," he announced, lifting his cup of ale.

Josiah nodded fondly at his son. "Go ahead, Benjamin."

All eyes turned to him, and Benjamin exhaled, a ribbon of warmth stitching through his heart as he looked at Clara and his son. "These past few years have been some of the hardest, yet most rewarding of my life," he began. "I learned to walk again, to hope, to yearn, to live… And in the very midst of war, I joined my life with the one person who overlooked all my ugliness." With a tearful smile, Benjamin lifted his cup in a salute. "Before your love, I was broken, Clara…shattered and useless, and then you made me whole. You made me somebody loved and with a purpose. In short, you saved my life."

Clara opened and closed her mouth, her eyes welling as Daniel squirmed in her arms. "Ben…"

"I love you," he said. "All four of you. Without your love and support, I know I never would've been able to lend my aid in this war…to pull through and survive, and fight for the principles I believe in." Raising his arm into a proper toast, he concluded, "Here's to those we have lost, and all we've gained along the way."

Everyone lifted their own cups of ale, their faces pensive as the past several years flashed behind their eyes, the pains, the triumphs, the loss, the reward.

After setting aside her drink, Clara rose with Daniel in her arms, her gaze wet as she regarded Benjamin with a lump in her throat. Caring little for their audience, she embraced him and buried her face into his chest, their son caught between them as Benjamin wrapped his arms around her just as strongly.

"I don't know how to live without you," he whispered, "and I pray I'll never find out."

"You won't," she promised, whimpering. "Not ever."

Squirming against her middle, Daniel exclaimed, "Don't squish the baby!"

Laughing amidst her tears, Clara withdrew and promised, "Of course we won't, darling. And we won't squish *you*, either."

"Oi!" Amos called over to them. "Are we gonna eat, or what?"

"'If we hope for what we do not see, we wait for it with patience,'" Josiah quoted.

The cabinetmaker scoffed. "That's some mighty nice scripture there, Reverend, but I think you've got it a little backwards. I do see the food. My question is, why aren't we eatin' it?"

Taking Amos's hand, Josiah reached across the table for Clara, who quickly wiped her eyes and reclaimed her seat, drawing her son back into her lap. When she and Josiah clasped hands, Benjamin sat and took Daniel's, who looked at him with an excited grin over the prospect of finally eating boiled beef, beans, and the promised apple tart.

Once everyone bowed their heads, the boy perked up and leaned toward Clara's belly. "It's prayer time, brother," he whispered.

Clara opened one eye with a smile. "And why are you so certain it's a boy, Daniel?"

"I want a brother," he replied as if it were obvious.

Expression fond, Benjamin murmured, "I hope you get a brother too, Danny. It's one of the greatest joys in all the world."

Josiah began their prayers, and tenderly, Clara curled her free hand over her son and husband's interlocked fingers, squeezing them until Benjamin lifted his head to spare her a warm smile.

This was it, he thought, the affection, the belonging, the sense of completion he'd sought long before he'd even known what he was seeking. And as he held his wife's and son's hands, he believed himself invincible. They were his heart, his life, his very breath, and the perpetual answer to all his prayers.

"Amen," everyone spoke, yet Clara didn't release his hand. Daniel drew away from them, eager for his plate, but the couple moved their hands under the table and remained entwined, their hearts full and their smiles bright as the chatter around the table melded into a warm, glowing symphony of good cheer. And as Clara's laughter joined in akin to silvery, tinkling bells, Benjamin found himself wishing to be in this moment forever, to be endlessly bound to her in hope, awe, and love.

Glossary

addlepate: an inconsiderate, foolish fellow

a pox on you: an expression of disgust, i.e. "to hell with you," or "curse you."

balderdash: nonsense

barmy: extremely foolish, half-witted

blackguard: a spy

bloodybacks: derogatory term for British soldiers, which colonists used to reference the floggings that officers used as punishment

bottle-headed: void of wit

bushel bubby: a full-breasted woman

by St. George: for goodness' sake; by God

carvel's ring: a woman's privates

casting up one's accounts: to vomit

chit: a young woman viewed as immature, or lacking respect

chub: a foolish fellow, easily imposed upon

claptrap: nonsense

clodpate: a dull and stupid person

clotpole: a very stupid person

codshead: a dupe, a fool

cully: a fool, a blockhead

cur: a surly fellow; a contemptible man

dandy prat: an insignificant or trifling fellow

dicked in the knob: silly, crazed

doddypole: blockhead

doggess: bitch

doxy / doxy-dell: she-beggars, a common strumpet / young, buxom, virginal wenches

fiddle-faddle: nonsense

fie: exclamation expressing disapproval or disgust

fribble: an effeminate fop

fubsy: plump

fudge: nonsense

gingambobs: testicles

glimflashy: angry, or in a passion

goosecap: a silly fellow or woman

grout-head: a blockhead

headrails: teeth

highwaymen: robbers

high-flyer: Tory or Jacobite

hob: clown

hulver-headed: having a hard, impenetrable head

in her flowers: menstruating

jobbernole: the head

jolter-head: a stupid fellow

jingle brains: a wild, thoughtless, rattling fellow

knight of the trenches: a great eater

lobcock: a dull, inanimate fellow

long shanks: a long-legged person

looby: an awkward, ignorant fellow

lout: a clumsy, stupid fellow

loyalist: an American colonist who remained loyal to the British Crown during the revolution

lushey: drunk

mutton: a woman's privates

nutting bag: testicles

pillock: a man's privates

poltroon: an utter coward

sennight: one week

shag: intercourse

strumpet: a female prostitute

Tory: an American colonist who remained loyal to the British Crown during the revolution (this term was primarily used by their patriotic/rebel opponents)

trollop: a female prostitute

zounds: a mild oath (surprise or anger)

About the Author

Madelyn Grey is a huge history nerd (she especially loves to geek out over historical medicine!), a former legal/obituary coordinator for the *Richmond Times-Dispatch*, and an occasional contributor for the home and garden section of this same newspaper. She is also a member of James River Writers and Quill & Scroll, and has contributed articles to *V Magazine for Women*. When she is not voraciously reading or writing, she's drawing concept art of her characters, or (lovingly) harassing her cats.

Madelyn is a historical romance writer—primarily for the late 18th and early 19th centuries—and is a tremendous fan of enemies-to-lovers (blame the series *Moonlighting* for this one!), friends-to-lovers, hurt/comfort, and snappy banter, so expect to find one or all of these in most of her writing.

Although she never achieved her childhood goal of being the world's youngest author, for as long as she's able, Madelyn intends to keep writing about love, laughter, and all the emotions in between. Feel free to follow her on Instagram @madelyngreyauthor!